Beyond the Sea

1116

Beyond the Sea

JoAnn Ross

ISBN-10: 1941134092
ISBN-13: 9781941134092

From *New York Times* bestselling author JoAnn Ross, the romance Shelter Bay readers have been waiting for!

While in Ireland to bake a wedding cake for movie star Mary Joyce, Sedona meets Conn Brennan, an Irish rock star who refuses to fit into any of her tidy, concise boxes. Unable to deny the sizzling chemistry between them, Sedona rashly throws caution to the winds, forgetting that she's never, *ever,* been attracted to bad boys.

When Conn learns a dark family secret that has stayed buried for over thirty years, the revelation has him questioning nearly everything he's believed about his life. But the one thing that hasn't changed is his intense attraction to Sedona Sullivan, the blond American he hasn't been able to stop thinking about. The woman he's destined to spent the rest of his life with.

But first he must break through Sedona's formidable defenses and convince her that their romance is much more than a summer fling. And Sedona must decide where her heart truly belongs.

1

Castlelough, Ireland

THE PUB ON the bank of the River Dathúil had begun serving rebels and raiders, smugglers and sailors, poets and patriots in 1650. Which gave Patrick Brennan, who'd bought and restored the crumbling stone building, a centuries-old standard to maintain. While rebels and smugglers might make rarer appearances these days, Brennan's Microbrewery and Pub continued to thrive.

From her spot at a small table across the room from the wooden bar, Sedona Sullivan could see a young couple share a kiss inside one of the two snugs by the front door. The leaded glass window kept the couple's behavior reasonably sedate, which didn't keep Sedona from briefly wondering what clandestine affairs the pub had been witness to over the years.

Whiskey bottles gleamed like pirates' booty in the glow of brass-hooded lamps, a turf fire burned in a large open hearth at one end of the pub, warming against the chill of rain pelting on the slate roof, and heavy wooden tables were crowded onto the stone floor. Booths lined walls covered in football flags, vintage signs, and old photographs, and in the library extension, books and magazines filled shelves and wall racks.

The man murmured something in the woman's ear, causing her to laugh and toss hair as bright as the peat fire. As the woman lifted her smiling lips to his for a longer, more drawn-out kiss, Sedona felt a stir of envy. How long had it been since a man had made her laugh with sexy abandon? How long since anyone had kissed her like that man was kissing the pretty Irish redhead?

Sedona did some quick mental math. Finding the sum impossible to believe, she recalculated. Twenty-two months, three weeks, and eight days? Seriously?

Unfortunately, given that she was, after all, a former CPA with excellent math skills and a near-photographic memory, Sedona knew her figures were right on the money. As were those additional sixteen hours she reluctantly tacked on to the initial subtotal.

How could that be possible?

Granted, she'd been busy. After leaving behind an accounting career in Portland, she'd opened a successful bakery in Shelter Bay, Castlelough's sister city on the Oregon coast.

But still...nearly two years?

That was just too depressing.

Unlike last evening, when Brennan's had been crowded to the ancient wooden rafters with family members and friends enjoying Mary Joyce and J.T. Douchett's rehearsal dinner, tonight the pub was nearly deserted. In addition to the two lovers, three men were watching a replay of a rugby match on the flat-screen mounted on the stone wall, and an ancient man somewhere between eighty and a hundred years old was nursing a foam-topped dark ale and singing sad Irish songs to himself.

And there was Patrick Brennan, owner, bartender, and cook, whose smiling Irish eyes were as darkly brown as the fudge frosting she'd made for the chocolate groom's cake.

Which was what had brought Sedona to her ancestral homeland. She'd met international movie star and award-winning screenwriter Mary Joyce when the Castlelough-born actress had visited Shelter Bay for a film festival featuring her movies. After Mary had gotten engaged to J.T., a former Marine who'd been pressed into service as the actress's bodyguard, Mary had asked Sedona to make both the groom's cake and the all-important wedding cake.

Happy to play a part in her friend's wedding, Sedona had jumped at the chance to revisit the land of her ancestors.

A cheer went up as a player dressed in a green jersey from the Ireland Wolfhounds scored against the England Saxons. After delivering her wine and taking her order, Patrick paused on his way back to the bar long enough to glance up at the screen, and even the old man stopped singing long enough to raise his mug before switching to a ballad celebrating a victory in some ancient but never-to-be-forgotten war.

Sedona was thinking that watching a game when you already knew the final score must be a male thing, when the heavy oak door opened, bringing with it a wet, brisk wind that sent her paper napkin sailing onto the floor.

Before she could reach down and pick it up, her attention was captured by the arrival of a man she had already determined to be trouble on a hot, sexy stick.

His wind-mussed hair, which gave him the look of having just gotten out of bed, fell to a few inches above his broad shoulders and was as black as the sea on a moonless night. As he took off his leather jacket, revealing a lean, hard, well-muscled body, testosterone radiated off him in bone-weakening waves.

"Well, would you look at what the night gale blew in," Patrick greeted him from behind the bar. "I thought you were leaving town."

"I was. Am," Conn Brennan clarified in the roughened, rocker's voice recognizable the world over. "I'm flying out of Shannon to catch up with the lads in Frankfurt. But I had a sudden craving for fish and chips, and sure, everyone knows there's no finer food than the pub grub served up by my big brother at Brennan's."

Patrick laughed at that. "Sure, with talk like that, some would think you'd be from Blarney," he shot back on an exaggerated brogue. "So how did the party go? I assume the bride and groom enjoyed themselves?"

"The party was grand, in large part due to the music," said the infamous bad boy rocker known by the single name Conn to his legion of fans around the world. He had been dubbed "Conn of the Hundred Battles" by the tabloids for his habit of getting into fights with the paparazzi.

"As for the bride and groom, I imagine they're shagging their brains out about now. The way they couldn't keep their hands off each other had the local band lads making bets on whether they'd make it to bed before consummating the nuptials."

The heels of his metal-buckled black boots rang out on the stone floor as he headed toward the bar, pausing when he almost stepped on Sedona's dropped napkin. He bent to pick it up, then when he straightened, his startlingly neon blue eyes clashed with hers.

And held for a long, humming moment.

"Well, fancy seeing you here. I would have guessed, after the busy day you've had, that you'd be all tucked away in your comfy bed at the inn, dreaming of wedding cakes, sugar plums, and all things sweet."

He placed the napkin on the table with a dangerously sexy smile he'd directed her way more than once as he'd rocked the reception from the bandstand. When an image of a bare-chested Conn sprawled on her four-poster bed at the inn flashed wickedly through Sedona's mind, something quivered deep in her stomach.

It was only hunger, she assured herself. Between putting the last touches on the towering wedding cake and working with the serving staff during the reception, she hadn't taken the time for a proper meal all day.

"I was in the mood for a glass of wine and a late bite." Her tone, cool as wintry mist over the Burren, was in direct contrast to the heat flooding her body.

He lifted an ebony brow. "Why would you be wanting to go out in this rain? The Copper Beech Inn has excellent room service, and surely your suite came with a minibar well stocked with adult beverages."

"You're correct on both counts," she acknowledged as the old man segued into "The Rare Auld Mountain Dew."

She took a sip of wine, hoping it would cool the heat rising inside her.

It didn't.

"But I chose to spend my last night in Ireland here at Brennan's. Besides, you're right about your brother's food. It's excellent." While the pub grub menu might be casual dining, Patrick Brennan had proven to be as skilled in the kitchen as he was at pulling pints. "There's also the fact that the inn's minibar is ridiculously expensive."

"Ah." He nodded his satisfaction. "Your parents didn't merely pass down an Irish surname, Sedona Sullivan. It appears you've inherited our Irish frugality."

"And here I thought that was the Scots."

"It's true that they've been more than happy to advertise that reputation, despite having stolen the concept from us. Same as they did the pipes, which, if truth be told, were originally intended as an Irish joke on the Scots, who, being dour people without any sense of humor, failed to get it."

"And didn't I recognize your famed Irish frugality the moment you roared into town in that fire-engine-red Ferrari?"

He threw back his head and laughed, a rich, deep sound that flowed over her and reminded her yet again exactly how much time had passed since she'd been with a man.

Your choice.

"And wouldn't you be a prime example of appearances being deceiving?" he countered.

"Don't be disturbing my guest, Conn," Patrick called out.

"We're just having a friendly conversation." Conn's eyes hadn't left Sedona's since he'd stopped at the table. "Am I disturbing you, *a stór*?"

Yes.

"Not at all," she lied.

The truth was that she'd been feeling wired and edgy from the moment he'd strode into the hall for a sound check before the reception.

"Though you do force me to point out that I'm no one's darling," she tacked on. He'd undoubtedly used the generic Irish endearment the way American men used "babe" or "sweetheart."

Even without having read about all the rich and famous women the rocker was reported to have been involved with, any sensible woman would keep her distance from Conn Brennan. Despite having grown up on a commune of former hippies and flower children, Sedona had always considered herself unwaveringly sensible.

Her knowledge of the endearment failed to put a dent in his oversized male ego. Instead, amusement danced in his electric-blue eyes.

"Would you have learned that bit of Irish from some local lad attracted by your charms?" he asked as he rubbed a jaw darkened with a day-old stubble that added machismo to his beautiful face. "Which, may I say, despite your short time in our fair village, would not surprise me in the least."

"My parents believe everyone should speak at least two languages," she responded mildly. "I'm fluent in Spanish, know enough French to order a baguette and wine in Paris, and thanks to a year studying abroad at Trinity College Dublin, along with the past few days having an opportunity to practice, I can carry on a bit of a conversation in Irish."

Raindrops glistened in his black hair as he tilted his head. "Mary wasn't exaggerating when she was going on about your charms," he said finally. "And aren't brains and beauty an enticing combination? As for you not being my darling, Sedona Sullivan, the night's still young."

"Perhaps for those in Dublin or Cork," she said, struggling against the seductive pull of that smile. The rugby game ended with a score by the redshirted Saxons. The men who'd been watching the TV shuffled out, muttering curses about allegedly blind referees. "But if you don't leave soon, you won't be able to drive your fancy 'frugal' import to the airport because Castlelough's cobblestone streets will have been rolled up."

He gave her a longer, considering look, his intense blue eyes narrowing as he scrutinized her in silence for what seemed like forever, even as some part of her brain still managing to function told her it must have only been a few seconds.

"Your order's up," he said without having even glanced toward the bar. "Since Patrick's occupied with my fish and chips, I'll bring your late bite back with my ale."

He smelled so amazing, like night rain darkened with the scent of leather and the tang of sweat from having played as energetically for his hometown crowd of a hundred wedding guests as he had to his recent sell-out crowd of ninety thousand in London's Wembley Stadium.

Tamping down a reckless urge to lick his dark neck, Sedona forced a faint smile.

"Thank you. We certainly wouldn't want your fish to burn while your brother's distracted delivering my meal."

Assuring herself that there wasn't a woman on the planet who'd be capable of not checking out the very fine butt in those dark jeans, she watched his long, loose-hipped outlaw's stride to the bar.

Not wanting to be caught staring as he returned with his dark ale and her plate, she turned her gaze back to the couple in the snug. The woman was now sitting on the man's lap as they tangled tonsils.

Why didn't they just get a damn room?

"Now there's a pair who know how to make the most of a rainy night," Conn said as he sat down across from her.

There was no way she was going to respond to that.

Instead, she turned her attention to the small white plate of deep fried cheese served on a bed of salad greens with a side of dark port and berry sauce. The triangular piece of cheese that had been fried in a light-as-a-feather beer batter nearly made her swoon.

As she'd discovered when making her cakes, Irish dairy farmers seemed to possess a magic that churned milk into pure gold. "This is amazingly delicious."

"The French claim to make the best cream and butter, but I'd put ours against theirs any day. That St. Brigid's cheese you're eating is a local Camembert from Michael Joyce's farm."

Michael was Mary Joyce's older brother. Sedona had met the former war correspondent turned farmer and his American wife at a dinner at the Joyce family home her first night in Castlelough.

"And speaking of delicious," he said, "I'm remiss in not telling you that your cake had me tempted to lick my plate."

"Thank you." When his words brought back her earlier fantasy of licking his neck, she felt color rising in her cheeks.

"Of course, I wouldn't have," he continued, thankfully seeming unaware of her wicked, too-tempting thoughts. "Because I promised Mary."

"You promised Mary you wouldn't lick your dessert plate?"

"Mary can be a bit of a stickler for propriety. So I promised to behave myself."

He waited a beat, just long enough to let her know something else was coming. "Which was the only reason I didn't leave a set to the lads and dance with you at the reception."

"Well, no one can fault you for your confidence."

"Would you be saying you wouldn't have given me a dance? If I hadn't been performing and had asked?"

Dance with this man? From the way he'd watched her from the bandstand, his eyes like blue flames, Sedona had a feeling that dancing wasn't precisely what he'd had in mind.

"I came here to work," she said. "Not dance." Nor hook up with a hot Irish musician.

"It was a grand cake," he said. "Even better than the one I was served at the White House." Where he'd received a presidential medal for his social activism, Sedona remembered. "And one of the few that tasted as good as it looked. Most cakes these days seem to have spackle spread over them."

She laughed at the too-true description. "That's fondant, which creates a smoother surface to decorate."

"It's shite is what it is. When I was growing up, my mam's carrot cake always won first prize at the county fair. With six children in the family, we'd all have to wait our turn to lick the bowl or she'd never have ended up with enough frosting to cover it, but I always believed that cream cheese frosting was the best part."

Sedona was relieved when Patrick arrived at the table with his brother's fish and chips, interrupting a conversation that had returned to licking.

"Something we can agree on," she said, dipping the cheese into the sauce brightened with flavors of ginger, orange, and lemon. "Which is why I used buttercream on the cakes for the wedding."

He bit into the battered cod. Heaven help her, somehow the man managed to make chewing sexy.

"So," he said after taking a drink of the Brian Boru Black Ale. "Mary tells me you make cupcakes back in America."

"My bakery, Take the Cake, specializes in cupcakes, but I've also added pies."

"Good business move," he said with a nod. "Who wouldn't be liking a nice warm piece of pie? Cakes are well enough, but pies are sexy."

Said the man who obviously had sex on the mind. Unfortunately, he wasn't alone. As Sedona watched him bite into a chip, she found herself wondering how that black face scruff would feel on her breasts. Her stomach. And lower still.

"Well, they've proven popular," she said as her pulse kicked up. "Which was rewarding, given that it proved the validity of months of research."

He cocked his head. "You researched whether or not people like pie?"

"Well, of course I already knew they like pie. I merely did a survey and analysis to calculate the cost and profit margins."

"Which told you lots of people like pie."

He was laughing at her. She could see it in his eyes. "Yes. Do you realize how many businesses fail in any given year? Especially these days?" They were finally in a conversational territory she knew well.

"Probably about as many people who don't succeed in the music business," he guessed. "Though I've never done a sales analysis before writing a song."

"That's different."

"Is it, now?"

She tried again. "What if you wrote a song that didn't connect with your fans?"

He shrugged and took another bite of battered cod. "I'd write it off as a mistake and move on. No risk, no reward. I tend to go with my gut, then don't look back."

"My father's the same way," she murmured, more to herself than to him.

He leaned back in the wooden chair and eyed her over the rim of his glass. "And how has that worked out for him?"

"Very well, actually."

He lifted the glass. "Point made."

"Different strokes," she argued.

"You know what they say about opposites." His gaze moved slowly over her face, his eyes darkening to a stormy, deep sea blue as they settled on her lips, which had parts of her body tingling that Sedona had forgotten could tingle.

"I have a spreadsheet," she said.

"I suspect you have quite a few." When he flashed her a slow, badass grin she suspected had panties dropping across several continents, Sedona sternly reminded herself that she'd never—ever—been attracted to bad boys.

So why had she forgotten how to breathe?

As the fantasy of him sprawled on her bed next door in the Copper Beech Inn came crashing to the forefront of her mind, Sedona reminded herself of those twenty-two months, three weeks, eight days, and sixteen, going on seventeen hours.

Every instinct she possessed told her that not only was Conn Brennan trouble, he was way out of her league.

"They're not all business related. I also have one for men."

Putting his ale down, he leaned across the small round table and tucked a strand of blond hair, which had fallen from the tidy French twist she'd created for the reception, behind her ear. The brush of fingertips roughened from steel guitar strings caused heat to rise beneath his touch.

"You put us men in boxes." His eyes somehow managed to look both hot and amused at the same time.

It was not a question. But Sedona answered it anyway. "Not men. Attributes," she corrected. "What I'd require, and expect, in a mate."

Oh, God. Why did she have to use that word? While technically accurate, it had taken on an entirely different, impossibly sexy meaning. Desperately wanting to bury her face in her palms, she remained frozen in place as his treacherous finger traced a trail of sparks around her lips, which, despite Ireland's damp weather, had gone desert dry.

"And where do I fit in your tidy little boxes, Sedona Sullivan?"

Although she was vaguely aware of the couple leaving the snug, and the pub, his steady male gaze was holding her hostage. She could not look away.

"You don't."

"I'm glad to hear that," he said in that deep, gravelly voice that set off vibrations like a tuning fork inside her.

Conn ran his hand down her throat, his thumb skimming over her pulse, which leaped beneath his touch, before cupping her jaw. "Because I've never been comfortable fenced into boundaries."

And growing up in a world of near-absolute freedom, Sedona had never been comfortable without them. "There's something you need to know."

"And that would be?"

"I'm not into casual sex."

"And isn't that good to know." He lowered his mouth to within a whisper of hers. "Since there'd be nothing casual about how you affect me."

She drew in a sharp breath, feeling as if she were standing on the edge of the towering cliff where J.T. and Mary's wedding had taken place in a circle of ancient stones.

"I'm taking you back to your room."

Somehow, her hand had lifted to his face. "Your flight..."

He parted her lips with the pad of his thumb. "It's my plane. It takes off when I'm ready." His other hand was on her leg, his fingers stroking the inside of her thigh through the denim of the jeans she'd put on after returning to her room after the reception. "I'll ring up the pilot and tell him I'll be leaving in the morning."

Then his mouth came down on hers and Conn was kissing her, hard and deep, setting off a mind-blinding supernova inside Sedona.

They left the pub, running through the soft Irish rain into the inn next door. As the old-fashioned gilt cage elevator cranked its way up to her floor, he continued to kiss her breathless, making Sedona forget that she'd never, *ever* been attracted to bad boys.

2

Shelter Bay, Oregon
Six weeks later

SEDONA WAS PIPING out buttercream frosting onto a row of salted caramel chocolate cupcakes when her cell phone began playing "Blowing in the Wind," her mother's ringtone.

She put down the frosting bag and dug the phone out of her apron pocket.

"Hello, darling," Skylark Sullivan said. "I had a thought at yoga this morning."

"Oh?"

"I haven't wanted you to think I'm pushing, but after the beautiful cakes you created for Mary Joyce, I wondered if you might want to add wedding cakes to your menu."

"You could never be pushy."

That might be an exaggeration. Sedona had watched her mother's soft-handed guidance of her father. Freebird Sullivan—who'd taken his first name from a poem written by the Indian Nobel Prize-winning poet Rabindranath Tagore years before the Lynyrd Skynyrd song—was handsome, intelligent, and talented. He'd even once appeared on the cover of *Rolling Stone*. He was also softhearted and generous. Unfortunately, he had no working concept of time or money, and her mother had often joked that the logical left side of her husband's brain was littered with warning signs reading *Here There Be Dragons*.

Fortunately, he'd married a woman who, while possessing artistic talents of her own, was as detail oriented as a rocket scientist, kept track of time like a Swiss watch, and made sure her husband remembered to eat and sleep while in the throes of creativity.

"As much as I enjoyed having some part in J.T. and Mary's wedding, wedding cakes take so much time, with all the consultations and the preparations, the profit margins wouldn't work for me."

There was also the problem that making wedding cakes would bring back memories she'd been trying to forget.

Her impulsive, reckless night with Conn Brennan had been totally out of character. Not only had she surrendered control to a man who was the antithesis of her ideal, she'd also insisted that it was a one-time event. She'd had no interest in pursuing a long-distance relationship. Especially one that involved not only an entire ocean but a continent between them.

However, although she'd rather run down Harborview stark naked than admit it, her insistence that she was only interested in a one-night stand hadn't stopped her from anticipating a call. Or an email. Even a text.

When weeks passed and Sedona still hadn't heard a word—or so much as a damn one-hundred-and-forty-character tweet—from Conn since he'd left for Germany and she'd returned to Oregon, she'd come to the conclusion that he'd taken her at her word. Which was exactly what she'd wanted. What she'd insisted on. So, why wasn't she happy?

Because, she answered her own rhetorical question, somehow, when she hadn't been looking, sometime during those hours together, Conn Brennan had gotten into her head.

But not her heart. No sane, logical woman ever fell in love just because she'd experienced a night of lava-hot sex. The way Conn Brennan had moved on without looking back at that rainy night in an Irish inn was proof that her decision to avoid any further contact had been the correct one. The only logical one she could have made.

"Perhaps you could take on a business partner," Skylark suggested, dragging Sedona's atypically wandering attention back to their conversation. She shook off a memory of Conn's wickedly clever mouth scorching a damp trail down her torso. "That would also prevent you from having to bake your own wedding cake when you get married."

"I wouldn't hold your breath waiting for that to happen, Mom." Sedona found it ironic that her parents—a hippie and a flower child—appeared to be so invested in marrying off their daughter.

"You just haven't met the right man," her mother insisted. "As it happens, now that we're on the topic, your father and I met this nice young man at the Farmers Market yesterday—"

"No. Period. Way. Period."

"You haven't even let me tell you about him," Skylark complained. "He's self-employed in the tech field and very creative."

"That's what you said about the last guy you set me up with, and while I appreciate you wanting me to be happy, I can't see myself spending eternity with a vampire."

There was a long pause. Then finally, "Please tell me that you're not serious."

"Believe me, Mom, I never joke about vampires. Well, unless they sparkle. Which seems an oxymoron for creatures of the night, but hey, who am I to judge?"

"I believe I read that the sparkling had something to do with vampire skin being different from human skin," Skylark mused. "It's created from a hard crystal that gives it that special glow in sunlight."

"Well, my date definitely didn't glow. And he wouldn't sit by the window, so perhaps his crystal shield isn't as strong as those up the Washington coast in Forks. Though he did assure me that he could hover."

"Oh, no. I'm so sorry. Why didn't you tell me earlier?"

Sedona shrugged. "I didn't want you to feel bad. And it wasn't that big a deal."

"Honestly, darling, I had no idea. I met his mother while buying essential oils for my candle making, and one thing led to another, and when we were talking about our children, she mentioned that he was very creative and imaginative."

"I'll give him imaginative," Sedona agreed as she began drizzling melted caramel atop the frosted cakes. "I think he's also more than a little unhinged."

"But harmless, I hope?"

"Well, he didn't try to suck my blood, so yeah, I'd say except for being a thirteen on a one-to-ten delusional scale, he was harmless enough."

What Sedona didn't share with her mother, whom she didn't want to worry, was that she wouldn't have minded if creepy date fail guy had decided to leave for Transylvania. Like yesterday.

"This is another one of those times when I so miss your grandmother," Skylark said with an audible sigh. "If my mother had only been with me, she would've immediately sensed his mother was holding something back." Along with being psychic, Sedona's maternal grandmother had been an empath. A gift the older woman had always insisted that Sedona herself possessed. A claim Sedona had, in turn, always resisted. She'd always lived by logic and reason and never acted on impulse.

Except once.

"Well, hopefully the next man will be your perfect soul mate," Skylark said.

"Mom. I don't need you to keep setting me up. I really can get my own dates."

She decided not to mention that shortly before going to Ireland, she'd actually tried one of those online dating services, assuming that their rigid selection process and algorithms—along with casting her net wider than the local coastal communities—might prove more effective.

Unfortunately, while they had screened out any vampires or other dates from hell, the handful of men she hadn't eliminated before a first meeting had proven duller than dirt.

The hot bad-boy Irish musician had been anything but dull. Though what she and Conn had shared, Sedona reminded herself firmly, hadn't been a date but an hours-long hookup.

"Sedona, this is your father," a deep baritone boomed out, suggesting that her mother had put them on speakerphone. As if she couldn't recognize his voice after having heard it her entire life?

"Hi, Dad. How's the music going?"

The last she'd spoken to him, inspired by the hulking shipwreck at Castaway Cove, he'd finished writing a folk rock opera about a ship captain who, furious when the woman he loved caved into her wealthy family's demands and refused to marry him, had cursed her and every succeeding generation of women in her family to never succeed in love.

According to local lore, the captain's temper had cooled by the time he delivered his cargo in Japan and picked up a shipment bound for Astoria. Unfortunately, when his ship had sunk in a Pacific storm, the curse continued, leaving him stuck between worlds unable to right his romantic wrong.

"I was having some problems for a while," he admitted. "Then your mother thought to get out the video we took the last time we visited you. The sight of that old shipwreck got me right back on track."

"Freebird's had ongoing interest from some New York theater producers," her mother said with wifely pride. "The talk's become serious about a Broadway musical, so we're flying to New York to hopefully close a deal."

"Wow. That'd be so cool."

It also had her thinking back on that conversation she'd had with Conn about both him and her father going with their gut. Which was fine for artistic types, but she preferred the predictability of numbers whose values never changed and always did what they were supposed to do. So long as you followed the rules.

Which was also why baking appealed to her. Cooking, which Chef Maddy Chaffee performed to near perfection at her Lavender Hill Farm Restaurant, allowed continual experimentation during the process, while baking was chemistry. It depended on exact measurements and controlled technique and was the one place in the kitchen where flavor and logic intersected.

"I had a client, when I was working in Portland, who produced some plays here in the Northwest. He made a very nice income, but nothing on the scale you're talking about," she said.

"I'm not letting myself think about the financial part of the deal right now," her father said. "I don't want to put the pressure of too-high expectations on my muse, which is temperamental enough. We were thinking we'd visit you again after we get through in New York."

"You know I always love to see both of you. As long as you're not bringing along a future husband candidate."

"Kenneth turned out to be a vampire," her mother informed Sedona's father, who had apparently missed the earlier part of the conversation.

"Well, damn. I hope you dumped him before you had to end up sleeping in a coffin."

"We didn't make it past dinner."

"Good. Because while I like to think of myself as open-minded, having Dracula for a son-in-law might just push the limits. Not to mention the possibility of you moving all the way to Transylvania…

"So," he continued, switching gears without missing a beat, "when are you going to make your mother happy and give her a grandchild? She's starting to envy all our friends whose children have been procreating like bunnies."

"I do not envy anyone," Skylark insisted. "*You're* the one who wants to play grandpa, Freebird Sullivan. He's already begun working on a child-sized guitar," she revealed to Sedona. Along with writing songs and performing an occasional benefit concert, Freebird Sullivan was an artisan guitar maker whose work, coveted by some of the biggest names in the music industry, had made him a wealthy man.

"Well, don't worry about taking too much time away from your opera," she said. "Because I haven't met anyone I'd want to marry, so there's no hurry for a tyke guitar."

"This is the twenty-first century. Lots of women have babies without husbands," he pointed out.

"I'm well aware of that. I'm also sure many are doing fine. But from watching friends, parenting appears difficult enough. If I ever were to decide to have a child, I'd want a partner to share the decision-making responsibilities."

Not that motherhood was in her future, but Sedona didn't want to get into that conversation yet again.

"Are you sure you're not a lesbian?" he asked. "Maybe that's why you haven't been able to find a man who appeals to you."

"Sedona's not a lesbian, dear," her mother broke in. "Not that there'd be anything wrong with that," she added quickly.

Sedona laughed at her mother's less than deft attempt at political correctness. "I believe I'd know by now if I were a lesbian," she said. "I'm merely choosy enough to hold out for what you and Dad have."

"Oh, what a lovely thing to say. Isn't it, darling?" Skylark asked her husband.

"Well, marriage is easy when your wife is the most beautiful, perfect woman on the planet," Freebird responded, on cue.

"And your husband the most challenging but exciting man," her mother responded.

And wasn't *that* what Sedona was holding out for? A relationship just like her parents had shared all these years. But perhaps with a bit less of the challenging part, she considered, as a certain Irish rocker's wicked grin came crashing out of that mental box she'd attempted, with scant success, to keep him locked away in.

"Trust your intuition, Sedona, darling," her mother said with her usual serene optimism. "You'll know the right man when you meet him."

"Though you might try being a bit more open-minded," her father, never one to hold back an opinion, advised.

And hadn't she heard that before? Most recently from Conn Brennan, who'd proven his claim that he wasn't one to fit in any tidy little box she might try to create.

"I've been thinking my criteria might be a bit stringent," Sedona admitted.

After all, who'd have thought Shelter Bay's sheriff would now be living in matrimonial bliss with the town's former bad boy? Or that J.T. Douchett, the community college teacher and son of a local fisherman, would marry an Irish movie star and screenwriter? And those were just two of the couples who'd become friends that she wouldn't have thought stood a chance in the beginning.

As her parents had proved, two people from entirely different worlds could form a strong and lasting bond. Which still didn't mean that she and an Irishman renowned for misbehaving could last once the sheets had cooled.

"So you're giving up those spreadsheets?" they asked in unison, as they so often did.

"I said I'm thinking about it," Sedona said, continuing to keep her online matchmaking failure to herself. Lifelong habits weren't easy to break, but surely there was a man out there who fit somewhere between Dracula and a bad-boy rocker. "And as much as I always love talking to you, I need to get back to baking. I'm catering a bachelorette party in Newport this evening."

After assuring them that she'd love to see them any time they could get away, Sedona got out a fresh mixing bowl and began preparing a batch of margarita cupcakes with tequila lime frosting. It was the third bachelorette party she'd catered this month. Love, apparently, was in the air on the Pacific Coast.

Not that she was the least bit envious.

Really, she wasn't.

Okay. Maybe just a smidgen.

But, dammit, it wasn't just her detailed spreadsheet that was at fault. While Shelter Bay might not be a bustling city, the recent uptick in the economy had new businesses starting up, bringing in a new crop of available men. Like sexy Luca Bongiove, who'd brought upscale Italian dining to Shelter Bay this past year.

There was also Captain Flynn Farraday, who, before joining the Shelter Bay Fire Department, had played basketball for the Navy Midshipmen and been a Navy SEAL. He was a nice guy and hot as the fires he put out, but during their one dinner date at the Sea Mist, Sedona hadn't felt a single spark.

While sexy Gabriel Lombardi, an heir to the Lombardi family vineyards, wasn't technically a Shelter Bay resident, he spent a great deal of time hosting tastings up and down the coast. Lombardi was the house wine at both Luca's and Maddy's restaurants and having returned home from a recent wine tasting with several bottles of smoothly complex Pinot Noir, Sedona had turned down his invitation to a private tasting in his suite at the Whale Song Inn because, dammit, she'd half hoped to hear from Conn.

As she hand mixed the batter with more force than necessary, Sedona decided the time had come to move on. Perhaps she'd ask Gabriel if he'd be interested in setting up a tasting of dessert wines to pair with her specialty cupcakes at catered events. Then, if he still seemed inclined to move their relationship to a more personal level, this time she wouldn't say no.

3

Castlelough

THE PAST MONTH had been like a never-ending Irish wake. Although the old clock that had been a wedding gift to Conn's parents had yet to strike three in the afternoon, whiskey was flowing like holy water in the baptismal font at the Church of the Holy Child. It seemed as if the entire parish had turned out, arriving with covered dishes of enough shepherd's pies to feed every shepherd in the county, stewed hens, stews, brown breads, soda breads, colcannon, and so many plates of biscuits and other sweets that Conn Brennan figured Dr. John Joyce and his physician sister-in-law and partner Dr. Erin Joyce, would soon be diagnosing a plethora of new diabetes cases.

Unlike a wake, however, the guest of honor refused to die.

Conn had flown home from Dusseldorf and moved into his old room for what he'd believed would be a few days, as soon as he'd gotten the call from Patrick that their father had returned to Ireland. For seemingly the final time. Fortunately, Celtic Storm had been wrapping up the tour that had done ninety-two shows in eighty cities in under five months, so he'd only had to cancel three events. Which had nearly given the band's manager and those suits at their recording company apoplexy, but as Conn reminded them at the time, taking care of such things was what they were all handsomely paid to do.

It wasn't as if touring made any money. This latest one, with an entourage of musicians, roadies, managers, tech folks, advance people, and publicists, would probably lose between one and two million dollars. On the flip side, touring always doubled or even tripled sales of his albums, which made the entire traveling circus worthwhile. At least to the label's bean counters.

Conn wouldn't lie. He had not an ounce of feeling toward the man currently propped up in what had once been Joseph and Eileen Brennan's wedding bed. He'd been gone most of Conn's life, only popping up like a bad penny every few years when he'd needed something from his wife. Usually money, which, for some reason Conn couldn't fathom, she'd always give him.

His mother had married while still in her teens and having given birth to six children, had never worked outside the home. But during all her husband's absences, when there'd been no money coming in, she'd turned their home into a B&B, taking in guests who'd kept the lights on and the fridge filled. Fiercely independent, she'd refused to let her grown children take care of her. Even once Conn started making serious money, she'd flatly turned down his offer of building her a new, cozy cottage with more garden space.

Until the ongoing death watch had put her business on hold, she'd liked running her B&B, welcoming interesting new people from all over the world, feeding them a hearty breakfast, sending them off to explore her beloved emerald island, then welcoming them home again in the evening with tea, wine, and pre-supper snacks.

"I'm doing just fine where and how I am," she'd insisted yet again over last year's Easter dinner of lamb stew. "Save your money for your own families, which, may I point out, I'd appreciate one of my sons to get started on so I can be a grandmother before I'm too old and decrepit to enjoy the experience."

And as always with their mam, that had been that.

Which hadn't stopped Conn and his brothers from buying her a new car for her birthday to replace the battered old wreck she'd been rattling around in. She'd fussed about the unnecessary expense but, being outnumbered, had finally caved in.

Conn was headed into the kitchen when a formidable roadblock appeared in front of him. Feck. Wasn't this what he needed? Lena Sheehan ran the local butchery when she wasn't browbeating her long-suffering husband.

"Well, if it isn't himself," the harridan said, planting her hands on her broad hips. Hair the color of steel was pulled into a tight bun at the back of her neck. "I'd have thought you'd have been long gone by now. Back to all those stadiums around the world filled with fans awaiting your lordly presence."

"Family comes first," Conn said, ignoring the dig. "As I'm sure you'd know well, Mrs. Sheehan," he tacked on mildly. "Having such a large family yourself."

Left unsaid was that three of her five sons had finally escaped to open their own shops in Cork, Limerick, and Dublin, while the youngest, Dolan, had managed to remain far from home by joining an order of missionary priests. Only poor Liam remained beneath his mother's iron thumb.

Lena Sheehan's eyes narrowed behind wire-framed glasses as she studied him, as if looking for the insult.

"It must be difficult, having your father suffering his last days."

When Joseph Brennan had first returned to Castlelough, despite having had his claim to be dying confirmed by both John and Erin Joyce, he'd appeared to be much the same as he'd ever been. Propped up in bed, he'd spun his tales to an avid audience, charming people who had to have become strangers to him after all these years, while managing to ignore the long-suffering wife who'd put up with so much for so long.

The past two weeks, partly thanks to the pain meds, he'd been sleeping more and more, which would have made things more peaceful were it not for the ongoing deathwatch. Which, thankfully, had begun to dwindle off as Joseph lost his entertainment value.

"It's been a challenging time," Conn said obliquely.

"You're probably not used to challenges. What with being so rich and successful and all, life's undoubtedly all peaches and cream."

"Success makes life easier," Conn said. "It doesn't make living easier."

"I suppose you'd be the one to know." The hard look she gave him suggested she didn't believe that for a moment. "I just dropped in to let you and your mother know that we've received a nice order of French pâté."

"With all the geese we have here in Ireland, you imported French goose livers?"

"Irish geese are domestic." She sniffed. "I thought it was appropriate. You being a celebrity. People all over the world will read about your father's funeral supper. I assumed you'd want to live up to expectations."

"You assumed wrong, Mrs. Sheehan." Conn thought, for not the first time, that if there was a God, and He or She were a fair judge of character, Mrs. Sheehan's husband should surely arrive at heaven's pearly gates with his sainthood already having been pronounced after surviving decades of marriage to this woman. "Truthfully, I don't give a flying fig what a bunch of forked-tongue gossipmongers might think of me."

"Well," she huffed. Her face flamed as hot as a turf fire. "I suppose, given your unsavory reputation, I shouldn't be surprised at your lack of respect for your own dying father." She shoved a white paper-wrapped package at him. "I brought your mother a rasher of bacon. Dermott cut it thickly, the way she likes to serve it to her more special paying guests."

"Thank you. I was on my way into the kitchen," he said as he accepted the package. "I'll take it with me. Good day to you, Mrs. Sheehan."

Her lips drew into a razor thin line at being so coolly dismissed. "Good day to you, Mr. High-and-Mighty Rock Star. And for the record, you're not the only person in this village who's appeared on the telly."

With that parting line, she marched across the room and out the door, which his mother had painted a cheerful green as a welcome to arriving guests. Conn knew that Patrick, the eldest of his brothers, touched it up every year right before St. Patrick's Day, which, despite March weather being miserable even for this rainy country, was one of the town's high tourist seasons.

"Well," a familiar voice behind Conn said, "that went well."

Conn turned and shook his head at his eldest brother. "I was thinking of suggesting the woman try selling some of her damn livers to you. To serve at the pub."

"And isn't that thoughtful of you? But I think I'll pass." Instead of smiling at the absurdity, as Conn had expected, Patrick's grim expression signaled a problem.

"How's Mam holding up?" Conn asked.

"She's a rock, as always," Patrick said. "It's Da. He wants to speak with you…alone."

"And if I don't care to speak with him?"

Patrick raked a hand through his black hair. "I can't say as I blame you. But you know his temper only too well. If you don't, and—"

"Mam doesn't need that." Conn handed Patrick the bacon. "Take this into the kitchen for me."

Despite Mrs. Sheehan's unrelentingly negative attitude, the butchery sold the best bacon in all of County Clare. Probably the entire country. Which was why the shop had been featured on acclaimed Irish Chef Paul Flynn's RTÉ cooking program. A fact the woman was not about to let anyone in town forget.

As he headed upstairs to the bedroom, Conn wondered why the hell his father couldn't have just stayed in America. Oh. Perhaps because the divorcee Joseph had left his wife for hadn't wanted to take on the burden of caring for a dying old man who undoubtedly hadn't managed to remain monogamous during *their* two decades together?

Despite Conn's reputation for womanizing, he'd never, *ever* cheated. Which, admittedly, wasn't that difficult when most of his relationships tended to be short-lived. Like that one-night stand he'd had with the American cake baker.

Going back to his teens, when he found out playing music could get him any girl he wanted, Conn had never apologized for his enjoyment of fast cars and fast women. As he'd gotten older, while the women he took to bed were no more eager to settle down in some cozy, thatched-roof country cottage than he was, he *had* grown choosier, moving on beyond the always available rock groupies to women he'd be able to have a conversation with the next morning.

Sedona Sullivan had been different from the moment he'd seen her. In the first place, she'd been so intent on putting the final touches on a white wonder of a wedding cake that she hadn't noticed he'd come into the reception hall.

Even when he'd gained her attention by turning the speakers to stun while blasting out a sound check, her only response had been a furrowed brow and a distracted frown. Then she'd returned to her work, proceeding to ignore him. Which *never* happened.

She'd continued to appear immune to him whenever he'd caught her eye during the reception. Wondering if she might be involved with someone, Conn had nearly given up on her when fate had gifted him with a second chance. Which he'd grabbed with both hands.

She'd made herself clear from the first that she wasn't looking for any relationship beyond a single night. An idea which, perversely, somewhere between making her come twice before they'd even gotten their clothes off and the next morning, had proven unsatisfying.

Not that *she* hadn't satisfied. The vexation was that Sedona had gotten beneath his skin. Which was why, by the time she'd left for America on that Aer Lingus jet the next morning, Conn had already determined to see her again.

Not wanting to give her an opportunity to turn down picking up where they'd left off, he'd decided against calling or emailing while on tour. Instead, he'd planned to use a visit to Mary Douchett as his reason for showing up in Shelter Bay.

Thanks to his bloody father, he hadn't gone to America. Nor had he managed to write any more on the score for Mary's film. His muse, it appeared, refused to visit so long as Joseph Brennan was in Castlelough.

4

JOSEPH BRENNAN WAS definitely fading. His once ruddy face was yellow with jaundice, as were the whites of his eyes, still veined with the red tracings of a long-time drinker. He'd always been hefty, with large, cruel hands that could wield a Rowan switch or wound by themselves. Now, due to the pancreatic cancer devouring his body, he looked like thin pastry dough spread over spindly bones.

He tugged down the oxygen mask when Conn entered.

"Sit," he said as he might to a dog. The hand that had left scars when he'd beaten a six-year-old Conn with a sally branch shook with tremors as he waved toward a chair beside the bed.

"I'd rather stand," Conn responded, remembering how Patrick, the quietest and most easygoing of the Brennan brothers, had come to his rescue that day, punching their father on his jaw, sending Conn's tormenter tumbling onto his ass. Fists flying, Patrick had bent over Joseph and things might have escalated into something far more dangerous had their mother not pulled him away.

In retrospect, Conn was grateful for the intervention. He'd often fantasized about someone killing his father, but he wouldn't have wanted his brother to spend the rest of his life in the gaol due to him. Or his mother to have to live with the thought of her eldest son murdering her husband. Even so, the memory of that day stayed in Conn's mind, as crystal clear as if it had occurred yesterday. Watching this man wailing like a newborn babe as he'd begged for mercy remained a high point in Conn's life.

"So you find this humorous?" His father's querulous question brought Conn's wandering mind back to the here and now and made him realize he'd been smiling at the memory.

"Not at all."

"Then sit the fuck down. How do you think your poor mam would feel knowing that one of her sons forced a dying man to strain his neck to look up at him?"

His father had always been a gambler. Horses, sports, lotteries, bingo (which was the only time Conn could remember this man entering a church), cards...it hadn't mattered. If someone said that the sun would rise tomorrow, Joseph Brennan would make book against it. And while he might be cursed with terrible luck and was a miserable poker player, he played the Catholic guilt card with a practiced expertise.

Conn cursed beneath his breath. Once again protecting his mother from unneeded drama, he caved to the emotional blackmail, threw his body onto a wooden chair, and folded his arms over his chest. "Patrick said you wanted to see me."

"Not particularly." Despite being a profligate liar, there were times when Joseph could be brutally honest. This, apparently, was going to be one of those times. "But since

I don't have much time left before I shuffle off this mortal coil, I feel it's time I tell you some home truths."

"And wouldn't that be a change?"

"You've always had an insolent mouth, boy."

"I suppose it's in my blood," Conn countered.

"That may be." There was a pause as Joseph's gaze drifted out the window to a rolling green pastoral landscape far more peaceful than this house had ever been when he'd been living beneath its roof. "But if that's the case, you wouldn't be getting it from me."

The past few days, as his life's clock had ticked down, his father had suffered hallucinations. From the sly look in those jaundiced eyes, Conn didn't think this was one of those occasions.

He curled a hand into a fist but kept it at his side rather than give in to the urge to slam it against bone. "My mother's never said a negative word in her life." At least none that he'd heard, although Conn had always hoped she had at least one close friend she could confide in.

"What makes you think I'd be talking about my wife?" This time the pause was longer. The older man's eyes drifted shut, whether caused by the dying, the pain medication running through his veins, or merely for dramatic effect.

"I never liked you," he muttered.

"Why don't you tell me something I hadn't figured out for myself by the time I was three years old?" Joseph had never been one to shower love on any of his children. But his sin regarding Conn's mother and brothers had been one of neglect. Toward Conn he'd been unrelentingly cruel.

"But then again, why should I?" the older man continued, as if Conn hadn't spoken. "When you weren't my own flesh and blood but some other man's bloody bastard."

The moment he heard the accusation, Conn knew that it was not born from any hallucination. Nor was it another lie.

It was the absolute truth.

"Do you know, I've waited all my life to hear one positive word from you," Conn said. "Just one." His eyes hardened enough to have his former tormentor cringing back into the feather pillows propping him up. "And while I suspect you meant to deliver one last, final wound to the heart, I'm tempted to thank you."

Rather than suffering emotional pain at the accusation, Conn experienced a rush of cooling relief that Joseph Brennan's blood was not flowing through his own veins. "However, bloody bastard that I am, I'll resist."

As he felt the heavy weight he hadn't even realized he'd been carrying his entire life lift from his shoulders, Conn stood up and left the bedroom. It was only after he joined the others that a thought belatedly occurred to him. If the man wasting away beneath his mother's roof was not his father, who was?

And right on the heels of that question came another. Did any of his brothers know the truth?

5

THE BRENNAN BROTHERS gathered at the pub, as they had at least once a day since the deathwatch had begun. As much as they loved their mother, no, *because* they loved her, it had become a necessity to escape the hypocrisy of pretending to grieve for a man who'd never given a second thought to any of them.

"I'm going to ask you all something," Conn initiated the conversation after Patrick turned over the closed sign and began pouring Powers Gold Label Whiskey into the glasses he'd lined up on the scarred wooden bar. "And I need each and every one of you to swear on our mother's head that you'll tell the truth. No matter what the consequences."

"That sounds serious," Roarke, who'd returned from Dublin for the dying, said. Having served both in Afghanistan and Syria as part of NATO's peacekeeping missions, then the Special Detective Unit (SDU), which was the country's primary counterterrorism and counter-espionage unit, he was undoubtedly the Brennan expert on what defined serious.

"Even dire." This from Aidan, who'd flown in from Barcelona, where he'd spent the past few months painting his exotic, dark-eyed Spanish muse in varying stages of undress. From what Conn had been able to tell, Aidan's models/lovers all seemed to be unable to keep their clothes from falling off.

"Why would we lie?" Declan, eleven months younger than Conn, asked. "We're brothers. We've always shared everything."

"Not exactly everything," Aidan suggested.

Although Conn realized he could well be opening a can of worms with his question, he had to know what each of his brothers knew. And how, if in any way, that had colored the way they'd thought of him.

Patrick momentarily forestalled the conversation by placing a glass in front of each of them, then lifted his own. "Here's to brothers. Never above you. Never below you. Always beside you." His gaze, moving down the bar from Brennan to Brennan, returned to land on Conn. "*Sláinte.*"

"To brothers," the others repeated before tossing down the whiskey.

The triple-distilled Powers went down smoothly, like a kiss from an Irish farmer's daughter.

"Would this question you're about to ask have anything to do with the private talk you had with our father?" Patrick, who'd always been the rock of the family, asked evenly as he refilled their empty glasses.

"Shite," Bram, who'd established a career restoring the country's old, derelict houses, muttered. "He had a private talk with Da?"

At least Bram and Patrick knew, Conn determined. Neither of them had ever been good card players. "As it happens, Joseph Brennan appears not to be my father," he answered Patrick's question.

Patrick's expression showed no surprise. Nor did Aidan's, Bram's, nor Roarke's.

On the other hand, Declan's eyes widened. "We're being punked, right?" He looked around as if expecting someone with a television camera to come popping out from behind a magazine rack in the pub's library.

"He told me himself. This very afternoon," Conn said. "While the man may be able to best the devil himself in a lying contest, in this case I believed him."

Declan shook his head as he speared a look at the four eldest brothers, one by one. "How did you all know and I didn't?"

"Because you're the youngest," Patrick said. "We overheard the fights about it back when you were still climbing Mam's lace curtains. We weren't old enough ourselves to get the entire gist, but later, putting two and two together, it sunk in."

"Still...Damn." Moving beyond the vexation of a family secret having been kept from him, Declan turned toward the subject of the lie. "How shitty do you feel?" he asked Conn.

"Actually," Conn said truthfully, "my initial response, and the one I'm still experiencing, is relief. I've experienced guilt from time to time for hating my father. Now I don't have to concern myself about that." He shrugged. "Besides, the bugger will be gone soon enough."

"Dust to dust, ashes to ashes," Bram said.

"Exactly," Conn agreed. And hopefully straight to hell.

"Meanwhile," Patrick said, "we're not to mention this to anyone. Least of all, Mam."

"I'm on board with that," Roarke said. "She's under enough stress. The last thing she needs is to have her secret exploding out into the open."

They were all as independent as they were stubborn. Yet as heads nodded, Conn knew they were in agreement. "There's a new question on the table," he said.

"We don't know who your father might be," Patrick answered before Conn could ask. "It was a busy summer, with everyone coming from as far away as America for the music festival. The house was so filled that Aidan, who, by the way, is a blanket hog, and I had to share a bed."

"As did Bram and I," Roarke said. "It was like trying to sleep in the middle of Grafton Street." Given that Dublin's main tourist area was made up of shops, pubs, restaurants, and street performers, and knowing how much work his mother had put into her B&B during a *slow* time, Conn wondered how Eileen Brennan had found the time to have an affair. Let alone get pregnant.

Then again, desire could always find a way. Hadn't he kept both his plane and his band waiting in Germany in order to tumble the delectable American cupcake baker?

Conn did the math and realized that it would be half past six in the morning in Shelter Bay, Oregon. They hadn't spent enough time talking for him to know her routine. Would she already be at work, mixing up dough and batters that left her smelling a bit like vanilla? Or would she just be waking up, her long, lean body warmed from a night's sleep, her hair tousled, her eyes heavy-lidded as she emerged from her dreams. Which, egotistical as it might be, he hoped would be of him. As his had been of her.

Did she sleep in something as practical as she'd tried to convince him she was? Or fancy, frippery bits of lace? The kind made for a man to take off? Or maybe, as she had in the feather-topped bed at the Copper Beech Inn, silky soft and perfumed naked skin? And wasn't that memory enough to make him go hard as a pike?

He should have called her. But what could he say? All they'd shared that night were their bodies. Yet instead of leaving him sated, those darkened hours had only left Conn wanting more. Not just sexually. He wanted to know more about Sedona Sullivan, the woman. He wanted to know about her life growing up on that commune Mary had mentioned. Had she run barefoot in wildflower-sprigged meadows? Had she fed chickens and milked cows? Gone skinny-dipping in a local pond?

He knew she would've had friends. Of both genders. Which brought up another thought that caused a spike of something that felt too much like jealousy for comfort. Had some teenage lad tumbled her in a hayloft or on a blanket beneath the trees of an apple orchard?

"Conn?"

Bram's voice jerked him from the fantasy of making love to Sedona in a meadow while the sun shone down between the branches of a gnarled old tree, illuminating her fragrant golden flesh.

"I'm grand," he said. At least a far sight better than he'd been yesterday.

"We'll be getting the pre-supper crowd here soon enough," Patrick said. "Since there's nothing I can do at the house, I'll be staying here for the evening shift, then dropping back in before bed."

"I'll be going straight back to the house," Conn said. Although Mary had offered him her guest cottage, he, Aidan, and Roarke were staying at the house to provide their mother support.

Aidan, who was the most like Conn, speared him with a narrow-eyed look. "Tell us you're not going to try to pry any details from Mam."

"I wouldn't do that." Which didn't mean that he wouldn't give his left nut to know who his father was.

Perhaps, once her husband was six feet under the Irish turf, she'd feel free to tell him about his birth father.

Or perhaps not.

Not that it mattered. Hadn't he made it this far without a father? He could easily go the rest of his life without knowing whose blood was flowing through his veins.

Or so Conn kept telling himself as he, Aidan, and Roarke drove together back to their childhood home.

6

Shelter Bay

MARY JOYCE DOUCHETT had first decided to be a movie star when her now brother-in-law, Quinn Gallagher, had arrived in Castlelough for the filming of his book about the village's sea beastie. Her father had rented a room to the American writer and during those weeks he'd changed all their lives.

Most of all her older sister Nora's, when the two of them had fallen in love. It hadn't been an easy courtship, but you'd never know that by their seemingly idyllic marriage.

Quinn had also changed her from a moody Goth teenager prone to outbursts and tears to a focused would-be actor. Not only had he casually, without any lectures, led her to see the folly of her ways that long ago night she'd slipped out of the farmhouse to meet the boy who hadn't been worth her virginity she'd been about to give away, but he'd gone on to cast her as an extra in the film.

After both Quinn and the director had declared that she had a face made for the big screen, her part had been expanded. By the film's release, not only had Mary forgotten all about the boy who'd dumped her right before the May Dance, she'd decided to become an actress.

It was later, while at university, that she'd become interested in screenwriting, and her first film, *A Secret Selkie*—the story of a motherless young boy who discovered his selkie heritage—had won the screenwriting award at the Jameson Dublin International Film Festival.

Her second film, *A Faerie's Kiss*, based on the folktale of Conla the Fair—son of Conn of the Hundred Battles—running off with a faerie maiden over the sea to the Plains of the Ever Living, had surpassed the awards of her first. It was her third, *Siren Song*, the first in her selkie queen trilogy, which had swept the awards season, ending with a Best Screenplay award at Cannes.

No longer was she the struggling actress who had to star in her own films in order to keep production costs down. Overnight she'd been thrust from being a struggling, independent screenwriter/filmmaker from the rural Irish West into the big leagues of American cinema.

Which, she'd discovered, brought new meaning to her grandmother Fionna's maxim of being careful what you wish for.

She was sitting with her husband out on the deck of the house overlooking Moonshell Beach, enjoying the brilliant display of the sun setting into the sea.

"It can't be easy losing a parent." J.T. brushed her hair to the side to give his lips access to the nape of her neck. If anyone had told her that she'd end up being married to an American Marine turned history teacher, she'd have accused that person of either being daft or having overindulged in Jameson's.

"Even worse when the parent was never the least bit kind. Even cruel."

"Yet Conn cancelled the rest of the band's tour when he got the news about Joseph Brennan's cancer."

"Only to be with his mother. I called him this morning to see how he was holding up, and the first thing he did was apologize for not getting any songs to me. I assured him that I didn't expect him to be working while he's sitting a deathwatch with his family."

"I'd imagine that might interfere with creativity. Especially when you're talking about a love story."

"Everyone's different. Escaping into fiction has been helpful to me during trying times. But I'd never put work before Conn. He's been with me from the beginning, refusing to take money back when I was a struggling newcomer, and again, doing the soundtrack for last year's *Selkie Dreams* for no charge."

Mary had bought that screenplay back from the Hollywood studio that had insisted on creative changes she'd refused to make, no matter how it might send her back to the minor leagues. Or, as Aaron Pressler, the hotshot studio head, had threatened, ensure she'd never work in Hollywood again.

The last part had proven true enough. But only because she'd returned to her Irish movie-making roots, and despite both Aaron's and *Variety*'s prediction that she'd destroy her "selkie franchise," the film had topped the box office charts for three straight weeks and gone on to unprecedented foreign sales.

Now, although she was still writing about selkies, she'd gone deeper, more emotionally tragic than the American movie-making machine would have allowed. Once filming had finished two months ago, post-production had begun. Now that she and the editor had completed their collaboration, all that was left was for Conn to create his usual magic capturing all the layered moods, highlighting emotions and even the plot's turning points. Working from the cue sheets she'd sent him, he'd been ahead of schedule, yet more proof that his hard-living days were in the past.

Then Joseph Brennan had returned to Ireland, and although Mary would never accuse him of lying, she sensed Conn wasn't being quite honest with her when he'd assured her that the score was coming along grand.

"I wouldn't worry," J.T. said. "Despite Conn's infamous reputation, he's too professional to bring a project in late."

"I'm not thinking about the schedule," she said, feeling a familiar melting inside as he began nibbling on her ear. "While I won't argue that it's important, there's enough time in the schedule to allow for delays. It's Conn that I'm concerned about. Despite the estrangement with his father, his father's death has to be affecting him on some level. He's never opened up easily, but if only I could be there, I might be able to learn what's troubling his mind."

And his heart. Mary had definitely sensed things during their brief conversation. Things Conn hadn't been prepared to share. Not even with her. Which could only mean that whatever was vexing him was serious.

"It's not like you chose to get chicken pox," J.T. said.

"And isn't that a ridiculous disease for a grown woman to be getting," she said on a flare of Irish temper she mostly kept banked since outgrowing her teenage tantrums. "I'm so frustrated not to be allowed to fly."

She sighed heavily. Then, as the sun set into the darkening pewter sea in a dazzling display of ruby and gold, she decided she'd fretted enough for one day. Putting her wineglass onto the table beside the wide wicker chair, she framed his handsome face between her palms and brushed her lips over his.

"Come to bed with me, husband," she said against his mouth. "And help me work off my vexation."

He cupped the back of her head with his hand as he deepened the kiss. Then stood up and lifted her into his arms. "I thought you'd never ask," J.T. said as he carried her back into the house.

7

SEDONA TOSSED AND turned as she dreamed, in vivid HD detail, of her last night in Castlelough.

By the time they entered her room at the Copper Beech Inn, she was weak in the knees and, although she'd always thought it was a cliché, the earth began spinning so fast she had to hold onto Conn's shoulders to keep from flying off into space.

Without taking his mouth from hers, he kicked the door shut, then managed to twist the lock and slide the chain into place even as his free hand roamed down her back, to her hip, pulling her closer against an erection that had every cell in her body screaming out yes!

She deserved this, Sedona told herself as he kissed her hard and deep, tangling his tongue with hers. Her sex life had been an arid desert for so long. She was due.

No, she thought as his hand delved beneath her sweater to cup her breast, even as he backed her against the wall and slid a knee between her legs, she was so overdue that even though she was still fully dressed, she was on the verge of shattering into a million pieces before they made it to the bed.

As if reading her mind, he reached between them and unsnapped her jeans. The sound of the metal zipper lowering in the stillness of the night and the brush of his knuckles against her bare stomach had her desperately needy body trembling.

"I never do this," she managed to say as he cupped her.

"And what would that be?"

"Have sex with a total stranger."

"Ah, but we've been introduced by a mutual friend." He stroked a slow, sensual touch against the dampened crotch of her panties. "And trust me, Sedona Sullivan, we most definitely won't be strangers after tonight's over."

She, who never, ever *lost control, actually whimpered as his thumb rubbed her through that soaked cotton. Couldn't she at least have been wearing something silky and sexy? Having had her body locked up all day in the breath-crushing spandex prison of a body shaper—which had undoubtedly reorganized her internal organs in ways she hadn't wanted to think about—when she'd dressed for supper at the pub, she'd been thinking of comfort. Seduction had been the last thing on her mind.*

"We haven't even made it to your bed yet and you're already wet for me."

"Are all Irishmen so arrogant?" she asked, struggling to regain some semblance of control over not just this situation but herself.

"Ah, I'm one of a kind, luv." He slipped a calloused finger beneath the leg band of her boy shorts while skimming his lips along her jawline. "And it wouldn't be arrogance if it's true."

Which he proceeded to prove. Making her come with his fingers, then again with his mouth—kissing, licking, sucking, nipping—until she flew apart in his arms and would've crumbled to the floor if he hadn't lifted her up and carried her to the bed.

"And now that we've dispensed with the preliminaries, it's time for me to make you fly."

Which he did. All night long.

By the time a pale, pinkish-lavender light was brightening the room and the bells from the Church of the Holy Child began to chime, Sedona had decided that not only had the rock star not exaggerated his sexual prowess, he was more of an indulgence than a baker's dozen of her death by chocolate cupcakes.

She'd also realized—correctly, it had turned out—that just as Conn Brennan didn't stay in any box a woman might try to put him in, he was not going to be easily forgettable.

SHE WAS JOLTED out of the erotic dream by the storm that slammed into Shelter Bay with the speed of a fighter jet, bringing with it howling winds and angry, churning waves that picked up driftwood logs like matchsticks and slammed them against the rocky coast. Rain hammered on the roof and battered against her windows like stones thrown from the fist of a vengeful sea god. The hundred-year-old building shook beneath the assault.

Sedona had never liked storms. Their unpredictability, especially here on the often wild and dangerous Oregon coast, always made her anxious. They also brought back memories of one spring when she and her parents had been traveling across the South to a Tennessee music camp for children where her father had been going to spend two weeks teaching.

They'd been camped out in a rural RV park outside Little Rock when, shortly after midnight, a tornado had cut a swathe across the small community. It had missed the park by a mere mile, but as she'd huddled in the dark with the other travelers in the small storm cellar beneath the park's store—which was being battered by the winds and hail of the thunderstorm that had spawned the deadly twister—she'd feared she'd be flung into the air, like Dorothy and Toto, at any moment.

She'd done her research before moving to Oregon. The state was listed as forty-sixth in the nation for frequency of tornadoes, and no one had ever died or been injured by one. Which had been an important factor in her ideal geographical location graph.

This particular storm, triggered by a Pacific typhoon off Hawaii, had been forecast for two days from now, which would have given it time and distance to blow itself out.

Proving the unpredictability of Mother Nature, it had, instead, traveled faster and, from the sound of it, was far more vicious than the Weather Channel and meteorologists at the National Weather Service Storm Prediction Center had forecast.

As bad as being alone in a storm was, it was much worse in the dark. Sedona had no sooner turned on the bedside lamp than the light bulb flickered.

Once.

Twice.

A third time.

Then, just as an enormous black cloud covered the full moon, the light went dead, plunging the bedroom into darkness.

"Damn," Sedona muttered as the storm lashed at the house and her blood thundered in her ears.

The flashlight was in the top drawer of the dresser a few feet away. Believing in always being prepared, she also had plenty of candles on hand. She'd gotten out of bed to retrieve them when the same wind that was rattling her windows blew the cloud away from the moon, offering a stomach-dropping view of an enormous white-capped wave racing across the harbor. Moored boats began bouncing up and down as if they were toys in a bathtub. One sailboat broke loose and tore across the bay as if motorized.

Transfixed, she stood at the window, her hand unconsciously pressed against her pounding heart, unable to move as the boiling, seething rogue wave approached the stone seawall. Then breached it.

Time took on an eerie slow-motion feel. Later, Sedona would not be able to remember exactly how long it took the wave to cross the street and pound into the building, but she did recall that the blow was staggering, knocking her off her feet and sending a framed painting of Castaway Cove crashing down onto her head. Stars exploded behind her eyes.

Then everything went dark.

8

Castlelough

CONN AWOKE BEFORE sunrise with a hard-on. Not unusual. He was, after all, a male in the prime of his life.

But this one had been inspired by erotic dreams of Sedona Sullivan. Enough that even with all that he had on his mind—Joseph Brennan's dying, Mary's movie score waiting to be completed, his music label starting to nag about when was he going to start writing on a new album, his band at loose ends waiting for him to decide what he was going to do about his career (which was essentially on hold), and a new project he'd taken to turn an abandoned Guinness brewery into a loft apartment and recording studio—the frustrating woman wouldn't stop plaguing his mind.

He knew, if he'd seek advice from his brothers, Aidan's immediate answer would be that he just needed to get laid. Which wasn't necessarily a bad idea. Some curvy, wild, fiery redhead who wanted nothing more than hot sex with a rock star. It had been a long time since he'd taken a groupie to bed and the part of him still managing to think with his big head pointed out that sex with strangers whose names he didn't know or wouldn't remember had become depressing a very long time ago.

Still, it needn't go backwards in time, the other voice—the pleasure-seeking one that was voting with the hard-as-a-stone little head who just wanted to get off—argued. He could ring up any number of sexy, intelligent women who shared his aversion to long-term committed relationships and be burning up the sheets at the Copper Beech Inn before breakfast.

The vexing problem that had him grinding his teeth nearly to dust was that Conn didn't want any of those women. What he wanted was a leggy, trim American blond who apparently had meant exactly what she'd said about only wanting a one-night stand. Because he hadn't heard a word, not even a text, from her since he'd watched her walk down the Aer Lingus jetway at Shannon Airport.

Which, of course, was exactly what they'd agreed on right from the start. So why was he so damn frustrated?

When the rooster on a nearby farm loudly crowed his believed success in causing the sun to rise, Conn crawled out of bed, threw on his clothes, crept downstairs, and made some coffee from the machine he'd bought his mother. She'd protested the expense at the time, but he'd argued that it would allow her guests to each have their own flavor, which had won her over.

Then he went out into the back garden and worked out his frustration by taking a hoe to attack the bishop weed that Eileen Brennan had been fighting for all the years she'd lived in this house. Conn had spent much of his childhood hoeing out the damn stuff, only to have it return with a vengeance, especially after a rain. Which, in this wet country, was most of the time.

If he'd hoped to rid Sedona Sullivan from his mind in the same way he was clearing the garden plot, he failed. Because he couldn't unsee the image of her as she'd slept snuggled up against him the morning after Mary Joyce's wedding.

Her hair, freed of that tidy knot she'd worn to the reception, had been splayed over his pillow like strands of spun gold. His morning erection had been pressing against the small of her naked back. Damn, but her fragrant skin had the most amazing color. Unlike so many Irish women these days who, for some unknown reason, insisted on fake tanning themselves to the hue of a Halloween pumpkin, the baker's pale gold hue could only have been natural.

Her chest, beneath his hand on her breast, had risen and fallen steadily, but as he'd stroked her nipple with his thumb, she'd purred as she slowly roused, seeming to float somewhere in those mists of half sleep. When Conn had pressed his mouth against the nape of her neck, she'd lifted her hand to cover his, encouraging him to knead the breast he'd been teasing. During their long, sex-filled night, she'd been an eager participant in everything he'd done to her, *with* her, but on that hazy, rainy morning, apparently she'd preferred to play the passive and let him make the moves.

Which he'd been more than willing to do.

Reaching behind him with his free hand, he'd groped for yet another one of the condoms he'd scattered over the top of the bedside table. When he'd ripped it open with his teeth, the heartbeat beneath his stroking hand had picked up its pace while his own blood had begun flowing hot and fast in his loins.

"Oh, yes," she'd sighed as he'd moved between those soft, silky thighs. A ragged, almost desperate moan had escaped from the depths of her throat as he'd slipped into her and her body tightened around him. Other than those two sighed words of encouragement, neither of them had said a word.

His fingers had tugged at her hardened nipple as he'd driven deep, the deepest he'd ever been. Even after they'd both floated down to earth, he'd still wanted her. Again. Even as he'd realized at the time that *again* would never be enough.

Like the bridge of a song that kept repeating itself over and over, she'd gotten into his head. And, Conn feared, his heart.

9

Shelter Bay

SEDONA HAD NO idea how long she'd been unconscious. Surely it couldn't have been that long. Over the screaming wind, she heard the sound of her storefront windows shattering as the water surged into her bakery downstairs.

Fighting vertigo and double vision, she made her way on shaky legs to the window. Outside, Harborview filled with water as surf continued to rush in from the boiling, churning dark sea. A sudden gust of wind snapped a traffic light pole in front of the neighboring store in half, sending the pole through the store's window and the light flying.

Retrieving her phone from the bedside table, she discovered she had no cell service to call for help. Even if she didn't feel as if she were trying to stand on a tilt-a-whirl, she didn't dare go downstairs, because trying to wade against the tide in the dark could end up with her swept out to sea when the waves ebbed. Making matters worse was the hurricane force of the wind that kept her from escaping her second-floor apartment with the emergency chain ladder she kept on the floor by the window. She was obviously stuck here for the duration. In an attempt to protect herself from glass flying all around the room if the window broke, she took the quilt from the bed, hung it over the drapery rod, then pushed the heavy antique armoire against the window.

Having done all she could, as the wind continued to gust and wail and the rain and hail pelted down and the house trembled beneath the storm's onslaught, Sedona huddled beneath the sheets, her knees drawn up to her chest, and prepared for a long, dark, frightening night.

SEDONA REALIZED THAT she'd finally managed to fall asleep when she was awakened by someone shouting her name from downstairs. Stumbling out of bed, she grabbed the flashlight and made her way to the door to the stairs and was unable to hold back the moan when she saw the still-flooded bakery.

"Don't try to come down," a man's voice called up to her.

"Who's there?"

"Flynn Farraday." Cooling relief flooded over her when she saw his face illuminated by his own flashlight he was shining up on it. "How are you doing?"

"I'm fine now that you're here," she said, deciding this wasn't the time to mention the demons drilling away with jackhammers in her head.

"The water's still four feet up the wall and it took out some of the stairs. I wouldn't trust the ones left to be safe. Go back to your window and we can get you out."

Making her way past the bed, where tangled sheets told of a wild and restless sleep, Sedona shoved the armoire away and yanked down the quilt just as Flynn, looking for all the world like a knight in shining armor (if knights wore red helmets and fireman turnout gear), rode up to her window in the department cherry-picker.

"Hey, pretty lady," he said, sounding as if rescuing stranded women were an everyday occurrence. "Kara suggested you might need a lift."

Sedona leaned out and saw the sheriff's car parked at the curb. Standing in the street still dampened by falling rain, Kara Douchett, clad in a bright yellow rain slicker over her uniform and high black rubber boots, waved up to her.

Sedona waved wildly back at Kara. "Am I ever happy to see you guys!"

She'd always considered herself a strong, independent woman. But sometime during the hours of pitch-black darkness and howling winds, she'd desperately wished that she'd had someone with her. Someone, she considered, remembering the hot dream she'd jolted out of when the storm hit, like Conn Brennan.

Which was totally illogical, given that a firefighter was far more useful in this situation than a rock musician.

"We live to serve," Flynn said. "Are you sure you're okay?"

"I told you, I'm fine now that you're here."

"Said the woman with dried blood on her head."

"What?" She lifted her hand to her forehead. Which, while throbbing, otherwise felt normal.

"Your hair's all matted," he said, reaching out a gloved hand to lightly touch the back of her head.

A faint memory stirred. That explained why the painting was on the floor. A chill skimmed up her arms as she thought about what could have happened if she hadn't chosen against adding glass when she'd had it framed.

"Why don't you gather up some things and we'll get you out of here," Flynn suggested. "We can talk about what happened once you're back on the ground."

"Did everyone survive?" she asked as she climbed into the bucket of the cherry-picker with an overnight bag of necessities.

"As far as we've been able to tell. Kara's had her deputies out door knocking in the areas that got hit the worst. We lost a lot of cell towers, but groups of amateur radio operators, including the high school radio club, have volunteered to help Mac Culhane coordinate emergency services." Mac was the midnight deejay and, Sedona knew, had gotten a lot of the kids building ham radios, as he had when he'd created his own neighborhood radio station when he'd been a boy.

"Other than a couple roofs blowing off in Depoe Bay and some streetlights being broken in Cannon Beach, most of the mid coast did okay. Astoria took a pretty bad hit, but they're getting assistance from both sides of the state border with power crews coming in from Washington."

From her perch high in the cherry-picker, Sedona could see rows of shredded shop awnings. Harborview Drive and the sidewalks were covered with debris. A huge driftwood log the surge must have carried in from the sea sat in the middle of the street. More than a few windows in the storefronts were either cracked or missing. A flashback memory of that shattered southern small town flashed through her mind. This was bad. But not nearly as devastating as that tornado had been.

The roof of Cut Loose Salon had lost most of its shingles, and the sign from Memories on Main—located on the corner of Harborview and Main—owned by Sedona's best friend, Annie Culhane, was lying on the sidewalk in front of the scrapbook store. Proving that the town's citizens were a hardy bunch, people were already out, beginning the cleanup.

Shelter Bay had been given its name because, having been settled around the small harbor, it offered more temperate weather conditions than the coastal side of the drawbridge connecting the bay and the sea. Those who enjoyed the drama of Pacific Northwest storms tended to live coast side. Others, like her, preferring a more peaceful existence, chose the town. Living in the small town had always made her feel sheltered from all of life's storms. Not just meteorological ones.

Apparently she'd been wrong.

Which brought up another thought. "How's your house?" she asked Kara as she reached a sidewalk covered in sticky Douglas fir needles and seaweed.

"It's survived over a hundred years," Kara said of the cliff house Sax Douchett had been deeded by his grandparents, who'd previously inherited it from the widow of an Oregon timber baron. "One puny coastal storm isn't going to take it out. You're staying with us, by the way. Unless you'd rather go visit your parents."

"They're in New York. In a hotel." She needed to call them, in case they'd caught news of the storm, to reassure them that she was all right.

Although she wasn't prepared to share it in front of the small crowd who'd gathered to watch her ride down from her apartment, there'd been more than a few times during last night's squall when she'd wanted her mommy. Now, in the shimmering rain- gray light of a new day, she knew that flying to Manhattan wasn't an option. She had the bakery to take care of. Her parents were undoubtedly consumed with the play, and as much as she loved them both, there was no way Sedona was going to move into their hotel with them so they could hover over her.

"Then it's settled. Bon Temps came out okay, but it's closed today so Sax can stay home with the kids while I keep patrolling. Meanwhile, after you're sprung from the ER, I'll have the deputy who's been doing house checks across the bridge take you out there."

"I don't need to go to the ER." Her vision had cleared. She just wanted some Advil and to be somewhere dry where she could start planning how to get Take the Cake up and running again. Surely there was someplace on the coast she could rent until her landlord had the building repaired.

"You've got a gash on your head. How's your vision?"

"Twenty-twenty."

Kara narrowed her eyes, giving her a hard look. "They'll be able to tell that at the hospital. No double vision?"

Sedona realized it would be foolhardy to lie. "Not this morning."

"Get in the SUV," Kara said. "The sooner we get to the ER, the sooner we can get you lying down at the house."

"I can stay at the inn."

"Since it's possible that talking crazy is just another symptom of your concussion, I'm not going to be insulted that you'd even suggest that. Even you aren't Superwoman and we're friends, right?"

"Of course."

"Well, this is what friends do. And it's not that we don't have room," Kara said. "That house is ridiculously large for two adults and a couple kids but it's been in Sax's family for ages, so there's no way I'd try to drag him out of it. One major advantage is that we have a wired-in generator that runs power to the entire place. Including the water. Did I mention my deep claw-foot soaker tub?"

Independent she might be. But no way was Sedona going to reject an offer to move into a warm, dry house. Especially one that came with a hot bath.

"Did Annie and Mac's beach house come through okay?" The house was on Castaway Cove, where the beached shipwreck that had inspired Sedona's father's rock opera was located.

"It's fine. Like Flynn said, Mac's working with the radio reach-out effort. He and Annie and the kids rode the storm out. They're all fine. Castaway Cove is more sheltered than our stretch of the coast. Enough so that old ship didn't even get shaken loose. They have some driftwood and seaweed to clean up, but nothing Mac can't handle."

"That's good news." Moving on to what she knew was going to be not such good news, Sedona turned back toward Flynn. "How bad is it inside?"

He shrugged. "I'm no insurance adjuster, but I'd guess you're looking at a total gut job."

She'd feared that was the case, but hearing the words aloud hit like a fist.

"We SEALs have a saying: 'The only easy day was yesterday.' So, try thinking of this as an opportunity," he suggested. "A chance to start over from scratch."

"I've been thinking of changing the interior colors." She would have to sit down and calculate costs. Make plans. But at the moment, what Sedona needed was to get the ER exam over with and settle down with a cup of tea and a long, hot bubble bath.

Then she'd think about what she was going to do tomorrow.

10

PHONE SERVICE WAS finally reestablished the day after the storm, Sedona's phone ringing while she was standing in the doorway of Take the Cake. She'd promised Flynn, who'd reluctantly let her past the red *danger* tape after plunking a yellow hardhat on her head, that she wouldn't go all the way inside. Considering the destruction she was viewing, entry didn't look all that possible anyway.

It was her parents, who'd heard of the storm on NPR news and had been trying to get hold of her all night. Not wanting them to worry more than she knew they would, she didn't tell them about her concussion. Still, unsurprisingly, her mother immediately insisted she come to New York and stay with them.

"It'll be such a wonderful experience for you," Skylark insisted. "The theater is so much more than just writers and musicians and directors and producers all doing their individual jobs. It's a very close-knit community."

"Sounds like life on the commune."

"Exactly. I honestly never imagined New York could feel like home."

"I'm glad you're enjoying yourselves," Sedona said.

"It's an eye-opening experience. And although New Yorkers have that reputation for being unfriendly, we certainly haven't found that to be at all true. Everyone has welcomed us with open arms."

"I would imagine the fact that Dad wrote the opera that's providing employment helped." Damn. Sedona wanted to call those uncharacteristically snarky words back the moment she heard them leave her mouth.

"It's reasonable for you to be experiencing some negativity after the wretched experience you've been through," Skylark said with typical calm. "I do wish you'd come here and let me mother you."

"I'm fine," Sedona insisted, leaving out the ER doctor's advice against unnecessary air travel for a few days in order to give her head time to rest and heal. "Thanks to Kara and Sax taking me in, I have a wonderful place to stay while rebuilding my bakery."

"That's going to be quite the project."

"True. But it's good to have a goal." Hopefully it would stop her rebellious mind from continually spinning back to the storm.

Sedona had never thought of herself as a coward, but for some reason, every time she had to think about the destruction of the business that her entire life had been centered around, her mind blurred.

Admittedly, not her *entire* life had been destroyed. She had parents who loved her and close friends, and even customers who cared for her and had already rallied to help her get Take the Cake up and running again. But that didn't stop all those unexpected moments when she wanted to weep.

"Are you sure you couldn't steal a few days for a getaway?" Skylark asked. "You deserve a break." She paused. Just long enough for Sedona, who'd turned away from the disaster inside the building to watch the workmen repairing the breach in the seawall, to sense something else was coming. "It would give you time to meet everyone. Especially Dan Forester, the wonderfully talented young actor who was chosen to play the part of Angus MacGrath."

The tragic hero captain of the doomed ship. Despite her situation, her mother's matchmaking attempt made her laugh. "I'm sure he's a very nice man who'll undoubtedly play the role wonderfully, but I don't believe in long-distance relationships. And nothing's changed my view on marriage since the last time we talked."

"Did anyone mention marriage?" Her mother's innocent tone didn't fool Sedona for a moment. Skylark Sullivan was, in her own way, as stealthy as a ninja. Which was how she'd successfully managed her husband for over thirty years. "Well, I realize you have other, more vital things than romance on your mind right now. But please know that we're here for you, darling. Thinking about it, I should come to Oregon—"

"That's not necessary. I'm fine. Truly." It might be a lie. But only a white one. And well-intended. Her parents deserved this special experience. No way was she going to rain on their exciting Broadway parade.

A silver Mercedes glided up to the curb in front of the building. As a man wearing a three-piece gray suit that had to have been custom tailored climbed out, chills ran up Sedona's arms.

"All is good," she assured her mother. She hoped. "And now I've got to run because someone's here about the building. You guys enjoy yourselves and I'll talk to you soon."

"Tomorrow," Skylark insisted.

"Tomorrow," Sedona agreed.

After ending the call, she turned toward the man from the Portland development company with whom she'd negotiated her lease. "Hello, Bryan."

"Sedona," he responded absently as he turned his gaze from the still wet, soggy mess where only days ago display cases had showed off brightly colored cupcakes. "This place is an even worse mess than I'd expected."

"I'm fine," she said. "Thanks for asking."

"Good to hear," he said, still obviously distracted. "I brought you papers to sign."

"An extension on the lease, I assume?" It would take at least a month or even longer to rebuild what the storm had washed away. With her lease term up in six weeks, an extension was the logical business response to the problem.

"No. Mr. Bondurant feels it makes more sense just to refund your deposit and pay you for the six weeks you'll be losing."

"Although that's generous, it's not necessary." It was also a surprise. Harlan Bondurant had always reminded her of Mr. Potter from *It's a Wonderful Life*. The only thing he cared about was making more and more money, no matter who he had to step on to do it. "I have insurance for loss of income."

"That's good to hear." He finally met her gaze. The near sympathy she viewed in his gray eyes was not encouraging.

"But the thing is, Sedona, Bondurant doesn't intend to renew the leases."

"What?" Sedona's heart dropped. "But I've been an excellent tenant. I've spent my own money on improvements—"

"Which all have either washed or blown away."

"That's why I've already contacted Lucas Chaffee and asked him to come up with a renovation cost estimate to send to Mr. Bondurant and my insurance company."

"You don't get it, do you?" He shook his head. "He'd already determined not to renew your lease. The storm just moved up the timeline."

His expression was calm and reasonable, but as he continued to talk, his words began buzzing in her ear like a hive of angry wasps. She'd made breakfast pastries for Kara and Sax this morning, wanting, in some small way, to repay their kindness. Now, the flaky, break-apart cinnamon roll she'd eaten turned to a rock-hard ball in her suddenly churning stomach.

"I don't understand. I've never been late with a payment. As I said, I've paid for improvements myself, and I've even brought business into the other stores on the block." A block Bondurant just happened to own. She admittedly hadn't had any way to run the actual numbers, but various shop owners had commented how their businesses had picked up once people had started coming to the bakery for cupcakes.

"I've no doubt you have. You make seriously good cupcakes. The best I've ever eaten, which is saying something, since Portland seems to be overrun with cupcake shops. They're becoming like Starbucks. One on every corner. But that doesn't really matter. Not when it comes to the big picture. If it helps, everyone's leases are being bought out."

"The entire block?" And didn't that squash her thoughts of hiring an attorney to fight her case. It also included, she realized, Annie's scrapbook store. "What's he planning to do with all that space?"

"He's going to raze the buildings and build bay-front condos."

"You're kidding. I can't believe the town council actually approved that." Shelter Bay had, after all, fiercely fended off fast-food restaurants, chains, and big-box stores over the decades. It had taken her three months of lobbying the council to get a permit for outdoor seating.

His gaze skimmed down the sidewalk toward the gift shop. "They haven't," he admitted. "Yet."

"I hope Bondurant's bought a pair of ice skates for when hell freezes over." While she couldn't imagine the developer being allowed to build multi-floored condos that would block harbor views, Sedona also didn't expect to be getting back into the storm-damaged building. "What's his plan B?"

"He fully expects to have his original designs approved."

She lifted a brow. And waited. She'd had enough dealings with Bryan White to know that he wasn't comfortable with silence. Which made him a less-than-efficient negotiator.

"Okay, the fallback plan is to build a boutique hotel."

While she'd rather chew the broken shells that had swept in from the sea and were littering the sidewalks like shattered dreams, Sedona privately admitted another hotel was something the town could use. As the economy had begun to pick up, they'd begun getting more tourism.

Like the song said, Sedona knew when to hold and when to fold and walk away. Fighting the developer would eat up her savings, her time, and her energy. Which was already at a low ebb. Even if she found an attorney to take on her case, Bondurant undoubtedly had a hundred high-powered lawyers at his disposal, and while David and Goliath might make a great story, in real life, an underdog's odds sucked.

He put his briefcase onto the top of a wastebin with one of Shelter Bay's resident whales painted on the front and pulled out a sheet of paper. And a checkbook. The check, she noticed as he ripped it out, had already been written.

"No one would ever fault the man for his confidence," she muttered as she took the gold pen and, after reading the page, signed her name and dated it. Pride had her wanting to tear the check into shreds. Common sense had her accepting it.

"That's how he got where he is," Bryan said. Once the deal was done and the paper was back in the expanding folder in the case, he shook his head. "I'm honestly sorry as hell this happened to you, Sedona."

"Are you referring to the storm? Or you being sent down here as a financial storm trooper to close me down?"

"Both."

He did not, she noted, argue her description of his job. Which was more flattering than how she'd always thought of him: Harlan Bondurant's trained lapdog. There'd been rumors that Bryan's ultimate career plan was to marry his boss's daughter and as much as Sedona disliked gossip, she wouldn't be surprised if it turned out to be true.

"But I know you'll bounce right back and have a new plan up and running by this time next week." His Hollywood-bright teeth flashed in what she supposed was meant to be an encouraging smile.

Sedona was still trying to process this unexpected new problem he dumped on her when he had the gall to ask her out. At least she thought he had. But surely while her mind had been reeling, she'd misunderstood.

"I'm sorry. What did you say?"

"I asked if now that we no longer have a business relationship, which could have been viewed as a conflict of interest, you'd let me take you out to dinner."

"Are you asking me out on a date?"

"Surely you're not surprised. I've always sensed a shared attraction. Now, thanks to the storm and Bondurant's plans for the town, we no longer have any reason not to act on it."

"You have got to be kidding." If forced to choose, Sedona would take Vlad the Impaler over Harlan Bondurant's slick, ass-kissing yes-man any day.

"I'm totally serious. I realize that Shelter Bay doesn't have the upscale dining options that the city offers, but I read about Madeline Douchett's James Beard Award in *Portland Monthly* and thought we might check out her Lavender Hill Farm Restaurant."

"Maddy's a close friend of mine, her food tops anything you could find in Portland, and what possibly made you think I'd consider going out to dinner with the man who just took away my livelihood?"

"Would that be a no?"

She'd been down this road before. During her previous career, which was what had landed her in Shelter Bay. "Absolutely. And for the record, Bryan, when a woman says no, she really can mean *no.* In your case, it means *not in this lifetime.*"

With that, she turned away from the ruined building that was no longer hers and walked away.

11

A WEEK AFTER THE storm, Sedona was sitting with Kara, Sax, Annie, and Mac out on the porch of the Douchett home overlooking the sea after a delicious Cajun comfort dinner of Dungeness crab jambalaya Sax had prepared when her phone played Celtic Woman's "From the Heart."

Excusing herself, she went into the house to take the call.

"How are you?" Mary Douchett asked. "I was so sorry to hear about you losing Take the Cake."

"Yeah. Me, too. But I'm not alone. We all lost our businesses."

"So, do you have any plans yet?"

"Not really. I'd considered finding a kitchen to rent, then setting up a booth in The Cannery, like Annie's doing while looking for new rental space, but…"

She shrugged. "Mostly I'm just taking time to sort things out." She left unsaid the fact that she hadn't been able to concentrate enough to follow through on the idea of setting up a temporary shop in the old cannery that had been regenerated into a shopping market.

"It's probably wise to take time off. To allow yourself to ponder all the possibilities," Mary suggested.

Sedona grasped onto that excuse like a drowning woman clinging to a life preserver. "Exactly."

"I've been hesitant to call about this, but since you sound as if you have some time on your hands, I have a huge favor to ask."

"Anything." Whatever Mary might need had to be better than this limbo she'd been mired in.

"I may be wrong, but I thought I sensed a connection between you and Conn Brennan at the wedding."

"And here I thought you'd only had eyes for J.T. that day," Sedona hedged.

"That's true enough," Mary agreed. "However, I seem to pick up on emotions from time to time...I'm not asking you to share specifics," Mary assured her when Sedona didn't respond. "It's just that I'm terribly worried about him. Enough that I'd be in Ireland now if it weren't for these blasted chicken pox keeping me off planes."

"Has something happened?" Had he been in an accident? Injured? But surely that would make news. Bono falling off his bike in Central Park had been covered like a major world event.

"Oh, he says he's fine. As if he's not at all affected by his father dying."

"I didn't know. I'm sorry."

"As we all are. More for his mother, Eileen, than for Joseph Brennan, who, if truth be told, was neither a good husband nor father. In fact, he's been away for most of Conn's growing up years."

"I think I read about an estrangement."

Although she wasn't about to admit it, she'd Googled Conn after returning to the Copper Beech Inn to change clothes after the wedding reception. She'd already heard of the musician, of course. Even if her father hadn't been an admirer of his music, a person would have to live in a different galaxy not to recognize his name.

Once she'd returned home to Shelter Bay, she'd downloaded all his albums and watched his music videos and couldn't deny he was amazingly talented. But after reading about all the supermodels and actresses he'd been involved with, she'd resisted additional searches.

She may have been foolishly reckless to spend that night with him, but Sedona was no masochist. He could be doing the entire Swedish Bikini Team in a hot tub and she wouldn't care because she wouldn't know. Ignorance might not be bliss. But there were times, and this was definitely one of them, when it was better than the alternative.

"Although he's never said anything, there were always rumors in the village about physical abuse," Mary broke into Sedona's thoughts. "And I've seen the scars on the backs of his thighs myself."

"Oh?" Sedona didn't want to know how Mary was familiar with the backs of the rock star's bare thighs.

"It's not what you're thinking," Mary quickly assured her, backing up her claim about being able to pick up on vibes. "We filmed *A Secret Selkie* in County Clare during the winter. Although that worked well enough for the interior scenes, when the sea became too cold and stormy in Ireland, chasing summer weather, we moved to Australia. Conn had already agreed to do the score, and although music is the last to get added to a film, and he could easily have waited until the final cut to get involved, since it was my first venture, he joined us.

"He claimed it was so he'd have a better idea of the story, which would give him a head start on writing the score, but he knew I was as stressed out as a cat watching two mouse holes, so I'm sure that the real reason he came along was for moral support."

"That was nice of him." Sedona wondered if he would've been so supportive if Mary Joyce wasn't so stunningly beautiful.

"It was lovely," Mary agreed. "There were days his steadying influence was the only thing that kept me from falling apart."

Steadying was not the word Sedona would ever use in regard to Conn Brennan. But it was yet more proof that the two were merely very close friends.

"At any rate, while some of us worked on the dailies, Conn and others in the crew would go surfing. That's how I saw the scars."

"Did he say what had happened?"

"I didn't ask. And he didn't tell," Mary said. "But putting two and two together, along with the way that he's never, *ever* once mentioned his father, led me to believe that Joseph Brennan was responsible."

"That's obscene. To treat a child that way."

She wasn't naive. Sedona knew such things happened every day. But having grown up the way she had, she'd never experienced anything but love and acceptance from all the adults in her life. Those who were family by blood and the others in the commune who'd become family by choice.

"Aye, isn't it just?" Sedona had noticed that despite Mary's years living in the States, whenever she became tired, upset, or had a second glass of wine, her accent and Irish syntax would become more pronounced. "And I'm certain the only reason he cut his tour short and went home was to support his mother."

"He cut his tour short?"

"He did. The band performed in Frankfurt after leaving Castlelough. The next day they played Dusseldorf and were booked for Hamburg two days later when he got the call from Patrick telling him that Joseph had returned home. Conn immediately cancelled the rest of the tour, flew right away back to Ireland, and has been there ever since."

Was that why he hadn't called her? Not because he was working his way through a bevy of European supermodels but because he was home supporting his mother? A dutiful son was not the first picture that came to mind when Sedona thought of Conn Brennan. Then she remembered the pride in his voice when he'd mentioned his mother's cake baking contest wins.

"I'm so sorry."

"I suppose I should be, as well," Mary said with a sigh. "But if truth be told, I suspect, in the long run, it'll be for the best for all of them. Except perhaps Joseph, who undoubtedly will be having to do a good bit of penance in the beyond." Her voice hardened in a way Sedona had never heard before.

"But that's not why I'd be ringing you," she continued. Sedona could envision her shaking off uncharacteristically negative thoughts. "I was wondering, although I know this is the worst possible time, if you could run over there, see how he's doing, and report back to me firsthand. Patrick's been like a damn clamshell when it comes to imparting any information about his brother, and Conn's down to mostly monosyllables when we speak."

Ever since they'd first met, Mary had never acted like the international movie star she was. But referring to flying across not only a continent but also the Atlantic Ocean as if it were no different from running down to the market for a quart of milk showed that, while the screenwriter/actress might have fit right into Shelter Bay life, another part of her dwelt in a very different world than ordinary people.

"I'd pay," she said when Sedona hesitated again.

"It's not that." Okay, it was. Even with the loss of income insurance and the unexpected check from Bondurant, she wasn't exactly rolling in money.

"I insist. You have to be financially strapped, with all the repairs and remodeling."

"That's a moot point, since I've lost the building." When Mary gasped at that bit of news, Sedona gave her a short version of events. "So, now I've got to come up with a new business plan." Which was even more difficult due to her uncharacteristic lack of focus.

"I can imagine. I face the same dilemma whenever I begin a film. What I can afford to put in, what to cut, how the timing will be. It involves a great deal of juggling of pie tins, to be sure. Which is why, I thought, perhaps a few days staying at my guest cottage in Castlelough would get you away and give you a fresh perspective on things.

"If I hadn't been here in Shelter Bay, away from Hollywood, when my former studio was trying to ruin my film, I doubt I could have seen my options as clearly. Distance, I've found, can be helpful…

"I think he's in trouble, Sedona," Mary said. "Although Conn comes off as bold as brass, he's always been an expert at holding his thoughts and emotions close to the chest, as you Yanks would say. Which is why I was hoping that perhaps you might be able to get him to open up."

"If, after your history, he hasn't told you what's going on with him, why would you think he'd open up to me?"

"Because he called the day after the wedding with plans to visit me here after the tour ended. Your name came up then, which gave me the sense that his reason for coming to America wasn't to talk about my film but to see you again."

And wasn't that an out-of-the-blue surprise? "Let me think about it," Sedona said as she tried to digest Mary's information. "I'll get back to you in an hour or so. But I still don't know how I could be any help."

"Conn's life has been complicated. What you'd be offering him is friendship without the burden of backstory drama that would come with someone who's known him for so many years."

Which was ironic, Sedona thought, since she and Conn had their own shared backstory. Granted, it was brief, but that night was going to be difficult to ignore. At least on her part.

"While you're deciding, I'll go online and find some flight options, just in case," Mary said.

After returning to the porch, Sedona shared the gist of the call with Kara and Sax.

"If you can help Mary's friend, I think you *should* go," Kara said. "And although I've tried not to put any more pressure on you, we've been worried about how you're coping after the storm."

"I'm fine." Sedona repeated what she'd been saying ever since she'd ridden to the ground on the fire department cherry-picker.

"No," Sax disagreed. "I don't think you are. I saw ghosts when I first got home," he said mildly, as if envisioning dead people were an entirely normal event. "My old battle buddies hazed me, rode around with me, they were pretty much in my face all the time. Even that time I came to you for business advice when I wanted to rebuild Bon Temps." When his gaze shifted to his wife, his eyes warmed in a way that reminded Sedona of how her father looked at her mother. "Then Kara came into my life, and they left."

"You certainly hid it well."

"That's what we all think," Kara said. "But to those who've been through it, it's obvious. You can say it was 'just a storm' all day long. But if that were true, you wouldn't have slid downhill from Malibu Barbie to Morticia Barbie."

"Ouch." Sedona rubbed her chest. "Direct hit, Sheriff." Not much remained a secret in Shelter Bay, so she knew of her nickname. But no one had ever said it to her face. Just as no one had ever compared her to the Addams family matriarch.

"We're worried." Kara covered Sedona's hand with her own. "If you're not going to get professional help—"

"I don't need therapy," she shot back. Okay, so that was definitely uncharacteristically snappish, but it was only normal that she'd be under some stress, Sedona assured herself as her stomach clenched in defense. All she needed was to get her damn life organized again. "I just have to put on my big-girl underpants and move on."

"Sometimes easier said than done. Especially when your life, which you pretty much take for granted, is threatened," Kara said in a way that had Sedona thinking there might be more to her friend's life story than having been left a widow with a young son.

"Your situations were different. Sax, you fought wars. You were also held prisoner and managed to escape. Kara, you faced dangerous situations as a cop. I sat out a storm in the safety of my own home." She shook her head, embarrassed to even be having this conversation. "I have a lot on my mind. I just need some sleep and I'll be fine."

"Sleep would help," Mac entered into the conversation. "But it might not solve your problem. After I got blown up at that market in Afghanistan, I relived the day time and time again in my nightmares."

"I can't imagine what you've been through," Sedona said. "But like Sax, you have a horrific war experience to recover from. I went through one night of a storm. I'm just tired, which makes multitasking more difficult."

"Before the storm, you could keep a dozen flaming balls in the air while doing tour jetés on a tightrope without blinking an eye," Kara argued. "Hell, you probably created spreadsheets in your sleep.

"Sedona, we've all experienced post-traumatic stress. I'm a police officer, Sax and Mac were both soldiers. We know what it looks like and we know how it feels. You don't have to be ashamed. Between the storm and the concussion and the loss of your shop and home, you've experienced significant trauma. But life moves on and sometimes, just when you least expect it, fate has a wonderful surprise in store for you. If you're not going to consider talking to a professional, getting away from the scene of the storm might prove helpful."

Hiding away in a colorful Irish cottage was appealing for many reasons. Conn Brennan could prove a problem, though it wasn't as if they were romantically involved.

"You're making valid points," Sedona admitted. If she were to be perfectly honest, even as her head was telling her everything was fine, she felt empty. And worse yet, useless. She was always the one who solved problems for others. She was a doer. A fixer. Not a whimpering whiner. For the first time in her life, she didn't have a plan. She might as well be adrift in a rowboat out there on that wide steely sea.

Okay. She did need a rest. Needed, as her mother would say, to find her center again. And where better than Ireland, a land that had always soothed her soul? Well, except for that reckless night with Conn that had been anything but soothing.

"You'd be helping Mary by easing her worry about her friend." Kara pushed yet another button in a way that had Sedona suspecting that the sheriff was probably dynamite at coaxing perps into confessing to crimes. "Conn Brennan could probably use some support during this sad time. And you can't discount that the guy's really hot. If I weren't happily married, I sure wouldn't turn down an opportunity to comfort him."

Sedona had to laugh at the way Kara had deftly lightened the mood. Perhaps she was right. Perhaps time and distance would help her regain her sense of purpose, and since she wasn't making any progress here, it couldn't hurt.

"And while you're over there, while I look for new space for Memories on Main, I'll also find possible space for Take the Cake two-point-oh for you," Annie volunteered.

Realizing that she was outnumbered, Sedona caved.

So she'd be returning to Ireland, despite not being nearly as optimistic as Mary that she'd be any help to Conn. Not when she hadn't managed to find a way to help herself.

12

Castlelough

CONN WASN'T SURPRISED by Mary's call. She'd been checking in on him for weeks. And not, he knew, because she was concerned about her film, though he was feeling guilty on that point. Things had been going well until Joseph had shown up. Then not only had the bloody man stolen his sleep, he'd apparently chased off Conn's muse, causing his writing to grind to a halt. Not that he was prepared to share that with Mary. There was no point in giving her something to fret about when he'd manage to get back on track. Somehow. Because failure was not an option.

After he'd assured Mary that he was doing grand, that his mother was holding up, and yes, he'd tell Eileen Brennan how sorry Mary was that she couldn't be there, she turned to the real reason for her call.

"I'm ringing you to ask a favor," she said.

"Anything for you."

"You always say that."

"Because it's always true."

He could see her smile at that. Imagine the color drifting into her cheeks. The mental image lifted his spirits for the first time in weeks. "So," he said, "what can I do for you?"

"Pick up a friend who'll be staying at my cottage for a while at Shannon tomorrow morning?"

"No problem. Who is it I'll be looking for?"

"Sedona Sullivan."

The name hit like a blow to the chest. "The baker?"

"That would be her. I believe you met her at the reception."

"I seem to remember a leggy blond Yank," he hedged with studied carelessness. "Why would she be coming back so soon?"

"Ah, and isn't that a tragedy?" she said on a sigh.

Conn knew Mary well enough to know when she was playing him. She'd obviously sensed something between them and was fishing. Well, she'd also known him long enough to know that he wasn't some stupid brainless guppy who'd jump at the bait.

He waited her out.

Mary was many things. She was gorgeous, intelligent, creative, and one of the most caring individuals he'd ever known. But when she got an idea in her head, the female hung on with all the stubbornness of an Irish terrier.

"There was a storm," she said finally, surrendering to the silence humming between them. Then proceeded, with many frustrating asides that had him wanting to shout at her just to get on with it, to tell him the tale with the skill of the born storyteller she was.

"So," she finally finished up, "Sedona was understandably a bit stressed, so some of us convinced her to get away for a short rest."

The irony was that Conn had intended to go to Shelter Bay after the tour wrapped up. He'd been thinking about Sedona Sullivan a lot. Wondering if that connection between them had just been an overload of romanticism from drinking the wedding Kool-Aid at the reception or if it might actually be something more serious.

Thanks to unforeseen circumstances, he still hadn't managed to get away, but now Sedona was coming to him. And while the timing couldn't have been worse, Conn was Irish enough to believe in fate. Which was why he was going to grab this unexpected opportunity to explore the chemistry that had tormented his sleep and had him waking up each morning as horny as one of his brother Declan's billy goats.

THE FLIGHT MARY had booked allowed a long enough layover in New York for Sedona to take a cab into Manhattan to meet her parents for dinner and a quick tour of the theater where Freebird's play would be performed before she continued on to Ireland.

Even booking at the last minute, Mary had somehow managed to score a seat in business class, which should have been a treat. Unfortunately, due to all the stress she'd been living with, nerves about seeing Conn Brennan again, topped off by a flirtatious Irishman seated behind her chatting up his seatmate all night long, Sedona arrived at Shannon Airport feeling like a zombie.

Fortunately, she wasn't going to have to drive to Castlelough. Since she'd have use of the car kept garaged at the cottage during her stay, Mary had insisted on sending a car and driver to take her to Castlelough.

After making her way through customs, she went to baggage claim to retrieve her luggage and meet her driver.

Sedona saw Conn the minute she entered the area. It would've been impossible to miss him. Wearing a white T-shirt that showed off the ripped torso she'd come to know well, worn jeans, and leather work boots, he looked hot, dark, and dangerous.

"You're my driver?" Terrific. And wasn't that a great start to encouraging him to open up to her?

"I am." Apparently unwounded by her sharp, negative tone, he held out a cardboard cup. "Knowing you'd be bringing luggage, I brought my own vehicle from Dublin rather than the Ferrari. Which, by the way, was a rental. Thinking you might have a jet lag on, I picked you up some coffee."

As seemingly every cell phone camera in the place began snapping away at them, Sedona accepted the coffee with a murmured, "Thank you." Inhaling deeply, she breathed in the fragrant steam. "I apologize for being rude." She glanced over at the young Irishman who was still talking as he and the young woman passed. "It was a long night."

"After some longer days, I hear."

"They've been trying. But not nearly as difficult as yours must have been." She took a sip and sighed. "This is exactly what I needed." What she didn't need, nor had she expected, was to immediately land in Conn's rock star spotlight.

"I also brought you sugar." He held up a bag.

Noticing he hadn't addressed the issue of his father, she looked inside the bag. "A scone."

Due to tangled nerves twisting her stomach in knots, she'd turned down the lovely airline breakfast served on Wedgewood china with fresh-squeezed orange juice in a Waterford crystal tumbler. But this was not a run-of-the-mill, everyday scone. Nearly as large as her hand, it was stuffed with blueberries and raspberries and sprinkled with powdered sugar.

"It is, indeed. Since the baker who was making sweets for Monohan's Mercantile, as well as Patrick's pub, ran off to Dublin and married her computer programmer sweetheart last month, Castlelough has been suffering a dreadful dearth of bakery goods. But when Nora Gallagher heard you were coming, she whipped these up. There are more at the cottage."

"That's incredibly nice of her." Nora, Sedona remembered from having met her at the wedding, was Mary's older sister, married to a best-selling American novelist.

"She was pleased to be able to welcome you back. If you'd prefer, you could save the scone for later, and we'll stop and get you a proper full Irish breakfast on the way to Castlelough."

"No." She shook her head and pressed her hand against her stomach, which had growled in response to the aroma of baked dough wafting from the bag. "This is perfect. Plus, I can eat it in the car so we don't have to waste time."

"Ah, but you know what we Irish say about time," he said with a glint of familiar humor in his neon blue eyes.

Even as some distant voice in her brain warned her against looking in that misty rearview mirror, Sedona's mind drifted back to how, when she'd been getting dressed to leave the inn for the airport, he'd talked her back to bed for just one more round. "When God made time, he made plenty of it," she repeated what he'd told her at the time.

"Aye. 'Tis true enough." His brogue thickened, the same way it had when they'd been making love. *No*, the rational, good angel told the frisky one sitting on her other shoulder. *Don't even go there.*

Easy for you to say, the reckless angel, the one Sedona had listened to that rainy spring night, shot back. *All you ever do is work and make those stupid spreadsheets. You never want to have any fun.*

I came here for peace and quiet, countered the stern voice of self-discipline. *And to help Mary out by seeing if you can make this time easier for her friend. Which doesn't mean picking up where we left off.*

Unfortunately, even as she fought to give herself very good advice, blood began to simmer in Sedona's veins.

"Besides, any time spent with you is no hardship, Sedona Sullivan." As she looked up into Conn's electric-blue eyes a long, humming moment, Sedona knew that keeping any emotional distance from this man was going to be easier said than done.

As they left the terminal, Sedona felt as if they were leading a parade and considered that he should have arranged for a contingent of ground troops to clear the way through the mob of fans. Unlike so many celebrities she'd seen behaving badly on Internet video clips or *ET*, Conn hadn't arrived with huge bodyguards to keep people away. Instead, every few feet, he'd stop, chat, sign autographs, and pose for selfies.

"Are you always so accessible to your fans?" she asked after he'd finally explained to the mob that his friend had just gotten off a long flight from the States and would appreciate some quiet to help overcome jetlag.

Amazingly, they obeyed, fading away, leaving the pair to walk to the car park alone.

He shrugged. "I'm only returning their loyalty, which has paid my rent and fed me well. I wouldn't want you to think I was boasting, but some actually travel across continents to attend a show. There's this one lad, from Germany, who's shown up in every single city over this past tour. He writes a blog titled 'On the road with Conn and Celtic Storm' chronicling his adventures with videos taken on his phone. Not only is it vastly entertaining, it's gained him thousands of followers of his own."

"All that traveling must cost a fortune."

"He gets paid for his YouTube hits, which pays for his expenses with some left over. It's a bit like making an indie documentary while bypassing film studios who'd want a significant cut of the profits."

"The times, they are a-changing," she quoted Dylan.

"And wouldn't that be the truth," he agreed.

"Mary told me about your father," she said as they reached his vehicle. That he could consider the big metallic black Porsche Cayenne SUV *frugal* only emphasized the vast difference in their lifestyles. And why, in this land of gray skies, did he need the dark tinted windows more suited to a rapper or a Secret Service agent? "I'm so sorry."

"That's kind of you," he said as he put her carry-on and larger suitcase into the back of the vehicle. "But no sympathy is necessary." He held the passenger door open as she climbed up in the seat. "If I were to be honest, I'd have to say that I finally have something to be grateful to the man for."

"Oh?"

"Had Joseph Brennan not decided to return home to Ireland for his damnable dying, Mary would've had no reason to send you here to get me out of my music writing funk."

"That's not the reason I'm here." Sedona also found it a bit odd that he spoke of his father by his full name. Then again, everything in her life the past weeks had been out of sync, as if ever since meeting Conn here in Castlelough, the entire world had tilted on its axis.

"Isn't it, now?" He shook his head in obvious disbelief, walked around the front of the car, climbed into the driver's seat, and headed out of the airport into the morning commute traffic.

Sedona decided this was no time to argue the point because while she knew every inch of that lean, mean body, she knew very little about the man himself. No way was she prepared to stumble around in such a conversational minefield while she was so jet-lagged.

13

Neither spoke as they drove north along the River Shannon estuary, through rolling pasturelands that had once been inhabited by cattle barons and, in times long past, ancient Celtic kings. Once off the highway, the narrow road twisted through a maze of hedgerow-separated fields, past whitewashed cottages, many of which, even in this twenty-first century, possessed thatched roofs.

After crossing a small stone bridge, they came to a sign welcoming them to Castlelough—home to the legendary Lady of the Lake. A second sign proclaimed the village to be the sister city of Shelter Bay, Oregon, America. When Sedona had first visited the tidy, medieval town and taken in the colorfully painted shops that brightened the soft days with hanging baskets of cascading flowers lining the cobblestone sidewalks, she'd been charmed. This time, she felt a vague inner click that she knew her mother would take as some sign from the universe, but since Sedona and the universe had not exactly been on talking terms before, she decided it was only a caffeine/sugar rush from the coffee and scone she'd polished off.

He slowed while driving past the gleaming white St. Bernadette Hospital, with its tall Palladian windows. Was he wondering how his father was doing inside? Did he feel guilty about driving her to the cottage instead of sitting vigil with his family?

"That's fortunate that the town has its own hospital," she said.

"It began as a workhouse, running from the 1800s until the second decade of the last century," he told her. "We have Quinn Gallagher to thank for its conversion. Before Nora's husband paid to have the building transformed, people were forced to travel to Ennistymon or Ennis for medical treatment."

"Which would have been more difficult for your mother in this situation."

"It would. Yet Joseph didn't go to hospital. He'd been staying at the house since arriving back in the country."

"Oh. Well." Mary had neglected to mention that part. "I imagine that can get a bit awkward."

"It was, indeed," he agreed. "But things will undoubtedly get back to normal soon enough now that he's finally gone."

"He died?" The past tense Conn had used belatedly sunk in.

"He was after dying last night. Which, of course, would have been while you were traveling here and out of pocket, so Mary couldn't reach you."

Having lived in Ireland, Sedona knew that the *after perfect* tense of the language signified the recent past. In this case last night. She pressed her fingers against her tired and aching eyes, regretting that she'd forgotten to check her email after the plane had landed. "Now I really am sorry," she said. "You should be with family rather than taking time away to fetch me from the airport."

"It was a relief to escape," he brushed off her apology. "My brothers are all there and probably half the town. Not so much for him as for my mother. And if there's one thing the Irish love, it's an excuse to get together and talk. The wake's tonight, but you needn't concern yourself about that. When you ring Mary, you can assure her I promise not to get drunk and cause a scene, so there'll be no need for a chaperone."

"I'm not here to chaperone anyone." For a man whose father had just passed on, he didn't seem terribly depressed. Then again, if what Mary had told her about those scars being a result of having been beaten by the deceased man was true, Sedona could hardly expect him to be crying in his Guinness.

While she was still trying to wrap her mind around what she was supposed to be doing here, if not to try to help lift him out of depression, Conn pulled over and parked in front of a hulking stone building. It was obviously unoccupied. The windows were boarded up with sheets of plywood that a teenage boy was currently tagging with a can of green spray paint.

"I'll be right back."

He walked over to the teen, who, instead of running away as Sedona might have expected, merely stood there, chatting away as if getting caught committing vandalism by a rock star was an everyday event. Whatever they were discussing, a peaceful accord appeared to have been made. After doing one of those mysterious male complex fist-bumping handshakes, Conn walked back to the SUV with the paint can while the teen pedaled away on a bike.

"I wouldn't have taken you for a member of the neighborhood watch," she said after he'd tossed the can into the back of the SUV and returned to the driver's seat.

"Sean Malone's a second cousin on my mother's side." Conn started the engine and continued rumbling down the cobblestone road through the town. "I merely told him that if he didn't hand over the paint, I'd be ringing his parents and letting them know what he was up to."

"Small towns," she murmured.

"Wouldn't that be true enough? One summer, I was returning home after taking a local girl to the movies. By the time I got to the house, no less than six people had rung up my mother to tell her I'd been speeding."

"I've no doubt she was shocked by that news alert," Sedona said dryly.

His answering chuckle confirmed her words. "Sean's a good enough lad. Certainly better than the hell-raising black sheep I was when I was his age. He's just mad about his father losing his job when Guinness shut down operations here. Which is how the brewery came to be abandoned."

"That's a shame."

"Since paid work has always been hard to come by out here in the back-of-beyond West, even more so since our booming Celtic Tiger economy crashed and burned, you'll be getting no argument from me," he agreed as he turned off the road onto an even narrower country lane. "Which is why I bought it."

"You bought a brewery?"

"No." He paused as a thirtysomething woman in jeans and a blue-and-yellow County Clare football jersey shooed a bevy of geese across the road in front of them. "Patrick, whom you've already met at the pub, is the brewer in the family and already has a much smaller, more modern operation to make his beers. I merely bought the building."

"Why?"

"I have plans for it." He waved to the woman, who smiled and waved back, then continued on.

"You didn't mention that when I was here for the wedding."

"We didn't spend that much time on conversation," he reminded her. "But it's a moot point because I hadn't yet bought it."

"But you did have plans to do something with it."

"Not at the time. But I do now."

She wondered how a man could buy an entire building without having done an extensive study. Then remembered whom she was talking to. The man who'd claimed to go with his gut. Which might be fine for musicians. Such a leap-into-the-mist music writing method had, apparently, served him very well. But something as conventional as investing in real estate? Sedona could more easily imagine sprouting wings and soaring over the Castlelough cliffs than behaving so irresponsibly.

"Are you going to share those plans?" Apparently Conn hadn't gotten the memo that the Irish were supposed to be talkative. "Or are they top secret?"

He shot her an amused look. "I finally have your attention. I was wondering what it might take."

"I don't know what you're referring to," she hedged. As his gaze dipped down to her lips, she resisted licking off any powdered sugar that might have lingered.

As if she'd been alone in feeling the jolt of chemistry that could have electrified the entire west of Ireland for a month, he returned his eyes to the road. "When you didn't call or write or text after our night together, I had no choice but to assume that you no longer respected me the next morning."

"We'd agreed," she reminded him. "Besides, *you* could have called *me*." Rather than move on without a glance back.

"Agreements can always be altered," he said conversationally. "I am surprised to discover that you'd be falling back on the old rules of waiting for the man making the first move. I seem to recall you informing me that you're an independent-minded woman who wasn't in the market for a lifemate but only up for some hot shagging that would be enjoyable by both parties. No strings or entanglements. No promises."

Was he actually laughing at her? "You're right, of course. That was our agreement."

"Perhaps you'd feel more comfortable if my solicitor wrote up an official contract for our time together during your visit here?"

"That won't be necessary." Wanting to get off this topic, she turned her attention toward a flock of sheep, marked with various flashes of fluorescent paint to signify ownership. "It was only idle curiosity. Whatever you have planned has nothing to do with me."

"I was only pulling your leg, luv." When he put his left hand on her thigh, her heart kicked up. Not as hard and fast as it had during the storm. But too close for comfort. Way more than she was prepared for. "And to answer your question, I'm going to be living there."

"In an abandoned brewery? Why?"

He shrugged the wide shoulders that strained at the seams of the T-shirt. "Why not?"

"Because, well..."

Sedona couldn't think of a reason off the top of her head.

"You'd expect me to be living in a designer-decorated bachelor flat with a mirror above my bed?" His tone was light, his eyes serious.

"Not exactly that," she muttered. Though he'd come close. She also did *not* want to think about Conn Brennan's bed. Nor did she want to remember being braced between those dark, sinewy arms as he'd taken her, hard and fast, up against the wall.

"Home never had a big attraction for me," he said as her rebellious body hummed at the memory. "I couldn't wait to get out of this village, and once we began touring, I'd look forward to all the different cities, the different hotel rooms. You open the door and you never know what you're going to get."

Which was exactly what Sedona had always considered the downside of travel. Not knowing what was behind any given door. Could they be any different?

"But being forced back here recently caused me to look at my sleepy hometown with new eyes," he continued in that husky voice known the world over. The voice that brought to mind too many unfiltered cigarettes in too many smoke-filled pubs, too many whiskey chasers, and murmured words of all the things he intended to do to her.

With her. And by the time the sun had come up the next morning, he'd definitely proven himself a man of his word.

"I've spent so many years wandering the world like an Irish traveler—which, as you undoubtedly know, having lived here, would be our gypsies—my flat in Dublin is mostly only used as a place to throw my bags. So I decided it was time for a change."

"Just like that."

"Exactly like that." His smile was the same one he'd bestowed on her when she'd explained her spreadsheets that night in his brother's pub. "I'm turning the top floor into a loft apartment. It has a grand view of the harbor on the other side, which you can't see from the street.

"Then the first floor will house various studios to record local Irish artists. Especially those from here in the West, who can't afford the high rates and living expenses in Dublin or London."

"You're actually moving here? For good?"

"For the time being," he said. "After I produced Celtic Storm's last album, other musicians contacted me and asked if I'd produce theirs, so since I'd enjoyed the creative challenge, I thought I'd give it a try, just for something different.

"Because, as you could tell, there's still a great deal of work to be done, the past weeks I've been staying in my old room in my mother's house with two of my brothers who've also arrived from out of town. We're also there to run interference with all the visitors. The plan was for me to move to Mary's after the funeral tomorrow. She invited me to stay in her guest cottage during the renovation."

The cottage *she* was staying in?

"And you needn't get upset about the possibility of sharing a bed with me again," he said as her nerves tangled and her hormones spiked at that idea. "When she first made the offer, Mary had no idea you'd be coming here. Yesterday we decided I'd move into the main house while you're visiting. I moved my things out this morning. Though I can move them back again so you can have the house. Whichever you prefer."

Her first thought was that she'd *prefer* to be as far away from this man as possible. Like back home in Shelter Bay. "The cottage sounds lovely," she said, turning her attention back to the rolling green hills.

Perhaps Kara and Sax had been right about her needing a break. Not that she had PTSD. She'd never been in a firefight, never witnessed anyone killed or blown up.

"It was only a storm," she muttered. Then realized she'd spoken out loud.

"We have our share of Atlantic gales here on the western coast," he said mildly. "Some worse than others. But when the rain is pounding, rattling windows like stones, the wind sounds like banshees screeching and the lights go out, a storm can get under your skin. Like snakes writhing in your head. It'd come as no surprise if you'd be having a bit of trouble getting past your experience."

"Is that what Mary told you?"

"She told me that you could use some away time after having lost your building first to the storm, then your greedy landlord. She shared that she was concerned about you. The same as she undoubtedly told you that she's concerned about me."

"Does she have a reason to be concerned about you?"

He waited a beat before answering. "Not anymore."

If that were true, Sedona wondered if any possible change of attitude had to do with his father's death. Not wanting to delve into complex, untidy family matters, she remained silent as the pastoral beauty, dotted with biscuit-brown cows, rolled by the window.

She needed this. The peace. The solitude. The irony was there was nothing peaceful about the way Conn Brennan made her feel.

14

MARY MIGHT HAVE worried overly much about him, but she was right on the money when it came to the woman who was pretending vast interest in the scenery. When he'd first seen Sedona Sullivan, focused like a laser on that towering white wonder of a wedding cake, the Beach Boys had begun harmonizing in his head. Having been writing songs nearly all his life, Conn knew that song lyrics were mostly fiction.

But despite being from the rainy Oregon coast, she had, in one leggy blond package, epitomized every male's fantasy of a Beach Boys' California girl. While she might not have given him an iota of encouragement, he hadn't imagined the chemistry between them. Not wanting to piss Mary off by hitting on one of her friends at her wedding, he'd reluctantly kept his distance. Until he'd walked into his brother's pub.

They might not have danced at the reception, but they'd damn well spent the rest of the night doing the horizontal tango. The following morning, she'd looked even more delicious than the wedding cake she'd made—all warm and sleep-rumpled, with her formerly tidy French twist tumbling over her bare shoulders.

The woman who had gotten off the flight from America this morning bore little resemblance to the one whose body he'd come to know so intimately that night. Despite Mary's fretting, he hadn't expected Sedona Sullivan to look so fragile. So lost. As slender as a sally willow, she appeared in danger of being blown over by a stiff wind and the deep shadows beneath her eyes gave her the look of one of the *tais* who populated the ghost stories he and his brothers would scare each other witless with.

Conn would be the first to admit to occasionally being self-centered. As a younger brother, he hadn't shouldered nearly the responsibility Patrick had taken up, and although it wasn't spoken about, except when he and his brothers had gotten into fisticuffs over some long-forgotten disagreement, he'd been his mother's favorite. Conn had always suspected that the extra attention he'd received had been meant to balance out her husband's cruelty. But now he wondered if it could have been born from warmer feelings Eileen Brennan had continued to harbor toward his birth father.

Which was neither here nor there, he reminded himself with a stiff mental shake. What he should be thinking about was how to help Mary help this woman. It went without saying that he'd have to try to be emotionally tender, something that wasn't second nature to him, having walled off softer emotions at an early age. And patient, which *definitely* wasn't his long suit. He'd also have to ignore the testosterone jolt that had surged through him the moment he'd seen her this morning.

That last requirement was going to be the most difficult to pull off. Because even as exhausted as she appeared, he still wanted her. Naked. In his bed. In the shower. On the kitchen table. Up against the wall. In front of a glowing peat fire. All those scenarios, and more, had tormented his mind ever since he'd made the mistake of letting her get away.

"The Irish tourism bureau should put this on a poster," she murmured, taking in the whitewashed cottage with its thatched roof, Irish linen curtains, and cranberry-red door as he pulled into the cobblestone driveway.

"It's a famine cottage. Left to crumble after its inhabitants either died or emigrated. My brother Bram is making a fine living restoring our old buildings that had the strength to remain standing after all who tried to destroy them. Unlike the poorly built fake cottages developers threw up to draw foreign real estate investments, our country's famine cottages have a history that's worth preserving. Bram assured Mary that this particular one has great bones."

As he carried her bags into the cottage, Sedona paused to read the framed blessing hanging on the wall in the entry next to a painting of Castlelough's harbor.

"May your troubles be less, and your blessings be more. And nothing but happiness come through your door," she read aloud. "That's lovely." She glanced around, her eyes sweeping around the front room. "It's like the *Quiet Man* meets *Modern Family*."

"Mary has very definite ideas on everything," he said, his lips quirking as he remembered some of their *discussions* over their differing interpretations of scenes he'd scored. "I know nothing about design, but she and Bram spent a great deal of time talking about how they wanted to remain true to the original cottage while updating it for both function and comfort."

And hadn't his eyes blurred over more than once as they'd shown him detail after detail? "So, they melded both old and new. This entry floor and the kitchen and baths are Irish blue limestone quarried in Kilkenny."

"The soft blue-gray color reminds me of a cool, misty morning."

"As it's meant to. The oak floors were reclaimed by an old abandoned mill on my brother Declan's farm. Ireland was once covered with forests, but now only about one percent of the few trees are native. Which is changing thanks to a program Declan works with, taking DNA from trees going back a thousand years to Brian Boru's time to create new stock. Ireland's experienced its share of tragedies over the years, but one of the longest-lasting was having forest people end up without their forests. But that's going to change. In time."

"I grew up on a commune," she told him. "We lived with reclaimed wood before it got cool. Make over, make do, or—"

"Do without," Conn finished up the quote. "We Irish have, for the most part, lived the same way. Modern life has its benefits, indoor plumbing and electricity being two of the more advantageous. But the past has much to offer, as well."

"Which is why your rock songs are often influenced by traditional Celtic tunes."

"Ah." He lifted a brow as he carried her suitcases down the hallway into the bedroom. She followed, running her hand along the antique oak dresser Bram had polished as smooth as a newborn's arse. "Someone's been reading up on me."

"It's hard to miss all the tabloid coverage while waiting to buy groceries," she said, more than a little defensively, Conn thought. "But my father's been a fan of your music since long before you began scoring Mary's movies."

"Your father being the one who goes by his gut."

"You remembered." She seemed surprised by that. How much of a shallow prick did she think he was? Conn wondered as she picked up a small Belleek china harp from the dresser, running a fingertip over the graceful curves.

"I do." He put the smaller of the cases in the adjoining bath and the larger on the little folding luggage stool Mary had bought for guests. "I remember *everything* about that night."

And didn't she, as well? Conn watched her pupils expand and darken in those gorgeous sky-blue eyes.

Unable to resist that siren's call, he gave into impulse and felt her shiver as he brushed his thumb along the curve of her jaw. Encouraged, he tipped her chin up and did what he'd been wanting to do since she'd gotten off that plane.

He kissed her. Mouth to mouth, as their breaths mingled, although it was as romantically fanciful as something Mary might write in one of her love stories, Conn imagined he could hear the singing of larks and the strumming of harps as the sea sighed in the distance.

Going up on her toes, she wrapped her arms around his neck and practically melted into him and he kissed her long and hard enough to draw a ragged moan from deep in her throat, which was when he almost lost it.

She was soft and warm and as sweet as one of her cakes right from the oven. The part of his brain still functioning reminded Conn that she was also the most dangerous female he'd ever met. Unfortunately, she was a great deal more vulnerable than she'd been their first time together.

"I'd best let you get a proper rest to catch up to the clock," he said as he backed away enough to put some distance between them. "I'm supposed to tell you that the fridge and pantry are well stocked. My mother's kitchen is overflowing with covered dishes brought by those who'd come to visit during the dying, so she thought you'd enjoy not having to forage in the village for food when you first arrived."

"That's very generous." Her arms dropped limply to her sides. Her wide eyes appeared more than a little dazed.

"She's a generous woman. Like another I know." How many people would fly across a continent and ocean to bake a cake for a friend's wedding? And later, drop everything during a personally stressful time and return to Ireland to ease the concerns of that very same friend?

Because he couldn't be in the same space without touching her, he brushed his thumb across those pink, parted lips he could still taste. And vowed to taste again. But, although it was one of the more difficult things he'd ever done, even more difficult than letting her get on the plane back to the States when he'd jetted off to Germany, Conn forced himself to walk past the enticing white feather bed and out of the cottage.

As he climbed back into the SUV, he made a mental note to send Mary Joyce Douchett the most ridiculously expensive basket of hothouse flowers he could find on the Oregon coast.

15

BECAUSE SHE WASN'T certain her knees would hold her up, as she heard the cottage door close behind Conn, Sedona sank down on the fluffy bed and pressed a fingertip against her lips.

It had only been a kiss. But it had left her lips tingling, nearly melted every bone in her body and left her head even foggier than when she'd arrived at Shannon.

She flopped back on the bed and flung an arm over her eyes, which were feeling sandy from the dry air on the plane and lack of sleep. "Houston, we have a problem."

Technically, she had more than one. But being thrown back together with the one person who'd had her reevaluating everything she'd always believed she wanted in a man had just shot up to the top of the list.

You're just jet-lagged, her brain assured her. *You'll be fine after a nap.*

She doesn't need to nap, her wicked body argued. *She just needs to get laid.*

"I do not." Liar.

Wanting to shut up the damn voices, she rolled over onto her stomach and hugged the pillow—which impossibly, because the bedding had obviously been changed, seemed to carry his scent. This country obviously messed with her head, stimulating her imagination in ways that weren't healthy. Or safe.

She turned her head, pressing her nose deep into the down and breathed in a deep breath. See? The lavender scent had nothing to do with Conn Brennan. But the pillow was a poor substitute for what, or, more to the point, *whom* she'd prefer to be cuddling up to in bed.

"Your agreement was one night, no strings, no commitment, no waltzing down a white satin wedding runner to a thatched-roof cottage for two framed with a white picket fence." Not that she'd ever seen a traditional Irish cottage with a picket fence. Which wasn't the point.

The point was that she and Conn had both walked away the next day like grown-ups. She wasn't some silly teen crushing over the latest boy band pop star.

Sighing, struggling not to remember the feel of his roughened hands warming her, all over, Sedona rolled back onto her back and stared up at the sun-and-cloud-dappled ceiling. It had begun to rain again. She could hear it dancing on the roof, a far cry from the hammer blows she'd endured during the storm.

The flashback was instantaneous, only lasting a second, but it caused her heart to start jumping around.

Since it was obvious she wasn't going to be able to sleep, Sedona dragged her wandering mind back to that kiss, which was definitely preferable to reliving the night of her bakery's destruction.

"It probably didn't mean anything." He was a male. A very hot, sexy male who'd kissed a great many women, no, make that a *legion* of women, and would undoubtedly kiss a lot more after her.

Not that she cared.

The hell she didn't. But just because they weren't going to have hang-from-the-rafters-sex ever again didn't mean that she couldn't enjoy the memory. Conn was a hot, swaggering Irish testosterone bomb. A woman would have to be six feet under not to experience explosions of lust.

Fantasizing is one thing, Sedona's voice of logic reminded her. *Acting on those fantasies yet another.*

As long as she remembered that, she'd be fine.

16

BACK WHEN HE'D been young and restless, Conn hadn't been able to get out of Castlelough fast enough. Even before his sixteenth summer, life outside his sleepy Irish village had been calling to him. During those early years, when he and the lads had been playing on Dublin streets for whatever coins passersby might toss into his guitar case and sleeping on floors at night, he'd considered himself the luckiest man on the planet. He was doing what he loved, in a bustling city bursting at the seams with a vibrant night-life and things to do and see.

And the women. Tempestuous redheads, sophisticated blond socialites, Black Irish brunettes with hair as glossy as a raven's wings—all had proven as ready for a tumble as he'd been.

The world had been his ripe, plump oyster, and he'd seen no reason not to savor all it had to offer. He'd worked as hard as a ploughman, writing his music during the wee hours of the morning after a night of partying. Then, ignoring the maniacs pounding away on bodhran drums in his head, he'd drag his equally hungover band mates out of bed, where, after a breakfast of eggs, bacon, and hash—at times their only meal of the day—they'd be back on the streets.

He'd also made daily rounds to the pubs, schmoozing with owners, managers, and bartenders, because as much fun as busking could be, he'd known they needed to expand their audience beyond just those who might be out and about on Grafton Street on any given day. On those occasions when his efforts had paid off, Celtic Storm, known back then as the Castlelough Lads, would jam themselves into an old milk delivery van and head off to play a gig. If there were times when the pay consisted merely of free pints, Conn had never complained. It was, he'd continually reminded the lads, just one more part of keeping their eye on the prize.

The hard work and focus had paid off. They'd achieved the success he'd dreamed of and more. Four lads from West Irish villages that were little more than pinpoints on the map had traveled the world, playing their tunes to legions of screaming, devoted fans who'd made them rich and famous.

And yes, infamous, as well, since the more salient of the entertainment presses and paparazzi thrived on scandal, exaggeration, and often downright lies. Considering them nothing more than fleas that survived by living on the backs of dogs, Conn had gotten into his share of fights. More so in his wild and wooly twenties. Which had only increased his reputation as a bad boy, leading to his being called Conn of the Hundred Battles. Which had perversely seemed to increase his appeal among women.

As he'd grown older, although Conn hadn't given up his pub-band mentality, keeping things from getting stale by changing up the song choices every night, he'd gotten better at not taking the paparazzi bait.

This past year, as he was turning thirty, he'd grown increasingly restless, with idle thoughts of home occasionally tugging at him.

Which was why, as he drove past Declan's farm, where cows grazed contentedly in the fields and the first crop of Christmas trees rose like shaggy green arrows in the distance, he decided that he owed Joseph Brennan a debt of gratitude. If he hadn't been forced to come home for the dying of the man he'd always believed to be his father, he'd still be on the road like an itinerant traveler.

He was well aware that buying the Guinness warehouse had struck not just those in the village but probably some in his own family as being recklessly impulsive. At the time, he'd not been able to deny it. But when he'd been telling Sedona that the building was *his,* the pride and sense of home he'd felt had been so strong he'd belatedly realized that it was meant to be.

Not that he was ready to take himself a bride, post the bans at the Church of the Holy Child, walk down the aisle, and nine months later bring his wife home from hospital with a newborn sprog who'd be getting him up all night long and taking a toll on his sex life.

Which had him, for the first time in his life, wondering what quality of sex life a married man might have.

17

SEDONA HAD ALWAYS been convinced that there were two types of people in the world. One who, upon arriving at a location away from home, immediately hung up their clothes and put them away in dressers. The other half seemed quite content to live out of suitcases for the duration of their trip.

She was in the first camp. After unpacking, she'd climbed into the white cloud of a bed and had instantly fallen like a stone into sleep. For the first time in weeks, she hadn't been jolted awake by the sound of glass crashing downstairs. Or had her dreams invaded by memories of the storm that had seemed never-ending.

She entered the cozy ensuite bath, eschewing the deep tub for the tiled shower. As Mary had promised, the cottage held every comfort she might need, including a locally made shampoo with a soothing, beautiful fragrance. Sedona decided to find a shop that sold it and have a crate shipped home.

Everything about the cottage—the view of crazy-quilted green fields stitched together by stone walls, the white cloud of a bed, the bath products arranged on a pretty tray that looked to be original mercury glass, all encouraged relaxation and calm. As the scented suds disappeared down the drain of the pebbled shower floor, Sedona could almost feel her cares washing away with her travel grunge.

Just as she returned to the bedroom, a rainbow appeared outside the window, framing the green fields, cliff, and sea beneath a shimmering, brilliantly colored arc. Sedona knew her mother would view the rainbow as a sign of positive things to come. What *she* saw was another postcard image and a sign that the rain had stopped long enough for her to take a walk and work out the last of the kinks from all those hours of sitting in airports and on planes.

She cranked the window open, welcoming the rush of salt-scented air. The temperature, which felt as if it was in the low seventies, was perfect. After dressing in shorts and a pink Take the Cake long-sleeved T-shirt with three colorfully frosted cupcakes across the front, she laced up her cross-trainers. Stopping long enough to eat a thick slab of brown bread slathered in grass-fed butter that made the baker in her nearly weep with joy.

She wrapped up another piece of bread and put it in her pack, along with a bottle of water, a plastic-coated map of hiking trails she'd ordered online. Then, pulling on a lightweight Gore-Tex jacket and a baseball cap over her still-damp hair, which she'd twisted into a tail, Sedona left the cottage, headed toward the sea.

After making her way on the narrow, winding, hedge-lined road, she'd reached the cliff. The climb to the top was just challenging enough to have the blood flowing comfortably in her legs while the brisk air and misty rain that had begun to fall again cleared the last of the cobwebs left over from her long nap.

The walk along the cliffs offered a spectacular view of the famous Aran Islands, which she'd always wanted to visit, ancient mountain domes, a stone tower and thousands of whirling, diving, calling seabirds. The scene was so magical Sedona wished her parents could be here to view it with her. Although she didn't know anything about the inner workings of the theater world, if Freebird's rock opera were to ever be performed in Dublin, she'd have to bring them out here to the West.

"Not that you'll be here," she reminded herself. She did, after all, have a full life back in Shelter Bay. It might be in pieces at the moment, but she'd started over before, when she'd escaped her life in Portland, which had become impossibly difficult. Both professionally and emotionally.

"You can do it again," she gave herself a little pep talk. And after she was back on her feet, what could be better than to share this land with the two people she loved most in the world?

She'd just turned to head back to the cottage when she caught a glimpse of the sun beginning to lower over Galway Bay, the inspiration for one of her father's favorite Irish folk songs. In her early childhood, she'd fallen asleep to his baritone crooning it to her. A music historian, Freebird had later told her that an Irish psychiatrist who'd served in World War I had written the song in memory of his beloved brother, who'd drowned in the bay. Sedona doubted the song would have become nearly as popular were it not for the later, romanticized spin to the lyrics.

Even as the rain picked up, falling now at a steady pace that soaked through her shorts, the memory of those lullabies made her smile. While she might become frustrated by her parents' insistence on finding her a husband, she knew that being loved unconditionally was a gift not everyone was lucky to have known. Conn Brennan being one of the less fortunate.

As if conjured up by her thoughts, Conn drove up at the same time she returned to the cottage. He pulled up beside her and rolled down the window. "So, you're up and about."

"I am. After a too-long nap, I took a walk along the cliffs," she said. "It's a stunning view."

"When I was younger, I gave my mother a great deal of concern because I firmly believed that if I concentrated hard enough, I'd be able to leap off and soar like the seabirds."

"I'm sure she's relieved you resisted the temptation."

"I suspect she was," he agreed.

In the momentary silence, she could view the shadow in his eyes. "How was the wake?"

"It's still going on and I've no doubt it'll last until the wee hours. Since my brothers, myriad aunts, uncles, and cousins have all flocked to pay their respects along with seemingly everyone in the village, I decided no one would miss me if I made my escape."

Recent fond thoughts of her relationship with her own father had Sedona's heart going out to him. She couldn't imagine being alone on the night before Freebird's funeral. How much more complex would your feelings be, she wondered, if you had good reason to hate the man who'd fathered you?

"I thought you're staying at your mother's house until after the funeral."

"I was. But since my brothers Aidan and Roarke are still there, I'm taking Mary up on her offer of her home."

Okay. Now that he'd be right next door, there'd be no avoiding him. Which might have been what Mary had in mind. Given that Conn didn't appear to be nearly as depressed as reported, Sedona suspected her parents weren't the only ones with a matchmaking plan in the works.

"I was about to heat up one of those dinners you brought," she said, uncharacteristically acting on impulse. "Would you like to join me? It's too much to eat by myself, and it would be nice having company on my first night here."

"Ah, and there you go again," he said. "Watching out for me for Mary."

"Ah, but you've already told me that you don't need watching out for."

"I don't. Not at all."

Despite his words, the bold and reckless male energy that had so attracted her seemed muted this evening. Sedona found herself missing it. "I'm not up to mingling at Brennan's, but sharing a meat pie and bread with you is preferable to eating alone in front of the television."

"You flatter me," he said dryly. "I'd enjoy another meal with you, Sedona Sullivan. I'd enjoy it even more if the evening were to end up like our last late supper."

Not sure whether or not he was kidding, she merely shook her head. "I'm offering shepherd's pie and a bottle of your brother's beer. That's all."

"Then that's what I'll gladly accept."

18

CONN FELT A tinge of regret when she excused herself to change into dry clothes. The wet shorts clung to her body in a way that had him wanting to carry her off to bed and spend the rest of the evening and night touching her. Tasting her. Steeping himself in her warmth, forgetting the vexing world still waiting for him in the morning.

They also brought up a particularly erotic memory of the way she'd climbed onto him, bare-arsed and prettily flushed from orgasm, riding him like a cowgirl astride a wild bronc.

From the moment he'd seen her, Conn had known that a woman with Sedona Sullivan's looks would be accustomed to men throwing themselves at her feet. Which is why he'd let her get away. His plan had been to let memories of their night together fill her mind until he was all she could think of. Then, after the tour ended and his obligations had been dispatched, he'd show up in the States to claim his prize.

Then bloody Joseph Brennan had shown up, shooting that plan to smithereens.

Which didn't mean that he couldn't revise it. Although he hadn't had any true experience having to go to the work of seducing a woman, Conn decided that seduction couldn't be that different from making love.

Or even writing music—sometimes slow and tender worked best. Other times hard, fast, and dirty. He and Sedona had already done the second. And as mind-blowing as it had been, apparently it hadn't left her so enthralled and needy she'd felt the need to track him down for another round.

So, the new plan, he considered, as he readjusted his too-tight jeans, was to try it the other way. Let her make the first step. That was the way to go.

When his mind drifted to her stripping out of those wet clothes, Conn slammed the door on the erotic mental pictures and found the shepherd's pie, which he recognized as being Sheila Monohan's contribution, and put it into the oven to warm. Since he and his brothers had grown up setting breakfast tables for B&B guests, he put out the placemats, napkins, and flatware on the table.

On impulse, he retrieved a small bouquet of wildflowers Mary had ordered as a welcome and put it, along with two white candles, in the center of the table.

Standing back to observe his handiwork, he decided there was something to be said for setting the scene for romance. Now that he'd decided to take a slow train to seduction, he was enjoying injecting a bit of romance into the mix. Though if his brothers were to find out, they'd undoubtedly rag him until his dying day.

He sifted through the selection of CDs in a small cabinet, passing over the more obvious Irish airs. Conn had introduced Mary to R&B while working on their first film together, and when it came to seduction, the genre had cornered the market. And no wonder, given that the smooth and soulful tracks were designed to have women's knickers dropping to their ankles.

Not that he expected knickers to be dropping tonight. But just because he'd determined to take his time didn't mean that Conn didn't want the lady thinking about it. A lot.

But apparently the thinking about sex worked both ways, because deep in a fantasy of his own involving wet bodies beneath a streaming hot shower, he hadn't heard her enter the room.

"Wow," she said, just as Barry White's rumbling, growling whisper was encouraging listeners to put aside fear and let love flow. Her openly astonished gaze swept over the table. "You didn't have to go to so much bother."

"Although it's undoubtedly difficult for you to believe, I haven't always existed on room service meals dished up on silver trays," he said. "My mother ran a B&B. We all grew up being assigned kitchen and cleaning detail."

"As much as I have trouble imagining you wearing an apron and washing dishes, it's lovely. And very considerate." Her smile was warm and softened her eyes as she took in the candles waiting to be lit. "And the pie smells delicious."

"Mrs. Monohan runs the mercantile. But despite not being a professional chef, she's one of the better home cooks in town. Her lamb pie is a regular competition blue ribbon winner."

"Like your mother's carrot cake," she said.

"Like Mam's cake," he agreed, surprised that she'd remembered that little detail. "And for the record, I never wore an apron. Would you like wine or beer?"

"There's white wine in the fridge. Which I suppose you'd know since you were the one who put it in there." She climbed up on a stool at the bar counter while he retrieved the *Pouilly Fumé* and a bottle of Brennan's Pirate Queen Red Ale. "That's interesting you all grew up in a B&B. Tell me more about your family."

"I'd rather talk about yours," he said.

She tilted her head, studying him for a moment, then shrugged. "I grew up on a commune."

"Your parents were hippies?"

"My father was a hippie," she said as he uncorked the wine and poured it into a Waterford stemmed glass. While Mary might not flaunt her wealth, Conn remembered her saying, after a school field trip to the Waterford factory, that someday she was going to have cupboards filled with the sparkling crystal. Ambition was another of the things he and Mary had always shared. "My mother was, and still is, a quintessential flower child. There *is* a difference between hippies and flower children," she said as if accustomed to being challenged on the topic.

"I'll be taking your word for that," he said. "What did you do on this commune?"

"A bit of everything. It was a very democratic lifestyle." She waved her fingers. "If you ever need someone to milk a goat, I'm your girl."

"I'll pass that on to Declan, being that he's the farmer in the family," Conn said before reminding himself that he'd declared his family off-limits for now. "From what I've heard of communes, most people bring certain skillsets to the community. Yours is obviously baking. What about your parents?"

"My mother's an artist," she said. "Watercolors, oils, metals. She's very versatile and extremely talented. She's also an avid gardener, but that's her avocation, not her vocation. My father's a musician."

"A musician who goes with his gut." She wasn't the only one who remembered every detail of their rainy-night conversation. "Would I be knowing his work?"

"Probably. His 'Unfinished Soldier' hit pretty big worldwide. There were many who considered it this era's quintessential antiwar anthem."

"Shite." Conn slapped his forehead. "Your father's Freebird Sullivan." Why the hell hadn't he put it together? Because, he considered, he'd been distracted first with making love to Freebird Sullivan's delicious daughter, then moved on with the tour, only to be called home and immersed in family drama. "He's a bloody genius."

She gifted him with a warm, genuine smile that lit up those remarkable lake-blue eyes. "You'd get no argument from him on that topic."

"I first heard his 'Time for Some Serious Disruption' when I was a lad of nine. It's what inspired me to get into rock."

"That's a bit young to decide to become a rock star bad boy," she said.

"Ah, but I was a prodigy."

"And what would your mother say about that?"

"That I was a challenge. But her favorite son."

Sedona laughed as he'd meant her to. Conn loved the sound of her laugh. It reminded him of sunshine sparkling on the sea. It was also hard to remain in a funk listening to her.

"I began playing all his songs on an air guitar," he said. "Music became my life. It was everything." He paused, shot a look at her. "Everything."

"That's impressive. To find your future so early in life. Most people might find it risky to set out on a single path."

"Ah, but I always knew what I wanted to do and where I was going. Anything other than music was a nonstarter for me. Would he be working on a new album now?"

"At the moment he's in New York working with producers to bring a rock opera to Broadway. *The Curse of Captain Angus MacGrath* is based on an old Oregon coast legend."

"Fair play to him." It also answered the question he hadn't thought to ask Mary when she'd rung him. Why Sedona hadn't simply gone home to her family rather than come to Castlelough.

Afterwards, giving it some thought, he'd imagined at the time that her home life must be as dark and complex as his own. Which would explain her need for control, with all those tidy spreadsheets with the rigid lines and boxes. But from the warmth in her voice, he guessed that she was fortunate to possess something he'd thought was as rare as a unicorn: a happy, united family.

He took another drink of ale. "You should advise him to tell the producers they should bring his opera to the Abbey or one of the other theaters in Dublin. We Irish love our theater."

"I'll bring it up the next time we talk. He'd love an excuse to visit his ancestral homeland."

"Tell him, in the event he doesn't already know, that the Sullivans were early royalty. Ancient myths have them arriving on the island in the 800s B.C. Eventually the Normans drove them out of their home in County Tipperary, sending them to Kerry, Cork, and outward from there. I know some Sullivans here in Clare. Perhaps you're related."

"Dad would love the idea of being royalty," she said on another of those sunny laughs. "And thank you."

"For what?"

"For giving me something to laugh about. While it's nothing like what you've been going through, this has been a difficult time for me...Mary told you about the storm."

"She did."

"I'm not sure why it affected me so much. What was lost was just stuff that's easily replaced and it's not as if I was ever in any real danger. I've certainly lived through storms before. But afterwards, when I took in all the damage, it was..." Her voice drifted off again. "Devastating."

"You hadn't planned for it," he offered. "Therefore, you felt helpless to fix it."

She looked at him in surprise. "That's true. Which is only more depressing because I'm always the person who fixes things."

"That's not at all surprising. But are you always so hard on yourself?"

She thought about that for a moment. "Do you know, the only people who've ever suggested that were my parents. Everyone else..."

She fell silent again, looking out the window at the sea, which was turning a choppy steel gray. Conn hoped they wouldn't be having a storm. Although she appeared much improved from when he'd met her at the airport, he wasn't certain she was ready to go through another coastal gale so soon.

"Expects you to keep calm and carry on," he suggested.

Her lips, which he could still taste and wanted to taste again, quirked. "I believe that's the British."

"The Brits do claim to be the stiff-upper-lip champions," he said. "While we Irish tend to have the reputation of being driven by pure emotion. Which only goes to show that you can't always count on stereotypes, because we're an infinitely pragmatic people. And didn't we have to be, what with all the different countries invading our island, which gave us the choice of adjusting to change or dying?"

He rubbed his jaw, allowing himself the pleasure of a long look at her. "I watched you creating that towering wonder of a cake. When you piped on the thin, intricate lines into the shape of a Celtic heart on the top, I kept thinking that one slight jiggle of your hand would ruin your work. But you were not only rock steady while everyone was bustling about around you and we musicians were warming up, probably sounding like cats shagging on a night fence, you remained as cool as ice."

"I was just doing my job," she murmured.

"And weren't you doing it perfectly?" he agreed. "But don't forget, I've witnessed the heat beneath that icy, controlled exterior."

It suddenly dawned on him that she reminded him of a blond from those midcentury American movies. While at first glance Sedona might appear to be the quintessential sunny California girl, she also gave off a definite Hitchcock blond heroine vibe. He suspected her male requirement spreadsheet wasn't the only thing that had kept her from marrying. How many men would fear frostbite from trying to get beneath that cool, tautly controlled exterior?

Fortunately, he was not most men. Having witnessed the fire, Conn knew that embers were still smoldering beneath the surface. Mary had merely told him to watch out for her, Conn rationalized. He'd been given no instructions as to *how* to do that.

"You're fortunate to have a loving father," he said. Since she'd shared something personal, it only seemed fair that he do the same. "There were many times I wanted mine dead."

"Because he beat you when you were a boy?"

"Ah. Mary told you more than the fact that I've fallen behind on her score."

"She's not concerned about the score." Sedona waved the thought away. "She's worried about you. She mentioned scars. And that your father was not the kindest of men."

"And wouldn't that be an understatement? For the most part, Joseph Brennan ignored his wife and my brothers. But he was nothing short of a monster to me. When I was a tyke, I'd lie in the bed at night and think up ways to kill him." All of which had been bloody and gruesome, slow and painful.

"That's so sad, that a young boy should have to think such dark thoughts."

"The thinking didn't disturb me. Indeed, it gave me a great deal of pleasure. What was a concern was not sharing those brilliant plots with Father O'Malley during Saturday confessions. I'll admit to fearing that I'd be going to hell if I was run over by a lorry in the street and died without an opportunity to make a true act of contrition."

Her eyes filled with a sympathy Conn neither wanted nor needed. "That's a terribly heavy burden for a child."

"It seemed so at the time," he allowed. "Which is why I quit my altar boy position to enjoy a lie-in on Sunday mornings while my mother dragged my brothers to mass and the old man was sleeping off a Saturday night drunk."

Conn had reveled in the silence that had allowed him to create more pleasurable fantasies of what life would be like when he became the new Bono or Springsteen.

She surprised him by laughing. "I'm sorry," she said. "It's not that I don't sympathize. Because I do. My heart aches for that child you were. It's just that I'm having difficulty picturing you as an altar boy."

"And isn't that the same thing Father O'Malley said on more than one occasion?"

Despite how the conversation had taken a dark turn, Conn smiled back on those memories. With his mind always making up tunes, he was admittedly not the most attentive of the lads. Nothing like Patrick, who, the priest would continually remind him, had achieved head altar boy status by the time he was a mere ten years old.

"Joseph Brennan wasn't my birth father."

Conn hadn't planned on telling Sedona this. At least not tonight, which was supposed to be about setting the stage for romance. But now the truth was out there and would have to be dealt with.

Sedona blinked. Slowly. As Conn watched her process that out-of-the-blue information, he could practically see the wheels turning in her blond head and realized, yet again, how she fascinated him on so many more levels beyond sexual.

"I see." But her tone suggested she didn't quite. And how the hell could she? "Is that why he was cruel to you? And the reason you wanted to kill him?"

"The first is probably true enough. But it couldn't have been the cause of me wanting to kill him because I didn't know the truth until recently."

"Oh." She blew out a breath. "Wow."

"That would be one word to describe it."

"I can't begin to imagine what you're feeling, but I'm so sorry."

He shrugged. "Your sympathy is appreciated but not necessary. In truth, it was a huge weight off my shoulders. I always worried that carrying Joseph Brennan's DNA could have me ending up as cruel as him."

"That could never happen."

"And you got to know me that well while we were scorching the sheets in the Copper Beech Inn?"

"DNA isn't destiny. But if we're talking about inherited traits, my mother passed on a strong intuitive sense. No matter how attracted I was, I never would've left Brennan's with you if you weren't safe."

"Safe isn't the most flattering description a man hopes to hear from a woman, luv." Jesus. He really liked her smile. It hit like an arrow to the heart.

"I didn't say there's not an edge of danger that's more than a little appealing," she assured him. "But beneath your bad-boy swagger, there's a thoughtful, caring individual."

"I wouldn't have thought you, of all people, would be one to act on intuition."

"Intuition and observation," she corrected. "When we first met, you'd returned home from a world tour to play for your close friend's wedding reception. Then, days later, you cancelled the rest of the band's engagements to come home to support your mother and brothers through a difficult time, even though you've already stated that you hated the man you believed to be your father.

"Since family has always been the most important thing in my own life, that speaks volumes. Plus, I doubt you hesitated for a moment when Mary asked you to pick me up at the airport and watch out for me."

"Any excuse to escape the house packed with gossipy visitors was welcome," he said. "An excuse to be with you again was a decided bonus. And while the last thing I want to do with you is argue, I have to point out that for such a logical person, there's a contradiction in your reasoning. If family's the most important thing, what do all those years of my hating the man I thought to be my father say about me?"

"That you also have very good intuition," she countered without missing a beat. "Surely there were times when you believed you must be another man's son."

Bull's-eye. And how could she know something he'd never, *ever* shared with anyone?

"I also believe that some people don't deserve either love or respect," she said firmly. "From what Mary has told me, Joseph Brennan had earned neither."

Falling silent, she began running her finger around the rim of her glass, looking down into her wine as she gathered her thoughts. Although the two women were nothing alike, Conn realized that she reminded him of Mary. Both were beautiful and sexy, each in her own very different way.

Mary was much more open, her emotions running closer to the surface, while Sedona was inclined to be keeping her feelings to herself. He wondered how many people, how many *men*, had taken the time and effort to look beneath the glossy blond exterior to the intelligent, complex, and, he sensed, *conflicted* woman beneath.

Taking her to bed would be easy. A long, lingering look, a light caress, the touch of lips against lips, and he could have her tumbling around on that feather-topped bed. But Conn wanted more. Much, much more.

"Does your mother know that you know?" she finally asked, meeting his waiting gaze.

"I don't believe so. He claimed he had no intention of telling her."

"Yet he was a liar."

"He was. Most definitely."

"Which puts you in an extremely difficult position."

And hadn't he thought the same thing himself? There was no way Conn wanted to dump more emotional upheaval on his mother. But surely she was wondering, even worrying, that her husband might have revealed the deeply kept family secret during his last days. Would bringing it up, assuring her that he was glad to hear that she'd at least enjoyed some pleasure during all those years, ease her mind? Or make things even worse?

"The man could have given Machiavelli lessons. Joseph Brennan did nothing without an ulterior motive. I knew, at the time, that he revealed the truth to hurt me. But his reasons were more layered. Even if I was happy to hear that he wasn't my father, I'd be left conflicted about whether to keep the knowledge to myself. Or tell my mother I know."

"And possibly release her from the burden of her secret."

"Or embarrass her, or worse, cause her pain. Because whoever my birth father may be, he certainly didn't stick around, either."

She gazed down into her wine again, as if seeking answers or advice she could pass on to him in the straw-hued depths. Since he enjoyed looking at her, Conn had no problem with the silence spinning between them.

"Would you like me to attend the funeral tomorrow?" she asked finally. "Or would having a stranger there be an intrusion?"

He hadn't realized, until she'd asked, that was precisely why he'd stopped by the cottage. Why he'd hoped she'd invite him in. Because while his pride wouldn't allow him to admit he needed an ally, the truth was he did. Desperately.

His brothers would always have his back. But they were invested in the family dynamics, which added several additional levels of tension. Particularly with Patrick, Roarke, Bram, and Aidan having known for years that he wasn't biologically a Brennan. Conn still hadn't decided how he felt about them having kept the secret for so long. While he understood their need to protect their mother, that didn't prevent him from feeling betrayed. And wondering if, in some way, they'd considered him not exactly one of them.

"I'd like for you to be there," he admitted. "But are you certain you want to sign up for this Brennan family reality show?"

"You obviously haven't watched the Housewives franchise if you think *this* qualifies as a reality show," she said. "At best it's a day in the life of your average American soap opera."

Conn laughed at that, her dry reply easing the renewed pain of his conflicted feelings toward brothers he'd always looked up to. "I'm believing that Mary had no need to worry her head about you," he said. "Because you're unflappable."

"Don't I wish."

A shadow crossed her eyes as she retreated again behind that high privacy wall she must have spent her entire life building. A thought hit like a bolt of lightning from the blue. Not only did Sedona remind him of Mary, she reminded him of himself. One of the reasons the tabloid exaggerations had never concerned him was that they were, in reality, much like a magician's illusion trick. By keeping the world's eyes on his alleged and admittedly occasional actual misbehavior, they distracted anyone from catching a glimpse of the real man behind the curtain.

"Then it appears Mary was right." As usual. Even knowing the actress as well as a sister, there were times when he was surprised at how the tempestuous, emotional Goth teenager he'd once known had matured into such a wise, self-possessed woman. "Assigning us to watch out for one another. I've already told you my deepest, darkest secret."

"I'll never tell anyone."

"That I believe. And the reverse is true if there's anything you'd care to be sharing."

"I'll keep that in mind," she said mildly. He didn't believe her. Not entirely, yet perhaps he had managed to make a faint crack in her wall.

"The service is at the Church of the Holy Child across from the harbor in the town center at noon. There will be a cemetery internment afterwards, then a funeral supper served by the women of the church's St. Brigid's Society."

"That's a long day for you."

"It is. But now that I'll be spending it with you, things are looking up."

"Should I meet you there?"

"That'd probably be best. I'll be leaving early to take the car with my mother to the church. That way you'll have your own transportation back here if you want to escape immediately after the funeral."

"I wasn't thinking of escape as much as the fact that you might want private time alone with your family afterwards." She covered his hand with hers. Her fingers were long and slender, her nails a pearly white at the tips. A memory of them exploring his body, moving down his chest, over his stomach, and lower flashed through Conn's mind.

"I'd rather be alone with you."

The flicker of heat deep in the blue pools of her eyes told him that he wasn't alone.

"It wouldn't be wise." Nor logical.

"Possibly not." He gave her the slow smile that had always worked on females from eight to eighty. "But we both know it would definitely be fun."

This time it was the quirk of her lips that gave her away, even as she shook her head and came just short of rolling her eyes. "You're incorrigible."

"You'll get no argument from me on that regard." At least he'd leave her thinking of it. "I'll see you tomorrow, then. At the church."

"At noon," she confirmed.

She walked him to the door. Conn could feel her standing in the open doorway as he walked away and knew that he could change her mind about being with him tonight. But worse than a lonely bed would be having her wake up in the morning with regrets. Reminding himself that she wasn't going anywhere, at least until after tomorrow, he beeped the horn, lifted a hand in farewell, then continued up the long, curving stone driveway to the house.

And for the first time during these past miserable weeks, the music he found himself humming along with was not coming from the Cayenne's speakers but inside his own head.

19

As soon as Conn entered the house, he went upstairs to one of the three guest suites and got out the guitar that had been lying idle in its case. Although Mary had a shiny white baby grand piano downstairs in the music room, he felt he'd have better luck playing on the old acoustic he'd bought with money earned cutting peat the summer he turned twelve. It had been hard, back-breaking work, and he'd been paid less than the traveler he'd been assigned to work with, but although he'd ended each day knackered, with every bone and muscle in his body protesting, by the time school started up again, he'd earned enough for an entry-level Gibson, which was what Bono had played in his early U2 days.

Like Bono, Conn, too, had graduated to the much pricier acoustic-electric Fender, but tonight, Irish superstition had Conn choosing the Gibson that had started it all.

Having spent his youth building internal walls and moats, Conn had always used music as a bridge to his emotions. His early work was rough and raw and loud, expressing the anger that had once manifested itself in more fistfights and school suspensions than he could count.

It had not escaped his notice that once he'd started writing songs for Mary, Celtic Storm's album sales had skyrocketed through the roof. People apparently preferred to hear songs about love to listening to him rage against the world. That wasn't to say that he'd sold out to write sugary pop tunes sweet enough to give listeners cavities. Love, he'd observed, tended to bring every bit as much angst and pain as it did happiness.

Take Mary's new film, a three-tissue story of the love between a fisherman from a small, Irish coastal city and a selkie. While there were several myths of seals taking on human form, in this story, if a selkie were to return to the sea, it would revert to being a seal and lose the ability to ever take on human form again.

Which foreshadowed the tragedy Mary had slowly set up.

Conn hadn't gotten to that fatal tearjerker part yet. Rather than create songs to a theme, then jam them into a score wherever they might somewhat fit, he preferred to watch the entire film through, once, twice, three, as many times as it took for him to get beneath the characters' skins and understand who they were. What drove them, which, in this tale, was—as with all Mary's screenplays—first and ultimately, unselfish love. Something he'd personally never believed existed. But the idealized concept sure as hell sold tickets and filled theaters, which was the important thing.

There might be those who would think that any songwriter with his cynical view of love wouldn't be able to write romantic ballads. They'd be wrong. Instead of exploring his own feelings, which would require risking deep-seated vulnerability, he transferred experiences onto the lives of fictional characters.

Had people left him? That would be a yes, beginning with his birth father, then the man he'd thought to be his father (which had been a cause for celebration), along with a few women who'd professed to love him but had finally given up waiting to hear the L word. There might be those who considered him a bastard, but no one could ever accuse him of being dishonest. Just as he'd never gone to bed with a woman without protection, he was always forthright about his disbelief in the concept of romantic love from the start.

Having never given his heart, Conn had never experienced jealousy, but having a vivid imagination, he could put himself in the place of a man being afraid of losing a special someone. He'd never wanted children, fearing he'd morph into the brutal, alcoholic man he'd believed to be his father, but that didn't mean that he couldn't understand the emotions a parent would have for a child. Which had allowed him to write his share of the joy of childbirth songs. And once, a rawly painful song about a couple's marriage disintegrating after the loss of their child that had won him a Grammy.

The closest he'd ever personally come to such a tragic experience was when the mangy stray Australian heeler he'd rescued from being attacked by a pack of vicious dogs had died. The day of the rescue, he'd stolen from his guitar savings account to have the dog's wounds tended to by the vet. Then he'd taken him home, fattened him up with discarded meat and bones from his mother's kitchen, and named him Finn, after Finn Mac Cumhail, the mythical Irish hero warrior and leader of the Fianna. Having no cattle nor sheep to herd, the Aussie had compensated by herding B&B guests, who were always slipping him a bit of bacon or roast beneath the table.

He'd adored his master unconditionally, waiting outside Holy Child School each day, greeting Conn with wild abandon at the end of the school day, his bushy curved tail wagging like an out-of-control metronome while walking him back home. Or to the peat fields.

Conn rubbed the heel of his hand against his chest, reliving the crushing ache he'd felt when Finn, after being hit by a car, had managed to make his way home, only to die in Conn's arms on the front stoop. It was the first and last time he could remember crying. Even his brothers hadn't ragged him when he'd spent the night bawling like a baby. He'd never told anyone his inspiration for those break-up lyrics, knowing that comparing the loss of a dog to the loss of a child would cost him a great many of his fan base and provide more grist for the tabloids' gossip mill.

Like the old Tom T. Hall lyrics, Conn had known trouble and he'd known pain. And when it came to trouble, he sure as hell knew rain.

But as he began strumming the strings, the memory of walking into that hall where the reception was to take place and seeing Sedona building that white wonder of a wedding cake came flashing back. As he stood there, taking in the sight of the tidy blond bathed in a ray of golden sun that had managed to break free of the quilted gray sky, although his rational mind told him it was impossible, he could have sworn he heard angels singing.

"He'd contentedly passed fifty years without taking himself a wife," he sang, stopping to write the notes and words down in his composing notebook. "Then, in one suspended, sun-gilded moment, an extraordinary woman changed his life."

As the sky grew darker and the night grew later, Conn lost himself in the words and the music that continued to flow like sparkling water from a secret, magical spring.

20

INSIDE BRENNAN'S, WHERE Conn and his brothers had gathered before meeting their mother at the house before the funeral, the mood was as dark as the clouds that were lying low over the village, weeping rain.

"I'll be damned if I say a positive effing word about the man," Conn said. His legs spread, arms folded across his chest, he dared any of his brothers to argue his declaration.

"Even if it'll make Mam feel better?" Declan, the peacemaker, asked.

Aidan lifted a brow. "You think a bunch of lies from us will make up for all those years he mistreated her with his other women and neglect?"

"You all can say whatever you care to," Conn said. "It's neither here nor there to me. But since I'm not Joseph Brennan's son, I feel no obligation to acknowledge him in any way."

"There's also the point that there's nothing any one of us could say that would make up for the humiliation he's caused her," Roarke entered the argument on Conn's side.

"And decades of being without a husband to share a loving life with," Patrick said.

"Since when do Catholic funerals have effing eulogies anyway?" Conn argued.

"They're not typical," Patrick agreed. "But Finn Joyce says that because it's become a point of contention and additional pain to loved ones, more and more dioceses have been allowing a family member to say a few words. Which is why he offered the option."

"It's enough that we're showing up at all," Roarke said.

"As it happens, he agrees that any of us sounding like hypocrites would be a worse reflection on our mother, and give everyone else something to talk about. So, we're sticking with tradition."

"Why am I not surprised you'd have already worked this out with Finn?"

Patrick shrugged, even as his resigned smile silently acknowledged his lifelong role as the eldest and parental surrogate. "While funerals are usually a sad time, this is a good day for this family," he said. "A shadow has been removed from our lives. Mam can move on, both emotionally and legally, and the rest of us can leave whatever negative memories we might have back in the past. Where they belong."

"Damn," Aidan drawled. "I think you just gave Conn a new song."

Even as Conn shot his brother a hard look, part of his mind had already begun spinning lyrics addressing that very same idea. So many songs focused on the grief of losing a parent. He suspected more than a few people would be able to identify with the darker side of family life.

As he left the pub with the others, it occurred to him that, once again, he was writing a song from his own life instead of some imagined event about some fictional character.

IT APPEARED THE entire village had shown up for the funeral mass. Both sides of the street in front of the church were packed bumper to bumper with cars, and there were bicycles parked on the sidewalk, leaning up against the gray stone walls.

Several of those present were people Sedona had met this past spring at Mary's wedding. Given what Conn had told her about his father, she assumed many of the people filling the pews at the Church of the Holy Child had come to morally support Eileen Brennan.

There were only a handful of floral arrangements on the altar. Mary had told Sedona during a call last night that she'd sent the spray of white lilies for the casket. Not for the man, she'd stressed. But to publicly support Conn, his mother, and brothers.

Eileen, seated in the front pew, flanked by her six sons, did not weep. Nor did she wear widow's black but a compromise gray the color of a winter sea. Although she portrayed a silent, calm composure rather than regret for years lost, Sedona thought she detected a sense of relief.

The priest, dressed in somber black vestments, greeted the casket at the door of the church, sprinkling it with holy water and intoning prayers asking for eternal rest given to the departed. Looking at the shadows beneath Joseph

Brennan's widow's eyes, it crossed Sedona's mind that *she* was the one who could use some rest.

After post-communion prayers, Father Finn stood at the foot of the coffin and granted the departed husband and father absolution, then sprinkled it again with holy water, swinging a censer that filled the church with the sweet scent of smoke and burning myrrh.

Once a final prayer for angels to bear the departed to paradise was said, six black-suited employees of the funeral home carried the casket out of the church into a nearly blinding sunlight that had broken through the clouds while everyone was inside. Either the irony or the perceived mystical sign of moving from the darkness to the light created a busy murmur among the gathered.

Outside, a lone piper played a soulful rendition of "Amazing Grace" that brought tears to Sedona's eyes. Conn had told her how, not that many years ago, men from the village would carry the casket from the church to the cemetery. Brady Joyce, Mary's father, had been honored that way.

However, either modern times had overcome tradition or perhaps they couldn't find enough willing volunteer pallbearers, but today the plain oak casket draped with Mary's flowers was driven away in a black hearse with Father Finn riding shotgun while the family followed in a shiny black town car.

An eight-foot-tall wrought iron fence surrounded the cemetery, undoubtedly to keep the grazing sheep in the adjoining hillsides from eating the grass and flowers left on graves.

As mourners crunched their way along a winding path made of crushed seashells past high stone Celtic crosses adorned with bas-relief interlacing designs and spirals, they passed older, rounded tombstones, their edges and the names and dates of the departed worn away by sea winds and rain.

Living up to the country's reputation for quixotic weather, the sun had disappeared again behind pewter clouds and a mist began to fall.

As a young man and woman clad in black business suits escorted the family to the front row of chairs that had been set up for the occasion, the men who'd carried the casket from the church moved it from the back of the hearse to the side of a dark, rectangular hole. Beside the hole, covered with a canvas, was a mound of freshly dug black dirt.

The only other people in the cemetery not here for the Brennan funeral were a couple, obviously tourists, taking photos of the high crosses, and a sixty-something man in a black trench coat and tweed fedora who was laying a floral bouquet at the feet of a stone angel marking a grave several rows away.

After the invocation and yet more sprinkling of holy water, the ancient man Sedona had seen singing sad songs to himself that night in the pub stood up and began to sing in Irish, his voice soaring and diving like the seabirds flying over the nearby cliffs. Captivated by the unaccompanied melody that was as fluid as the designs carved into the surrounding stone Celtic crosses, Sedona wished she'd known about it ahead of time so she could have recorded it for her father.

Suddenly, like a stone dropped into the sea, he abruptly stopped and the bagpiper broke into a plaintive rendition of "Danny Boy." After singing along to the last lingering note, everyone drove back to the church hall, where volunteers had set up a bountiful funeral meal.

Despite Brennan not having been the most admired former resident of Castlelough, it appeared no one was about to turn down a free lunch. Tables were groaning with baked salmon, sliced beef brisket, shepherd's pies, fresh vegetables, roasted and boiled potatoes, a variety of salads, breads, and enough cakes and pies to have kept Declan Brennan's cows and chickens working overtime to produce all the cream, butter, and eggs that must have been used in the preparation.

"That singing you did was amazing," Sedona told the rosy-cheeked elderly man, who was basking in a well-deserved spotlight.

"It's *sean-nos*," he responded, his chest puffing up like a bantam rooster. "My own da, who learned from his da, taught me when I was just a lad. While I don't have any sons of my own to pass it on to, more and more young people are taking it up. Enough that I earn my pint money giving lessons."

"Which I'm sure everyone appreciates," Sedona said. "Traditions are important."

"Aye, they are indeed," he agreed. He turned toward Conn. "It was an honor to sing for your family."

"It was an honor to have you grace our family with your song," Conn said with sincere formality. For a supposed bad boy, his mother had obviously taught him to respect his elders. Sedona doubted there were many in the village older than the singer.

"You can't have a funeral in Castlelough without Fergus Molony," Conn told Sedona as he slipped an envelope into the pocket of the singer's tweed suit pants.

"Being that I'd be older than peat is another reason I'm teaching a new generation," Fergus confided. "So there will be someone to send me off. And while we're speaking of my passing—"

"That's premature," Conn broke in.

"For you, perhaps, laddy. But others of us need to be thinking ahead." He turned a sharp eye on Sedona. "I'm told you'd be having a head for business."

"I have a bakery," she said. "But—"

"Having tasted Mary's cake, you're a grand baker," he cut her off. "But I overheard at the wedding that you're also an accountant."

"I was."

"Then you're just the person I need."

"Fergus," Conn said. "This isn't the time."

"Did you hear me mention that not all of us have all the time in the world?" Fergus shot back. "God may have made plenty of time, but even here in the Irish West, it's not infinite. So, I need someone to help me with *Cnoc an Chairn*."

"Oh, Jesus." Conn blew out a long breath.

Okay. Although Conn was obviously less than thrilled by the turn the conversation had taken, Sedona was curious enough to have to ask. "What's *Cnoc an Chairn?*"

"It's my Molony family home. The name means 'hill of the cairn.' It's in need of a bit of repair—"

"Which is putting it mildly," Conn muttered.

Fergus shot him a withering look. "As I was about to explain to Ms. Sullivan here," he continued. "My family had our home confiscated during the Penal Laws in the late 1690s. It's taken all this time to regain possession. Unfortunately, I entered into a partnership with a Dublin developer who claimed to share my vision for it. But he got overextended and declared bankruptcy before the final papers were signed. Unlike here in the West, where deals are often done with nothing more than spit and a handshake, his bloody damn bankruptcy solicitors insist that he'd not be owing me the money he'd promised for his share of my partnership."

"That's a shame," Sedona said.

"Aye, it is, sure enough." He shook his head, which was covered with what appeared to be white dandelion floss. "It's not as if I was in the need for funds in the first place, which makes it even more embarrassing to be caught being too trusting. Especially at my age, when I should know better."

He lowered his voice and bent toward her. "There are some that would be saying I've gone daft in my old age, but you know the saying about Satan being the most beautiful of all the angels?"

"I've heard that expression."

"Well, in this case, the devil himself was wearing his most charming face when he talked me into selling a portion of the property. Which I never would've done if I hadn't needed his expertise to restore *Cnoc an Chairn* to its former glory. And now the bloody bankers are sniffing around trying to get their grubby, ink-stained hands on it because of the money he owes them."

"I doubt they're all that ink-stained these days," Conn suggested mildly. "What with banking being computerized."

"That's not my point. My point is that he can't very well deny we had a contract to avoid paying his agreed-upon buy-in while at the same time trying to use my *Cnoc an Chairn* to try to solve his financial woes with all his creditors."

"That doesn't sound at all fair," Sedona said. "Though, admittedly, I don't know anything about Irish real estate law."

"And isn't the damn law as twisted as our roads?" His already ruddy cheeks flamed as scarlet as molten lava. "I've a team of solicitors fighting them on that score, claiming that there's no deal since no papers were signed."

He winked. "That little bit of legalese can work on both sides of the coin. But I'm in need of help with how to best utilize my finances. And from what I'd be hearing, you're just the lass to solve my problem."

"Real estate and building loans aren't my area of expertise."

"Oh, I won't be needing a loan, so you needn't bother your pretty head about that." He waved the idea away with an age-spotted hand. "I'm looking for someone with a keen eye who can help me develop a business plan to have in place when Bram Brennan begins restoring it to its former glory."

"That's what bankers are for," Conn pointed out.

"Did you not hear me, Conn Brennan? I don't trust those wretched folk not to be lining their own pockets in the deal," Fergus shot back. Then he treated Sedona to a sweet, sly smile. "Perhaps you can come for tea and biscuits. Just look the place over. It would make a fine inn. Or even, for those with deep enough pockets, a five-star resort. The lawns could make a grand golf course."

"The so-called lawns are an impenetrable tangle of gorse and weeds," Conn said. "And that billionaire New

York American has already bought the Doonbeg golfing club and named it after himself. You'd be facing stiff competition."

"How many battles and sieges has that golf club survived over the centuries?" Fergus asked. "*Cnoc an Chairn* has better history, going back to the sixteenth century. They've only been hitting little white balls around the sod at Doonbeg since 2002.

"So"—he turned back to Sedona—"would you be willing to come take a look at it?"

"I can't promise I can give you any helpful advice," she warned. "But I'd love to see your home."

"When?"

She exchanged a look with Conn, whose upward gaze suggested he was praying for patience. "Perhaps the day after tomorrow?"

Fergus rubbed his white-stubbled chin. "I'm afraid I have an appointment with my solicitors in Dublin that day." His lie was as transparent as Irish crystal, but Sedona chose not to call him on it. "How would tomorrow suit you?"

"I suppose I could do that."

"Ah, that'll be grand." His satisfied smile suggested he hadn't expected any other outcome. "About half past three? I'll have Finnola, she'd be my sister, prepare something for us to enjoy while we discuss business."

Before Sedona could repeat that she doubted she could help on the business front, Conn placed his hand on her back and forestalled her answer.

"Now that we've got that settled," he said. "I want Sedona to meet my mother."

"Oh, Eileen's a lovely woman," Fergus told Sedona. "A saint, considering what Joseph put her through. May God rest his soul," he quickly tacked on, making a sign of the cross, as if to cover any sin he might have committed by talking ill of the dead.

"I'm sorry about that," Conn said as they walked across the room.

"Don't be. I'm admittedly intrigued. I know looks are deceiving when it comes to wealth, but I never would've taken him for a man with the kind of funds to do what he's suggesting. Especially if the place is in as bad a shape as you say."

"It's worse. I was trying to be polite because he honored my mother by singing at the burial. As for the money, I suppose you could consider the thirty-point-two million Euros he won in An Crannchur Náisiúnta, which would be our Irish lottery, a fair piece of change."

She glanced back over her shoulder. "That little old man is a multimillionaire?"

"He doesn't flaunt it, as you can tell by that ancient and miserable ratty tweed jacket he's wearing. But the property, as run down as it is, means everything to him. I swear his determination to restore it to glory has been keeping him alive into his nineties."

"Well, then, the idea of helping him celebrate his centennial birthday there is appealing."

"Why did I have a feeling you'd be thinking that?"

With his hand still on her back, Conn shepherded Sedona through the crowd to a large round table in the center of the room, where Eileen Brennan was seated with the rest of her sons, each of whom could have claimed his own month on a *Hotties of the Irish West* calendar. Put them all together on a travel brochure, and she had not a single doubt that female tourism to the Emerald Isle would triple.

Sedona had no idea what Joseph Brennan had looked like, but it was obvious that the Brennan brothers had inherited a great many of their mother's genes. Even after having given birth and raised six grown sons and being in her fifth decade, Eileen possessed the type of beauty that didn't fade. Her ebony hair was shot with silver streaks, her eyes were as emerald as the fields that had given the country its nickname, and her high cheekbones were sharp enough to cut crystal.

"So you're the young woman who made that stunning, delicious cake for Mary's wedding," Eileen said after Conn had introduced them.

"I am," Sedona confirmed. "I'm delighted you enjoyed it."

"I certainly did. As a home baker myself, I was also pleased that you'd chosen to go with a buttercream frosting rather than the more fashionable fondant."

"People may eat with their eyes first," Sedona said, smiling as she remembered having this same conversation with Conn, "but in the end, it all comes down to taste."

"And isn't that the truth." Eileen shot a teasing look up at Conn. "Of course the music at the reception was passable, as well."

"We aim to please," Conn said.

"I'm sorry for your loss," Sedona said. She wasn't certain Conn's mother would consider losing that particular husband such a terrible loss, but it seemed the proper thing to say.

The older woman shook her head. "It hasn't been an easy time for anyone. But in truth, I believe Joseph's passing was a blessing. He'd been ill for some time before he returned home, and I had the feeling that he was ready to move on."

"It was lovely to meet you," Sedona said as others came up behind her to pay respects to the widow Brennan. "I hope to see you again while I'm here."

"I'd enjoy that. Perhaps we can have lunch together."

"It's a date," Sedona agreed. She handed Eileen a card with her cell number. "Feel free to call me whenever it's convenient for you."

"We're going to *Cnoc an Chairn* for tea tomorrow," Conn said, sounding like a sailor about to walk the plank.

"Oh, dear." His mother's gaze softened with sympathy. "I'd suggest you eat a good lunch beforehand."

"Well," Sedona said as they made room for a middle-aged man wearing a tweed jacket and dark slacks, "that wasn't exactly encouraging."

"I tried to stop you from agreeing," Conn said.

"I'm not going for the food. I love old houses."

"Then you'll love *Cnoc an Chairn*. I just hope you are also fond of rats and spiders."

She stopped on their way to the door. "You're joking."

"I wouldn't discount the possibility. The place should be called *lár choinne*, which is Irish for 'the middle of nowhere.' They moved in last year, before the financial problems. Before then, he was living in an apartment over the Sheehans' butchery. His sister, who'd been living with a long-time friend, moved into the apartment when his wife died, but it's not as if they did any entertaining even before moving into the estate. You could well be their first guest."

"When did his wife die?"

"I wouldn't be sure. But he'd already been widowed when I left town at sixteen. His sister has never married."

"That's a long time for him to have been alone." She couldn't imagine either of her parents doing well without the other for any length of time. The other part of what he'd said belatedly sunk in. "You left Castlelough at sixteen?"

"So it says on Wikipedia."

"Well, if it's on the Internet, it must be true," she said dryly.

"In this case, it is."

"That's very young to be out on your own."

"I was in a hurry," he said. "And I wasn't on my own. My band mates went with me."

"Where did you go?"

"Dublin. Which is like a magnet, much like New York City or Hollywood is in your country."

"Dublin's a wonderfully alive city, with so much to do that I can understand the attraction." She'd certainly enjoyed her time at Trinity College. "Still, your mother must have worried about you."

"I've no doubt. But isn't that what mothers do? She would have worried just as much if I'd stayed here. Even more," he tacked on.

If he'd remained in Castlelough, wouldn't he have been under Patrick's guiding influence? Sedona considered as he walked her to her car. Yet perhaps that was another reason he'd left. His birth rank in the family could have subdued his chances for finding himself. For creating a separate entity, even as it was clear that he hadn't entirely cut ties. Even as she wanted to know more, she sensed that this wasn't a topic Conn was prepared to discuss. At least not now.

They'd reached her car, which she'd been forced to park in the public lot at the harbor. The white boats bobbing on the water reminded her of Shelter Bay, and as a sailboat skimmed by, the memory of that runaway sailboat the night of the storm was enough to make her feel as if her heart had stopped.

"Are you all right?" Conn asked.

"I'm fine." She mentally shook off the feeling of impending doom and forced a smile she knew looked as feigned as it felt when he took off those dark glasses and gave her a long, narrowed-eyed look. "Grand, as you Irish would always say." Which, she'd also figured out long ago was also a polite way to avoid sharing less-than-positive emotions.

"You went as pale as a *tais.* A ghost," he translated.

"I have a headache from the incense," she said. Which was a half-truth. "I'll be fine after I have some tea and aspirin."

He continued to study her, looking hard. Looking deep. Then, thankfully, slid the rock star shades back on his face. "I'll be back at the house in a while. If you'd like someone to share another one of those casseroles with."

"I'd enjoy that," she said as she slid into the driver's seat and pressed the ignition button. "I'll be seeing you later, then."

"Later," he agreed. Then turned and walked back toward the church hall.

21

ON THE WAY back to the cottage, Sedona stopped by the mercantile just as Sheila Monohan was turning the *closed* sign to *open.*

"Good afternoon to you," she said with a warm smile. "I saw you at the funeral but didn't get an opportunity to welcome you back to Ireland."

"It's good to be back," Sedona said. "Although Mary ensured the cottage is well stocked, I do need some basics. And something besides a casserole for dinner."

"Eileen told me she'd sent a great many over to you," the shop owner said with a nod. "But it's always nice to be able to whip up something yourself. I imagine that's even more so when you're a professional chef."

"Pastries are different from cooking. But I can manage to bake a potato and cook a steak without burning down the house."

"Ah." A light brightened Sheila Monohan's eyes. "I'm sure Conn will be appreciating a manly red meat and potatoes after the day he's been through. Not that the past weeks have been easy on any of the family. I don't want to speak ill of the dead, but Joseph Brennan would never be called the easiest of men."

Not wanting to let on that she'd been told anything about Brennan or admit she was cooking for Conn, Sedona didn't respond as she followed the shopkeeper to the vegetable department.

"You'll be needing to get your steaks at Mrs. Sheehan's," Sheila said. "She should also have duck fat you can use for roasting your potatoes the Irish way, if you'd have a mind to. It's very simple and I can tell you the instructions."

"I'd appreciate that," Sedona said.

"We Irish do love our spuds," Mrs. Monohan said as she put two medium-sized white-skinned ones into the red basket she'd taken from the front counter. "And all cooking methods are grand, but my personal favorite is roasted. And these Queens, from Declan Brennan's farm, have a beautiful floury texture and wonderful taste."

She moved onto another display. "You'll also be wanting some garlic and flat-leafed parsley. For some reason, Mrs. Sheehan has never chosen to give out recipes with her meats, but I have a recipe for whiskey and onion-glazed steak you might enjoy making. Patrick serves it at the pub. He learned it from Eileen, who learned it from her mother."

Two opposing ideas flashed through Sedona's mind. The first being that having grown up eating that particular steak, Conn would probably enjoy it. The second, and more daunting, was the fact that trying to duplicate what the Brennan women had perfected over the generations could lead to a major culinary fail.

"Let's go for it," she decided, throwing caution to the wind.

"You're a brave woman, Sedona Sullivan," Sheila said, flashing a warm, approving smile. "I believe that our Conn has met his match in you...Do you like buttered peas?"

"If they're fresh." One of Sedona's fondest childhood memories was shelling peas with her mother, popping raw ones that tasted like sugar into her mouth as they worked.

"Declan brought in these Waverex *petit pois* yesterday." A handful of pods went into a brown paper bag, then landed in the basket. "We Irish, like the Brits, have an unfortunate reputation for turning all our peas into mush, but these just need a quick flash in boiling water. They're heavenly with his farm's butter."

"I have a brick of that at the cottage," Sedona said. "It's unbelievable with brown bread."

"It is," Sheila agreed. "Declan's beginning to make quite a name for himself. Darina Allen, who's known as the Irish Julia Child and runs the Ballymaloe Cookery School, is always featuring his farm on her television program."

"When I was a child, if we didn't grow it, we pretty much didn't eat it," Sedona said.

"And isn't that the way it should be?" The older woman nodded her approval. "Food is not only healthier but so much tastier when fresh." She moved on, adding a bottle of Irish whiskey and other items she felt Sedona would need to the basket. "Would you be making a dessert?"

"Normally, I'd make a pie." Baking was, after all, her forte. "But the dinner's already heavy." Skimming a glance over the freezer, her eye landed on a carton of blood orange sherbet. "I'll take this," she decided, adding it to the bounty Mrs. Monohan had collected. "With those almond chocolate cookies."

"I've never met a man who'd turn down a biscuit," Sheila said.

After leaving the mercantile with her groceries, Sedona ducked into the butcher shop, where Liam Sheehan, a friendly, balding man in his mid-forties sold her two bacon-wrapped filets that he promised would melt in her mouth and a jar of duck fat.

"Although I shouldn't be saying this, because of him losing his da, Conn Brennan's a lucky man," Liam said as he wrapped the steaks in waxed white paper and tied the package with a string.

Rather than be offended by the fact that everyone seemed to know her business, Sedona laughed. "Small towns seem the same wherever in the world they're located."

"Aye. I'd suspect that's the case," he agreed cheerfully. "I've not traveled as much as many, but enough to know that while everyone in the village lives in one another's pockets, which isn't to everyone's liking, it's where I belong."

"You're fortunate," she said as she handed over her credit card. "To be able to make a good life where your roots have been planted." Sedona had thought she'd found her place, but somehow she'd lost her moorings and was now drifting aimlessly.

At least, she thought as she drove back across the bridge, out of town toward the cottage, she'd planned a meal. Now, if she managed to cook it without burning Mary's cottage down, she'd have accomplished more today than she'd managed during all the days since that tidal wave had washed the ground out from beneath her feet.

CONN SMELLED THE aroma wafting from the open cottage window as he walked up to the door. The familiar sound of Enya's "A Day Without Rain" floated like feathers on the salt air.

"It smells like heaven in here," he said as Sedona let him in. "And nothing like a warmed up casserole."

She'd changed into a summery sleeveless white dress emblazoned with poppies with a short, sassy skirt that showcased her wraparound legs, and a frilly white apron she'd found somewhere that managed to be both retro and hot at the same time. Her cheeks were prettily colored from the heat of the stove and strands of blond hair had escaped the tidy little twist she'd worn to the funeral. She looked flushed, a bit disheveled, and a lot tastier than whatever she might have been cooking up.

"It's not. I did some shopping on the way home. I thought you might appreciate a home-cooked meal after the day you've had."

It didn't escape Conn's attention that she'd referred to the cottage as home. It was probably just a slip of the tongue. Or perhaps a subconscious wish? Deciding not to derail the evening with details, he kept the question to himself. For now.

"I would. But you needn't have gone to the trouble."

"I wanted to. For you. And also for me."

"I like the idea of having a place in your equation." He put his hands on her hips and drew her to him.

"It's the first thing I've actually accomplished in weeks." She seemed a bit surprised and decidedly pleased by that idea.

"I'm even more honored by the effort."

"Actually, thanks to Mrs. Monohan's help, it's not that much of an effort. But it feels good to have managed it."

"I'm glad." There'd been a time when her smile alone would have had kings fighting battles to win her hand.

Her gaze shifted out the French doors Mary had talked Bram into installing, never mind that they weren't true to the cottage's original architecture, to a pretty walled garden patio. "It's such a lovely evening, I thought we might eat outdoors…I hope you enjoy roast potatoes, fresh peas, and steak with whiskey sauce."

"I'm an Irish male. Meat and potatoes essentially make up my food pyramid. And as grand as dinner sounds, I came here hungry for something else entirely."

"And what would that be?" Her lips curved in a devastating female smile designed to weaken a man's knees. And wasn't it working on him?

"You." He wrapped one of the curling tendrils of cornsilk hair around a finger.

She put her hands on his chest. He'd already discovered her to be a woman who guarded her personal space. Which, perversely, made breaching those barricades all the more rewarding. "This wasn't what I'd planned for tonight."

"I have a suggestion." He framed her face in his hands, his fingers stroking her cheekbones.

"You're going to tell me to stop trying to plan every moment and go with the flow." Her usually cool and calm voice turned breathless in a way that had been tormenting his sleep.

"That was my intention." She was trembling. And, dammit, she wasn't alone.

Conn had certainly bedded other women. But he'd never met any other who could turn his knees to jelly and cause his body to quake like with fever. Nor had he met one who intrigued him more, with her day planner, spreadsheets, her warm and generous heart, and, he wouldn't lie, her beach-girl blond looks.

"There's thirty minutes left on the potatoes," she said.

"Which isn't nearly enough for what I had in mind." As Enya was coming home, he lowered his hands to Sedona's waist and this time she did not stop him from pulling her close. Letting her feel a hunger that had nothing to do with roasted spuds. "But having been a lad who was guilty of being late for dinner more often than not, I recall they can be kept warm for some time longer."

"I suppose they could…"

"I hear a 'but' coming up." Releasing her, he rubbed his jaw. "You've knocked me off my feet, luv. In a way no woman has ever done before. I want you—"

"Want is easy," she pointed out. What woman wouldn't want this man? Millions the world over undoubtedly had fantasies of Conn of the Hundred Battles. Hadn't he been voted *People* magazine's Sexiest Man of the Year twice? "Easily triggered and capable of being easily satisfied." After all, sex with Conn had been amazing. "But you don't know me." It was her turn to hold up a hand. "And before you say that we got to know each other that night at the inn, it was only physical."

His bullet-quick response was curt and rude. "It was more than that. If it weren't, we wouldn't be wasting time having this conversation. We'd be shagging our brains out right now. There was a connection there, Sedona Sullivan. One that I couldn't get out of my head." He plowed his hand through his hair. "Just because I didn't call or write after that night, it doesn't mean that I don't have a major thing for you."

The quiet force behind that declaration started the fluttering in her stomach again. It would be so easy…

"Even if that were true, I'm not the same person I was back then."

"You've been through a rough patch." He smoothed a hand down her hair, over her shoulder, his fingers massaging the muscles that had bunched into a knot. "From the little Mary told me about the storm, anyone would have been affected by what you went through. Also, having taken a tumble and cracked my head myself, I'm familiar with at least some of the residual physical effects you may be experiencing."

"You had a concussion?"

"Two. The first was when I was fifteen and the car I was in took a corner too fast and ran into a stone wall on the road to Galway."

"You weren't wearing a seatbelt?"

He laughed at that, slid his fingers beneath her hair, dipped his head, and gave her a quick, hard kiss that had her toes curling in her pink ballet flats. "No. Neither was the woman who was driving and ended up hitting a wall on the way back to the village."

"And you received that concussion because you'd been willing to risk your life rather than appear unmanly," she guessed.

"Brigid Logan was eight years older than I was at the time. But to my surprise, she didn't seem to think of me as a mere lad, so I suppose that factored into my decision. Unfortunately, word of the accident got back to my mother. Who threatened to sentence me to house arrest until I was thirty if she were to hear so much as a whisper about me being anywhere with Brigid ever again."

"Good for your mom." Sedona knew that older women seducing underage boys weren't taken as seriously as men with girls, but had never agreed with such a double standard. "What was the other time?"

"I took a tumble off the stage at Copenhagen's Parken Stadium. That was my first time drinking *akvavit*. And the last time I performed drunk."

"You could have broken your neck."

"I could have, indeed. But I didn't and learned my lesson from the experience." With just that light touch on her neck, he drew her closer again. "I may not share your fondness for spreadsheets and überplanning, but I do take my career and my responsibilities to the lads in the band far more seriously than the tabloids suggest."

She'd sensed that when he'd told her about the brewery. Granted, it appeared to be an impulsive decision by a man with more money than he could spend in several lifetimes. On the other hand, when he'd talked about producing local artists, she'd gotten the feeling that he'd been thinking about the possibility for a long time. It had just been when the opportunity presented itself, in the form of Guinness moving on, that he'd acted.

As she'd admittedly done when she'd impulsively accepted Mary's request to come to Castlelough.

"Which brings up the point that I suppose I don't know you, either," she murmured.

"You'd be knowing a great deal more about me than I do you," he countered mildly. "A situation we should go about rectifying. Beginning tonight." He kissed the crown of her hair. "You've already bought the food and set the table. Why don't I grill the steaks while you pour us each a glass of wine and make the whiskey sauce?"

He made everything seem so easy, Sedona thought with a faintly envious sigh. Then again, as she poured the Irish whiskey into the measuring cup up to exactly fifty-nine milliliters, which the online conversion chart assured her was just .147 short of the quarter of a cup the recipe called for, perhaps she was making their situation more difficult than it needed to be.

It was just dinner. And if a shared meal and conversation were to lead to a night of mutually enjoyable sex between two adult, single individuals, what could be wrong with that?

After lining up the rest of the ingredients Mrs. Monohan had sold her—parsley, garlic, peppercorns, Worchester sauce, butter, and kosher salt—she took the glasses of wine outside to the garden patio, where Conn was lighting the stainless steel grill that looked large enough to feed the Irish Army.

The garden right outside the doors was a kitchen garden, redolent with herbal aromas. She set the lacy white wrought iron table with sunshine-yellow placemats and white plates with a green strip around the rims. Then, since her sauce, along with a bowl of fresh steamed peas that tasted like bright pops of green sugar were keeping in the warming oven, and the potatoes were done to a golden crisp, she sat down, sipped the ruby pinot noir, and watching Conn sear the steaks with an easy expertise that suggested he'd done far more cooking than she had, Sedona tried to remember the last time a man had cooked for her. Other than her father making her scrambled eggs when she'd been in bed with flu at age ten, she couldn't remember *any* man cooking for her.

As the meat sizzled, bees buzzed lazily around the gaily bright cutting flowers that had been planted beyond the herbs, and songbirds trilled their twilight songs in the branches of the leafy green trees, Sedona discovered that for the first time in weeks, she was beginning to feel like herself again.

22

FINALLY. EILEEN BLEW out a long breath as the last guest left the house. For the past weeks, she'd felt like a ringmaster in a three-ring circus. She'd always liked people, and although she'd stumbled into turning her family home into a B&B, the life suited her. Rather than get stuck in a rut, like so many other people she knew who woke each morning facing the same monotonous long hours ahead of them, each day was different, just as her guests were different.

She'd always wanted to travel. Hadn't her parents chided her for always having her nose in a book and her head in the clouds? Visiting the library in Ennistymon had been like taking a ride on a magic carpet that took her soaring to different times and exotic places.

Her future plans were always changing. When she'd been four, she was going to ride an elephant in the circus. By six, she'd decided to live on the tippy-top floor of a grand hotel, the way Eloise lived in New York's Plaza Hotel. At nine, she was going to be an adventurer, exploring tombs in Egypt's grand pyramids.

She'd flirted with other larger-than-life possibilities until that memorable summer of her twelfth year, when she'd turned on the TV and seen Rudolf Nureyev dancing the prince in *Sleeping Beauty*.

His tiger-like leaps and powerful pirouettes had radiated an arrogant masculine charm that had stirred feelings that, when she was older, Eileen would recognize as lust. A topic that had certainly never been discussed beneath her strict Irish Catholic family's roof.

While all of her friends took step dancing lessons, Eileen had ridden her bicycle nearly sixteen kilometers, round-trip, to Lisdoonvarna, to study under the elderly Doreen Lynch, who'd toured for two seasons with the English National Ballet.

Subscribing to the traditional teaching method that professed dancers must be broken down, then built back so they'd be tough enough to withstand the demands of a professional career, Miss Lynch had routinely verbally and even physically abused her students. There'd been many days when Eileen would pedal back home with red rod marks on her thighs along with her blistered feet, but driven by the romantic fantasy of Nureyev holding her in his arms as he lifted her across the stage, Eileen had refused to surrender her dream.

When she was sixteen, she'd performed a variation as Titania, from *A Midsummer Night's Dream*, for the talent portion of Castlelough's Oyster Festival queen competition. That night, the ballet's Queen of the Fairies had been crowned Oyster Queen. Giddy with happiness, she'd willingly surrendered her virginity to Joseph Brennan in the ruins of the castle that had given the town its name. That she'd imagined Joseph to be Rudolf Nureyev was a secret she planned to take to her grave.

When she'd missed one period, Eileen hadn't worried. Dancing, after all, was demanding, strenuous, and emotionally draining. It also caused irregular menstruation. Even after she'd passed out from dizziness while practicing chaînés turns after missing a second period, getting deeper and deeper into denial, she'd brushed away the niggling anxiety.

By the third missed period, when Miss Lynch had berated her for the swollen breasts that had risen on her previously flat ballerina chest, Eileen had accepted both the truth of her situation and her fate.

A week later, after the parish priest had dispensed with the usual posting of the bans, Eileen Hayes had stood at the altar of Holy Child Church and vowed to take Joseph Brennan as her lawful wedded husband, "to have and to hold, from this day forward for better, for worse, for richer, for poorer, in sickness and in health, until death do us part."

By the time divorce finally became legal in Ireland, her boys were grown, so it was easier to stay married to a man who stayed away for months at a time. Then, after raping her during a drunken evening, leaving her pregnant with Declan, he'd left for America. She'd thought he was gone for good.

She'd been wrong.

But now, after more than three decades locked into a sham of a marriage, she was truly, finally free. Reveling in the silence broken only by the liquid trills of a nightingale, she filled the claw-footed tub. Then opened the glass jar of outrageously expensive French bath salts that had been a Christmas present from Conn. After tossing in a handful, she sank into the fragrant, silky-smooth water, leaning her head back against the curved rim as she sipped a glass of wine from one of the bottles Patrick had brought over from the pub to serve the visitors who'd been streaming in to see her dying husband.

The funeral itself had been a surreal event. Of course part of her had been sorry at how Joseph had suffered in the end. But by the time he'd been laid to rest in the ground, her eyes had remained dry and she'd felt relief. Along with a heady sense of freedom that in younger days, in fear for her immortal soul, would have had her confessing.

Having spent so many years in various stages of limbo, purgatory, and even hell after she'd become pregnant with Conn, she'd moved past the need to seek dispensation from any priest, bishop, cardinal, pope, or even from God for her failure to mourn a husband not worthy of whatever the modern equivalent of sackcloth and ashes might be.

Her life was finally her own, and it was up to her, and her alone, to decide how to spend however many years she had left.

When she first heard a knocking on the front door, she ignored it. She'd done her wifely duty and she refused to allow anything or anyone to interfere with this well-earned indulgence.

The knocking continued. Sipping on the velvety burgundy, Eileen tried to shut it out. Finally, thinking that it might be one of her sons, concerned about how she might be holding up, she reluctantly rose from the fragrant water, retrieved the heavy robe from its hook, went back downstairs, and opened the green door that always lifted her spirits on the darkest of days.

At the first sight of the man standing in the spreading yellow glow of her front porch light, Eileen's mind was wiped as clear as glass. She couldn't think. Couldn't move. She was tempted to look down and see if someone had glued her bare feet to the floor.

It couldn't be true! Surely she'd fallen asleep in the bath and was dreaming, as she had on so many nights for so many years.

"And aren't you still the most gorgeous woman in all of Erin?" the deep baritone voice greeted her.

Gazing up into those all-too-familiar electric-blue eyes, Eileen allowed herself to hope that she was, indeed, awake. "Dennis?"

"'Tis me, my love," he assured her. "In the flesh."

The only man she'd ever loved, the only man she *could* ever love, stepped into the house and wrapped her in his arms as if he had every right to. Which, Eileen thought as her heart soared and an entire host of angels singing the Hallelujah chorus drowned out the nightingale's pretty song, he did.

"I can't believe you've come."

"Ah, didn't I tell you that I was a patient man?"

He had. But having learned that pretty words came easily, and certain that such a special man would not stay single forever, she'd never expected him to wait. But wait he had, and although there was so much to discuss, such as how he knew to come to Castlelough today, of all days, right now they had decades of separation to make up for.

Their lips met in a kiss so sweet that, as she clung to Dennis Byrne, who'd come from Dublin for her as he'd promised so long ago, Eileen wept. But unlike the last time they'd been together in this house, her tears were born not from sorrow but joy.

23

THE DINNER HAD turned out as well as promised, and Sedona sat drinking in the fragrance of the rioting cream, white, and pink roses around the far edges of the patio. For the first time since the storm, she felt the tensed muscles in her shoulders loosen.

"I can't remember when I felt more relaxed."

"I'm glad." As he topped off her glass, Conn flashed her his bad-boy smile, letting her know he was thinking of a time when she hadn't been the least bit tense. "The dinner was grand."

"You grilled the steak, which was the main part of the meal."

He dismissed that with a shrug. "That's easy enough." He lifted his glass in a slight toast. "Those rosemary roast potatoes were even better than my mam's, though if you ever tell her I said it, I'll deny it to my dying day."

She laughed and enjoyed the satisfaction of having managed to cook a dinner he'd so enjoyed. "My lips are sealed."

"And tasty." He leaned across the small bistro table, touching his lips to hers, creating another of those little zings between them that went all the way to her toes. "It's pleased I am to see you enjoying yourself."

"I am. Although I admit to feeling a bit guilty about not having even thought about how I'm going to reopen my bakery."

"You've no reason to feel guilty. A rested mind is more agile at solving problems." He laid his long-fingered musician's hand on hers. "And may I suggest that while you're resting that clever mind, you might consider treating yourself with the same generosity of spirit with which you treat others?"

"I don't know what you mean." She stalled, taking a sip of wine. The truth was that she *did* know. Weren't her own parents always telling her that perfection was impossible and that she'd always been too hard on herself?

Conn lifted a brow, clearly challenging her statement. "You're not only drop-dead gorgeous, with the most amazing eyes I've ever seen, you're remarkably kind and generous. Hell, didn't you jump on a plane and fly across the sea days after suffering a concussion because Mary was worried about me?"

"Maybe that wasn't the only reason." Torn in a dozen directions, most of them involving cutting off this conversation and jumping on *him*, Sedona ran a fingernail round the rim of her glass. "Maybe I just wanted an excuse to see you again."

"You're not alone there, since I'd decided that morning after that I needed to see you again." Her flash of thigh as she crossed her legs caused a spike in Conn's heartbeat. "But your agreeing to have tea with Fergus and his sister tomorrow proves my point. You'd never even met him."

"In my former profession, I worked with several clients I'd never met before they showed up at my office."

"The key word is *former*. You're no longer an accountant. You're a baker. Which, by the way, is quite a drastic career change."

She shrugged. But Conn could tell by the way she'd tensed up that there was more behind the story than she was letting on.

"Okay," she said when he let the silence drift out between them. "Since you shared the story of Joseph Brennan not being your birth father, I'll tell you something I've never told anyone but my very best friend. I didn't even tell my parents." She took a deep breath. "I enjoyed my work. And I was good at it."

"I have no doubt you'd be good at anything. But I can easily envision you spending your day balancing numbers. And actually enjoying it." Which was another difference between the two of them. Conn would rather be tarred and feathered than budget accounts. Which was why he had a financial manager to take care of the details of tour sales, expenses, royalties, and taxes. "So, what precipitated the change of plans?"

"After I was moved to the partnership track, I was assigned to work directly with one of the managing partners, who turned out not to have gotten the memo about proper workplace behavior."

"Meaning he hit on you?"

"On a regular basis," she confirmed. "Of course I realized that his behavior was illegal, but there were complications. One being that I was so focused on my goal of making partner I was willing to overlook his inappropriate comments. At least until I gained more internal power."

Conn wasn't naive. He'd witnessed women in the music business having to deal with much more. Which had, on more than a few instances, involved him getting into one of those tabloid-making brawls. But that didn't stop him from hating the idea of her having to put up with a misogynist wanker. "I'd have been more than happy to have punched out his lung for you."

"As much as I appreciate the sentiment, I didn't know you then," she pointed out.

"True enough." Though having yet more proof that logic appeared to be her default thought process, Conn found those times when he'd succeeded in breaking her free of that rigid mindset even more appealing. "And yet you eventually moved on."

"I did. And although it isn't that often in my mind, I'll admit that there are times when I am sorry that it had me leaving a career I not only enjoyed but that allowed me to help people...

"It was tax time and we were all working 24/7. Which was the same as every year. But one night, March thirteenth—"

"You remember the day and date?" Conn couldn't even remember the exact day his first song had hit number one on the charts. Then again, sober hadn't exactly been *his* default behavior in those days.

"It was a Friday the thirteenth, which makes it easier, though I'd probably remember anyway. Everyone else had gone home, and we were working on this very complex, very lucrative corporate return. The information had come in late, and the filing date was March sixteenth, so he and I were still at the office after midnight when, after he'd drunk too much, the situation turned physical."

A red haze of temper burned in front of Conn's eyes. Realizing that this was difficult enough for her to talk about, although it took a Herculean effort, he banked the flames. Just barely.

"The fucker tried to rape you?" Even the word was an abomination that threatened to put the damper on an evening that had begun so well.

"It didn't get that far."

"But he did put his hands on you?"

"He ripped my blouse. But let go fast enough when I hit him with a paperweight, then left him with his testicles tickling his tonsils." The smile teasing at the corners of her lips suggested she could still enjoy that memory. "I guess he hadn't known that all the kids on the commune took self-defense training every year."

"Fair play to you. And your parents. And then you called the cops?"

"No. I seriously considered it for about a minute, but there were complications. He had a three-week-old baby at home." She held up a hand to forestall his next comment. "And before you point out that's not an adequate excuse to let him get away with committing assault, I wasn't protecting him but his wife. Who'd been diagnosed with breast cancer in the final trimester of her pregnancy."

"That's problematic, to be sure. But it still doesn't excuse his behavior."

"No, of course it doesn't. But his behavior was an indication that the marriage was already troubled. Along with a newborn, his wife had a six-year-old daughter and a toddler son at home and was scheduled for her first chemo the following week. She'd have to have been Superwoman to deal with having her husband arrested. I wasn't prepared to do that to her. Especially since my own mother is a breast cancer survivor.

"So, I went home, let him sweat overnight worrying about whether I was planning to report him to the police, to the other partners, or file a sexual harassment case which would seriously damage his career.

"The next day I went into the office and presented him with a contract I'd drawn up requiring that he undergo counseling. If he didn't sign it, and comply with the conditions, I'd essentially blow up his life both at home and at work."

"How would you know if he complied?"

"One of the conditions was that he'd have to send me copies of the insurance charges, or if he chose to pay outside the company insurance to keep the fact that he was seeing a counselor private, I'd need to see copies of the receipts for treatment. Then I resigned, cleaned out my desk, and returned to my condo to come up with a new life plan."

"Of course you did." When she shot him a sharp look, Conn held up both hands in defense. "That wasn't a criticism," he insisted. "I was merely stating that I'd expect you to do exactly that. Though I doubt if I'd have guessed that you'd jump from accounting to baking."

As serious as the conversation had been, she smiled at that. "I enjoyed baking growing up. Enough that it became one of my jobs on the commune. As it happened, I was beginning over again just as cupcakes began taking off. Portland was already getting crowded, and by then I wanted out of the city anyway, because it just seemed time for a totally new start.

"So, after doing some market research, I decided that Shelter Bay was ideally situated between Newport to the south and Seaside and Cannon Beach to the north. Business took off from day one, and ironically, I'd been putting money aside to buy my own location when the storm took out my shop."

"So, that's what you're planning to do? Buy your own location?"

"Probably."

Conn could tell that, for some reason, she wasn't entirely on board with the new program. Which was just as well. The longer it took her to tick off all the boxes on all the spreadsheets and ledgers that were undoubtedly filling her head, the longer she'd be staying in Ireland. And the longer he'd have to explore whatever was happening between them.

"So," she said, exhaling a long breath. "It feels good to have told someone."

"I'm glad I was here to tell. As you were here when I needed someone other than my family to know about the lie I'd been living all my life."

"It's only a lie if you knew," she pointed out. "Which you didn't."

"True enough." And wasn't that still a salient point? Eventually he was going to have to have a heart-to-heart talk with his mother. As much as he hated the idea of causing her more discomfort than she'd already suffered, he deserved to know the truth.

Which didn't mean he had one damn idea what he'd do when he found out who the mystery man who'd fathered him was.

"But that's enough talk about negative things," he said, putting the vexing problem away for now. He stood up and held out his hand.

"Dance with me."

"There's no music." And wasn't he coming to love her practical mind? Fortunately, apparently her heart was more fanciful, because she took his hand and went into his arms.

"Now, I wouldn't be wanting to put a damper on such a lovely evening by arguing with such a bold and beautiful woman," he murmured as he began swaying to the tune that had been echoing in his head ever since he'd escaped the funeral potluck. "But I always hear music when I think of you."

"You must have kissed the Blarney Stone sometime during your life, Conn Brennan." She laughed softly even as she twined her arms around his neck. "Because you're an incorrigible flatterer."

"It's not flattery if it's true." His hand, splayed on her back, drew her closer. He felt her momentarily tense. "Relax, luv." He murmured the endearment as he nuzzled her neck. "Dancing is supposed to be fun." He nipped at her earlobe. "Like other things men and women might choose to do together."

"Incorrigible," she repeated. "I knew when I first saw you that you'd be trouble." She sighed and tilted her head, giving his roving lips access to her mouth. He kissed his way from one corner to the other. Then kissed her top lip. Then nipped at the plump pink flesh of her bottom lip.

"But there must be something in this village's water," she said, "because just like the last time I was here, I'm finding trouble irresistible."

Rather than plunder, his lips fluttered as soft as butterfly wings against hers, drawing her into the mists. It was so nice. Better than nice to feel this man's arms around her. For this moment in time, Sedona was going to take everyone's advice and stop struggling to direct the stream and simply go with the flow.

Her body was softened against him, yielding to the practiced seduction, when he drew his head back, his eyes still on hers. Serious. Watchful.

He shook his head, his half smile seeming to be directed inward. Then took her mouth again, easing her back into the kiss that had her head spinning like a leaf caught in a whirlpool.

And now the entire world was spinning as he waltzed her, with the same expertise he brought to his lovemaking, back into the cottage and down the blue limestone hallway to the bedroom, humming a tune against her mouth that had her imagining the weep of violins and the plaintive sound of an alto sax floating on the breeze of a cloud-scudded lonely night.

"I hear it," she said breathlessly as he stopped when he reached the bed, where freshly washed and turned-down sheets confessed her own hopes and plans for this evening.

"The music," she managed to say as his hands skimmed down the sides of her body, from her breasts to her thighs. "But it sounds so sad."

"It's a man considering his life without a woman." He slipped those clever hands beneath the hem of her dress and began to lift it up. "Not just any woman." The evening breeze was cool and soft on her thighs. Beneath her skin, her blood was running hot and wild. "The woman he loves."

He raised the skirt higher, then stepped a couple inches back to take in the white lace she was wearing beneath it. "The woman he's terrified he might lose. The one he'd rather die than live without."

His voice was deep and rough. A storm as dangerous as any she'd ever known swirled in his eyes, but the way he was looking at her, as if she were that woman in the song, the one he was afraid of losing, made her feel not merely desired. But powerful.

"And you wrote it?"

"I did." When his stroking touch stopped just short of her tingling bits, leaving her aching, she bit back a moan. "For Mary's film," he clarified. "Only last night. Thinking of you like this, wet and hot for me, proved a grand inspiration."

He cupped her, this time his thumb stroking her through the silky material, which was all it took to make her come. He'd already shown the ability to play her with the same familiarity and expertise that he used on that lipstick-red guitar, and the idea that he'd been thinking about her in this way made her feel sexy. With all the women he could have wanted to write about, to make love to, he'd chosen her.

As she'd chosen him.

"I'm glad you were thinking of me." There'd been a time, when they'd first met, when she would have thought he was tossing out a line. But because she was coming to know him well enough to believe him, she was able to share her own truth. "Because I've been thinking of you for weeks."

Her fingers were steadier than the last time they'd been together as she began unbuttoning the black silk shirt he'd worn to the funeral with a black tie. He'd dispensed with the tie while he'd been cooking the steaks and heaven help her, she'd found that little triangle of bare skin far more enticing than the smoky aroma that had wafted from the grill.

She went up on her toes, and as she'd wanted to do that first night in the pub, she licked his neck. Then, baring more and more warm male flesh as she unfastened the buttons, one by one, she worked her way down his chest.

Her fingers moved to his belt. Instead of unbuckling it, she slipped them beneath his waistband, teasing him as he'd teased her.

He sucked in his gut, making room for her touch to go lower. Yet when she went to unfasten those unfamiliar dress trousers, he caught her hands in his.

"I want another full night with you, *a stór*. Which is why, since I wouldn't want to risk the humiliation of an early blast-off, I believe it would be time for us to be making use of that bed you so conveniently have already turned down."

She looked up at him with fake coyness from beneath her lashes, loving the idea that she could not only inspire a song but bring him to the edge of control. "You knew I was a planner from the first."

"Aye, I did," he agreed as he tangled his hands in her hair and kissed her long and hard and deep. "And isn't that only one of the things I've come to love about you?"

As they tumbled onto the sheets that smelled of lavender and the fresh air they'd been dried in, Sedona wondered if he'd meant that all-important word, which he'd professed never to have said to any woman literally. Or if it had merely been an expression tossed out in the moment.

Then, after he pulled her pretty dress over her head, he professed grand admiration of her lacy bra and panties before deftly dispensing with them. While she, in turn, stripped him of his clothes. Taking in the rock-hard body that had inspired women all over the globe to toss their underwear at the stage, Sedona stopped thinking and surrendered to the moment. To Conn.

24

MUCH, MUCH LATER, feeling as boneless as water, Sedona managed to roll onto her side to kiss his damp chest. "Did I tell you that first night how much I love your body?" His hot, hard, mouthwatering body.

"You did, indeed." He stroked a broad hand down her spine and squeezed her butt. "As I told you how I felt about yours. What I kept to myself was the idea that I could spend the rest of my life getting to know every silky, fragrant inch of it."

"You didn't tell me because of our agreement," she murmured as her fingers toyed with the arrowing of hair bisecting his ripped torso.

"True." With one deft move, he pulled her on top of him, adjusting their positions so the parts of her still quaking were pressing against an erection that demonstrated amazing recovery powers. "But I was already considering rewriting the rules before you walked away."

Those black curls stimulated her ultra-sensitive nipples, causing her to want him again. And again. And again. It crossed Sedona's mind that after having gone over two years without missing sex, she might possibly be turning into a nymphomaniac. Even more surprising was that she couldn't find anything wrong with that idea.

"I felt the same way. But when you didn't call…"

"You assumed I'd lived up to my highly exaggerated womanizing reputation and moved on."

"I did. And it bothered me. More than I'd expected. More than it should have." She trailed her fingers around the lips that had created such havoc on her body. "I knew when you sat down at my table in the pub that night after the reception that you'd never fit into my male criteria spreadsheet. What I hadn't expected was that you'd blow it to smithereens."

"And isn't that gratifying to know?" She could feel his deep, satisfied chuckle. "But while we'd be sharing home truths, I'll be telling you from that fateful, ill-ended joy ride with Brigid Logan, I've enjoyed the pleasure of women."

"We'd best call the *Castlelough Celtic* and tell Duncan and Cassandra McCaragh to stop the presses." Even as she kept her tone dry, Sedona experienced a sharp sting of jealousy. "Because that's definitely a newsflash."

"Smart arse." He treated the ass in question to a quick, playful spank. Then his brows furrowed and his gaze turned as somber as one of those stones she'd seen today in the cemetery. "I've tried telling myself that the reason everything seems so different with you is because the rest of my life has been turned upside down and inside out, so nothing feels the same.

"But it's more than that." He rubbed his jaw thoughtfully and gave her a long, deep study that reminded her, in a way, of Kara when she was digging for secrets. "I haven't figured it out yet. But I will."

"Not that I'm claiming to be an expert, but from personal observation, it seems that when a man decides he's ready to put down roots, he tends to set his focus on the first woman who sashays by."

"I can't decide which of us that sweeping statement about my species insults more. Me, for being thought of as some shallow, idiot wank who'd pluck the first available egg-bearing female off the street in order to cage her into lifelong monogamy because I might be considering settling down. Or you, for not giving yourself credit for being an exquisite, remarkably unique woman." He ran a hand over her shoulder and down her arm, linking their fingers together. "However, if you'd care to put your theory to the test by sashaying around this bedroom to see if I'm stimulated to start nest building, I'm bloody well not going to stop you."

It was her turn to slap him. Lightly, harmlessly, on the boulder masquerading as a bicep. "See, now you're dodging the issue by turning it into a sexist challenge."

"More an invitation," he said easily. "Meanwhile, I'd best research the issue more deeply." He rolled them over again so that her legs were on the outside of his, their bodies pressed together so closely even the slightest zephyr of the sea breeze fluttering the white curtains couldn't have gotten between them. Not that she would have wanted it to. "What would you say to conducting more experiments?"

She might not be just any woman, but as he began rocking against her, Sedona doubted that there was a woman on the planet who could resist that suggestion.

He'd already ruined her for any other man. After tonight, she might as well start researching convents in need of a baker. As anticipation rose, she wrapped her arms around him and hung on tight, ready for her next breath-stealing, mind-melting, heart-hammering ride on the Conn Brennan Irish rocker roller coaster. "Since we're acting solely in the interest of clinical observation—"

"Absolutely." This time he didn't start out slow and coaxing. He crushed his mouth to hers, demanding, taking, sweeping her into the smoke and flames.

When he finally came up for air, she managed, just barely, to finish the response he'd cut off. "I wouldn't say no."

Blue fire flamed in his eyes while his mouth curved in a bold, wickedly satisfied pirate's smile.

Then he took her mouth again, and it was the last thing either of them would say for a very long time.

25

CONN WAS BRACED on one elbow, deciding he wouldn't mind staying in this rumpled, feather-topped bed, watching the delectable woman lying in his arms peacefully sleeping. From the blissful smile on her face, he could only guess that her busy-bee brain had shut down long enough for her to dream of last night. Catching up for lost time, they'd made love until a lavender-pink light was filtering into the room, bathing her in a soft glow.

She awakened slowly, glanced up, and rather than tense when her eyes met his, she shared a slow, seductive smile. At least he thought it might be seductive. As far as he was concerned, watching her balance a spreadsheet would probably turn him on.

"It's so much lovelier to wake up to meadow birds than the buzz of my phone alarm," she said. "As lovely as the nightingale was, its song sounded a bit sad. All these trills and warbling are far more cheerful."

He ran a hand down her hair, over her bare, silky shoulders. "The birds would be skylarks."

"Oh, that's wonderful." Her smile lit up her eyes. "I'll have to record them for my mother, since that's her name."

"One she took when she became a flower child?"

"No, while my father changed his name from James to Freebird, not from the song but after some old Indian poem, coincidentally my grandmother named my mother after Shelley's 'To a Skylark.'"

"Hail to thee, blithe spirit," he quoted the poem. "Bird that never wert, that from heaven, or near it, pourest thy full heart in profuse strains of unpremeditated art."

She lifted her hand to his cheek, her expression one of both surprise and pleasure. "You know it?"

"Just because I left school at sixteen doesn't mean that I don't read. Especially poems, which can be inspiring because I can hear the music of the cadence."

She sighed. "I'm sunk."

"Why would that be?" He tugged the sheet down, trailed his fingers over her breasts, pleased when her nipples tightened in response to the light caress. He'd known from the beginning that they'd be a perfect match in bed. What was proving a surprise was how well they fit in other ways.

"Because both my parents are going to love you."

He liked that she was assuming they'd meet. Another wall breached. "In all honesty, I'd prefer that to them disliking me. And not believing me good enough for their daughter."

"Oh, that's not going to be a problem." She turned into his touch and lifted her lips to his. "The problem is that they've been trying to set me up with husband prospects for ages, despite me insisting that I have no plans to get married."

"Then there shouldn't be a problem." He drew her into his arms, mentally doing the math to figure out how many more condoms were on that tabletop.

"You haven't met my mother," she insisted. "She's like a silken bulldozer."

"I believe I can resist." He slipped a hand between them. All it took was a single stroke for her to become as wet as he was hard. "But what do you say we blow up that bridge when we come to it?"

Her fingers curled around him, stroking him in a way that suggested she was no more eager to waste the morning arguing than he was. "And relish this moment," she said throatily.

"Aye." As he slid into her, while the rising sun gilded the green fields and the skylarks sang their morning song of joy, it crossed Conn's mind that this moment with Sedona Sullivan could well be the most perfect of his entire life.

"I have a favor to ask you," he said as they dressed after a long, luxurious round of shower sex.

"Anything," she said without hesitation as she fastened a white, lace-trimmed bra with a front opening that would take him two seconds, tops, to undo.

"You've already reminded me of Mary. The more I get to know you, the more I understand why you've become friends."

She smiled up at him. "I'm taking that as a compliment."

"Which is exactly how it was meant...Would you be willing to work with me on her film's score?"

"Me?" She turned toward him. "I'm not a musician."

"Yet you grew up with one."

"I also grew up with an artist," she countered. "But my drawing ability pretty much stopped at stick figures."

"The woman in the movie has a major life decision to make," he said. "I can understand intellectually why she responds to a crisis in the only way she considers possible, but there are a lot of conflicting emotions crashing against each other, and I'd enjoy a female's point of view while working on it.

"And not just any female," he quickly said, not wanting her to think that was the only reason he wanted to work with her. "But one whose mind and heart I admire. And respect."

"There you go with the flattery again."

"Again, it's the God's truth." He lifted his right hand. "There's also the fact that being with you has brought back my temperamental muse. Since I'd admittedly found myself in a frustrating creative dry spell, I've decided she likes you."

"If she's even partly responsible for the music in Mary's films, I believe I'd like her, too."

A thought occurred to him. One that hadn't crossed Conn's mind until this moment. Yet more proof of how much Sedona had disrupted not just his body but also his brain.

"There is one thing. I honestly didn't think of it until now, but it could well prove a problem and I want you to feel absolutely free to say that you'd rather not work with me."

She tilted her head. A crease appeared between her brows. "That sounds serious."

"It is. It's the black moment in the film, when a dangerous situation brings about an epiphany and has her forced to confront a lie she's been telling herself. And decide what action she's going to take. I think it's the best work Mary's ever done, and I know you could help me live up to the bar she's set.

"But here's the thing..."

He sucked in a deep breath. Dragged his hands through his hair. What in God's name had he been thinking to even suggest she collaborate with him on this particular part of the film after what she'd suffered through?

"It takes place during a storm at sea."

"Oh." She paled a bit at that. Damn. Why didn't he just take Bram's heavy framing hammer and pound it into his dense eejit's head? "If it's a black moment, I take it that it's a pretty bad storm?"

"Very bad." The hell with the hammer. He should just throw himself over the cliff. "Damn. Forget I said anything. It was a spur-of-the-moment idea and obviously not well thought out."

She looked out the window at the waves, which this morning were as still as glass. But they both knew that those rugged cliffs hadn't been carved and chiseled away by a glassy, calm sea. But an angry, tempestuous, dangerous one.

"I'd love an opportunity to preview any of Mary's movies," she said finally. "Let alone actually have a part, however small, in the making of it."

Surely there had to be a *but* in there somewhere. Conn waited, then, when it didn't seem to be coming, had to ask, "Are you certain?"

"I am. Absolutely. I'm not fragile, Conn. Other people have been through far worse. And don't they say that the best way to overcome your fear is to face it?"

"I suppose that would be one way." As rocky as his own life had been, he'd never been forced to face a situation that had left him traumatized.

"Let's say it does trigger a flashback," she suggested. "Wouldn't that make my responses more real? Which, in turn, would be helpful to your scoring?"

"My scoring isn't the damn point." Did she truly think him that self-centered?

That small furrow formed between her brows again. Conn's fingers itched with the need to smooth it away, but every time he touched Sedona, he wanted her. And as impossible as he would have thought it just days ago, this conversation was more important than a vigorous tumble with a hot woman.

"If it wasn't, then why did you ask me to work with you?"

"For the very reason I asked. And, truthfully, because I wanted an excuse to be spending more time with you."

She laughed at that confession. "You needn't come up with excuses. Sometime during the night, I considered tying you to the bedposts to keep you from leaving this cottage."

"I wouldn't be one to stop you. If you're still inclined."

Damn, he liked her sunny laugh. "I'll keep that in mind. But to get back to your concerns, was I traumatized? Yes. I suspect I wasn't the only one on the coast that night who was.

"Was I injured? Slightly. Do I still have nightmares? The occasional flashback. Wouldn't anyone? Though"—her eyes took on a sexy gleam—"I didn't have any nightmares last night. Which, given the eroticism of the dreams I did experience, I attribute to having made love with you."

And didn't that make him feel like an effing king of the world? "You'd not be alone in those dreams," he said.

"Thank you...I assured everyone, and myself, that all I needed was rest. And time. Which I'm definitely getting today. Bakers keep early hours. Usually I'd be long done with my morning run and already at work. But sleeping in past sunrise has me feeling like a lady of leisure from times past. Especially since the day includes tea in a centuries-old Irish manor house."

"Which will undoubtedly inspire a new nightmare," he said dryly.

She laughed. "Your Fergus is an intriguing character." Her succulent lips turned down for a moment. "I wish I'd thought to bring a hat. Not that I actually own anything but ball caps, but a nice, wide straw hat with a ribbon and flowers around the brim would be lovely."

"You'll be lovely without a hat. Whatever you're wearing." Or not wearing. Conn had already determined that he especially liked her with her clothes off. "Although I do have to warn you that you may be over-romanticizing the tea party part of the day."

"Perhaps," she said with an easy shrug of her bare shoulders. "Whatever happens, I'm going to think of it as a new experience."

He shook his head and decided that she had to be one of the most positive persons he'd ever met. Right up there with

Mary and his brother Declan. Although a screenwriter/movie star and farmer might appear to have nothing in common, they were both unrelentingly optimistic. And whenever they did get knocked down, whether by a Hollywood studio or powerful summer storm that wiped out a season's oats, didn't they pick themselves right back up and keep on going? Just as Sedona had done. And, Conn knew, would do again.

The question, one that was becoming increasingly important to Conn, was where she'd choose to build her new life. In Shelter Bay, closer to family, where she had so many friends who cared about her and whom she obviously cared about? Or here in Castlelough? With him?

Which, for a man whose lifestyle tended more toward hit-and-run short-term relationships with women equally disinclined to settle down, sounded eminently appealing.

He was still pondering that new thought when his mobile rang.

"It's your mother," Eileen announced, as if both her ringtone and the screen hadn't already identified her.

"What's wrong?"

"Not a thing. Can't a mother call her son without there being a problem?"

"It's been a difficult time." And wasn't that an understatement?

"It has. But now it's over and it's a new day and time for a new start. Which is why I want you and your brothers to come to breakfast. I have news to share."

When she'd first mentioned the new start, he'd wondered if she was about to tell him who his father was. But if the others were invited, as well, she must have something else in mind.

"I'll be there. What time?"

"I've already talked to Declan to make sure he's done with his milking, so he can join us. What would you say to half past?"

He paused, his attention drifting to Sedona, who'd just pulled a snug white tank top over her head, covering up what, a moment ago, had been the best view in Ireland. Having gotten the gist of the conversation from his side, she mouthed, "Go."

"See you then," he said. After ending the call, he crossed the room, took her in his arms, and dipped her, as if they were posing for a cover of one of those romance novels she read. "Thank you," he said after a long, deep, wet kiss.

"Thank *you*." She touched her white-tipped fingers to lips his kiss had left the hue of strawberries. "I'll say this for you, Conn Brennan, you are definitely a world-class kisser."

"You inspire a hell of a lot more than just my music," he said as he resisted the urge to take her full bottom lip in his. One nip and he'd be taking her back to bed, and although Conn couldn't think of anything he'd rather do, he knew that his mother wouldn't have called all her sons together if she didn't have something important to tell them.

His confession caused Sedona's mouth to curve up as she rolled her eyes. Needing her to understand that he wasn't just talking blarney, that his words weren't shallow flattery but the absolute truth, he snagged her wrist when she would have turned away to finish getting dressed.

"We've both agreed that our first time together turned out to be much more than the rainy-night hookup we'd initially agreed upon."

The laughter left her eyes as they met his. "That's true."

"And I've told you that I've never felt the same about a woman…any woman…before."

"You did." She glanced down at his hand braceleting her slender wrist. Was she remembering how he'd held her hands over her head as he'd taken her against the tiled shower wall? He stroked the inside of her wrist and felt her pulse leap. Which was all it took to make him hard as stone. "And the feeling is mutual," she said.

Her staccato pulse, along with her admission, had him drawing her closer even as he struggled to ignore the tempting, rumpled sheets only a few feet away. "There's something between us."

He tunneled one hand beneath her sleek hair, his fingers curving around her neck while his other hand moved down her back, below her waist, pressing her even closer. When she cupped his jeans-clad butt and shifted against him again, lifting one bare leg around his, Conn gritted his teeth.

To hell with the bed. It would be so easy to yank down the white lace knickers that matched the bra and take her right here and now where they were standing, her twined around him like Irish ivy.

"I'd best go," he said with an eye on the clock as he slowly, reluctantly released her.

"Yes." Her throaty tone assured him that it wasn't her first choice, either. Her eyes, with their dark, expanded pupils, drifted down below his belt, zeroing in on his erection. "You might want to work on that during the drive into town."

"And wasn't I thinking the same exact thing?" His laugh was rough and pained. He now knew exactly how

Mary's male characters felt when they found themselves drowning in a selkie's sensual spell. "I shouldn't be long."

"I'll be here," she said as she walked him to the cottage door.

"In bed? Naked?"

She lifted a brow. "Perhaps you've confused me with a groupie." Before he could protest he'd never, *ever* thought of her that way, her lips curved in a seductive smile that would bring any male to his knees. When she touched a fingertip to her tongue, then trailed it along the neckline of the tank—teasing, tempting, tormenting—Conn felt his own knees turn to water. "Which, for some reason, I'm not finding all that unappealing…I'll have to give the idea some more thought."

Her nipples, God help him, had hardened, pressing like pearls against the tank. Either she was really cold or the idea turned her on. Her purred response suggested it was the second.

"Why don't you do that?" The metal zipper of his jeans was growing increasingly painful. Conn knew that if he so much as touched himself to adjust the damn pressure, with her looking at him that way, his intentions of being a dutiful son would go up in smoke.

Unable to resist her siren's call, he kissed her one last time before leaving, to give them both something to think about.

He was halfway to the SUV when she called after him. "I have one question."

He glanced back over his shoulder. Conn had visited the Taj Mahal, ridden a camel past the pyramids, tossed a coin in the Trevi fountain, and performed a concert on China's

Great Wall. But never had he seen anything as stunning as the sight of Sedona Sullivan framed in the cottage doorway, her long legs and feet bare, looking good enough to eat.

"When you say naked, are you talking absolutely nothing at all? Or is the perfumed lotion I found on the bathroom vanity allowed?" Her fingers trailed teasingly over the golden skin above her breasts again.

"You do realize," he said as his tightened jeans began to threaten any future possibility of procreation, "that you're killing me."

Her slow, sultry smile hit him like a double shot of Jameson's. "Good. Hurry back. I'd hate to have to start without you." With that provocative vision hanging in the air, she shut the cranberry-red door.

And wasn't that thought enough to torment his turned-on mind all during the drive into the village?

He was so screwed.

And soon literally would be again. If he managed to make it through the upcoming family breakfast without self-immolating.

26

EILEEN HAD GONE all out with a full Irish stir-up. If nothing else, she'd thought as she'd covered the old oak farm table with Irish sausage, rashers of bacon, black and white pudding, eggs, and potatoes, with brown bread to soak it all up with, the fuller her sons' stomachs were, the less energy they'd have to argue against her plan. Or to ask questions she wasn't yet prepared to answer.

When Conn had come in a tad later than the others, looking like a man who'd had little sleep and enjoyed every moment of it, she wanted to ask how Sedona Sullivan was doing this morning. But fairness demanded that she not inquire about her son's love life if she wasn't willing to discuss her own.

Which she most certainly was not. She and Dennis had, in fact, enjoyed an amazing night. Despite all their years apart—her choice—they'd come together with the ease and sense of "rightness" that they had the first time they'd made love.

"This is just grand," Declan, who'd probably used up a thousand calories before he'd put the cows out to pasture this morning, declared.

"It's always a special time when I can have all my boys together under this roof for a meal together. At least one I've cooked myself." She went around the table, refilling orange juice glasses.

She'd been getting the Spanish oranges from Mrs. Monohan to serve guests for years. The first time she'd discovered that Americans, who were blessed to live in the land of plenty, were willing to settle for concentrated orange juice, or even worse, *frozen,* Eileen had been stunned. Ever after that momentous morning, she'd never failed to keep fresh oranges in her fridge.

"You said you had news?" Conn asked around a mouth of fried pudding. He'd been rushing through the meal like a ploughman. Either he was starving or, more likely, he'd left Sedona Sullivan waiting for him back at Mary Joyce's cottage.

"Aye." She made a second round, filling coffee cups, then sat down at the table with her own cup of stout tea. Although she'd burned a great many calories herself last night and should have been starving, the nerves tangling in her stomach had done away with her appetite. "I'm taking a holiday."

"That's a grand idea," Aidan said. "Where to? Italy? The Greek Islands? If you'd like recommendations—"

"That's lovely of you to offer. But I've already made plans." She took a deep breath and resisted glancing toward the stairs, which went up to her bedroom on the third floor, where Dennis was waiting for her to return. She took a long drink of tea to calm her nerves, then said, "I'm going to Dublin."

"Dublin?" Six male voices spoke in unison. From their expressions, she might as well have suggested she was taking a spaceship to Mars.

"Is there something wrong with our country's capital city?" she asked. Then realized she'd come off overly defensive.

"Nothing at all," Bram said quickly. A bit too quickly, Eileen thought. "It's a grand city. It's just that, after the circus this house has been, I'm sure the others join me in thinking that you might be after a bit of peace, quiet, and sunshine."

"That's one idea," she said. And hadn't Dennis suggested the very same thing this morning as he'd sat in bed and watched her pin up her hair? When she'd caught his lusty gaze in the mirror, she'd known they were both thinking of last night, when he'd freed her hair, pin by pin, and sent it tumbling down her naked back. "But I'm after a bit of diversion."

"Well, Dublin certainly offers that," Conn allowed. "Would you like to stay at my flat?"

She shook her head. Folded her hands together in her lap below the table, so no one could witness that they'd begun to tremble. "Again, that's a lovely offer, darling, but I'll be staying with a friend."

"You have a friend in Dublin?"

"I have quite a few friends in Dublin. Some I met through dancing while growing up, others who moved to the city from here, and then there are always those who stayed here on holidays whom I became close with."

Roarke's eyes narrowed. Although she'd worried about Conn having suspicions, because heaven knew what Joe had told him during those last days of the dying, having served in the military, and now being an investigator on the government terrorist task force, Roarke was the least likely of her sons to take anything at face value.

"Which of those types of friends would this be?" he asked.

She smiled. "A former guest." And didn't that have Conn sitting up a little straighter? She should have listened to Dennis when he'd argued that she'd be better off just telling Conn the truth first. Then filling the others in later.

But weary from the past weeks and wanting some stolen time away from family drama, she'd opted for stalling for just a fortnight. Perhaps three weeks at the very most. A mistake, Eileen now realized. She felt as if she'd stumbled into quicksand and was sinking fast. Seeing no choice, at least for now, she forced herself to forge on.

"Denise has a townhouse near Trinity College." She said a quick, mental prayer of indulgence for the lie about his name and gender, just in case God might have nothing better to do on this morning than to check out her family breakfast. Unfortunately, having already lied, she had no choice, for the moment, but to stay with it.

"Does she teach there?" Patrick asked.

"Aye." What a tangled web she'd woven, Eileen thought miserably, even as she pasted a smile on her face. "She's a music historian." Finally! A true statement.

Conn's attention sharpened enough to cut crystal. "I'd like to meet her."

"I hope you will." Another truth. She was on a roll now. Beginning to feel relieved, Eileen took a sip of her milk-laced tea.

"I'll be taking part in a benefit concert in the city three weeks from this coming Saturday," he said. "Since it sounds as if you'll still be there, I'll leave tickets for you and your friend at the box office. And afterwards, I'll be taking you both for a late supper at Troc."

Trocadero Restaurant had been a favorite of Dublin's theater world for as long as Eileen had been alive. As a young ballet student, she'd often dreamed of someday dining at the glamorously appointed restaurant after performing in *Swan Lake*. She'd imagined the sound of champagne corks popping as celebrities from all over the world feted her brilliance. Dining there with the man she loved, and her son, far surpassed even those childhood fantasies. However…

"That sounds lovely." Also tricky, since there was no way she could spring the news of his parenthood on him in a public place. Which meant she'd have to risk telling him beforehand. "But I don't remember you mentioning an upcoming concert."

"It's been planned for a while," he said easily. "A charity event to fight childhood hunger. A significant share will be going to the rising percentage of food-insecure Irish children."

Snagging another piece of thick brown bread from the basket in the center of the table, he slathered it with Declan's creamy yellow butter, then used it to scoop up the remainder of his eggs.

"I had my name taken off the program as soon as I got called home from Germany, but"—Conn shrugged broad shoulders so like the ones she'd run her hands over just a few hours ago—"now there's no reason not to play. I'd already planned for Sedona to come with me. Having my mam there will make the evening even more special."

"Sedona's planning to still be in Ireland then?" Aidan asked with a knowing gleam in his eye.

"If I have anything to say about it," Conn said. "She's agreed to help me with Mary's score."

"What would an accountant-turned-baker know about music?" Roarke asked.

"Her father's Freebird Sullivan. And, as a woman, she undoubtedly knows what she's looking for in a love story," Conn said.

"I'm sure she does." Eileen felt a small measure of relief as the interrogation appeared to turn Conn's way. A lifetime of practice had him easily able to handle his brothers. She could only hope that he'd deal with her news as well.

Her nerves coiled like snakes in her belly for a moment. It was a familiar feeling and one she'd lived with more times than she cared to count since she'd made that momentously poor decision to mistake the rush of post-performance teenage euphoria for love.

She'd been a child having a child. Though, looking back on that time, even if she could have legally gotten an abortion, even if she hadn't been brought up to know doing such a thing would be a fast ticket to hell's eternal fires, if she were facing the same situation today when she'd at least have the opportunity to travel to Britain to have the procedure done, the only change she would have made is to never wed Joseph Brennan.

Still, she'd never think of Patrick, who was conceived that first rash night, to be a mistake. He, like all her sons who'd come after him, was a blessing. Even Conn. *Especially*

Conn. Because whenever she looked into his beautiful eyes, she remembered that she'd once loved. And been truly loved.

Having grown used to carrying the family's burdens on her weary shoulders, even as her boys grew older and would find ways to help despite her assurances that things were going grand, Eileen was not comfortable sharing her private burdens. And she definitely wasn't accustomed to the idea of a man staying by her side. Through good times and bad.

But Dennis had proven himself to be a man of amazing patience and honor. Though she strongly doubted he'd lived as a monk these past thirty years, his heart had always belonged to her. As hers had to him. He'd promised he'd wait. He had. He'd promised he'd return when she was ready for him. He had, he'd told her, read the obituaries in the papers, then later, online every day. After reading about Joseph Brennan's demise on the *Castlelough Celtic* website, he'd driven straight away from Dublin to keep that promise.

When he'd shown up at her door last night for the very first time in so many years, Eileen had believed in miracles.

And when he'd sworn to her that he'd manage this latest dilemma so as not to hurt Conn or in any way damage her relationship with her sons, or Conn's with his brothers, Eileen trusted him. Absolutely.

Now, as she watched her boys clear the table, as they had for so many years as she'd fought to keep her family above water, Eileen had not a single doubt that love was the truest miracle of all.

27

After Conn drove off to breakfast with his mother, Sedona picked up the phone and called the States.

"Talk about great minds," Annie said when she answered the phone. "I was just about to call you. It's tricky with the time zone difference, but I wanted to tell you that Marcy found me a new location. It's up the hill a bit farther on Main, next door to Tidal Wave Books."

"Yay Marcy! That's certainly quick work." The real estate agent was married to Ken Curtis, the local hardware store owner and head of the high school athletics booster club. She also happened to know every inch of the coastal market from Banning, near the California border, to Astoria, across the Columbia River from Washington State.

"That's a great location," Sedona said. "It's got a view of the bay, you won't have to change the shop's name, you'll still get tourist foot traffic, and you and the bookstore probably share much the same customer base."

"That's what I was thinking. I also looked at a couple spaces for you. As you know, it's more difficult to find a commercial location that comes with both foot traffic and space for your kitchen."

"I discovered that the first time Marcy helped me find a location. I was thinking recently of expanding into the gift shop when Monique told me she was going to retire and take off in an RV to visit all the national parks with her husband. But then the storm and Bondurant threw a monkey wrench into that plan."

"He's made a lot of people unhappy."

"Not that he cares."

"There is that," Annie agreed. "Though Marcy said several members of the council are against giving him his permit, so we'll see what happens. Anyway, one of the places that would work for you is in Depoe Bay. Close to The Sea Witch."

The popular restaurant drew a lot of tourists who came for the chowder. People who might choose to have a cupcake or piece of pie for dessert, Sedona thought. But…

"It's across from their seawall."

"Yeah." Annie sighed. "I thought that might be a problem for you."

"It might be, at first. But it's also a great location, not just for foot traffic visiting all the other shops but it's on the main drag so the seawall isn't a deal breaker. Where's the other place?"

"In Cannon Beach near the museum, which puts it more back from the water."

"It's also two hours away from Shelter Bay."

"I know. And I'd miss you like crazy, but with a little work either one could be a great space. I'll send you some photos and you can call Marcy for more particulars."

"Thanks. But I didn't call for a real estate update."

"Are you doing all right?"

"I'm fine. Seriously," Sedona said before her best friend could challenge that statement. "Better than fine…I slept with Conn."

"I know. You told me about that one-night hookup when you came back from Mary's wedding."

"No. I mean I slept with him again."

"You. Did. Not!"

"I did. And more than once. A bunch of times, actually. I think I'm becoming a sex addict. Another few more days here and you're going to have to come stage an intervention."

"I'd never try to talk you out of sex with such a hot guy. Especially after all those major loser dates you've suffered through."

"Thanks for pointing that out," Sedona said dryly.

"I'm sorry. But I only brought those up because, as your BFF, I'm thrilled for you. In fact, if you were here, we'd be mixing up a pitcher of margaritas and doing high fives and fist bumps…So, are you guys are just expanding your original agreement? About it being all about the sex and nothing more?"

They'd been friends long enough that Sedona's slight hesitation tipped Annie off. "Oh, wow," she said. "You're serious."

"No. Maybe." Sedona dragged her hand through her hair. "I don't know. We have something. But who knows what we'll both be feeling in a few weeks? Or days. Or even tomorrow? So, if I had to give it a label, I'd say it's probably just an affair."

"You had to point out to me that I'd fallen in love with Mac," Annie reminded her. "Maybe something we have in common is an inability to recognize love when it's staring us right in the face."

"It's not love," Sedona insisted. "It couldn't be. Not this fast." It wasn't logical. And Sedona had always considered herself a sensible, logical person.

"Looking back, I fell in love with Mac that first night we talked on the phone when I called the station."

"But you really disliked him when you met him in person before that," Sedona pointed out.

"I had no way of knowing he was the station's midnight deejay. When we literally ran into each other, he was in a rotten mood that day, dealing with a lot of family problems, what with having become a single parent to a daughter he hardly knew and a grandfather with Alzheimer's. I seem to remember you telling me to give him a break about that."

"I did. But Mac and Conn are completely different."

"I'm not so sure. Mac returned to Shelter Bay partly because of his grandfather. And so his daughter could get to know *her* grandfather. You told me that Conn cancelled his band's tour to go home to be with his dying father."

"Technically, he went home to be with his mother while his father was dying."

"Same thing. It sounds as if he's as devoted to his family as Mac is to his. Which is, to be honest, partly what had me falling in love." Annie laughed. "But I have to admit that him being hottie Midnight Mac on my radio sure didn't hurt."

Sedona suspected that hearts had broken up and down the mid-Oregon coast when the late-night deejay with the sexy, dark, velvet voice had gotten married.

But while Mac had settled down and become a devoted father to his own daughter and the twin boys he and Annie had adopted, Sedona wondered if Conn would ever actually be willing to give up his rock star lifestyle.

Sure, he might have bought that brewery with the idea of setting up an apartment and recording studio, but she had a hard time seeing him staying in that same small coastal village he'd been in such a hurry to leave at sixteen.

"Everyone keeps telling me that I need to learn to live in the moment," she said, putting away those thoughts for now. Trying to analyze or second-guess what a man who'd buy a brewery on a whim would do was a sure road to insanity. "So, that's what I'm going to do. I'll simply enjoy this time together. And when it's over, I'll be on my way."

"Where have I heard that before?" Annie mused. "I know...It's the Beatles. And they got it wrong in that song. True love does last. Your parents are proof of that. As are Mac and I. And Kara and Sax. And don't forget Charity and Gabe, Maddy and Lucas, Claire and Dillon. Kelli and Cole. Mary and J.T...."

"Okay!" Sedona laughed at the strong defense of love from a woman who'd fought falling every step of the way to the altar. "You don't have to name every happily married couple in Shelter Bay. But maybe I'm different."

"You're unique," Annie returned without missing a beat. "And special. You also make the world a special place."

"Now you're sounding like one of those sentiments you're always stamping on greeting cards."

Annie laughed as she was supposed to. "I miss you," she said.

"I miss you, too." It was the truth. Annie was truly like a sister. Which was why she was the only person who knew about Conn. And the reason Sedona had left Portland.

"I'd like to tell you to hurry back home," Annie said. "But far be it from me to deny you all the sex you can get. You were way overdue when you met the guy at the wedding."

"Well, my long personal drought is definitely over."

"I'm glad. Now I don't have to feel guilty about my insanely glorious multiple orgasms this morning." They shared a laugh, then Annie's voice turned serious again. "Does he make you happy?"

"Yes." Deliriously.

And hadn't that come as a surprise? Conn Brennan had triggered a lot of emotions that first night, but Sedona never would have put "happy" on the list. But she had found herself humming along with Enya while roasting potatoes. And waltzing with him in the garden had made her feel like a Disney princess. Not that she'd share *that* fanciful idea with anyone. After promising to call again tomorrow, Sedona hung up. And went to get ready for Conn's return.

Just as she'd promised, she spread lotion over every inch of her body. Then blew her wet hair dry, straightening it to silk. Just imagining him running his hands through the strands caused a flush to rise in cheeks that had no need for artificial blush. Keeping a deft touch with makeup, she settled for a quick swipe with a mascara wand to darken her pale lashes and a touch of strawberry gloss that would probably last all of two seconds once he got in the door.

Because the hands of her watch seemed to move impossibly slow waiting for Conn's return to the cottage, she went online and looked up the history of the house she'd be visiting today. Fergus hadn't been exaggerating when he'd told of its history. He hadn't put up a website, so she couldn't trust either the woodcut illustrations she'd found on Wikipedia or the earlier black-and-white photos. As far as she could tell, no one had bothered to take any pictures in this century. At least none they'd wanted to share online.

Which wasn't a positive sign, since searches for Irish manor houses certainly brought up pages and pages of photos ranging from ruins to glorious estates with formal gardens. Deciding to withhold judgment until she saw the place in person, she located the golf course resort Conn had mentioned and took a few notes. Then she went on Bram Brennan's website and looked through his portfolio of past and present projects. Conn hadn't exaggerated his talent in restoring the crumbling famine cottages. What did interest her was the work he'd done transforming Brennan's Microbrewery and Pub, updating his mother's B&B, along with a Georgian manor house in Cork, a Victorian mill in Limerick, and a Regency-era police barracks in County Mayo. Even if Conn was right about the condition of Fergus's home, architect and contractor Bram Brennan was definitely the man for the job.

THE BREAKFAST TOOK longer than Conn had expected. It also left him with questions that he wasn't going to think about now. Not when he had a beautiful, sexy woman waiting at home for him.

Home. Once again he considered how that word, which had once been something to escape, sounded so right. Neither Mary's cottage nor her big house was actually his own home, but he had no problem imagining Sedona in the loft penthouse he and his brother had planned for the top floor of the warehouse.

His original plan had been to have his offices downstairs and leave the loft mostly open. Maybe with a few sliding wall units here and there to add a bit of privacy to the bedroom. But now, having been trained by Bram—who'd graduated with a master's degree in architecture from University College Cork—to envision a three-dimensional space from a set of blueprints, Conn could imagine setting up a commercial kitchen and bakery in some of the space he'd allocated for studios. Or perhaps she'd prefer to open a shop in the center of the village. Although the economy was coming back, there were still several available storefronts she'd be able to lease for a good price.

If she decided to stay. And wasn't that the only vexing thing on his mind at the moment? Conn knew his plan—for his own life, his career, and not only the village but West Irish musicians and traditional music—was a good one.

The problem was that, more and more, he was having difficulty picturing his life without Sedona Sullivan in it. Although creative types were thought to be solely right- brained, childlike individuals living in their imaginary worlds, actually earning an income required problem solving. Didn't writing a song, planning a performance, or checking the receipts and business balance sheets each bring their own challenges?

All he had to do was find a reason, other than chandelier-swinging sex, for Sedona Sullivan to want to stay here in Castlelough with him.

As he walked into the cottage and found her lying in bed, the snowy-white sheet arranged provocatively to reveal enticing bits of breast and leg, Conn decided there'd be time for planning later.

For now, as he stripped off his clothes, he was going to celebrate the moment.

28

"SO, WHAT WAS your mother's news?" Sedona asked as they lay, wrapped in each other's arms, basking in the golden afterglow of a lovemaking that, amazingly, just got better and better. Of course there was a lot to be said for the anticipation that had had her wanting to run outside and jump Conn the moment she'd heard his SUV drive up.

"She's going on holiday to Dublin."

"What a wonderful idea."

He shifted onto his side, bracing himself up on his elbow. "You don't think she'd be wanting someplace more quiet?"

Sedona had to hold back a purr as he smoothed a hand down her hair and over her shoulder. "While peace and quiet is turning out to be exactly what I needed, everyone's different. I can't begin to know what your mother's past years were like, but I can imagine the unrelenting stress she's been going through since her errant husband returned home for her to care for him during his last days. So, perhaps she's looking for a diversion. And Dublin certainly fits that criteria."

"True." That wicked hand continued down, a finger trailing along the crest of her breasts. He followed the erotic path with his eyes, seeming fascinated by the way her nipple pebbled at a mere stroke of a touch.

"What hotel is she staying at?"

"She's going to be visiting a friend." His eyes turned to blue flame as he stimulated the other nipple.

"That's nice." With every molecule in her body on full alert, waiting for where his caress would move next, Sedona could barely get the words out. What were they talking about again?

"Nice." He palmed a breast. "What would you say to continuing this conversation later?"

"Later," she agreed breathlessly as his leg covered hers, pinning her to the mattress. Apparently all that dancing around he did on stage paid off because even his amazingly defined quads had muscles.

"Grand answer." As he rolled over onto her and she ran her hands down his back, over a butt that should come with its own warning label, Sedona totally forgot the question.

Much, much later, Sedona was leaning back against the pillows while Conn, wearing knit boxers, sat cross-legged amidst the rumpled sheets, playing her a song on an acoustical guitar. Although it had no lyrics, the melody sounded so sad it made her want to weep.

"Please tell me the film has a happy ending," she said after he'd strummed the last chord, leaving it hanging on the air like a shimmering raindrop clinging to a leaf.

"I suppose that depends on your definition," he said. "It's more serious than Mary's usual fare. But it's a story she's wanted to tell for some time and, I believe, one audiences will respond to."

"If that song is any indication, I think I'll be buying stock in Kleenex," she said.

"The DVD's up at the house. I can run up and get it."

"I'd love to see it." She sighed as she glanced at the bedside clock. "Unfortunately, we don't have time before we leave."

"We can always cancel." He leaned forward and brushed a kiss against her frowning lips, which curved beneath the feathery touch. "Tell Fergus that something's come up."

She glanced down at the tented part of his anatomy the guitar had covered and laughed, feeling any lingering sorrow from the sad air evaporate at the kiss. This man could make her ache. He could also make her burn. Then, minutes later, have her feeling as if she were about to float up into a bright, sunlit sky on brilliant crayon-colored balloons.

"Which wouldn't be a lie."

He shrugged shoulders as well cut as the rest of his body. So much for rumors about his supposed escapades on tour. There was no way he could spend as many hours as it must have taken to have chiseled that body, travel to venues all over the world, and still have any time for anywhere near the amount of womanizing he'd been accused of.

"It's you." He wrapped a strand of hair around his finger, then tugged, drawing her to him for another kiss that ended far too soon. "You have me feeling like I'm a horny fifteen again."

"A prodigy," she said dryly, remembering his story of the older woman and the car wreck.

"Perhaps." His easy tone and hot grin suggested the reports of wild living might have been close to the truth in the band's beginning days. "But one advantage of having sampled my share of willing females is that I can recognize when a woman is one of a kind."

Oh, the man was good with words. But she'd expect a songwriter to know exactly what to say to seduce a woman. Still, having always been a good judge of people, Sedona believed that, from that first night in the Copper Beech Inn, he'd been nothing but honest with her.

Conn Brennan might not be a perfect man. Yet, as Annie had pointed out, the attributes Sedona was discovering—loyalty to family and friends, generosity, a sense of humor, and yes, the way his lovemaking could both make her fly and feel cherished—more and more made it appear he might be the perfect man for her.

Which could also be hopeful thinking, her logical mind intruded once again. On the other hand, hadn't her mother warned her that if she didn't get more open-minded about choosing a husband, she could end up eighty years old, living all alone with a houseful of cats?

"What would you say to a jaunt to Dublin?" Conn asked, yanking her from a depressing thought of a possible future in a cramped studio apartment with doilies on the furniture and fur balls everywhere.

"With your mother?"

Conn could tell that his out-of-the-blue question jolted her mind out of whatever private place it had wandered off to. "I'm sure you two would have a grand time. But I was thinking you'd be going with me. I'm taking part in a charity concert there, and I thought you might enjoy it. Then, afterwards, unless she finds some excuse to back out, I'm taking my mother and her friend for a late supper."

"I'd love to go." Even as he'd felt her loosening up, her immediate response surprised him. He'd half expected her to draw up a whiteboard pros-and-cons analysis of accompanying him to the bustling capital. Instead, he was finding her impulsivity encouraging. She snuggled closer. "Where would we stay?"

"I was thinking the Shelbourne."

"On St. Stephen's Green?" And didn't she sound suitably impressed? It was, after all, the most luxurious and most famous of any hotel in Dublin.

"That would be the one. I rang reservations on the way home from breakfast. The Princess Grace Suite unexpectedly became available."

Outside the cottage, rain had begun falling. Inside, her light laugh brightened the bedroom with sunshine. "And what president, prime minister, potentate, or movie star did they kick out to make room for you?"

"I didn't ask." He put his arm around her, drawing her closer, thinking how right it felt to be this way together. "And they didn't tell. Though, I wouldn't mind if it happened to be Bono."

"But he's a fellow countryman!" She appeared truly shocked. "And surely an inspiration."

"He is, indeed."

More than an inspiration. The musician had been a mentor in Conn's early years and they'd grown to be friends, sharing the stage on more than a few charitable occasions. "He's also the countryman who got me evicted from that very same suite five years ago when he showed up at the lobby desk without a reservation."

"Hotel karma," she decided. "If it does turn out to be him…I had afternoon tea there a few times while I was at Trinity College. Once with my parents when they came to visit. I was worried my father would find it overly stuffy, but it somehow manages to be formal yet intimate at the same time."

"I've never had the tea. I'm more likely to be in the Horseshoe Bar." He pressed his lips against the top of her head, enjoying the fresh scent of her shampoo, which reminded him of the linen sheets his mother had dried outside on the line while he was growing up. "We'll have to make time. The idea of you eating sweets from my hand is more than a little enticing."

"I've been feeding myself for some time now," she informed him with a toss of her sunny hair.

"And doing quite a fine job of it, I've no doubt. But surely you wouldn't deny me a bit of enjoyment? I am, after all, going to be singing my heart out to earn all that money for hungry children."

"Which is a good cause and it's wonderful that you're taking part. Yet, as lovely as tea with you sounds, it also seems more than a little hypocritical to be enjoying tea in a luxury, world-class hotel while children around the world are starving."

That small line Conn was beginning to recognize appeared between her brows again. Loving her earnestness, admiring her huge heart that felt such concern for others, he rubbed it away with his thumb.

"I doubt they'd all fit into the Lord Mayor's Lounge. But now that you've brought it up, I'm hearing one of your father's protest songs playing in my head, so I fully understand where you're coming from.

"Yet, speaking as the son of a mother who worked extremely hard, from dawn long into the night, to put food on her own children's table, why don't you think of it as providing an income to those families whose jobs depend on their hotel salaries? And I promise, we'll add an outrageously generous tip to soothe your guilt."

He felt her rigidness loosen as she lifted a hand to his cheek. "You're very logical for a creative type."

"I've never found a distinction."

"I would have argued that if you'd claimed that during our first conversation at the pub, when you talked about going with your gut. But having watched you in action, I've changed my mind." She sighed. "I also realize that you don't want to be put in any box, but that duality ticks off another one of my criteria. Although I had it turned around."

He took her hand, turned it, and pressed his lips to her knuckles. "And how would that be?"

"I was more thinking of a logical man who was also, at least in some small way, creative. You flipped it."

"And aren't I glad to hear I passed your test? So, to celebrate my achievement, how about I flip *you*?"

Which he did, with one deft movement, turning them so she was lying on top of him, her smooth, silky bare legs on either side of his thighs.

Her brow arched as she felt his erection against her.

"So soon?"

"As you just pointed out, luv, I'm a creative man." He nuzzled her neck. Licked that little place behind her ear he'd discovered was directly connected to that hot spot between her legs. "So you'll just have to blame it on my muse."

Her musical laugh was like silver flowing through his veins as he proceeded to demonstrate exactly how inspired he was by his sexy blond Yank muse.

29

"YOU PROMISED TO tell me the story of Mary's film," Sedona reminded Conn as they headed out into the country to *Cnoc an Chairn*.

"I did, indeed. Since you've watched her movies, you'd be knowing that seals have the ability to take on human form."

"I do."

"Well, in this version of the tale, although selkies need to live near the sea, if they actually go back into the water, they revert to being seals and lose the ability to ever take on human form again."

"That opens up an opportunity for a serious decision down the road."

"And doesn't it just? Mary's story revolves around this fisherman who'd lived his entire adult life, into his fifties, all alone. There were those who'd known him when he was a younger lad, who said that he'd been born a bachelor.

"Then one fateful day, he went out to sea, fishing far beyond the breakers. A few days later, he returned to port with a wife. Now, being a coastal village, there were those who recognized her as being one of the seal people. Still, she proved to be a fine wife to the fisherman. She was also a good, although shy, neighbor who didn't speak more than need be on market days."

"It would have been a very different world for her," Sedona murmured as they drove along a reed-rimmed river winding its way down the nearby mountains on its way to the sea. A family of ducks bobbed on the water, still-downy babies swimming in a straight line behind their parents.

"Wouldn't it just? Especially as we Irish are known for our loquaciousness. She also never attended Sunday mass nor mingled with people at the pub in the evening."

"A loner was the fisherman's wife," Sedona said, her heart going out to the woman. She remembered, when she'd first moved to Shelter Bay, being worried that she'd have trouble fitting into such a small and close-knit community. But she'd found everyone to be warm and welcoming. Of course, she admitted, it hadn't hurt that she'd brought cupcakes to the people.

"Indeed," Conn agreed. "Yet those in the village had kind feelings toward the fisherman, who'd always shared a bit of his catch with those in need. As they saw him happier than he'd ever been, she came to be accepted by one and all."

"So far, this is a heart-warming love story set in a seaside village populated with generous, openhearted people without prejudice." Now that they'd left the village behind, cottages and houses became more sparsely located, looking like whitewashed boats bobbing on an emerald sea.

"Aye. Though, in a remote coastal village, people might have been more accepting of the selkies living among them."

Sedona noticed that he'd slipped more and more into Irish lexicon as he told the story. Conn may have traveled the world, but his roots obviously went deep into the rocky soil of the Irish West.

"Yet the song you played me, as well as the one you hummed while we danced, were both so sad. So, obviously something goes wrong."

"Wouldn't it be a short story otherwise?" An elderly man paused from the task of cutting peat—which she'd learned was layers of plants that had decayed over thousands of years—to wave as they passed a bog. "As you might imagine, being a bachelor for so many years, as much as he adored his wife, the fisherman wasn't open to changing his ways."

"A male resistant to change. I'm shocked."

His laugh was rich and deep and had heat curling inside her. Heaven help her, a few more days in this country and she really would turn into a raving nymphomaniac.

"At any rate," he continued, "the fisherman would take his dory out to sea for several days at a time, which worried and saddened his wife. As the seasons passed, nightfall came sooner, signaling the relentless approach of winter.

"Now, whenever her husband was away, those who saw her walking alone on the cliff swore they heard her calling to him in an eerie, haunting language no human had ever heard."

"A seal's song. And now you're making me nervous."

"As I hope audiences will be since part of my job is to portend impending danger."

"Like those ominous two notes in *Jaws*."

"Precisely. Which was done much earlier with those nerve-gnawing strings in *Psycho's* shower scene."

"Ever since I watched that movie, I've gotten nervous if I hear a strange sound when I'm taking a shower," Sedona admitted.

"That was the point. Hitchcock originally didn't want music in that scene, but the composer convinced him to try the violin and cello."

"I've bought movie soundtracks before, and even though I'm a musician's daughter, I never gave much thought to how a musician planned the score."

"You're not supposed to. Nobody goes to the movies to listen to the score. The score is simply assisting them in watching the film. The entire point of the music is to further the story. It has to be there for a reason, or it isn't necessary."

She turned toward him. Put a hand on his thigh. "You enjoy working on Mary's movies." She'd heard it in his voice when he talked about his work.

"I do love it. Not just because she's a good friend but also because she gives me a movie with such a wide range of emotion that, while it can be frustrating and have me ready to slam my head through a wall, suddenly I'll have an epiphany. When all those scattered pieces finally fit together, it's the second best feeling in the world."

"What's the best?"

He flashed that wicked, bad-boy rocker grin that had proven so irresistible that rainy night and slipped a finger beneath the hem of the white gauze skirt she'd worn for tea, slowly tracing a curving design up her thigh. "Let me turn back toward the cottage at the next roundabout and I'll show you."

"Good try." She caught his hand before it went any higher and she found herself taking him up on his suggestion. "But we're sticking to the plan. You tell me the story, we have tea with Fergus and his sister, then we're going to try working together."

"Spoilsport." She heard the laughter in his tone. The look he shot her as his stroking touch began creating havoc at the back of her knee was overbrimming with devilish amusement.

"I'm not going to deny that the idea of going back to bed is tempting," Sedona allowed. "But after you asked me to offer input on the selkie's character, I realized that as much as this time away from my problems has been therapeutic, I still need to work."

"Another thing we have in common," he said. "Just in case you'd be writing down a list."

"Which I'm not." Which was true enough. But it didn't mean that she hadn't been thinking about it. "And speaking of work, the fisherman didn't stop going out to sea, did he?"

"No. He adored his wife, but fishing was as much a part of his life as breathing. He assured her, as they lay in their bed, warmed by the glow of the peat fire, that he'd been fishing in those very same waters since he was a lad and promised to return."

"Have you written the music for that scene yet?"

"No. I've been guilty of putting it off."

Sedona wondered if the scene was proving difficult because he'd spent a lifetime hiding his own emotions, perhaps even from himself.

"So, he went off to sea and got caught up in a furious temper of wind and sea that ripped down his sail and broke the mast into splinters."

"You've written this part, haven't you?" Sedona asked.

"I have. While the grand and rousing music sections may capture people's attention, they're easier to write."

"Perhaps because fear is a more basic and straightforward human emotion than complex issues of the heart," she suggested.

He slanted her a look. "There is that," he agreed.

"He didn't make it home, did he?"

"Ah, now, wouldn't that be tragic?" he said, not telling her she was wrong. "But straightforward."

As she thought about what he'd told her thus far, and knowing Mary Joyce Douchett's movies as well as she did, Sedona realized that she'd been so distracted by his stroking touch and the deep, rough voice telling her this tale that she'd lost track of the basic premise of the film, which Mary had set up in the beginning.

"If it ends with him drowning, it would be a Man against Nature story. Which is not what Mary writes."

"No. That would not be her genre. But that doesn't mean that there aren't rousing, roller-coaster moments as the fisherman battles against sea and wind, even as snow and ice pelt him like stones. Every time his adversaries seemed to be winning, the fisherman, who was as stubborn as he was wily, would outsmart them.

"It wasn't until the dory began to fill with icy water that he knew his pride had brought about his downfall. His heart broken at the idea of never seeing his beloved wife again, he shouted out his love, then lay down on the bottom of the dory and prepared to die.

"Although he had no way of knowing it, his last words of love reached the cliff where she'd been pacing. Tearing off her confining human clothing as she ran down the cliff steps, she dove headfirst into the waves and swam into the storm."

"She went into the water."

And made an eternal choice, Sedona thought as they passed an old stone castle crumbling to ruin, broken open by trees reaching upward toward the light. The once strongly defended castle ruins dotted the countryside, inspiring legends and myths, along with the acknowledgement that, like the marriage of the fisherman and the selkie, all things must pass.

"She did, indeed. Saving him in the only way possible," Conn agreed. "By sharing her warmth. The morning after the storm, the fisherman was found safe and sound, sleeping on the bottom of his boat, which had drifted back onto the shoals. A seal was covering him like a blanket, while a blanket of snow lay on her back. When the townspeople approached, it leaped over the side of the boat and disappeared beneath the water."

"That's so sad."

"True. But they had, for that time together, shared a grand love. Which is, after all, more than many of us are granted in one lifetime."

"My parents have that."

"They're fortunate."

"True. There was a time, when I was very young that I thought they were the norm. Later I came to realize how exceptional their relationship is."

And wasn't that what Sedona wanted for herself? And why she'd admittedly set the bar so high when it came to choosing a man she could fall in love with. Was Conn that man? He was certainly the first man she'd even considered making a life with.

Which was illogical. It was too soon to be thinking along those lines. Obviously sex was clouding her brain.

30

Conn turned off the road, onto a narrow, twisting lane leading up a hill. Unlike so much of the land, which had long been deforested, huge, ancient oaks that had somehow escaped the ax arched majestically over the roadway, creating a leafy green tunnel.

He'd opened the moon roof, and over the hiss of the tires on pavement still wet from the earlier rain, Sedona heard the trilling music of songbirds.

As they came around a tight corner, the view suddenly opened up to a grand stone house with tall Palladian windows adding importance to the first two floors. Detached symmetrical wings swept away from the main house on both sides, connected by colonnades.

"Oh, my God," she breathed, "it's Downton Abbey."

"More *Dumpton* Abbey," Conn corrected with a sweep of a hand that took in what should have been an expansive front lawn lined with flowering hedges and gardens that would soften the aged stone. Instead, as he'd claimed at the funeral luncheon, brambles, yellow gorse, tangles of nettles, other weeds she couldn't identify, and moss had claimed the space.

"And you profess to be creative," she scoffed. "Try looking at what could be rather than what is." Sedona had no problem imagining a young woman in a white dress seated on a bench beneath what she could recognize as a pear tree—which in spring, would undoubtedly be covered in lacy blossoms—while the woman's friends played a game of tennis on an emerald-green lawn.

"You'd need a spreadsheet the size of this entire county to begin to plan how to turn this place into anywhere any sane person would want to stay."

"Ah, but I wouldn't be doing it." Was that truly a crumbling and pitted helicopter pad on the front grounds? "I'm merely here as an advisor." An advisor who, while Conn had been at breakfast with his brothers and mother, had done some homework. It wouldn't be easy. But with Fergus's surprisingly endless supply of funds and some clever planning, Sedona could envision a few ways to restore this manor house to its original glory.

And wasn't that the type of thing she'd enjoyed about accounting? Not that anyone would necessarily link home restoration, gardening, and accounting ledgers. But they were all about solving problems, finding new ways to meet a goal.

She had, after all, managed to help Sax find funding for Bon Temps. And helped several others in Shelter Bay reboot their lives. Why couldn't she do the same thing for an old man who'd apparently been such a vital part of Castlelough?

The wide front door opened as they climbed the steps. "You've come," Fergus Molony, dressed in the tweed suit he'd worn to the funeral, greeted them.

"I'm happy for the opportunity to visit," Sedona said. "Your home appears in remarkable condition." The grounds, while needing a great deal of work, would be much easier to reclaim.

"An advantage to the Brits taking our trees for their ships and buildings is that we were forced to build with stone. Did you notice that the main house is created from a white-gray limestone, while the pavilions are a darker, more goldish brown?"

"That struck me right away."

"And you'd have thought perhaps that was because the builder had run out of either money or the pricier white stone?"

"Or to highlight the more important center building," she suggested.

"Aye. That would be the case. Instead of the Portland stone that was being used all over the British Isles at the time, this would be Ardbraccan stone from County Meath." He gave Conn a look. "Your lass is not only a beauty, she's intelligent, as well."

"You don't have to convince me of that," Conn responded.

"Hopefully you're smart enough to see that she's a keeper."

Conn put a lightly possessive arm around her waist. "Again, you'll be getting no argument from me."

Despite being discussed as if she weren't standing right there and being referred to as one might talk about one of the salmon fished for in Irish rivers, Sedona couldn't deny that she enjoyed his touch.

The old man stepped aside, inviting them in with a sweep of his hand. "Welcome to *Cnoc an Chairn*. One of the largest and certainly most splendiferous country houses in all of Ireland."

Cnoc an Chairn might resemble an aging dowager who'd fallen on hard times, but as they entered the two-story entrance hall, Sedona had no problem envisioning the beauty the grand home had once been.

"It's based on the sophistication of Palladianism, which was brought from the continent," he told her. "But being proud of his heritage, my ancestor chose an Irish architect rather than an Italian, as so many were doing at the time. He also specified that it would be built using only Irish materials. It took eleven years from start to finish to construct, but it was a work of art when finished. Which is why it was the model for your own country's White House."

Sedona had read that. She'd also found three other houses in Ireland making the same claim.

"And didn't your Thomas Jefferson refer to Palladio's concepts as the bible for his own work, including his own beloved Monticello, which you may have been fortunate to visit?"

"I have." She decided not to mention that Jefferson had later covered the Palladian facade. "How much land comes with the house?" she asked as she viewed yet more tangles of brambles and woodlands through a pair of tall French doors as Fergus led Conn and her across the entrance hall to a curved, cantilevered stone staircase she'd read was one of the largest in Ireland.

"It's forty-eight and a half hectares, which would be one hundred and twenty acres."

"That's a hell of a lot to restore," Conn said.

Fergus bristled. "I prefer to think of it as a grand opportunity."

"Much of the woodlands would stay," Sedona said as they climbed the stairs. "They undoubtedly provide a habitat for wildlife."

"Aye. That they do." Fergus bobbed his head. "Finnola and I saw a fox just last evening while we were having our supper. I was considering offering fox hunting to guests to bring in more tourist trade, but Bram advised against it."

"He and I are in full agreement there," Sedona said.

"Even if you don't want to get into the morality of fox hunting, the negative press, probable demonstrations, and even sabotage by animal rights groups would take away from any possible business you'd receive," Conn said.

"And didn't Bram say the very same thing?" Fergus admitted, his frown adding yet another set of wrinkles to his weathered Puck's face. "Which brings us back to the golfing."

"I have an idea about that I'd like to discuss over tea," Sedona said after giving Conn a warm smile for having jumped in to back her up. Although he'd kept his voice neutral, she'd come to know him well enough that she could see his distaste for the fox-hunting idea in his eyes. Another box ticked. Not that she was keeping score.

Of course she was. A personality, she was discovering, was not that easy to change.

Surprisingly, the interior of the house was in much better condition than the grounds. Although the silk on the walls was water-spotted, undoubtedly from the roof leaking, the limestone floors looked as if all they needed was a good cleaning and polishing, and most of the plaster on the walls appeared to be in good shape. Including the high coffered ceiling on a long room they'd entered at the top of the stairs.

"A young American who'd sold his company for millions bought the house in the late 1990s and poured a lot of dollars into it," Fergus said when she mentioned being surprised. Which explained the helicopter pad. "But then the U.S. tech bubble burst, so he ended up losing it in a bankruptcy procedure and although there was a bit of interest during our own boom, when our economy crashed, it became yet another ghost estate."

"Until you won the lottery."

"God works in mysterious ways," a tall, thin woman with her gray hair pulled back in a braid said as she entered the room pushing a wheeled glass and black wicker Victorian teacart.

"This would be my sister, Finnola," Fergus stated. "Finnola, may I introduce Sedona Sullivan, the savior of *Cnoc an Chairn*."

"It's good to meet you," Sedona said, shaking the woman's hand, which had all the heft of a sparrow's leg. "And I'm afraid your brother's overstated my ability."

"And hasn't he always been the master of overstatement?" she asked. "Hyperbole could be his middle name."

"Yet didn't I get *Cnoc an Chairn* back as I always said I would?" Fergus countered.

"You did, indeed, for all the good it's doing us," she huffed. "Why you couldn't have bought a nice cottage or even a modernized home with a decent kitchen in the village is beyond my comprehension."

"Oddly, for an artistic person, Finnola has been known to lack vision," Fergus said. "But she's been a grand companion since my wife's passing, and I'm grateful to have her for a sister." He patted the birdlike hand Sedona had released with a speckled one of his own. "Enough that I won't be pointing out all those times when she badgered me about wasting money on the Irish Sweepstakes and *An Crannchur Náisiúnta* tickets."

"And didn't you just point that out?" his sister shot back in a way that had Sedona suspecting they had been having these types of conversations for decades.

"Well, it's lovely to have been invited to tea," Sedona said.

"It's no bother." The woman began pouring the tea from a porcelain pot painted with flowers. As much as she preferred order, Sedona found the mismatched cups and saucers brought interest and charm to the tea set.

Along with the tea, they were fed cucumber sandwiches with butter on stale brown bread, scones with currents so hard they threatened a broken tooth, and obviously store-bought shortbread cookies—or biscuits, as the Irish called them—even more perilous to bite into than the scones. Sedona would have thought the food would have backed up the woman's expressed desire for a modern kitchen were it not for the stale bread. Apparently, culinary skills were not Finnola Molony's forte.

"This is a wonderful space for entertaining," she said, glancing around at the long room that went the length of the main part of the house and, like the French doors on the ground floor, overlooked the grounds. From this higher vantage point, it was possible to see the acres of woodland and what appeared to be a weed-and-reed-choked pond. Even with its current limitations, Sedona's mind was whirling with possibilities.

"It used to be the print room," Finnola said, showing that, despite her outward disdain for the manor house, she still held some family interest and even pride. "In the mid-sixteenth century, the fashion was for women to get together to paste engravings and mezzo tints onto the walls as something to do during long winter days."

"My best friend owns a scrapbook art supply store," Sedona said. "She has parties to work on scrapbooks and make greeting cards. She says attendance always goes up during Oregon's rainy winter days."

"I suspect that was much the same for women of the time," Finnola said. "Printing not only changed the world by making books more available, it also made art more accessible."

"My sister has a PhD in art history from University College Dublin," Fergus said with pride. "She also studied in Florence, has a grand reputation as a painter herself, and has taken on the job of being art curator for *Cnoc an Chairn*'s collection."

"As if you gave me any choice," she muttered.

"You didn't say no," her brother reminded her.

"I may not approve of this folly you've undertaken," she countered. "But that doesn't mean I would let you waste even more money by filling it with horrid dreck."

"Did I mention she also has a mind of her own?" Fergus asked impishly, not appearing at all wounded by his sister's criticism.

Something clicked in Sedona's mind. "Do you sign your work FM?"

"I do, indeed."

"I've seen a painting of Castlelough Harbor in Mary Douchett's cottage and a similar one in her Shelter Bay home."

"That would be my work. She was Mary Joyce and living in Los Angeles when she commissioned the one that's in her home in the States. She asked me to paint a similar one for the cottage."

"I love the way those brightly colored houses seem to be coming down the green hillside to greet the sea."

"Our village houses are painted in those hues in order to cheer and warm returning fishermen," the older woman revealed. "And you'd be correct that I painted them to appear to be coming down the hill."

"They take on a life of their own. I also like the dappled sky and your subtle use of contrast with sunlight and shade."

"There's an old saying that our Irish sky is always preparing for the acceptance of prayers. Which is what I was attempting, in my small way, to portray in that work."

"You definitely succeeded," Sedona said. Imagining how Mary must also share a great many feelings in common with those returning fishermen whenever she returned to her homeland, Sedona understood why she would have commissioned those particular paintings. "Coincidentally, my mother's an artist. Skylark Sullivan."

Finnola, who already seemed to possess a spine of steel, sat up a little straighter at that revelation.

"And wouldn't this be a small world? I'm an admirer of your mother's work," she said. "I have a landscape of a shipwreck at sunset hanging in my bedroom."

"She'll be so pleased to hear that. It's a ship that went down in the waters outside Shelter Bay. My father's written a rock opera of the story." Sedona shared a quick synopsis.

"It's obvious he's Irish," Fergus said. "We are fond of our tragic love stories."

"It appears so," Sedona agreed, thinking of Mary's latest selkie tale. "My mother has a birthday coming up. I'd love to buy her a print of the harbor painting if one's available in a gallery somewhere."

"There are prints available. But I'd prefer to give you a signed one as a gift." Finnola flashed a laughing smile that reached her dark eyes. "To make up for the dreadful tea I've served you."

"It's fine tea," Fergus defended his sister. "Stout enough for a mouse to trot across, it is."

At least strong enough for a spoon to stand up in, Sedona thought, having taken a sip when it had first been poured.

"My mother would be honored to have a signed print."

"As would I, to have you find my work worthy of being hung in your mother's home...At any rate, once the room was no longer used as a formal art gallery, it became what you Americans might call a family room. People held parties and informal dinners, played billiards and card games, read books, and, of course, ladies undoubtedly did needlework."

"It's a wonderful party space," Sedona said, imagining a wedding reception.

"It is, indeed," Fergus agreed. Enthusiasm brightened his ruddy cheeks to the color of ripe cherries. "We could have banquets to celebrate winners of golf tournaments."

"That's an idea."

Caught up in his own plans, Fergus missed the hesitation in Sedona's voice, which his sister immediately caught. "We invited Ms. Sullivan to *Cnoc an Chairn* to hear her ideas. Not yours."

"Of course we'd be wanting to hear what you have in mind," he said.

"Well, as Conn pointed out, there's already a golf course nearby."

"Which, as I pointed out at Joseph Brennan's funeral supper, doesn't have nearly the history of *Cnoc an Chairn.*"

"Exactly my point." Sedona watched surprise followed by curiosity chase away his frown. "There's so much you could do that would draw in more than merely golfers, who, if they wanted to spend their time hitting a little white ball around the grass, could always drive down the road.

"But with all these grounds, you could create a skeet shooting range, which would be popular with sportsmen and women alike. And to appeal more to women, who are often the ones actually planning vacations, you could become a location for destination weddings, with couples and guests coming from all over Europe and America. Perhaps even Australia."

"I met a couple from Sidney just last month at Brennan's," Fergus said. "They were researching the husband's roots. His many times great-grandfather, James Lynch, landed there on the British prison ship *Anne I* in 1801. Officially he was found guilty of larceny, which was a catchall phrase at the time for being a rebel."

"The fact that his family knows that piece of their ancestry and came here researching their roots would make them even more eager to visit an estate that would give them a sense of that time," Finnola said, catching on quickly.

"Exactly," Sedona agreed. "You wouldn't try to create an exact replication of the life at that time, but you could maintain the sense of it. *Downton Abbey* has stimulated a tourism boom for Highclere Castle, where it's filmed. You might be wise marketing *Cnoc an Chairn* as Ireland's very own Downton Abbey. It would also add to the experience if Fergus sang for guests during the evening wine and tea time."

"That does sound more appealing than golf," he agreed.

"You could also tell stories, just as you do in conversation at Brennan's. But these would be about your family and the estate's history." Sedona turned to Finnola. "You'd want a gift shop, of course. It only makes sense that your prints would be for sale. Along with postcards and greeting cards."

"And coasters," Conn broke in. "Celtic Storm started selling those at our concerts along with T-shirts and the usual souvenir items. Until then, I had no idea how many people collect the bloody things."

"Imagine people all over Ireland, even the world, wearing T-shirts with a silkscreen of *Cnoc an Chairn* on it." Dispensing with his golf plan, Fergus grabbed the idea and began running with it.

"When we were starting out, we played a fair in County Wexford," Conn said. "I met a lass who was acting the role of a blacksmith's wife in a reenactment of the Battle of Vinegar Hill. Over three hundred people took part over two days, which is when I learned that there are groups all over not just this country but the world who do the same thing. We also played at a reenactment of the Battle of Kinsale. This would be a natural venue to stage similar events."

"I was born to play the rebel," Fergus claimed, surprising no one.

"There's just one problem," Finnola said. "Look around. This project could take as long as it did to build the estate in the first place. You might behave as if you're nine years-old," she told her brother, "but you're far closer to ninety. And while God may have given the Irish plenty of time, he didn't make it infinite."

"I think we can get much of the house and grounds restored sooner than you might think," Sedona said. "Conn and I are meeting with Bram after we leave here because I want to discuss his plans, but—"

"We're meeting with my brother?" Conn asked.

"Yes. At the pub. Did I forget to mention that?"

"You did, indeed. I thought we'd had plans for this evening."

"We do." Sedona dearly hoped the others couldn't see the color rising in her face at thoughts of exactly what Conn's plans entailed. "But we have to eat," she pointed out. "So I thought this would be killing two birds with one stone…

"Also," she forged on when Conn didn't argue the point, "when I was here for Mary Joyce's wedding, I stayed at the Copper Beech Inn, which I learned was restored by the Georgian Society."

"It was, indeed," Finnola confirmed. "As was Castletown, a manor house much like this one. The society supplied volunteers and money they raised from all over the world. Even your own country."

"So the president of the governing board told me," Sedona said. "She also said that they're looking for a new project and thought this one presents an interesting challenge members would enjoy."

"That's fabulous news!" Fergus clapped his hands and bounced up and down in his chair like a four-year-old boy who'd just been told he was going to Disneyland.

"There's more. University College Dublin is interested in making a special-interest course and giving credit to landscape horticulture students who sign up to work so many hours on the project. They also gave me a list of other schools that would probably be interested in doing the same. I only had time to talk with one, but the chair for horticultural studies at Cork Institute of Technology not only signed on right away, he also offered to work with UC Dublin on an overall design plan based on any drawings you can find of the original estate.

"My idea is for you, or better yet, someone you hire as a grounds coordinator, to contact as many post primary schools in the region to find volunteers who'll work on weekends and during summer holidays. I suspect that things aren't so different here than in the States, where high school students are all scrambling to enhance their college applications with volunteer work. Restoring such a large part of Ireland's history would gain a great deal of notice."

"You did all this while I was having breakfast with my mother and brothers?" Conn asked, clearly impressed.

"It only took a bit of time online and a few calls," she said. "I've always enjoyed strategizing. It's like solving jigsaw puzzles. You find each piece that works, put them all together, and you end up with a completed picture."

"People told me you were smart," Fergus said. "But they failed to mention that you're bloody brilliant."

"Now there I'm going to have to accuse you of that Irish hyperbole Finnola mentioned," Sedona said with a laugh, even as she was pleased that he had taken to her ideas. "Although you say you have the funds to do it yourself, you should think of this estate as part of Irish heritage. My advice would be to set up a charitable foundation, and eventually, to prevent it falling back into disrepair, since neither of you have any immediate heirs, turn it over to the government and let the Office of Public Trust take care of it. You could also provide for that part in your wills.

"Down the road you'll be wanting to get with other departments to hire event planning and hospitality and such, but at this stage of the game, I'd suggest you narrow your vision to getting the more important rooms in the interior of the house and at least the front and part of the back grounds in order."

"So we wouldn't have to have the entire thing done and polished before we open for business?" Finnola asked.

"No, I believe you can set up public areas in the beginning. I wouldn't suggest overnight guests while you're doing the work, but you could hold events and have tours."

"And outdoor weddings?" Finnola asked.

"Absolutely. And if the day turned to a soft one, you could always move inside to this room."

"I've always dreamed of a wedding on a rolling green lawn beneath a flowered arbor," Finnola said wistfully.

"It would be lovely." Sedona found herself feeling a little sad that the elderly woman's chances for that happening were slim. But not impossible.

"And now I can achieve my dream." Finnola's smile lit up her eyes and turned the gray to a gleaming pewter. "Thanks to Ireland passing the marriage equality referendum."

"You'd be marrying Magdalena?" Fergus asked.

"Well, we have been a couple for forty years," she said, a bit huffily, Sedona thought. "With our parents already passed, you'll be having to give me away."

"I'd be honored. And of course you'll want me to perform the singing."

"Of course." She turned to Sedona. "We'll have to get started right away. My partner and I have waited a very long time and we're not getting any younger."

"I'll pass that on to Bram when we meet," Sedona said. "If you wouldn't mind me sharing your news."

"Of course not. Especially since I'll be stopping by the butchery in the next few days. We're in need of a chicken and some bacon."

"Mrs. Sheehan will also save you from having to go door to door to spread the news," Fergus said slyly.

"There is that," his sister agreed.

"Well, this makes the project even more personal and exciting," Sedona said. "What fun will it be to have the first wedding for a member of the family who originally owned this home?

"I'd also suggest hiring someone to build you a website and a blogger to keep people up to date on how the project is progressing. I was considering using your family crest with its armor, torch, and bow as your buy button, but while you should include it on the merchandise, I think a bright green, white, and orange button would stand out better."

"The colors of our Irish flag," Fergus said. "That's clever."

"Thank you." Sedona blew out a breath. "So, if you're agreeable, I'll talk with Bram so he can start planning a schedule, and I'll email you a list of contacts, including a couple headhunters I know who can find you the people you need to head up various pieces of the final picture of a stately, beautifully restored *Cnoc an Chairn*."

"That's grand," Fergus said. "I knew you were the lass to solve my problems. Now I can see that developer welshing on his deal was a blessing."

Finnola only murmured a response as she gazed, lost in thought, out the tall windows at the grounds. Sedona knew the older woman was imagining the estate as it would become and was heartened by the fact that she'd just met another person who seemed to have found the secret to a lasting love.

31

"THAT WAS QUITE a pitch," Conn said as they drove away from the manor house. "I've always agreed with Finnola's assessment that Fergus is the poster child for Irish embellishment and overstatement. But he's right about you. You're bloody brilliant."

His words shouldn't make her feel so warm and fuzzy. Sedona knew she was intelligent. She also took pride in her ability to problem solve with logic and strategic planning. But hearing Conn, who was first attracted to her because of an undeniable chemistry, sincerely appreciate her for being more than what she knew was merely a lucky DNA inheritance when it came to her looks, did exactly that.

"Your suggestions helped move him over from his golf course idea." Sedona had enjoyed feeling like part of a team. It reminded hwe of what she'd enjoyed about her work in Portland. "It's pretty much what I did during my accounting days. I thought I'd gone there as well prepared as possible in the short time I was given, but Finnola threw me a curve with the wedding news."

"They've been together so long I doubt anyone in town will be surprised," he said. "When Finnola moved into the flat with Fergus, Magdalena kept her own place a few blocks away. But now that they're in the manor house, I heard they have their own suite of rooms on the first floor. Unfortunately, word is that Magdalena, who handles their business affairs, including being Finnola's agent, is an even worse cook."

"It's too bad Maddy's in Shelter Bay. Her school has turned equally bad cooks into people who can prepare a meal without the risk of poisoning their families. But it does make helping them even more special."

"Your plan definitely surpassed a mere golf club. And here I thought accountants mostly just filed taxes and chided you for spending too much."

She laughed, having been given an insight into Conn's own client-accountant relationship. "I did that, as well. But what I really enjoyed was business planning. Helping a client make the most of his or her assets and become even more successful."

"Tricky business, that, I'd imagine," he said.

"It helps to have a relationship where you get to know the client well," she allowed. "Not everyone wants to share the type of information needed to get a sense of what they'd be comfortable with."

"My manager was Celtic Storm's original drummer," Conn said. "Diarmuid was my best mate since we were in nappies and our mothers would visit back and forth to each other's houses next door for morning tea. His was where I'd escape to when things got rough at home.

"He was the first person to join my original band, the Castlelough Lads, then came with us to Dublin. But once we were competing with higher-level bands, it was obvious that he was not very good about keeping time and needed replacing."

"That must have been difficult, given your long personal history together."

It was Conn's turn to shrug. "Not so much. He'd always been good with numbers, even earning a mathematics award in *rang a sé*, which would be the final year of primary at Holy Child School.

"As a bonus, while I've always preferred to let my music do my talking for me, Diarmuid's nearly on a level with Fergus when it comes to pitching a good story. So I put him in charge of finances, and eventually, when I found trying to book gigs took too much time away from writing the songs, I promoted him to being the band's manager. So, he's still with us and handling the business end quite admirably."

He took his attention from the road cutting through the alley of green trees to flash her his bad boy grin that caused warmth to pool inside her. "Of course it helps that he mostly always agrees with what I want to do."

"That would help," Sedona agreed, even if she wondered if it *was* the best business arrangement. Although she'd found that many clients preferred a sycophant yes-person, she'd often helped them see better ways to achieve the same goal. Then again, having been together essentially all of their lives, close enough for the drummer turned manager to know many of Conn's secrets, perhaps they thought the same way. Which might also be counterproductive.

Not that he'd asked for any advice on the business level. And from what she could tell, having built a powerhouse brand from a small, back-of-beyond teen band to the third wealthiest, and possibly, according to *Forbes* magazine, the most socially influential band in the world (depending on what politically social effort Bono was taking part in on any given year), Conn Brennan didn't need her help guiding Celtic Storm.

"It does, indeed," he agreed. "Are you sure you want to stop by the pub?"

"I could do with a bite. I should have listened to your mother about eating something before we went to tea."

"There's still a wealth of meals we can heat up in the cottage freezer." He slid his left hand beneath her skirt and began tracing those enticing loops on the inside of her thigh. "And while they warm, we could see about satisfying other hungers."

"That is so tempting," she admitted as she felt herself melting into the leather seat. "But I'm the one who asked Bram to meet with me. Since he's on his way to Donegal tomorrow, it was either this evening or right before he leaves. Which would be at dawn."

His stroking hand went higher, wickedly toying with the elastic band of her boy shorts. "Which would cost us a long, lazy morning in bed before I show you Mary's film."

"That was my thought."

Not that she was certain she was going to be able to think coherently since she'd be reduced to a puddle by the time they reached Brennan's. She was tempted to reach across the center console, undo Conn's fly, and treat him to the same sensual torture, but not wanting to risk driving into one of the stone walls lining either side of the road, which twisted like a snake past the quilted green patches of farmland, she resisted.

"I have a question," she said.

"If it's to ask me to pull over, I'm there in a heartbeat," he said.

She managed a shaky laugh. "There aren't any turnouts. We can't have sex in the middle of the road."

"Must you always be so practical?"

"You, more than anyone, know I'm not always." He was cupping her through the white cotton that was becoming more drenched by the moment. "And if you don't stop that, I'm going to retaliate by doing the same to you, and we could both end up dead in this non-frugal rapper SUV of yours."

"Caught me. It's admittedly not the least bit frugal. When I first heard Ludacris's 'What's Your Fantasy,' I was all of fourteen, and like boys of that age are prone to do, I started fantasizing all the ways he sang about making love to his woman. But the one that really stuck, for some reason, was doing it on the roof of his Escalade. Which got me thinking I might want to get one for myself. But by the time I could afford it, they were impossible to find in Ireland. I was told by a car guy that it's because they don't make a diesel model. So, I pretty much put it out of my mind.

"Fast forward sixteen years and a few months ago, I recorded a duet with Ludacris, and we got to talking about that song. I told him that Cadillac should've paid him a royalty on every Escalade they sold back then. Leaving the studio, I passed a Porsche dealership, saw this, which is the same idea, pulled in, and bought it."

He slanted her a hot, wickedly appealing leer. "Want to help make a poor West Ireland country boy's fantasy come true?"

Sedona laughed and put her hands over her ears. "I am *not* listening to you."

He took a hand away, capturing it in his. "Because you know you want to do it."

"Not listening."

"Maybe you'll change your mind after your hear the song," he said helpfully. "I could sing it to you. Maybe not the same way he does, but enough that you'd get the idea."

Oh, she got it. Only too well. "Not listening."

"You know you're tempted."

"I am not." Which was not the truth, the whole truth, and nothing but the truth. She also suspected that she did not want to hear the rest of those lyrics.

"That's okay." He lifted her hand to his lips. "I'm a patient man. And you know what we Irish say about time."

The cocky, arrogant rocker from the pub was definitely back. "Maybe you've also heard of the American expression, 'In your dreams'?"

"And haven't I already done that?" He waved to the man who'd been cutting peat earlier and was now taking it home in the back of a donkey cart. "And as grand as it was, it's not exactly the same as reality."

"I wouldn't hold your breath," she said as visions of her own erotic dreams starring this man flashed through her mind.

"Now see?" Conn treated her to another of those knowing alpha male smiles and returned to creating sexual havoc on her bare inner thigh. "We're making progress. Because that was not a definite *no*."

"What it is is a ridiculous conversation," she stated.

"Have I mentioned that I love it when you pull out that bossy duchess-to-peasant tone? When we do make love on this Porsche, you can be on top and instruct me on everything you want me to do."

Heaven help her, didn't she have a few ideas of her own about exactly that?

"We were talking about the risk of dying if you run us into a stone wall because you don't have both hands on the wheel," she dragged the conversation back to where it had been before he'd sidetracked it with talk of sex on the SUV's rooftop. Which was a bad, bad idea.

But, dammit, enticing.

"Our backcountry roads are risky," he allowed as a delivery truck passed with a toot of the horn, making Sedona grateful for the darkened windows, now that her white gauze summer skirt was bunched up practically to her waist. "But I'm not sure I could think of a better way to go."

Rather than return that roving hand to the wheel, he breached the cotton barrier and touched her, a quick stroke of his thumb, exactly on the spot that he knew would have her coming undone. Which it did.

"You are so impossibly wicked," she gasped when she returned from whatever plane he'd sent her to back into her limp body.

He bent over the console and took her lips in a quick but still enervating kiss. "And you love it."

"Aye," she admitted, echoing the exaggerated accent he always took on when making love. "Dammit, I do."

"Then my work, for now, is done. You've no idea," he said, as he withdrew his hand and tidily pulled her skirt back down, "how hard it was to keep my mind on your earlier conversation when I kept picturing doing that to you in the gallery.

"Not in front of Fergus and Finnola," he quickly assured her, "but someday, when we're all alone, I want to take you on that billiard table while that framed photo of St. Patrick looks on."

"You're not only an exhibitionist, you're a heretic," she accused, her smile softening her words. She could not deny that she was more than a little attracted to the bad boy dwelling inside the surprisingly sensitive man.

"And proud of it," he agreed. "But it's you who'd be bringing that out in me, *a stór*."

When he'd first used the term, that rainy night after Mary and J.T.'s wedding reception, she'd believed he'd meant it generically. Now she knew that, at this moment in time, which was all she was going to allow herself to think about, she truly was his darling.

"It's the same for me. With you," she admitted. "But getting back to my original question," she said as her brain caught up with her body, which had gone racing ahead when he'd taken control of it yet again. "How is it that Fergus's ancestors ended up with so much land, when so much of what we're driving through appears to be small farms, some seeming little more than a cottage with a garden plot?"

"There's a complex answer to that," he said, returning both hands to the wheel. "After the Williamite War in Ireland in the late1600s, which brought about the accession of William and Mary, the crown confiscated land belonging to Jacobite supporters of King James II to pay for the cost of the war. Around six hundred thousand acres, which was nearly five percent of the land area of the country, were put up for sale. For those with ready cash and an aptitude for speculation, it wasn't that different from Fergus winning the lottery.

"Dermott Molony, who'd foreseen the futility of the Jacobite cause, had already converted to the Protestantism for business reasons. He ended up the second largest individual buyer, behind William Conolly, who would go on to be speaker of the House of Commons. Squire Molony, as he was called, kept a thousand acres for the building of *Cnoc an Chairn* and leased out the rest."

"A thousand acres is significantly more than it is now."

"True enough. Especially since Dermott used his rents to buy more and more land, making him one of the wealthiest and most influential men in Ireland. When he died, his son, Dermott Junior, proved equally skilled in making money. Unfortunately, he was a gambler, a drinker, and a whoremonger.

"Each generation appeared to have less work ethic than the previous and lost more land, until, while not penniless, no one could call them well-off. When it was sold for back taxes, the estate was down to the acreage it is now."

"That's sad but, I suppose, not so unusual," Sedona said. "Our history may not go back as far as yours, but we certainly have our own tales of black sheep among our wealthiest one percent. So, that's how the farms got so small? Too many leases?"

"In part. But another reason was the Popery Act, which required Catholic inheritances of land to be equally subdivided between *all* an owner's sons. So those lands became more and more divided. Making matters worse was even if one could afford to buy an additional plot of land, it was against the Penal Laws to do so.

"The Brennans, as well as my mother's family, the Hayes, lost our lands during that time, but when Declan announced that he was meant to farm, we all got together and bought some farmland originally owned by a Hayes. We've been adding to that over the years, and since he's proven farsighted in his agricultural choices, including going organic before farm-to-table became a popular movement, he's becoming one of the larger private property owners in the county. Second only to the Joyces."

"So much for Irish stories ending tragically," Sedona said as Conn pulled up in front of the pub. "Between Fergus getting his land back, Finnola's upcoming nuptials, and Declan's successful farming, this has been a very positive day."

"And just think," he told her as he cut the engine and leaned over to kiss her and set her head to spinning again. "We still have the entire long Irish summer evening ahead of us."

32

As much as he enjoyed his band, Conn had always relished his solo film work. Not that he and Mary didn't collaborate, but usually he'd send her scenes with the proposed score, and she'd weigh in. Because they'd proven creatively in tune, she usually found his ideas perfect. There were, however, those occasions when she'd suggest a more nuanced emotional feel.

He'd been right thinking that emotion was what Sedona brought to the table. As they spent the next two weeks working together, he also discovered that they created a strong partnership. If he was going to be locked away like a hermit for days at a time, he couldn't think of a better person to be locked away with. Not only had his creativity returned with her arrival, what he hadn't expected was that collaborating with her opened floodgates to emotions he'd kept locked up for years. They poured through his racing fingers over the synthesizer keyboard into the scenes Mary had so beautifully crafted for the screen.

When they weren't working their way through the ninety-nine minutes of music he and Mary had decided she needed for the one-hundred-and-twenty-minute film, they were making love. And because even they couldn't live on love alone, they'd occasionally take time to work their way through the store of frozen meals in the cottage.

Sedona had never experienced anything like her collaboration with Conn. If it weren't for her daily phone calls with Annie and her parents, they could have been whisked away to a desert island. Even back in her previous life, when she'd lived on Thai takeout during tax season, she'd never immersed herself so deeply, so completely, in work. And although her role was merely that of a sounding board, Conn's intensity was contagious, and she found her moods wildly swinging from joy to despair, to hope, to fear, then back to joy, depending on the scene.

A perfectionist himself, even when she thought a particular bit of music couldn't be better suited to a scene, he'd continue to work certain phrases, rearrange a bridge here and there, change a few notes from a major to minor key. She also noticed, as he wrote the music onto staff paper, that it wasn't that different from her keeping track of numbers in a ledger.

"I realize you and Mary decide where music should go," she said. "But how do you determine what to write? Obviously a film is different from a three to four-minute song to be played on the radio."

"It's the difference between night and day," he agreed. "Which is why trying to shoehorn blockbuster pop songs into a movie can often fail. My process has stayed the same since her first film, when, knowing nothing about the craft, I was going solely by instinct. The first thing I do is hole up all alone and spend a week watching the film without even trying to think about what music I'll be putting with it. I want to watch it over and over, until it talks to me. When it begins telling me what to do, I get to work and see where the story and characters take me."

"Following your gut instincts," she murmured. For not the first time since that conversation with Conn in the pub, Sedona envied him that ability. Perhaps she was too controlling, she'd been forced to consider. Her mother was always telling her to trust her instincts, but she'd preferred mapping out a plan.

And look where that had gotten her. She'd never imagined that her first career, which she'd enjoyed on many levels, would end up the way it had. And then, after diligent planning, it had only taken one storm and one greedy developer to bring Take the Cake crashing down on her.

"I am surprised, after you played one of the songs for me acoustically, that so much of the work you're doing is electronic," she said after heating up their third shepherd's pie of the week. As much as she appreciated routine, she had to admit that she wouldn't mind a hamburger or salad for a change. But that would involve shopping and she was discovering that scoring made for some long days.

"There's a lot to be said for technology," he answered as he tore off a piece of crunchy bread with his strong white teeth. Thinking that the man could even make eating sexy, Sedona took a long drink of ice water to cool down.

"People had been playing with synchronizers for a while, using them as accents, or to create a special, unusual sound, but when *Chariots of Fire* came out, entirely electronically scored, it proved a game changer. A lot of musicians lost work because most movies went electronic.

"But, as always happens, after the initial rush to new and shiny, the pendulum swung back the other way, and orchestral works began being incorporated into electronic scores. Which makes sense, because, while a very good electronic string section can fool an audience playing beneath an action scene or under dialogue, if it's in an exposed place, where there's little else in the soundtrack to compete, it can sound dry and artificial. I've booked an orchestra in Dublin to record the final scene."

"But I just watched you create an orchestral piece."

"That's only a sample piece for the orchestrator, to use as a suggestion, along with my sheet music to write it for actual instruments. I've worked with Brigit Cavanaugh on the past two movies before this one and we make a good team."

"I'm impressed with all the research and work that goes into all this." And wasn't that an understatement?

He laughed, a rich, hearty laugh that had every atom in her body tingling. "And here you thought I was just a pretty face."

"Your face is pretty," she agreed. "But I've also come to admire other parts, as well."

The blue flame was back. "We're down to the final scenes," he said, pushing his chair back from the farmer's table. "What would you say if, instead of going back to work, we call it a day and tackle it in the morning?"

"That's the best idea you've come up with all day." Hungry for more than reheated meat pie, Sedona put her napkin on the table, stood up, then went around and straddled his lap.

"I think you just topped me," he said as his hands cupped her bottom through the dress.

"That's the plan," she said, laughing against his mouth. "I've been wanting you ever since I watched that hot scene between the fisherman and his wife making love." She reached beneath his T-shirt, splaying her hands against his chest. "Once I got past the idea of watching a close friend rolling around on a bed with Gerard Butler."

Mary had always seemed so *normal*, fitting into the rhythm of the small Oregon coastal town, showing up at local events, helping to raise money for school arts programs, attending J.T.'s college functions as a faculty wife, simply being a friend, that it was easy to forget that in her other life she was a star who appeared on Sedona's TV every year at the Oscars, being singled out as a fashion icon while walking the red carpet. It was strange how, even after Sedona had met the screenwriter/director/actress, she'd managed to lose herself in the story and whatever role her friend was playing. It was only as she and Conn watched a scene over and over again that she'd wondered how long it had taken J.T. to make the disconnect between the character Mary was playing and his wife.

"I learned early on to never think of her as my Mary in those scenes." Conn's hands slid into the opening of the casual cotton wrap dress she'd put on that morning. "It would be like watching my sister…

"But I will admit that I've been thinking of you whenever I write the fisherman's feelings for his wife."

His *wife*. Sedona wondered if he'd thought about any possible future that might last beyond this stolen time together, as well.

Don't go there. Not when it was proving easier and easier to live in the now. Especially a moment as exquisite as this one.

Leaning forward, she took his mouth again, sucking at his tongue, which drew a rough moan from deep in his chest. Beneath her palms, his skin grew hot, and she could feel his heart begin to hammer.

One hand that had been teasing her nipple thrust beneath the skirt and discovered the secret she'd been keeping all day.

"You seem to have forgotten your underwear." His voice was rough and deep and sexy and had her close to coming all by itself.

"I did." Growing more and more impatient, she went to work on his belt. "On purpose. For this," she said as she began unfastening the buttons of his fly.

Conn sucked in his gut. "I knew you were dangerous," he managed on a strangled half laugh, half moan. "But I didn't realize exactly how dangerous until now."

"Don't worry." Despite her confident tone, she struggled for patience, realizing that if she wasn't careful, she could seriously wound him with those damn metal buttons. "I promise not to hurt you."

With that promise, she freed him and found him hot. Hard. Ready. When she wrapped her fingers around him, he bucked into her stroking touch.

"I've wanted you like this," she said, reaching into the side pocket of the dress she was still halfway wearing to pull out the condom she'd been carrying around all day. "For hours." They both watched as she rolled it down his stone-hard length. "And hours."

"You'd not be alone there." He gripped her hips, his fingers digging into her flesh as he lifted her as if she were as light as a feather, then, with darkened eyes, watched their joining as he lowered her onto him.

And wasn't this exactly where she belonged? Sighing happily, she would have laid her head on his shoulder before starting things up again when he lifted her off him just enough to cause those tingling nerves to tangle all over again.

"Conn..." She whimpered as he took his damn time, holding back, just barely letting her swollen, aching sex brush against his tip.

"Please." She'd known he was strong. She'd loved watching the play of tendons and muscles in his arms. But who knew that, along with strength, he possessed such vexing control? "I *need* you." Sedona had never begged any man. But she'd never been as desperate for any man the way she was for Conn Brennan.

Her head was thrown back, her eyes closed tight as she tensed. Waiting...Waiting...*Waiting*.

And then, oh, God, as she watched him watching her, as he slid her up and down his shaft, he thrust up his hips at the same time he brought her down hard and fast, detonating an orgasm that had her seeing stars.

His hips bucked against her. One, two, three more deep, hard strokes was all it took. Sinking his teeth into that soft, fragrant curve between her neck and shoulder, he gave in to his own forceful release and followed her into the void.

33

SEDONA AND CONN were finishing up breakfast the following morning when there was a knock at the cottage door.

Sedona opened it to a woman in her late thirties, with long, copper-hued curls and emerald eyes set in a heart-shaped porcelain face. She was wearing a pert green suit with a fitted jacket and a white porcelain locket painted with shamrocks. "Ms. Sullivan?" she asked, her Irish accent touched with what appeared to be nerves.

"That's me," Sedona said.

"I'm Abby Collins. And you'd be the baker who made Mary Joyce's wedding cake?"

"I am." Sedona smiled, hoping to ease some of the tension swirling in the other woman's eyes. "Would you like to come in?"

She glanced past Sedona, into the cottage, as if concerned she might have interrupted something. Small towns, Sedona thought with an inner smile. Nothing stayed private.

"We've just finished breakfast," she said. "But if you'd like a scone or some tea..."

"Oh, no." Bright color stained her cheekbones. "I wouldn't want to be interrupting."

"You're not. Truly." Sedona stepped aside to echo her earlier invitation.

"I can't be staying but a moment," Abby said. "I'm due at work at the tourism office." Which explained the suit, which seemed formal for everyday Castlelough attire. "I've just come to ask a question."

"Abby, darling," Conn greeted her as she followed Sedona into the kitchen. "It's good to see you. How's your sister?"

"Deidre's grand. She's going to be having her second baby in a few weeks. It's a girl."

"Who'll undoubtedly be as gorgeous as her mother and aunt," he said, handing her a cup into which he'd already poured tea. "Deidre Collins and I attended school together," he told Sedona. "She broke my heart when she went off and married some doctor she fell for in Cork."

Abby laughed as, from his broad grin, Conn had obviously intended. The tension eased from her face as her eyes sparkled. "Conn's joking," she assured Sedona. "Everyone in Castlelough knows that my sister gave her heart to Sean Murphy when they were assigned to sit next to each other their first day at Holy Child School."

"True enough," Conn said easily. "I always wondered how they avoided running into classroom walls with all those little red hearts circling their heads."

Sedona joined in the laughter as she picked up her own cup from the table. Once again Conn had demonstrated his generosity, making an extra effort to relax the other woman.

"You came to ask me a question?"

"Aye. Yes," Abby said, shooting Conn a grateful smile as she slipped onto the chair he'd pulled out for her. A touch of nerves was back. She took a long drink of tea, as if seeking calm. "I was wondering if you ever teach baking?"

"I have, on occasion, at a friend's cooking school," Sedona answered. "And occasionally on her television show."

"Would you ever be giving private lessons?"

"I haven't."

"I didn't think so." The color touched her cheeks again. "This was a mistake. I shouldn't have been after bothering you."

"It's no bother," Sedona assured her. "Are you asking for yourself?"

"I am. I'm getting engaged," she said. "To the kindest, most wonderful man in Ireland. But Liam's mother... Wouldn't she be another story?" She sighed and dragged a hand through her springy curls. "She's a bit negative."

"Liam?" Conn lifted a brow. "You're getting engaged to Liam Sheehan?"

"I am, indeed." She beamed. There was no other word for it. But despite her obvious happiness, seeds of worry had gathered in her expressive eyes again. "We're going to be breaking the news to his mother and father at supper. At Liam's flat. He's taking care of the main part of the meal, because, being a butcher, he's cooked meat and potatoes since he was old enough to reach the stove.

"But I promised to make dessert. And I've been known to burn bloody box pudding mixes." That confession came out on something close to a wail.

Sedona's heart went out to her. Having met the butcher's wife briefly at the funeral supper, she suspected it would take more than a tasty cake for Abby to win her prospective mother-in-law over, but no way was she going to refuse to help.

"Don't worry," she said. "I met your Liam when he helped me choose steaks and instructed me on how to cook them. He was a huge help. Together you and I will come up with something that'll have your fiancé's mother eating out of your hand."

At least, Sedona thought, she was going to give it her best shot.

"Well," Conn said as Abby left with a list of shopping ingredients. "Do you think she'll be able to pull it off?"

"The recipe? Absolutely. My chocolate lava cake is so easy a six year old can do it. I taught it to my friend, Annie, who could burn water, to make for her boyfriend and his little girl. They're now happily married with three kids.

"I also have these other friends, Lucas and Maddy, who had a rocky courtship due to a misunderstanding in their past. When she kept balking on marriage, he finally issued a cooking throwdown. She's a famous TV chef with her own television show and a bunch of cookbooks, so it looked like a slam dunk for her. Especially since he was a former Navy SEAL whose culinary expertise was mostly limited to heating up MREs and ordering takeout. But he definitely won the audience over with the bananas Foster I taught him."

"SEALs are probably good at setting things on fire."

Sedona laughed. "That's pretty much the same thing he said."

"So, what happened with the throwdown?"

"Well, the ending wasn't exactly straightforward, but they *are* happily married."

"Fair play to them," he said. "And while I've no doubt your recipe will be delicious and you'll be able to teach her to prepare it with the proper amount of panache, having known her all of my life, I feel the need to point out that Mrs. Sheehan is a formidable woman."

"So I sensed from our brief meeting at the funeral supper."

"Where she was, for her, on good behavior," Conn said. "You probably should have Abby put a pitcher of water on the table, as well."

Sedona lifted a brow. "Why?"

"Because if things get too difficult, she can always melt the harridan by dumping the water on her."

"You're terrible."

"But I made you laugh."

"You did, dammit."

Sedona may have been fighting depression when she'd arrived in Ireland, but during her time here, the dark cloud of doom hovering over her had lifted. Her life back home might be upside down, her future completely uncertain, but here with Conn, she was content. More than content. Indeed, there were moments when her heart was so light she felt as if she were walking on the soft air.

"I'll be wishing Abby good luck," Conn said. "Not that she needs it where Liam's concerned, since she's a wonderful lass who's already obviously won him over, but food's still one sure way to a man's heart," Conn said. "You had me the minute I walked into the cottage and saw you looking like a hot housewife in that apron."

Enough that he'd later had her wear it while making love. Sedona had always thought that fantasy sex would feel silly and had never been tempted to indulge. Until Conn. But as she'd stood in the middle of the kitchen, wearing only the apron and high heels while he'd fastened a pearl necklace he'd shown up at the cottage with, she'd fallen head over stilettos into the role of a hot housewife. She'd also never had sex on a kitchen counter before, but there'd definitely been nothing silly about that, and she knew she'd never be able to look at a squeeze can of whipped cream without thinking of this man.

"Then we're even. Because just looking at you when you strode into the pub in that kilt nearly made me come right on the spot," she said.

It had been her idea—when he'd coaxed her into coming up with an idea for their next role-playing scene—for him to show up at the pub, pretend to be a stranger, and send a drink over to her table. He'd have his usual pint, she'd have wine, then, when he invited her home, she wouldn't say no. To anything.

But trust him to put a twist on her carefully choreographed plan by striding into Brennan's wearing a badass black leather kilt with manly metal chains and belts buckled on one hip instead of that typical tartan plaid she'd imagined. His chest, beneath a studded leather vest, had been bare, and he'd been wearing those same black motorcycle boots he'd worn the night they'd met.

Although female voices had called out to him to let them touch that kilt, he'd kept his glittering eyes directly on her, holding her stunned gaze with the sheer strength of his will as he'd stopped at her table and, going off script to forego the preliminaries of pints and wine, simply held out his hand.

You could have heard a pin drop. The buzz of conversation ceased, and even the musicians hired for the night had stopped warming up. No glasses had clinked. No one had moved a muscle. The only sound Sedona had been able to hear was the pounding of her lust-crazed heart in her ears.

Without a word, she'd lifted her hand, which disappeared in his much larger, rougher one. Then she was standing, and together they'd walked back across the ancient stone floor, out the door, and into the night.

And although she and Annie shared almost everything, being erotically ravished by a Celtic warrior was something Sedona was keeping to herself. The memory of all the things he'd done to her, all the things she'd *begged* him to do injecting itself into what had begun as a conversation about cake baking was enough to start her bones melting.

"You were a wicked woman to come up with that idea," he said as his heavy-lidded gaze took in her tightened nipples, which seemed to have taken on a memory of their own.

"Not as wicked as you were once we got back here."

"And you loved every minute."

More like hours. And there was no denying it. "I did."

He slid his thumb along her wrist, reminding her of how, after he'd instructed her to undress, he'd looped those black leather belts around her wrists and tied her to the headboard. Kneeling above her on the mattress, clad only in the leather kilt, his legs spread on either side of her hips, he'd spun a bawdy tale of how, being the leader of his band, he'd captured her during a raid on her village.

"And now," he'd warned, leaving a trail of flame as his hand had run down her body, "you're my wench. To do with what I will."

And hadn't he lived up to his promise? He was right. She'd loved it. And wouldn't mind doing it again.

"I still have the kilt," he said, reading her mind. Or, more likely, her face, which probably had *lusty bad wench* written all over it in flashing neon lights.

"We have to get to work," she said sternly. "You told me you want to get the score finished today."

"So I did." He huffed out a deep sigh and shook his head. Then flashed her a grin. "Did anyone ever tell you how sexy you are when you pull out that good-girl-follow-the-rules tone? Maybe if we finish early enough, I'll let you tie me up. Sauce for the goose, and all that."

Sedona might have filled the glass front cases in her bakery with a wide variety of flavors, but she'd come to the sad conclusion that when it came to sex, she'd been strictly a vanilla girl. Until Conn had her tasting all the flavors of the rainbow.

She tilted her head. Chewed on a fingernail as she gave him a slow study from his head to his feet. She did not have to pretend to be imagining him in that black leather. "That sounds intriguing...Bring the kilt."

"I will, indeed."

If she could only bottle his grin, she'd never have to worry about coming up with a new business plan.

34

"I TELL YOU, IT'S love," Annie repeated during a phone call while Conn was up at the house, writing down some details for those final scenes that had come to him during his sleep.

"I think you might be right," Sedona admitted. "But it's so soon. And there's always the chance I'm merely in love with being in love."

"I've noticed that people who are in love with love tend to repeat the pattern. Have you ever felt that before?"

"Not since I was fourteen and had a *10 Things I Hate About You* movie poster on my wall." As had probably every other teenage girl that year. Including Maddy, Sedona had discovered during one of their girl DVD movie nights with Kara and Annie.

"Heath Ledger's Patrick Verona character was a bad boy, too," Annie pointed out.

"What makes you think I'm not talking about Joseph Gordon-Levitt?"

"Because his Cameron was more like the sweet, smart boys you probably grew up with on the commune. Ledger played the wounded alpha male with the sensitive marshmallow heart."

She'd nailed the character's appeal, Sedona admitted. Though Ledger's hotness couldn't be denied. She also belatedly realized how closely Conn matched Annie's profile.

"Okay. You're right. But that only backs up my point that what's happening now could be merely chemistry."

"Don't knock chemistry," Annie said. "It's what turns coal into diamonds."

"I hate to break it to you, but Superman lied to us all those years. Coal doesn't turn into diamonds."

"Must you be so literal?" her friend huffed. "And as much as I've been all for you doing that live-in-the-moment thing, perhaps it's time to at least consider a more long-term relationship."

"Which is impossible, since I have no idea what I'm going to be doing a week from now."

"Here's a newsflash for you. People adjust."

"I know." But that didn't make it any easier.

"When Mac proposed, he finally got through my fears by giving me that blank scrapbook that we could fill with photos of all the days of our future life together. That was the first time I realized that I wasn't alone. That *none* of us really know what's going to happen down the road. Which is when I realized that a life without him in it would be as empty as those blank pages."

"You two were meant to be," Sedona argued. "Everyone could see it."

"We didn't. Even Mac told me he was all wrong for me in the beginning. And I knew, or thought I knew, that I was the absolute wrong woman for him. But fortunately, he didn't give up on us."

"Conn and I haven't discussed any future." Sedona decided that his statement regarding his thoughts about wanting to spend the rest of his life getting to know every inch of her body didn't count.

"Maybe he's afraid he'll scare you away."

"I sincerely doubt that." Sedona laughed at the idea of Conn Brennan being afraid of anything. The mantel clock gonged, reminding her that he was waiting up at the house. "I've got to go. If you see Mary—"

"As it happens, we're going to the first annual Shelter Bay clambake and music festival on the beach with her, J.T., and the kids tomorrow."

Caught up in the events of her own life, Sedona had forgotten all about the clambake, which the mayor had talked Sax and Maddy into putting together to draw in more tourists.

"It sounds like fun." And ridiculously domestic. Which didn't stop Sedona from envying her best friend. Just a little.

"I think it will be," Annie said. "Maybe next year you can get Conn to attend. That would have the mayor over the moon."

"Now you're projecting too far into the future," Sedona protested. "Right now I'm just looking forward to going to Dublin." She'd told Annie about the trip in an earlier call. "The reason I brought up Mary is to have you tell her that I think she's going to be blown away by the work Conn's done on her film."

After Annie had promised to pass on the word, Sedona walked up the cobblestones to the house, where she found him at the keyboard, working on the storm scene, which she'd thought he'd finished two days ago.

"You've changed it." For the better. It was even more riveting than the original version, but she couldn't exactly tell why.

"I was putting the last touches on the orchestration suggestions when it dawned on me that the music should switch points of view the same as Mary's scenes do. It's still the same tune, connected but separate. So, if the conductor puts the musicians in their own isolation booths, the drums and Uilleann pipes in one, then violins and a pennywhistle for the selkie in another"—he played the instrument sounds on the keyboard—"instead of the music all coming from the center of the screen, it'll shift back and forth."

"As if it's being carried between the fisherman and his wife by the storm's wind," she said.

"Exactly." He rewarded her with a grin that Sedona knew would still have the power to thrill her when she was eighty. Not that they'd necessarily be together then, but—

Stop overanalyzing!

"Now it matches Mary's story. You're brilliant."

Another hot grin crinkled the corners of his eyes. "You'll be getting no argument from me."

After they'd gone back to work, Conn surprised Sedona yet again when they got to the final scene. Where the couple was found after the storm had passed.

"I just realized that you've been scattering fragments of the final theme throughout the movie in various scenes," she said. "Then they all come together as a completed theme in the climactic scene with the boat on the beach."

Conn liked that she'd heard what he'd spent weeks working out.

"I always see the music developing along with the plot. Mary set up the ending very early on when she presented her rule regarding what happens if selkies become human. Every piece along the way led to that final moment, but the audience won't hear it as a complete song until the storyline is complete as only it could be."

"But you said music should fit the scene," she said.

"As it should," he agreed. "And while Mary may disagree, which is her perfect right, I realized that the music, which I first came up with weeks ago, was all wrong. My original idea was too somber. It was a dark, sad air all about loss."

"She *did* die, in a way," Sedona pointed out. "At least she couldn't return to her human form."

"She sacrificed that pleasure in the name of love," Conn argued. "But during their time together, they shared an exceptional bond. And who of us knows how much time we have together?

"I realized that the love the fisherman and his wife shared was too special, too valuable to have people leaving the theater burdened down by grief. Will they shed tears? Unless they have hearts of stone, they will.

"I have no way of knowing what Mary was thinking when she first conceived this tale, which was before she went to Shelter Bay and met that Marine who turned out to be her soul mate. Which is, perhaps, how she ended up with a celebration of love between a man and a woman. Which is why the audience should be encouraged to leave feeling the joy in that. And a sense of how that magic of love can transform lives. Which is why I changed it to more an ode to joy."

As Mary's and, even more so, the emotionally wounded J.T.'s lives had been changed, Sedona thought.

"Do you believe that?" she asked. "That love can transform lives?"

"I've never seen it in person," he said after a moment's thought. "Yet, while I wasn't here when Quinn Gallagher arrived in the village to make his movie, Mary insists that he was a very different, closed-off, cynical man before falling in love. So, let's just say I wouldn't be entirely disbelieving."

And wasn't that a non-answer? "Well, whatever, you've just nailed Mary a best picture Oscar."

"No, she's done that on her own," Conn corrected. "I merely followed the breadcrumbs she left along the story's path." He framed her face in his hands. "With the assistance of my brilliant, sexy muse, who had me seeing so many parts of the tale in an entirely new light."

He leaned over and gave her a brief kiss that still possessed the power to unfocus her eyes. "And now, as soon as I send this MIDI file off to the orchestrator in Dublin to finish up the last bits, what would you say we call it a wrap, go back to the cottage and celebrate? Then drop in at the pub for a bite? Like a real date."

Which, except for perhaps the tea at Fergus's manor house, which had been more business than social, they'd yet to have an actual date during the two and a half weeks she'd been in Ireland. Conn was, she realized, moving their relationship, whatever it was, to a new level.

She swept the tip of her tongue across his lips, tasting. Teasing. "I'd say yes."

35

THEY ARRIVED AT Brennan's during the later afternoon lull. After taking their order of a warm scallop salad with cider dressing for Sedona and lamb with basil dressing and a roast potato for Conn, Patrick stuck the pencil behind his ear and took advantage of the lack of business to take time for some idle conversation.

"So, I hear you're going to save Liam Sheehan's bacon," he said. "Giving Abby a cake to win over his mother."

"I have absolute faith in her," Sedona said, ignoring the way Conn rolled his eyes up at the wooden rafters, as if suggesting the bride-to-be was going to need more than a hot chocolate lava cake to pull that feat off.

"As do I. She worked here pulling pints for a while. A more determined lass I've never known," Patrick said. "I will warn you that she was here earlier, sharing the news with a table of girlfriends, all of whom will now be coming to you for help with their own baking."

"I enjoy teaching and wouldn't mind." Sedona sipped her wine and avoided meeting Conn's gaze. "If I'm still here."

"Then you'd be returning to America soon?" Patrick asked.

"My plans are fluid right now." She made a waving motion with her hand. "But I'm in Ireland until at least after Dublin."

"Ah, yes. Where this one will be strutting the stage and you'll be having a meal with our mother and her friend. The very same friend, Roarke has pointed out on more than one occasion, that none of us knew about."

Conn hadn't mentioned that.

"I suppose even mothers are entitled to private lives," she said mildly.

"True enough," Patrick said, even as he exchanged a quick look with his brother.

"She knows." Conn tilted his head toward Sedona. "Not about the friend in Dublin, who we'll be meeting soon enough. But about my father."

Patrick lifted a brow. "I see."

There was no way Sedona was going to inject herself into this family issue.

"Fergus was in again last night," Patrick said, breaking the silence that had settled over the table.

"Now there's a surprise," Conn muttered.

"He was telling one and all about the plans for *Cnoc an Chairn*. Bram had dropped in as well and verified them."

"It's an amazing property," Sedona said. "I have no doubt that Bram will do it justice. Fortunately, price doesn't seem to be a problem."

"No. Not with the old man's winnings," Patrick agreed. "But Fergus said you advised him to set up a charitable organization."

"To bring in outside groups," Sedona agreed. "Who'll raise funds, but more importantly, the more people involved in a project like this, the more who'll have a vested interest in keeping it going years down the road."

Patrick nodded. "That's clever…You must have been very good at your other occupation. Before the baking."

"I like to think so." Sedona took another sip of wine, studying him over the rim of her glass.

"Would you happen to do any freelance consulting work? As you did for Fergus?"

Now they were getting down to the real reason for the conversation. "I do from time to time," she said. "Back home in Shelter Bay. But it's for friends. And I never charge."

"I'd be willing to pay."

She remembered what Conn had told her about Patrick having been the surrogate male parent for his five siblings, which meant that he was undoubtedly not accustomed to asking for help. That he was doing so now suggested that Brennan's might have a serious problem.

"I told you I don't take payment from friends. Is there a particular problem?" She glanced around the empty pub.

"It's not the customers," Patrick assured her. "It's always quiet during this time of day, which is good, because then I can start prepping evening meals and working on the books. Which are proving more and more vexing due to the fluctuation of ingredient costs, in great part due to other EU countries' prices."

"I know about that," she said. "No matter how small a business is, it's difficult to avoid international pricing. The spike in sugar costs alone has become a challenge. Unfortunately, I can't bake without it."

"Just as I can't brew beer without wheat and malt barley," he said. He dragged a hand through his dark hair. "At the moment the barley prices have gone down. But with farmers threatening to sell to France and South America to make up the deficit, I doubt that will hold."

A thought occurred to her. One she couldn't share without more knowledge. "Would you mind if I took a look at your accounting books?"

"Mind? I'd welcome it. And give you free meals the entire time you're here. "That's quite an offer," she said with a laugh. "Maybe I'll have a sign made up: *Will do accounting for food."*

After they'd finished their dinner, Conn sat at the bar, watching a football match while Sedona disappeared into the back room with Patrick. Although cheers went up from the crowd that had begun to gather for the evening, lost deep in his own thoughts, he hadn't seen the kick that had tied the score.

"Would you be liking another pint, Conn?" Donovan Fitzgerald, who was behind the bar, asked.

What he'd like was to be back at the cottage, in bed, with Sedona Sullivan. He hadn't missed the way she'd deftly dodged his brother's remark about the free food as long as she was here in Castlelough. Which he could only take to mean that she was intending to return to America.

And wasn't that idea like a dagger to the chest?

He loved her. And although he suspected it might be a bit of his rock star selfishness popping up, he also loved who he was when he was with her. Despite the way he'd dodged her earlier question, he knew that these weeks with her had transformed him.

He'd never realized that while he'd always thought he was running away from this village, in truth he'd been running away from himself. From the boy who, having never been good enough to please the man he'd believed to be his father, had given up trying before he'd hit his teens. The man who'd been nicknamed for those fights, which, he admitted looking back, he considered just a heritage for violence passed down from Joseph Fucking Brennan. Even after he'd bought the brewery, the voices whispering in his head had reminded him that he didn't deserve the fame that had given him the wealth to spend such money on what many considered a whim.

But then Sedona had come into his life just as it had been turned upside down by a withered, dried-up old man on his deathbed.

Once again Mary's instincts had proven spot on. Because had she not sent the American baker here, asking Conn to take care of her, he might have wallowed in a dark morass of might-have-beens. Of lost possibilities.

He could admittedly be a brooder. But rather than deny that character flaw, he'd accepted it and turned it to his advantage. Some of his strongest songs had come from dark places inside him. Except for those he wrote for Mary, many of his lyrics dealt with not getting what you wanted, a feeling he was well acquainted with. Because, as he'd told Mrs. Sheehan, while success might make life easier, it bloody damn well didn't make living easier.

Sedona had brought sunlight into his life, brightening all those dark corners. He'd been serious as a grave when he'd told her that she was the one who'd had him see the only way Mary's story could end. Not in grief and death. But in celebration of the type of joy not everyone was fortunate enough to experience.

Finally, at the age of thirty, Conn knew that joy. And it had turned out to be an emotion so much deeper, richer than those he'd faked while writing love songs. Because of Sedona. And selfish SOB that he was, there was no way he was going to let it get away. Let *her* get away.

But he'd also come to realize that no one made up Sedona Sullivan's mind for her but herself. Which was only part of her appeal and he wouldn't want her to change.

So, as the room erupted in another raucous cheer, Conn decided to do everything in his power to make her realize that they belonged together.

Forever.

36

"THAT WAS A grand idea you had," Conn said as they drove back to the cottage from the pub. "Bringing Declan into part ownership of Brennan's, then having him grow and supply the barley and hops for the microbrews."

Apparently she'd called his younger brother, who'd shown up at the pub and disappeared into the back office. Thirty minutes later, the three of them had come out, and Conn had joined them in a toast to the new venture.

"It's a type of vertical supply going back to Andrew Carnegie's steel industry," she said. "Apple probably does it best of anyone today, and while Brennan's is a much different situation, the concept should work well for both Declan and Patrick.

"Patrick can control the quality of his final product by being part owner of those acres set aside for his crops. Which is important for building his brand. He also now has control over the cost.

"Declan can sell whatever hops and barley Patrick doesn't use on the international market and since he's also part owner of Brennan's, some of those profits go into the pub's till, which allows Patrick to spend what it's going to take to expand his market beyond just the pub and Monohan's. And those extra funds can shore up the farm whenever outside markets destabilize for a time. It's a win-win for both of them."

"And for those who'd have more access to Brennan's brews," Conn said.

"Exactly. Though he was adamant about not wanting to become a giant like Guinness. Or be bought out by a major brand who'd merely re-brand Brennan's brews as their artisan label and take away his control."

"He's never been into making a fortune. Though I won't deny that it would be grand to be able to go into a bar in Paris, Copenhagen, or Berlin while on tour with the lads and order a Brennan's Brian Boru Black Ale."

"Those decisions are down the road," Sedona said. "According to Declan, it's much too late to plant for an August or early September harvest. In case you're thinking of touring again soon."

"I'm still working that out," Conn said, not wanting to tip his hand by telling her that much of what he was planning to do would depend on her. "At the moment, having finished Mary's score, I want to focus on building my new flat and studios so I can take on more of the producing jobs I've been offered. Along with writing a new solo album."

"That's all very ambitious. It sounds as if you'll be staying in Castlelough for a while."

Was that a hypothetical question he heard in her voice? Or was she asking for more personal reasons?

"I've grown weary of touring."

"But surely that's always the case at the end of a long tour," she suggested.

"It is. But being the ringmaster of a traveling circus is also beginning to lose its appeal. I've been running on fumes for years."

"From the outside looking in, that seems to be the rock-and-roll life."

"It is, in many ways. And if you're not careful, you can get blinded by all the hype and lose track of what's going on, which is when it can become self-destructive. I've been earning my living with music nearly half my life. There was a time when I was happy if we brought in a hundred Euros a night. Then we broke out of the pack and were making several times that. Which was the good thing. The bad thing is no one warns you that making that money brings you several times that number of problems.

"The irony is that I started out writing and singing about real life. But the whole fame star system, the life I ended up living, with the limos, magazine covers, red carpet interviews, supermodels, and all that shite, is totally *unrealistic*. You don't sell out with your first limo ride. You sell out when you forget to stay true to what got you there. What's important. Writing, then sharing your vision with others."

"Where have I heard that before?" she murmured.

"Probably from your da. In fact, I wouldn't be surprised if some of it wasn't lifted from an interview with him I read when I was a kid...

"I'm not knocking performing. It brings a lot of satisfaction, but right now, what I'm after is jumping off the hamster wheel and clearing my head enough to write.

"I still have things to say. Things about inequality, about people like my mother, who worked eighteen hours a day to feed her kids, about the fisherman who goes out on his boat in all kinds of weather to bring cod to Brennan's for my brother to cook and serve to more people who work their arses off day after day after day and are lucky if they can have the coin and time to stop into the pub for a pint. People living small lives, eking out a living on the fringes of a more and more stratified society.

"And although I know it's going to sound as if I'm not taking my own advice about not feeling all puffed up and self-important, I want to let them know that everyone needs dreams. And wherever you are, whatever you're doing, you need to hold onto those dreams and fight for them, if that's what it takes."

"It sounds as if you're describing an anthem."

"I believe I might be," he agreed. "Which is why I need the time away to make it my best work. Because the people downloading the music and showing up at concerts deserve only my best. Not a watered-down version designed to satisfy record executive bean counters who are just after selling the most albums."

Sedona knew about musicians going rogue, forging their own creative path. Hadn't her father done it many years ago? And although he'd always seemed content, he'd obviously been proud and undoubtedly pleased to have his music performed on Broadway.

Conn sounded sincere. Watching him score Mary's film these past two weeks, Sedona had no doubt that whatever he created would be amazing. But would he ever be satisfied with settling down, slowing the pace, and enjoying icon status at only thirty years old? Or would he have to keep pushing the envelope as new players and new sounds came into the music stream?

And why did the answer matter so much to her?

Because, dammit, Annie was right. No matter how illogical it might be, she'd fallen in love with Conn as surely as Mary's selkie had totally given her heart to her Irish fisherman.

37

A WEEK BEFORE leaving for Dublin, while Conn was out picking up food for a beach picnic, Sedona called her mother to see how the play was progressing.

"It's so exciting," Skylark said, her voice ringing with enthusiasm. "I have to admit that when we first arrived, the openly skeptical producers expected Freebird's book would have to be entirely rewritten." The book, in playwriting terminology, Sedona had learned during her parents' experience, was essentially a script without the music. "In our initial meeting, the first thing they said was how nearly impossible it is for any one person to write the music, lyrics, and book and do all of them well."

"Obviously they never met Dad," Sedona said. "How did he respond to that?"

"You would have been proud." This time it was wifely pride Sedona heard over the phone. "He merely calmly told them that two others with a single writer—*Music Man* and *Rocky Horror Picture Show*—hadn't done too badly."

"Ha!" Sedona laughed. "Go, Dad!"

"Of course, not knowing your father, they remained unconvinced. But they did take both the book and the CD with them."

"I'm surprised they had you come to New York without asking for those first," Sedona said.

"You'd think they'd want to, wouldn't you? But apparently when word got out that he was working on a rock opera, that was enough to get people willing to invest, just on his name alone."

"In his case they were right. Though it's not very logical. Not that anything about the music business seems logical. The least of which being that it's called a business."

"That's true," her mother agreed. "Needless to say, the next morning they called to tell Freebird that he had, and I quote, 'knocked it out of the park.'"

"Of course he did." Another trait her father and Conn shared was both did not consider failure an option. God help her, she thought, wondering why she hadn't seen it before. She'd fallen in love with a man just like her father. Which brought up another thought.

"Was it easy falling in love with Dad?"

"Too easy," Skylark said without hesitation, not seeming at all surprised by the change in topic. "Which I'll admit was more than a little unsettling. While it's true I was never going to marry that stuffy banker my parents had selected to be their son-in-law, I'd also never been the type of woman to get swept off my feet."

"I know the feeling." Sedona sighed.

"So, that's how things are with your Irishman? I was wondering," her mother admitted. "But I assumed you'd say something when you were ready to talk about him."

"He's special, Mama." Sedona couldn't remember the last time she'd called her mother that. Certainly the childhood term hadn't lasted into her teens. She took a deep breath before saying the words she'd only kept inside her head until now. "I'm pretty sure I love him."

"Oh." Skylark let out a long breath. Of relief? "I'm so happy for you." The sniffles Sedona heard over the air suggested she'd teared up. "I so wish we could come to Dublin when Conn performs. It would be wonderful to see you and meet him. But an unexpected opportunity to open three weeks earlier just came up, so now everything's suddenly rush, rush. In fact, they're starting casting today."

"That is fast."

"Well, you know what they say about New York being the fastest-paced city in the world," Skylark said. "It's true." She paused. "May I tell your father about Conn? Or is it still too early?"

"I'd prefer you not," Sedona said. "I hate to ask you to keep things from him, but he's obviously got a lot on his mind right now, and since Conn and I haven't even talked about any future together, the last thing I need is Dad showing up to grill him about his intentions and ask when we're going to produce a grandchild...because you fret."

Skylark laughed at that. A rich, warm laugh that had always possessed the power to assure Sedona that whatever current problem she was going through, things would turn out for the best. "I've never fretted about you," her mother said, turning serious. "Ever."

After Sedona passed her love on to her father and ended the call, she found herself wondering if the reason her mother had never worried about her was because she'd always been too careful, too boring to give her parents any cause for concern.

She'd always been the good girl. A good girl who'd now fallen for the town bad boy. And wasn't that a cliché that had provided a plotline for so many romantic stories over the centuries? Including Cathy and Heathcliff from *Wuthering Heights*, Rick and Ilsa from *Casablanca*, and, of course, Captain Angus MacGrath and Isabella Lombardi. And look how those had turned out.

There you go. Analyzing again! Shaking off those negative thoughts, Sedona boxed up the chocolate mint cupcakes she'd baked for the picnic and turned her mind to having an entire week without a single thing on her to-do list other than enjoy herself with the man she was falling deeper in love with every day.

38

After gracing the island with a soft morning, Mother Nature gifted the coast with sunshine.

"This is wonderful," Sedona said as she walked hand in hand with Conn along the hard-packed gold sand at the edge of the lacy surf. She breathed in the crisp salt air and felt every muscle and bone in her body relax.

"I'm glad you think so," he said, squeezing her fingers. "It occurred to me, while I was in Monohan's, that perhaps inviting you to picnic on the beach was a bad idea, given what happened to you."

"I told you, I'm mostly over that. And besides, that happened at night. In the dark. During a storm." She glanced at the wavelets the sun had turned to diamonds, then up at the robin's-egg blue sky, where raucous gulls wheeled overhead. "I love being here." Though admittedly, she wouldn't want to be on the beach in the winter, when the currently glassy waves would beat against the cliffs like warrior invaders from the sea. "I especially love being here with you."

She also should have tied up her hair, she thought as a gust of wind caused it to whip around like a flag. Putting down the picnic cooler, he grasped the blond strands in his free hand and used them to tug her close.

"And I with you." He brushed his lips over the top of her head. "I love the smell of your hair."

"It's the local seaweed shampoo." She tilted her head, encouraging him to skim lips over her cheekbones. "It goes along with the lotion and bath salts."

"I spent the first sixteen years of my life breathing in the scent of seaweed from this beach." Releasing her hair, he put his hands on her hips to draw her closer. "Which is enough time to know that it's your own seductive scent that has me wanting to pull you down onto the sand and make love to you. Here." Her breath hitched as he skimmed his hands down her thighs, over the gold dust silk of her skin, then back up again.

She swayed and, for one fleeing, foolish moment, was inclined to throw caution to the wind and risk it, when the sound of laughter came drifting on the salt air.

"Don't tempt me," she said, pulling away with a half laugh. "Are there wizards in Ireland? Because I swear, you've put a spell on me."

"Here in Erin we call our wizards *Draíodóir*. And wouldn't you be carrying their blood in your own Sullivan veins, since I've been bewitched by you from the beginning."

She was saved from coming up with an answer for that when a young boy, his wild, wind-blown curls the color of roasted chestnuts, came running up the beach, his arm above his head, holding a kite as it soared toward the sun.

"That's a wonderful kite," Sedona told him as she took in the seahorse with the shiny green scales flying amidst the gulls.

"It's the Lady," he said, referencing the creature that supposedly lived in the lake by the crumbling castle that had given the town its name.

"I can see that." The Lady was a familiar image, appearing on souvenirs all over the village.

"She grants wishes." He turned his attention to the kite for a moment, letting it dive toward the surf, pulling it back up again at the last minute. "Not the kite. But the Lady. I went to the lake every day for a week and asked her for this very same kite I'd seen in Monohan's window for my birthday." He let out more string, allowing the kite to climb higher and higher until it was over the top of the cliff. "And didn't my uncle John bring it to my party for a gift?"

"You'd best be watching out," Conn said, as it seemed headed straight toward the lone tree at the top of the cliff.

"No problem," the boy said. "Faeries live in that hawthorn tree. And everyone knows that faeries are best friends with the Lady. They'd never eat one of her kites."

Giving credence to that local myth, at the last minute the kite took a sudden sharp swerve, bypassing the tree to climb even higher.

"See?" A grin lit up the freckled face. "It's the magic."

"Aye, it surely couldn't be anything else," Conn agreed as the boy continued running down the beach, pausing just for a moment to pet the enormous head of an Irish wolfhound who'd been chasing sandpipers along the surfline.

"I know it's fanciful and totally illogical, but there *is* magic in this place," Sedona said. "Not just this beach but the entire island."

"You'd not be the first to notice that."

He took a green tartan blanket Sedona had seen displayed in the window of the mercantile from the outside pouch of the cooler and spread it out onto one of the many dunes dotting the sand. Although Sedona had assured him that being on the beach didn't make her nervous, Conn decided against telling her that these dunes had been created by a tidal wave that had swept Europe after the Lisbon earthquake of 1755.

"What can I do?" she asked.

"Just sit your lovely self down and provide me with gorgeous scenery while I lay things out."

"As if all this isn't scenery enough," she said, waving a hand to encompass the scene.

As she laughed again, Conn thought how much difference time could make. When she'd first arrived, she'd looked drawn and exhausted, with bruised, sad bags beneath eyes that had lost their sparkle.

But now the bags were gone, her eyes sparkled like a sun-spangled glaciated lake, and her face glowed with happiness. She was, in all ways, inside and out, the most beautiful woman he'd ever met.

Patrick had made them a light ploughman's lunch of slices of baked ham and rich porter cheddar cheese from Declan's farm arranged on mixed salad greens. He'd included a loaf of crusty brown soda bread and grapes. Conn had tossed in two bottles of Pirate Queen Red Ale for himself and, for Sedona, a pricey rosé from Provence, which Mrs. Monohan had assured him would be the perfect wine for a summer picnic.

"This is wonderful," she said after taking a bite of the sandwich he'd put together for her. "Did Patrick bake the ham at the pub?"

"He did. It's become quite popular, even getting a write-up in some travel guides."

"It's no wonder." Her gaze turned thoughtful as she looked out over the water. "I'll bet my friend Maddy would love to feature Brennan's on her TV show. If she came here to visit, do you think he'd be willing?"

"I think my big brother would be willing to do whatever you asked," he said. "I suspect he's fallen a bit in love with you." Conn couldn't blame him.

Nor could he blame his younger brother for his obvious infatuation. Declan had always been the quietest of the six brothers, which was probably why he'd turned to farming, where days could go by when he'd only have his cows to talk to. Still, he'd clammed up more than usual, barely managing to speak ten words the entire time they were toasting the new partnership between the pub and farm. Conn imagined Sedona had that muting effect on a great many males, which could explain why she was still single.

And wasn't he grateful for that?

"I've been in love with Patrick since that first night," she said.

Although her tone was mild, Conn felt an unwelcome spike of jealousy in his gut. "Have you now?" He poured her wine into the plastic glass Mrs. Monohan had included, then handed it to her.

"Thank you. Patrick's easy to fall in love with," she said. "He's handsome, smart, kind, warm-hearted, uncomplicated, and he really knows how to feed a woman."

"Fortunately, I'm not a jealous man, or I'd have to toss him into the lake to keep him from stealing my woman."

"You would not." She did not, Conn noted, protest his claim that she was his woman.

"It wouldn't be the first time. And before you go scolding me for living up to my brawling reputation, I feel the need to point out that he tossed me in far more times. In truth, I only managed to turn the tables and wrestle him into the water after he threw me in."

"So you both ended up wet." She took a sip of wine, then broke off a piece of brown bread.

"Aye. As did Roarke and Declan." Conn smiled broadly at the long-ago memory. "It was a grand day."

"Although I had a wonderful childhood, you and your brothers make me wish I'd had siblings."

"So you could throw a sister into the lake?"

"No. Because I envy you all your closeness." She took another sip. "This is a wonderful wine."

"Mrs. Monohan recommended it."

"That woman is a wonder. I wonder if she's ever considered writing a food blog? She has a wealth of knowledge to share in a way ordinary home cooks could easily understand. It'd undoubtedly gain attention from tourists visiting nearby towns, who'd drop into the store and then visit Brennan's for a brew and Patrick's excellent pub grub. Perhaps he could even share some of his recipes on her blog, which would benefit both their businesses...

"And how did Aidan escape the unplanned swim?"

He almost laughed at how her busy mind was already working up ways the shopkeeper could increase her business. What particularly amused him was how natural it was for her. So natural she didn't even appear aware of doing it.

"I seem to recall him being at the cinema with some comely lass from Doolin that day. Aidan has always preferred loving to fighting."

Conn waited for Sedona to mention his own Brennan black sheep womanizing reputation, but instead, she merely took another sip of wine and gazed out at a fishing boat chugging along the horizon.

"Your mother must be a strong woman," she said. "Raising six boys mostly on her own."

"Patrick did his best to shoulder a lot of the burden." And none but Declan had made it at all easy on him. Conn hadn't realized, until he'd returned to Castlelough, how much his eldest brother had sacrificed for the rest of them. "He also stayed here at home, when he could have become rich and famous himself."

"Really?" She turned back toward him. "As a chef?"

"No. As a footballer. That would be a soccer player to you."

"That's quite a sacrifice."

"It is, indeed. One the rest of us took for granted more than we should have."

"I doubt he sees it that way." She leaned forward to touch her mouth to his. All her intentions to keep the kiss and the mood light evaporated as his tongue eased between her lips and his arms went around her, pulling her against him.

The wine spilled, unnoticed, as he lowered her down onto the blanket, kissing her slowly, deeply, as if they weren't on a public beach, where anyone could walk by or watch them from the cliff above.

Noisy, squawking gulls followed a fishing boat toward the channel leading to the harbor. Offshore, a pod of dolphins dove and danced as if in celebration of the sun. Puffins, their short stubby black wings flapping furiously, leaped off the cliff and went diving deep into the sea for fish.

But neither Conn nor Sedona noticed. As her eyes closed, her mind emptied, and her body melted beneath his, Sedona let time and place drift away until there was only now. Only Conn.

Hundreds, maybe even thousands of heartbeats later, he lifted his head and smiled down at her. "To be continued," he murmured. He ducked his head again to skim the tip of his tongue over her swollen, still-tingling lips, drawing forth a ragged moan of protest that he'd stopped.

"We're about to have company." He nodded toward the cliff, where a group of laughing, shouting teenagers were clambering down the steps to the sand.

Sedona's still-dazed brain scrambled to catch up to events, even as her body continued to feel as fluid as the water that was flowing higher and higher onto the beach.

He arched a brow, devilish amusement in those electric-blue eyes. "In the meantime, did you mention something about cupcakes?"

39

THE PERFECT DAY at the beach spun out into a perfect week as Conn took her on a sightseeing trip of the Irish West.

Galway City, across the county border north of Castlelough, was a lively seaport town reminiscent of San Francisco, if that California city had boasted a sixteenth-century Spanish Arch, narrow medieval cobblestone laneways, and a plaque commemorating one of the city's most famous legends: James Lynch Fitzstephen hanging his son Walter for the murder of a Spanish sailor who'd become involved with a female family member, thus giving name to the "Lynch Law."

They spent the day strolling the streets that had provided such inspiration to Yeats and other poets and writers, stopped into shops bearing hand-painted wooden signs that reminded Sedona of Shelter Bay, stood on a stone bridge over River Corrib, watching rubber-wader-clad anglers fish for salmon, and dropped into the Nora Barnacle House, where James Joyce's lover and eventual wife had lived with her family before moving to London, where she'd met the Irish writer.

Although it was obvious that Conn was recognized everywhere they went, out here in his part of the country, it appeared an unspoken privacy zone had been agreed upon, because with the exception of an occasional nervous young musician asking to take a selfie, they were left to their holiday.

After a visit to the lush green Eyre Square Park, which had officially been renamed John F. Kennedy Park after the former president's visit to Galway, they ended the day at a seaside resort.

With the summer tourist season fully in swing, Sedona suspected he'd pulled yet more strings to book them a room, but when she worried aloud about what family he might have taken it from, he assured her that hotels always kept a few rooms on standby and it had been their good luck to snag one.

"I've always enjoyed working," she mused out loud as they watched the bustle of activity along the promenade while eating supper.

Parents pushed prams while older children ran ahead and enjoyed ice cream cones and pink cotton candy. Teenage boys tossed Frisbees and played beach volleyball, just as they did in the States, obviously trying to gain the attention of bikini-clad girls who were lying on towels, working on their tans, and giggling while pretending not to notice the boys.

"I may not have the detecting skills of Roarke, who was a military intelligence officer," Conn said, "but I figured that out watching you put together that cake. I've never seen such intense concentration."

"I wanted it perfect." *Needed* it to be perfect.

"I feel the same about my songwriting," he said, licking a bit of sauce from the barbecued ribs he'd ordered off his thumb. Which immediately had Sedona thinking about how he'd licked his way down her body just last night.

"But I've learned to give myself a break. If for no other reason than if I ever actually succeeded in achieving perfection, then I'd have to stop. Because what would be the odds of pulling such a miracle off a second time? And wouldn't it be too frustrating to try to repeat?"

"Good point." And hadn't that always been her problem? She'd stayed so busy chasing that illusive moment of perfection that was always floating just ahead of her in the mists of her mind, she'd never taken time, like she had these past days, just to take life as it was.

"Although," she said, after she'd taken a bite of a delicious local Kinvara mussel steamed in white wine and shallots and finished with cream and parsley, "this may have been as perfect a day as I've ever had in my life."

"I'm glad you've enjoyed yourself. Even if you've now set a challenge for me to finish it off just as perfectly."

"I'd be having no worries in that regard," she said, falling easily into the syntax she'd been hearing all around her.

And, as every time, not a worry was needed.

THE FOLLOWING DAY they drove through a kaleidoscope of natural beauty, past sapphire-blue lakes, vast bogs, and sculptured mountains that were the "Wild Atlantic Way."

"This is stunning," Sedona said. "And it certainly lives up to its wild billing." Which had her thinking how much freer her heart and spirit had become since she'd arrived on the island.

"The Connemara is the heart of Gaeltacht Ireland," Conn said. "It's where native people were banished to by Cromwell in the seventeenth century. It's told that one of his generals informed him that there wasn't enough wood here to hang a man, not enough water to drown him, nor enough ground to bury him.

"But we're a stubborn people, we Irish, and those banished at sword point risked their lives by continuing to speak Irish after it was officially banned. Now, of course, it's our official national language, and we owe a debt of gratitude to those who suffered such treachery.

"People around the country send their children here to stay with families during the summer in order to learn to speak it firsthand. When I was twelve, teenage twin sisters from Wexford stayed at our house for a month with their tutor. Unlike other guests, who we were only to speak to when spoken to, we were encouraged to interact with the girls." He shot her a sideways look. "Which admittedly was no hardship since they were lovely lasses with glossy black hair and gypsy dark eyes."

"You were definitely a prodigy," Sedona said with a laugh.

"I've always been able to appreciate beauty, whether it's a natural landscape like this or a lissome female. Though I was too young for them to notice me, there was a bit of a scandal when Aidan took them swimming in the lake."

"Why am I not at all surprised by that?"

"It was summer." He shrugged. "They were young and carefree, and when they returned wet and laughing, it appeared a grand time had been had by all. Though the stiff-necked tutor, who had them on the train the next morning, didn't seem to share that assessment. And Aidan did spend the next two weeks cutting peat for a local farmer to make up for the money our family lost by them leaving a week early."

And didn't that story define the Brennan brothers? Even those who might have tended to sow more wild oats than the others appeared to be responsible men. Conn had certainly proven diligent about safe sex, even that one time when things had turned hot and heavy so fast he'd interrupted long enough to take out a condom when a lesser man might have chosen to go for immediate gratification, then offered an apology afterwards.

"Your mother did a remarkably good job in raising you," Sedona said.

"I'll have to tell her you said so," he said. "Since she's accused me of being responsible for more than a few of her gray hairs."

Of that Sedona had not a single doubt.

Although a soft drizzle had begun to fall and fog was swaddling the SUV in silver mist, she couldn't resist asking him to stop at a huge stone set atop two upright stone pillars.

"It's a dolmen," he said as they approached. "A portal stone. There are over a hundred scattered here and about across the country."

She stopped about ten feet away. "Do you hear that?" It was a low humming, a bit like the sound of freeway traffic heard from a distance. Which it couldn't because, since leaving Galway behind, they hadn't come across any highways, merely these meandering roadways, many of which were barely wide enough for a single car.

"Aye. They're said to be restless souls. And although many might find it fanciful, like Castlelough's Lady, I wouldn't be disbelieving it."

"My parents once took me to Little Big Horn," she said. "That's a battleground in Montana."

"Custer's Last Stand," Conn said. "I've read of it."

"It had the same feel. As if the voices of ghosts were floating on the high plains breeze...But this would be much, much older."

"It was built, it's thought, around 3500 B.C. What you're looking at is the skeleton. When it was built, it would have been covered with earth to the capstone, and the vertical stones would frame the entrance of the tomb. This is one of the larger, with its capstone weighing in at approximately one hundred tons."

"How did they do it?" she asked. "Lift that enormous stone without any machines?"

"And isn't that the mystery?" He put his arm around her as they stood there, studying the tomb, the low hum echoing in the fog surrounding them. "And perhaps the magic."

"Other than the voices, or whatever they are, it's so quiet out here."

"That could be perhaps why they're able to be heard," he suggested. "What if spirits are always talking amongst themselves, or even to us as we go about our days, but our lives are so filled with noise we can't hear them?"

"That's an intriguing idea. Especially since, even in my quieter moments, my mind is always buzzing with thoughts." Or it had been, until this week.

"I know that feeling well. There was a time, after the band began to gain notice but before we'd become what the money people like to refer to as an 'international brand,' when, before beginning a new album, I'd steal time away from the lads, just on my own. I'd take myself off somewhere and just walk. And read. I read a lot in those days, which is probably when I learned about your General Custer.

"Whenever I feel the walls caving in, I try to walk through woods, meadows, along the sea, whatever's available, and after a few days, everything looks new to me. Fresh, as if reborn."

"And that's when you find your inspiration?"

"No. It's when I remember what I already know but had forgotten because all the bedlam surrounding me had walled me off from my instincts. That night, in the pub, I was far more interested in getting you into that bed at the inn, so I wasn't going to waste time explaining what I meant when I said I went with my gut.

"But if we hadn't been otherwise engaged, I would have told you how I believe firmly in instinct over intellect. Those times I've made a mistake I go on to regret are the same times I've listened to my head"—he tapped his temple—"rather than my heart. The silence allows me to hear my internal voice again.

"So, when I begin to write a new song, I don't spend time worrying whether or not people will like it or whether it will sell albums. I know it's going to be my thoughts, in my voice. And that's all I can hope for."

"It probably won't come as a big surprise to you that I've always gone for intellect over instinct. Knowledge over impulse."

"Spreadsheets over your feelings," he supplied.

"Exactly." And hadn't her analytical process worked well for her for many years? Until it hadn't. "I know I can't become an entirely different person."

"Leopards and spots," he agreed without a hint of judgment.

"True. But that doesn't mean that I can't open myself more so I might hear those other voices in my head." The way she was hearing the ghosts.

"That's a grand idea. Knowledge is necessary for decision-making, but I'd be betting that your instincts are informing your intellect even if you don't sense them." He brushed a kiss atop her damp head. "And now that you're opening up to them, I've no doubt those voices will be telling you what an excellent choice you've made in me."

Sedona laughed at his exaggerated brogue as they turned back toward the SUV.

A few kilometers later, she drew in a breath as they approached a huge, sprawling riverfront castle hotel surrounded by acres of wooded grounds.

"Oh. My. God. You're going to spoil me for anything less than top star luxury," she accused.

"I enjoy spoiling you," he said mildly. "The manor castle dates from the eighteenth century. I fear it's what Fergus has in mind for *Cnoc an Chairn*."

"I'm not going to worry about that today," she said. "Actually, the project is out of my hands."

He reached out and ruffled her hair. "That's what you say now. Just wait until Fergus learns the international calling code to the States."

"Not worrying," she insisted. "I'm working on my Zen, finding my bliss, whatever other clichés you might think up."

"Isn't that your best plan yet? Why don't we check into our room and get about locating your personal bliss."

As the doorman came out to retrieve their bags, Sedona couldn't imagine how making love with this man could get any more blissful than it already had been.

She was soon to be proven wrong.

40

After two days in the gloriously wild woodland solitude surrounding the Connemara, they continued up the coast to where, after hearing that Sedona had grown up riding, Conn had arranged for two horses to be waiting: a dappled gray native Connemara pony for her and to accommodate his height, a larger, black Irish Sport Horse for Conn.

They changed into the riding clothes and boots the man had brought, then rode along the beach, across green fields dotted with sunshine-yellow flowers, down curving dirt roads past cows and colorfully painted sheep. A castle on a hillside loomed over a quaint fishing village with livery posts erected in front of the brightly painted storefronts. After stopping for lunch at Molly Malone's Ale House, which offered a dazzling view of both sea and mountains, they wended their way back to the beach, riding on sugar-white sand in and out of the Caribbean-blue, crystal-clear water.

Having been away from home for so many years, Sedona had forgotten the joy of riding, the easy pace of sitting aside the pony as it walked in and out of the water. She'd moved on to a canter, not thinking about anything but the up, forward, down rhythm, her body's movements matching, becoming one with the animal beneath her. As quickly and unexpectedly as a bolt of lighting from the clear blue sky overhead, a reckless abandon struck.

"Race you to that rock and back," she challenged, clamping her legs against the gray pony's wide sides. She pointed toward a towering limestone outcropping which a circus of puffins had claimed as nesting grounds.

"You're on."

As if reveling in its freedom, the Connemara pony leaped forward in a sudden burst of speed into a headlong gallop, like an arrow released from a bow.

The pounding of racing hoofbeats on the hard, wet sand reverberated through Sedona. It was intoxicating. Thrilling. What it was, she thought, as she leaned low on the pony's neck, was *freedom*.

The sturdy animal's short legs covered a surprising amount of ground, but Sedona was not surprised when she glanced over her shoulder and saw Conn, on his much larger horse, beginning to gain on her.

Once he'd drawn even, he pulled up ever so slightly, allowing the two horses to ride neck and neck toward the rock. As hooves kicked up sand and manes flowed in the wind, Sedona felt every bit as much one with Conn as she always did when he was inside her.

At the last minute, he dug his heels into his horse's flanks and beat her, just barely, to the rock. Then guided his mount over to hers and caught hold of the reins.

"Consider yourself vanquished, lass," he said with a bold, Celtic warrior's triumphant grin. "What will you be offering as a forfeit?"

As he bent down toward her, leaning across the space between them, she wished he'd just pull her down into that foamy surf and have his wicked way with her. "I'd be offering myself."

His rough, rich laugh vibrated through her as he claimed her lips. "And isn't that a forfeit I'll gladly accept?"

STAYING WITH THE horse theme, Conn and Sedona ended their holiday with a visit to The Monohan and MacKenna Stud, where Triple Crown Winner Legends Lake (who'd been born at the stud), spent three months a year. In the interconnected way of the Irish, Kate MacKenna, Legends Lake's breeder and half owner of the stud, was close friends with the Joyce family, including Mary.

Kate and her trainer husband, Alec MacKenna, spent nine months of the year at their horse farm in Kentucky, then, once the Belmont had run, they'd return to Ireland for the summer racing season.

They spent the first day enjoying the peaceful harmony surrounding the stone house and barns where horses roamed the pasture, cropping the grass.

"I could stay here forever," Sedona said the first evening as she sat out in a garden, enjoying wine, cheese, and crackers with Conn, Kate, and Alec.

"You're welcome to stay as long as you like," Kate offered. "It's a big house, and with our daughter Zoe now grown and training horses in the States and James in law school at Trinity College, we've only Brigid and Connor at home. And being teenagers, they're often away. Especially in the summer when they're off catching up and staying with friends."

"That's both generous and tempting," Sedona said. "But I've taken enough time away from my business."

"You've had a difficult time," Kate said mildly as she leaned forward and topped off Sedona's glass. A stunningly beautiful woman in what Sedona guessed to be her early fifties, Kate had flowing black hair and eyes as deep and blue as the lake the land overlooked. She was wearing a colorful flowing skirt and tunic top that reminded Sedona of her mother. As did the aura of calm that surrounded her. "Not many could go through a storm such as the one you went through, especially after that youthful experience with a tornado, and not be left on edge."

"How did you know about that?" Since the two women were close, Mary had undoubtedly told Kate about Shelter Bay's storm. But Sedona had never mentioned the tornado to anyone.

"I'm sorry." Kate's berry-red lips twisted in a slight grimace of regret. "I'm usually much more discreet with my words. My only excuse is that I was feeling so comfortable with you they just slipped out."

"But how did you know?" Sedona pressed, exchanging a glance with Conn, who, in turn, glanced over at Alec, who merely shrugged. Obviously there was a secret here. One neither of the men appeared prepared to share.

"I'm fey," Kate said as mildly as she might have mentioned breeding horses for a living. "I see things."

"About other people?" Suddenly Sedona wasn't nearly as relaxed. Could this woman also read her mind?

"Often. Not on purpose, mind you. I'm not one to ever pry, in case you'd be wondering."

"I was," Sedona admitted.

"Of course you were." When Sedona tensed again, wondering if Kate *had* read her mind, she smiled. "It would only be expected. Especially given that I'm often referred to as Castlelough's witch, which I'm not one to mind, although my beliefs, which go back three millennia to the Celts, are not so easily defined."

"My maternal grandmother supposedly saw things." Sedona wished, yet again, that her mother were here in Ireland so she could meet Kate. "My mother insists that I inherited her talent, but I believe that's mostly hope on her part."

"Now, I'm not into arguing with a guest. But I'd have to disagree with you on that regard, which is neither here nor there, because don't we all have to find and accept our gift in our own time?

"It was passed down to me by an ancestor on my grandmother's side, Biddy Early, a healer who practiced white magic for those in the West who came to her with problems. When I was young and still dealing with the idea of what to do with such a gift, I developed a crush on Peter Quinlan, who just happened to be as handsome as an ancient king. All the girls at school dreamed of him, but I was the one he'd chosen to take to the beach."

"No surprise there," Alec said, reaching to take his wife's hand and link their fingers together.

"What happened?" Sedona asked.

"Well, just when his beautifully carved lips were a whisper from mine and we were looking into one another's eyes, I viewed little Kevin Noonan floating facedown in the surf. I'd just called out a warning to his mother, who was distracted by packing their supper things back into their picnic basket when a wave swept the toddler off his feet back into the sea."

Sedona's blood went cold. She could picture it as clearly as if she were there. Which only meant that she was overlaying her own experience with Kate's story.

"Fortunately, Mr. Noonan, who was closer to the surf and a strong swimmer, was able to reach him in time, and except for swallowing a bit of salt water, he was fine."

Not wanting to be rude to her hostess, Sedona didn't point out that Kate could have been nervous about kissing in public and had glanced around, even for a second, to see if anyone was watching. Or, perhaps, remembering her own teenage years, she'd wanted to see if any other girl might be watching her being kissed by the same boy the others could only dream about.

"You never got your kiss," she said instead.

"No. At the time I was heartbroken, even though I later accepted that he had no choice in the matter. His mother, who could give Mrs. Sheehan lessons on son smothering, had always insisted that Peter was destined to wear the red cardinal robes in Rome. Being raised in such a strictly devout home, with such expectations put upon him, he wasn't about to be caught kissing the village witch."

"But surely he knew what you were, and what others called you, when he asked you to the beach."

"He did." Her smile brightened her eyes. "Later, once my heart had unbroken itself, I understood that I represented the forbidden. And wasn't that an enticing temptation for a seventeen-year-old boy who'd always been kept beneath his mother's strong thumb?"

"You should have made a Peter voodoo doll and stuck pins in it," Conn volunteered.

Kate laughed. "We druids are not into voodoo dolls." She turned back to Sedona, her expression turning more serious. "The only reason I told the story was to explain that since I came to realize that day that there was no way to send back my inheritance, my only choice was to accept it as part of who—and what—I am. It's no different from having inherited the color of my hair and eyes. Or being left-handed."

She lifted her left hand, revealing an unconventional wedding ring created of three colored stones set in a gold Celtic woven band.

"There's also another reason Peter had no chance," Alec said. He lifted the hand he was holding to his lips. "Because destiny had already predetermined that I was the only man for Kate."

Sedona watched as man and wife shared an intimate thought. Then laughed with the others as Kate told him that she'd certainly wished she'd known that the day her fifteen-year-old self had been crying buckets of tears into her feather pillow.

Sedona's last thought, just before drifting off to sleep wrapped in Conn's arms, was that she could ask Kate if she could envision Conn Brennan in her future.

Then, not wanting to risk spoiling whatever time they had left together, Sedona decided to let destiny take its course. Wherever it might lead her.

41

Conn had mentioned a private plane their first night, but Sedona had assumed he'd merely hired a charter to take him to Germany. Despite the luxury he'd treated her to during their travels around the Irish West, he was so easy-going, so *normal*, that it was easy to overlook how wealthy he truly was.

It was only when the pilot and flight crew greeted him as if they knew him well that she realized this was no charter.

"You actually own this plane?" she asked as she settled into a glove-soft gray leather seat.

"It's the middle-size of three," he said after thanking the male flight attendant, casually dressed in pressed jeans and a polo shirt, who handed them both a printed menu with the Celtic Storm logo. "I might have been tempted to pull out the one with the separate bedroom and shower just to impress you, but unfortunately it's in Japan at the moment."

Although she'd never been star-struck, Sedona was duly impressed when he named the celebrity who'd booked the larger, more luxurious one to travel from Los Angeles to Tokyo for a movie opening.

"So much for frugality," she decided, scanning the menu, which included champagne and Irish trout caviar. Along with a selection of liquor and wine, all the beer, she noticed, was from Brennan's. Which made business sense on both a marketing and promotional basis.

"Believe it or not, each of the planes bring in a nice profit," Conn said. "Would you like to try the caviar? Despite all our streams filled with trout, we Irish don't have a history of eating the roe. But thanks to the growing local food movement, farmers have discovered that there's a market. Our trout caviar has even impressed Russians, who've begun importing it."

"You've talked me into it."

Sedona couldn't wait to call Annie and tell her about this. Her parents were well off, but for the most part, they lived as they always had. Although she'd never been a fan of fairy tales, as the flight attendant returned with a platter of caviar, crème fraîche, toasted triangle points, and slices of local smoked Irish salmon. And, of course, champagne, which Conn assured her she must have because it accentuated the flavor of the caviar.

The plates were Wedgewood, the crystal Waterford, the spoons mother-of-pearl because, the server volunteered when she mentioned it, caviar oxidizes sterling silver.

"Okay," she said after Conn had prepared her a plate and the glistening, round gold-orange beads had popped in her mouth. "This is delicious. But again, not very frugal."

"Granted. But the people who lease my planes aren't into frugality or they'd be flying commercial," he pointed out. "A bit of caviar and high-end liquor earn back their cost and much more."

"How did you happen to have a plane-leasing business in the first place?" The champagne sparkled like sunshine on her tongue.

"Ah, and wasn't that something Kate might well call a twist of destiny." He scooped more caviar onto another triangle of toast, topped it with the cream and held it out to her to bite into. Which, she considered, had her literally eating out of his hand.

"We started with a small five-seater, because we were losing so much time in airport gates and we'd have to always arrive a day early to allow for flight delays. Which, when we began doing three hundred and twenty shows a year around the world, got difficult."

"I can imagine."

"But when it was sitting idle in the Dublin hangar, it was still costing money. So, I got the idea to lease it to friends."

"That's a very clever idea."

"Coming from a woman who probably dreams of business plans, I'll be taking that as a compliment."

"It was meant as one."

"So, then we needed a larger one, so we bought this seven-seater. And although it's true we didn't actually need the model with the full bedroom, it proved a plus because I could get away and have a quiet space to write or just think about concert logistics. In that one, the lounge area seats fold down into flat beds, so each of us arrives at a new town in much better condition to perform. Especially since most of us have put the drinking and partying behind us."

Sedona decided that asking which ones hadn't moved on wasn't germane to the conversation.

"Since we couldn't be in all three at one time, and demand for leasing was escalating as commercial airline travel became more and more problematic, I went to our solicitor and had him set up a separate company. Which, as I said, pays a nice dividend, along with having transportation at my disposal whenever I need it."

"That's very clever. Plus, with the larger one, you essentially have a flying hotel room." How many women had slept in that bed with him? Although it was none of her business, Sedona couldn't help wondering.

"I never took a woman to bed on the plane," he answered the question she hadn't let herself ask. "It wouldn't have been respectful of her, the lads, or the flight crew."

Sedona knew she was getting in deeper every moment she spent with him when that assertion caused a cooling relief to wash over her. "I'll say this for you, Conn Brennan," she said as she lifted her glass to him, "you're turning out to be one surprise after another."

He lifted his glass to hers. "As are you, *a stór*."

THE SHELBOURNE'S PALATIAL brick facade, colonnaded entrance, and intricately fashioned wrought iron fence was Dublin's Victorian grande dame and, some curmudgeons might suggest, a monument to the excesses of the Victorian age. Having discovered how hard Conn worked for his money and how much thought he gave to the handling of his millions, as the top-hatted doorman carried their bags into the even grander foyer, Sedona wasn't about to fault him for his extravagance. Or his taste. Because despite the gleaming marble floors, crystal chandeliers, more columns, gold gilding, and intricate moldings, the hotel had managed to keep up with the times and be both sophisticated and modern.

As the desk clerk greeted him with a friendly familiarity, she wondered what it must feel like for a man who'd come from a small village on the West Irish coast to be able to stroll into such a place and be treated as if he belonged. For many, such privilege would go to their heads. Which didn't seem to be the case with Conn.

And while he seemed perfectly at ease in his faded jeans and black T-shirt, Sedona felt underdressed in her black-and-white-striped sleeveless blouse, summer white cotton capris, and red flats.

They'd no sooner entered the white-and-gold-decorated Princess Grace Suite—which, at fifteen hundred and thirty square feet was larger than Sedona's apartment back in Shelter Bay and came with its own butler who'd discreetly left them alone—when Conn's phone rang. While he took the call, she checked out the stunning marble master bath with double vanities and a couch. She was imagining making love to Conn in that oversized shower when he appeared in the doorway.

"I was just thinking of you," she said. "I usually unpack the moment I arrive in a hotel room." The butler had offered to do her unpacking, but Sedona had declined the service, deciding that having a man she didn't know put away her underwear was too weird.

"Now why doesn't that surprise me?" Conn asked with a quirk of his lips.

"I've no idea." She tossed her head. "Anyway, I was thinking that you might like to try out that shower. Before our tea."

"There's nothing I'd like more." When his faint smile faded, she looked closer and saw the shadow in his eyes. "But that call was from my mother."

"Is she all right?"

"Yes. As far as I know. But she said it was important that she speak to me before our dinner tonight and asked if I'd mind coming over to her friend's flat. Which isn't far from here."

"That sounds serious."

"It does. Which is the only reason I'm even asking if you'd mind if I were to leave for a bit."

"Of course not." Sedona's first thought was that the mystery friend would turn out to be male, in which case it only made sense Eileen Brennan would want to avoid springing any romantic relationship on her son in public. "I should unpack, anyway."

This time his smile was broad. And rakish. "So you'll be saving the shower for me?"

"I wouldn't take one without you." She crossed the small space between them, went up on her toes, and kissed him. "Now, be gone with you." She made a shooing motion with her hand. "The sooner you leave, the sooner you'll be back to get wet with me."

"That image is going to stay with me the entire time I'm gone."

"And isn't that what it's supposed to do?"

Once he'd left, Sedona unpacked the clothes she'd brought for tonight, grateful that her admittedly occasional over-planning had her arrive in Ireland prepared for whatever might come up. Years of attending business conferences had taught her the art of combining a few pieces into a wardrobe that would work for any occasion over several days. The underwear she'd been reluctant to have the butler put away were admittedly bought at Shelter Bay's Oh, So Fancy lingerie boutique after Mary had asked her to go to Ireland. Not that she'd been planning to have sex with Conn. But it never hurt to be prepared.

42

CONN'S MOTHER OPENED the red door of her friend's townhouse, and if he hadn't known her all of his life, Conn would have had to recheck the address on the side of the building to make sure he'd come to the right location.

Her hair, which she usually wore up but fell below her shoulders when loosened, had been cut and styled into a short bob. The silver streaks had been turned into a bright burgundy. She was wearing a purple sweater and black leggings that stopped mid-calf, eyes shone like emeralds, and high pink color brightened her cheekbones as she threw her arms around him and welcomed him with an enthusiasm that would have had strangers thinking it had been weeks, months, or even years since they'd last seen each other.

"You look amazing," Conn said. "And happy."

"I am. I'm even more happy now that you're here," she said, taking him by the hand and leading him into the two-story foyer, down a short hallway into a wood-paneled room that could have been a Georgian Irish gentleman's library. Or, in this case, Conn thought, taking in the books that not only overflowed the shelves but were piled on the desk, side tables, and even the floor, a writer's office.

A tall man wearing a black sweater and gray slacks was standing by the desk, looking far more hesitant than Conn's mother about this meeting. Conn's first thought was a lack of surprise that the house was owned by a man. That explained the way she'd been less than open about her friend during the breakfast when she'd announced her plans.

His second thought was that he knew this fifty-something man his mother introduced as Dennis Byrne. "You interviewed me."

The man's smile warmed his blue eyes. "I did, indeed. A very long time ago. I'm surprised you remember."

"I'd not be forgetting my first interview in *Celtic Music Scene* magazine." The magazine was, after all, the country's equivalent of *Rolling Stone*. "Especially when you were the first to predict I'd be a superstar."

"And wasn't that a prediction that came true?" the older man said. "Could I get you something to drink?"

"I'm grand." Conn slipped his hands into his jeans. Despite his mother's dazzling smile and Dennis Byrne's easy manner, a tension was humming in the air. Like a low ohm tuning fork. "I have a rule about not drinking before a performance."

"That's undoubtedly wise." Byrne's comment had Conn also remembering he hadn't exactly been entirely sober during the interview in the magazine's conference room.

Conn turned toward his mother. Who, he noticed, was squeezing her hands together so tightly her knuckles had turned white as bone. As he looked between the two, every instinct he possessed kicked in, and he knew why he'd been asked here.

"You've known my mother a long time," he said.

"Nearly thirty-one years," Byrne confirmed. "I was researching old native Celtic tunes that had stayed alive because of those who'd refused to obey the ban during the bad times."

"That wasn't all you did while in Castlelough." Conn had the answer he'd been wanting ever since that deathbed statement from the man he'd grown up believing to be his father. Now he couldn't decide how he was supposed to feel.

"No." Dennis held out his hand to Eileen, who took it. "I fell in love with your mother."

"And I with Dennis," Eileen said, lifting her still-firm chin as if expecting censure for that declaration.

Conn met Byrne's gaze. "I have your eyes."

"You do. When you walked into the magazine's offices that morning, it was like looking in a mirror. Though"—he glanced over at Conn's mother—"thanks to this one's genes, you're much handsomer."

Compliments weren't going to cut it. Conn fucking wanted answers.

"Yet you left. And stayed away all these years." Could *he* ever abandon his own child? Never.

"Only because I begged him to," Eileen said. "It wasn't Dennis's choice, and we argued about that our last night together. I wasn't going to be getting a divorce. At the time it wasn't allowed, and later…"

She shrugged. "I'd made my bed. It was up to me to lie in it. I could have easily lived with people calling me names, but I had you boys to think about."

"That's a sacrifice none of us would have expected." Deciding it would make no difference now, Conn resisted pointing out the years of pain that would have been prevented if she had left Brennan. But then, on the other hand—and wasn't there always another damn hand?—Declan wouldn't have been born. Which would have been a loss to the family she'd been struggling to keep intact.

"It's a decision that wasn't yours to make," she countered, proving yet again the steely strength he'd admired over his thirty years. "Dennis told me he'd wait. I had no idea, until he showed up at the door the night of the funeral, how sincerely he meant those words."

"With every fiber of my being," Byrne said emphatically. His expression as he looked down at Conn's mother was as warm and open as any a man had ever shared with a woman. It was, Conn realized, the same way he felt when he looked at Sedona.

"Yet you met me," he said to Byrne. "And didn't say a word."

"I'd promised your mother, and you should know, interviewing you wasn't my choice. It was an assignment given to me, which I admittedly knew I should turn down." He held out his hands, palms up, as in supplication. "But I proved weak and couldn't resist an opportunity to meet you. I needed to see if my suspicions regarding your parentage were true."

Another surprise. As comprehension struck, Conn turned back toward his mother. "You didn't tell him?" His tone, which he instantly regretted, was harsher, colder than he'd ever before used with her.

"No." She briefly closed her eyes. Was she regretting her decision that had altered all their lives? "Because I firmly believed that it would be better for everyone involved, most of all you, who'd have been branded a bastard, if I kept my secret."

A secret that had caused them all unnecessary years of pain. As pent-down resentment threatened to flare from an ember into a flame, Conn remembered Kate's words about destiny. It was possible, hell, *probable*, that if he'd discovered the truth about his father back when he was young, angry, and reckless, his reaction could have broken his family apart.

"That attempt failed," Conn said. "Given that many have used that same word to describe me." And hadn't he, on all of those occasions, wished that it were true.

"It's not the same," Eileen said weakly. The color that had been blooming in her cheeks when he'd arrived had turned to chalk.

"You never interviewed me again," he said to this man who gave Conn an idea what he, himself, would look like in thirty years.

"No. I had many opportunities to do a follow-up to that original one, but I avoided them," Byrne said. "Not because I wasn't interested in your future, because I was, but because my strong personal desire to spend even the smallest amount of stolen time with my son wasn't as important as keeping my word to your mother."

Considering how many couples had been openly living together without marriage in the years when divorce from original spouses wasn't an option, Conn believed his mother had worried too much about what others thought. Then again, he understood she had a business to protect, due to the B&B providing income to the family.

Of course, another voice in his head argued, if she'd just left Castlelough and taken off to Dublin with her lover, they could have started a new life in a city where their every move and word wouldn't have provided gossip.

Bygones, he thought, remembering Kate's story of meeting Alec MacKenna. If his mother, brothers, and he had moved to Dublin, he might not have grown close to Mary. Which would mean that he wouldn't have played at her wedding, which, in turn, would have prevented him from meeting Mary's wedding cake baker.

"I felt a connection, a kinship, when we first met," Conn said, remembering that day clearly. Wanting to look like Celtic Storm was a real band, not a bunch of ragtag country kids trying to make music, he'd bought a blue-and-green-tartan tie at a Dublin flea market to wear to the interview. "I decided it was because we shared the same interest in music."

"It was more than that," Byrne said. "I didn't want to mention it at the time, but I'd played with The Clancy Brothers."

"You did?" Conn ran through the list of Clancy family members who'd played with Ireland's first internationally famous band. They'd definitely gone through some roller coaster times, but he didn't remember a Dennis Byrne.

"Oh, it was only a couple appearances. I was a casual mate of Bobby Clancy's son Finbarr, who'd joined the group and he brought me in to play the accordion. But since I came off sounding like a cat in heat screaming on a fence, we all agreed that I was better off writing about music than playing it."

Conn laughed at that, even as he realized that since he was the only musical person in the Brennan family, at least that he knew of, just as Kate claimed to have inherited her gift from her ancestor Biddy Early, his had, indeed, come from this man.

"My family's always had a connection to music in some way," Dennis—Conn was now thinking of him in first-name terms—said. "So it's possible that your talent came from my bloodline. But it's *you* who enhanced and elevated it far beyond anything any of the Byrnes, past and present, could achieve."

A pregnant silence settled over the cluttered wood-paneled room as all three of them seemed to be taking in the fact that they'd come together as a family. While his brothers—who'd turned out to be half-brothers—would always be one hundred percent the true brothers of his heart, Conn also knew that from this day forward, the three of them here in this room would be forging their own bond.

Eileen was the one to finally break the silence. "I think we should all have tea."

And wasn't that her answer for everything? As she left to bring in the tray she'd undoubtedly already prepared, Conn realized that Sedona didn't just remind him of his best friend. But his mother, as well. Both of whom were, until he'd met the woman waiting for him at the Shelbourne, the only two women he'd ever loved.

And now, like the trinity he'd been taught in Holy Child School, and the leaves of his nation's symbolic shamrock, there were three.

43

SEDONA WAS WATCHING the marble mantel clock, impatiently waiting for Conn to return when her phone started playing "Memories." Sedona had selected the song from Annie's store's name as a ringtone.

"If you can't talk, I'll hang up in a sec," Annie said. "I just have some important news."

"What are you doing up so early?"

"I was so excited I couldn't sleep, so I finally just decided to call you...The zoning board refused to give Bondurant his condo permit."

"So he's going to build an inn, instead?"

"No. I was at the final hearing when he actually showed up in person instead of sending his weasel minion. After all the comments from townspeople, he got huffily egocentric and declared that if he wasn't granted the permit for the condo, he was going to wash his hands of a backwards, stuck-in-the-past fishing town that would only tarnish his high-profile reputation for excellence."

"Ha." Sedona laughed. "The man's ego has always outsized Mt. Hood. So, what's going to happen to the block?"

"That's the exciting thing. Gabriel Lombardi's buying it."

"Gabriel? But he's a wine guy."

"True. But apparently Lombardi Winery's been diversified into Oregon property management outside wine country. He said he's always enjoyed visiting Shelter Bay, and when the opportunity came up, he jumped at it. He's redoing the entire block while maintaining the seaside look. And Marcy called last evening and said that he'd love to have you build out to expand into the space next door. Which would increase your kitchen area, along with more outdoor service space."

"Wow."

And hadn't this news come from out of the blue? After she'd lost her lease, Sedona had been too overwhelmed and depressed to think about what she wanted to do about rebuilding Take the Cake. Then, once she'd gotten here and started working with Conn, and especially during their holiday, all thoughts of business had evaporated from her mind.

Conn Brennan was the only man she'd ever had sex with who could make her stop thinking. Unfortunately, they couldn't spend all their time on vacation or in bed. Especially now that reality had come crashing back into her life.

"You don't sound as if you're doing the happy dance," Annie said. They'd been friends long enough she could catch the nuance in Sedona's single-word response. "I thought this was what you wanted. What you'd been planning for since before the storm."

"It was."

"And now?"

"I honestly don't know."

"Because of your hot Irish rocker?"

"Again, I don't know. Maybe it's because he's so different. Maybe because it's just the best sex I've ever had. And probably ever will have...Maybe because our time together hasn't seemed quite real. More like visiting Brigadoon. Maybe it's not meant to last."

"I can't believe I have to be the voice of logic in this conversation," Annie huffed. "In the first place, Brigadoon was in Scotland and only appeared for one day every hundred years. You've been there over three weeks."

"Which isn't that much in the whole scheme of things."

"It probably depends on the people and the situation," Annie argued. "And by the way, although you tossed it off, I didn't miss that comment about the sex. Is it really that good?"

"Better." Sedona sighed. "But Conn's already setting down roots here. Roots that involve so many others he can't just pick up and leave to follow me back to Shelter Bay. And you know how I feel about long-distance relationships."

"It's about time you had great sex. So, yay for that. But I can also tell that you're going to start making lists of pros and cons."

"Of course I am," Sedona said, a bit dispiritedly. As Conn had pointed out, leopards weren't known for changing their spots.

"Of course you are," Annie echoed. "So, while you're making those columns, don't forget that at the ending of *Brigadoon*, Mr. Lundie appears to a distraught Tommy and tells him that when you love someone deeply enough, anything's possible. Even miracles. Then they disappear off into the Highland mist so Tommy can be reunited with his beloved Fiona to live happily ever after."

"*Brigadoon's* fictional."

"You're the one who brought it up," Annie shot back. "And now who's being too logical? Besides, fictional or not, the part about love is absolutely true. Mac and I are all the proof I need of that."

"I'll think about it," Sedona said. "On the flight home after tonight's concert."

"You do that. And Sedona?"

"Yes?"

"Don't keep Conn in the dark while you're thinking. Tell him what's happened because it sounds as if he's earned a chance to weigh in."

"I don't want to tell him before the concert."

"See?" Annie crowed. "You just admitted the idea of you returning to Shelter Bay would distract him. Which means you know, in your heart of hearts, that he cares."

Hearing that accusation out loud, Sedona couldn't deny it.

"I'll tell him in the morning," she said. After what might possibly be their last night together. "On the flight back to Castlelough."

44

CONN HAD NO sooner returned to the hotel than one of the receptionists came out from behind the counter as he passed on his way to the elevators.

"I hate to disturb you, Mr. Brennan—"

"No problem. What can I do for you?"

"A Mr. Hennessy showed up to speak with you about ten minutes ago. He said he's your solicitor, but one never knows for certain about such things, and the Shelbourne has always been diligent about respecting our guests' privacy. When I couldn't confirm you were staying here, he asked me to tell you that he'd be in the Horseshoe Bar."

"Thank you, Tara. I appreciate your diligence."

Wondering what was important enough to drag Brendan Hennessy out of his glass Grand Canal Square office building, Conn walked into the dimly lit, dark red-walled pub. When he spotted Brendan, not at the horseshoe-shaped bar that that had given the pub its name but in a leather booth at the far, dimmer corner of the room, he realized that his lawyer hadn't come here today to see about complimentary concert tickets.

"I'd think that the only reason for you being here is that you'd have missed having a pint with me while I've been away in the West," he said in greeting. "If it weren't for the fact that you've moved up to drinking whiskey."

"You might want to, as well, when you hear what I'm about to tell you."

"You know I don't drink before a performance." Conn slid into the booth. "And it can't be that bad that you'd bring it to me hours before I'm due to go on stage."

"I would have waited. But some business reporter from the *Independent* rang me with a story he's about to break."

"If it's about my buying the Guinness warehouse, that's old news."

"It's about Diarmuid."

"What about him?"

"He left the city last week. Apparently to go tend to his mother, who'd been taken to hospital with a stroke."

"I'm sorry. I also wish someone had thought to ring me." If he'd gotten a call from his longest friend other than his brothers, he definitely would have answered.

"The message on your phone said you were on holiday and not to disturb you unless it was a matter of life or death. Since no one had gotten word that her condition had worsened, the lads and I decided it could wait until you arrived in town for the concert."

"And this is what drove you to drink? Did she die?"

"No. She's quite well, actually. Or was when she called my office three days ago to ask if I knew how to get hold of Diarmuid. Apparently she's been trying to contact him for the past week. She's in Italy and late with the rent on a house she's been living in for the summer. She was hoping he could wire her some funds before she's tossed out into the street."

"Perhaps he's on holiday himself," Conn suggested.

"That's what I was thinking. Until I received a visit yesterday afternoon from two grim-faced men from Revenue's investigation and prosecution division."

"What would the tax cops be doing visiting you?"

"It seems they contacted Diarmuid two weeks ago regarding some irregularities in the income on ticket sales on last year's tour. He assured them that he'd send in receipts to be audited."

Conn had never considered himself a coward. Yet he would guess that anyone, anywhere in the world, would experience cold fingers of fear on the back of the neck to hear that they were about to undergo a tax audit.

"How much income are we talking about?"

"Close to a million. And change."

"Fuck me!" Conn's raised voice drew interest from a trio of businessmen seated at the white-topped bar. He immediately lowered his voice. "It has to be a mistake."

"That's what I told them. They gave me a copy of the paperwork and I had my accountants examine them. We didn't have time to do an in-depth audit, but from the irregularities we found on the receipts from this latest tour, he was definitely skimming significant profits at least going back to last year. Which explains how his mother could afford to be summering at a villa in Tuscany."

"Could he have been playing dodgy with the books even earlier?"

"I wouldn't be at all surprised." The solicitor dragged his hand through his dark red curls. "I could so use a cigarette. Damn the bloody government for banning smoking even in pubs."

"That was over a decade ago. Long enough that I'd gotten so I hadn't missed it. Until now." Conn scrubbed both hands down his face. "You'll need to call Revenue. Tell them we're working on it and ask for an extension to uncover the extent of the problem."

"I've already done that," he said. "Fortunately, it turns out that you visited one of the investigator's daughter last year when she was a heart surgery patient at Our Lady's Children's Hospital."

"I remember her," Conn said. "Four-year-old Erin McIntyre?"

"That would be her."

"She was a precious tyke with curly red hair and a face that could have belonged to a cherub on the ceiling of Holy Family Church. I've wondered how she's doing."

"Her father reports her new valve is working perfectly, and she still has the teddy bear you brought her." The teddy bear had been wearing a shamrock-printed dress and green hair bow. The woman in the shop where Conn had bought it had willingly sewn a bright red heart onto the front of the dress.

"Well, that's some good news for the day. I'm pleased to hear it."

"So was I. Especially since, I'm sure due to your act of kindness, he's agreed to give us a bit more time to get our ducks in a row...Unfortunately, that's the only spot of good news. One of the investigators on my staff, who specialized in financial crimes when he was in the guards, uncovered the fact that Diarmuid bought a plane ticket to Rio de Janeiro. One-way."

"He's gone on the lam, as the thrillers might put it," Conn muttered.

"It appears he has. And perhaps he took those films too literally, because while Ireland might not have an extradition treaty with Brazil, didn't that country send Michael Lynn, the archetypal prince of the Celtic boom who fled with debts of eighty million Euros back here to stand trial for fleecing his investors?"

"It's not the money," Conn said. "I've got enough to cover whatever's owed. It's the fact that I thought we were best friends."

"The news is going to hit big," Brendan warned. "Like Lennon and McCartney breaking up."

"That was a personality conflict. Even Lennon called it a divorce. Granted, it got nasty, but neither of them out-and-out stole money from the other. When's the news story going to come out?"

"I told the reporter if he held off for a day, so as not to take attention away from hungry children the focus should be on tonight, that you'll do an exclusive interview before you leave to go back west tomorrow."

"Not that I can tell him anything at this point," Conn said. "He probably knows more than I do." He drew in a deep breath. Heaved it out. "Well, there's nothing else I can do at this time. Of course you'll have to be handing over the records to the Revenue. But I'll need your people to go through every line with a fine-tooth comb. Start with the year being challenged. Then this year. Next you can start working your way back."

"We'll do that."

"And make sure Diarmuid's name is taken off all bank accounts."

"That's already been done."

When the solicitor tossed back the last of the whiskey, Conn almost wished he hadn't taken a vow about drinking before performances. But with the anger bubbling hot lava inside him, he didn't dare take a drink. Because one would lead to another. Then another. And there he'd be, drunk on his arse during a concert that would be watched all over the world. Which was not an option.

"Well, it sounds as if you have things under control. Thanks, Brendan." He held out his hand. "There's no one I'd rather have handling this affair, which I know couldn't have been easy for you to break the news."

"I'd rather drink drain cleaner," Brendan said as he clasped both his hands around Conn's.

That earned a rough laugh. "In all the years we've worked together, that's the first bit of Irish exaggeration I've ever heard from you. But don't worry. Haven't we survived a great deal together since you first took on an unknown ragtag group of musicians? We'll get through this, as well."

Conn patted Brendan on the shoulder of the charcoal-gray Brioni suit, which he knew had been hand-tailored to duplicate the one Daniel Craig had worn in *Skyfall*. Once, back in the days when they'd both been younger and had drunk more, the lawyer had admitted he always wore striped suits because that's what James Bond had worn ever since *From Russia With Love*. Suggesting, Conn thought as he left the bar, that every man had his fantasies.

And despite Diarmuid's treacherous disloyalty, as he got into the elevator, Conn felt like the luckiest man on the planet. Because *his* personal fantasy just happened to be waiting for him upstairs.

45

SEDONA SENSED THE simmering tension the moment Conn entered the suite. "Can I get you something?" she asked. "Tea? Coffee? This place is more equipped than my apartment." Former apartment, she reminded herself. But it could be again. Even bigger and better. "There are also soft drinks and both still and bubbly mineral water in the fridge."

"I'm grand, thanks."

Which was a lie. He'd returned from his meeting in a dark brood. With their futures seemingly at cross purposes, Sedona knew that if she and Conn were to have any future with each other, they'd both have to be completely honest with one another.

"Do you realize that you Irish use the word *grand* as a multipurpose adjective? It can mean spectacular, good, just okay, or *I don't want to talk about it.*" She folded her arms. "Which case fits this conversation?"

He rubbed his sexily stubbled jaw. "Your mother may be right. About you inheriting your grandmother's gift." He did not sound at all pleased by that idea.

"You're discounting the possibility that I'm more than capable of using logic. You went off to an unplanned meeting with your mother, who, more than thirty years ago made love with another man, which resulted in your conception. A fact about your birth she, for whatever reason, failed to tell you. Did she share her secret today?"

"She did."

"And was it her friend? The mystery one she's staying with?"

"It was. And I'd tell you that the meeting went grand, but, you're right, that's a catch-all phrase. In truth, the situation was uncomfortable as hell in the beginning but ended well enough. I'll also share the details, at least the ones I know, but right now, if you don't mind, since today's unexpected events have me running late and I'm due at the hall for a sound check, I hope you won't mind if we postpone our tea in the Lord Mayor's Lounge."

"Of course I don't mind." Sedona didn't think it wise to mention that they might have to postpone it for a very long time if she took Gabriel Lombardi up on his offer to expand her rental space on Harborview.

"Good. Because I want you. Naked and beneath me. Screaming my name. Right. Now."

His tone was rough. Harsh not merely with lust but with pain.

Something else had happened while he was gone. Something he wasn't yet prepared to tell her. But Sedona was, by nature, a fixer. And at this moment all she could think about was doing whatever she could, giving him whatever he needed, to fill the dark, lethal place in his heart he'd returned with.

She was drowning in those stormy blue eyes and had not a single desire to be rescued. "Now," she said.

Before she'd even gotten the word out, he cursed, then as one large hand palmed her head, he crushed his mouth to hers. He didn't tempt. Nor tease. Without the finesse she'd come to expect, his tongue plunged deep, hard, filling her. His teeth grazed hers as he backed her against the wall, cradling her legs between his muscled thighs.

Sedona felt a raw rush of need as he tore her blouse open, sending buttons flying. Then unhooked her bra with a quick flick and filled his hands with her. Gasping against his plundering mouth, she arched her back, offering him more. Offering everything.

There were no tender touches. No murmured words of endearment. No gentle kisses luring her into the mists. The testosterone-driven hunger driving her into the flames was savage, possessive. And thrilling, as he dragged her down to the floor and with teeth and tongue on her bared breasts, created a hot, primitive bloodbeat that flowed through her veins.

"Say it," he said, one hand fisting her hair as the fingers of his other dug into her waist. "Tell me you want this."

"I want *you*," she moaned as the tension coiled inside her. She was about to come from his strong, harsh voice. "Please." She lifted her hips as she felt the zipper lowering. "Take me."

With a primitive grunt that had her imagining being ravished by a caveman on animal skins as flames from the fire created dancing shadows on stone walls, he stripped off her capris, then cupped her.

"You're wet for me." He stroked a thumb over the soaked ivory of the thong she'd bought in hopes that he'd be taking it off her. Little more than a postage-sized triangle, it only took a tug of the ribbons at her hips to completely expose her to the blue flames of his eyes.

"Always," she gasped as he spread his hand on her inner thigh, and with his gaze intent on his motions, he stroked her. Again. And again. And again, increasing the pressure until she was writhing beneath him, on the verge of coming.

"Not yet," he said.

She heard herself whimper as he took that gloriously treacherous hand away to retrieve a condom from his back pocket of his jeans and unzipped them. Transfixed, she watched and waited as he ripped the package open and rolled it on.

And then she was pinned between the gold carpeting and his still fully clothed body as he surged into her, filling her in one strong thrust that caused her vision to blur at the edges. Her nails digging into his shoulders, she yielded to him, her entire world narrowing down to this place. This moment. This man.

She could barely drag air into her lungs as his strokes went deeper. Faster. Wrapping her legs around his hips, she opened to him completely, matching his rhythm as he took everything she gave. Tension coiled tighter as she raced with him, on and on, and on, her brain fogged, her body taking on a mind of its own, demanding even as it surrendered still more.

"Look at me, Sedona...I want to watch you when you scream my name." His raw growl, along with the erotic feel of him pulsing as he buried himself deep inside her and reached a shuddering release, had her screaming his name as she shattered.

While she lay there beneath him, damp, boneless, and entirely defenseless, he left just long enough to dispense with the condom, then returned to lie on the carpet beside her and touched his lips to her hair. "You are the most stunning woman I've ever met."

Although she still couldn't quite summon the strength to open her eyes, her brain did click in enough to manage a faint smile. "You're not so bad yourself."

"Should I apologize?" He trailed his fingers down her thigh, which she knew would show bruising by this evening.

That had her opening her eyes. "Never." Her still-limp arm felt as if it were levitating as it lifted to the side of his face. Her thumb brushed against his frowning lips. "I can, admittedly, be a bit of a control freak."

She felt his lips curve beneath her touch. "Are you now? I never would have guessed."

He'd made her ache. Burn. He'd also taught her she could fly, and at this moment, although she had something serious she needed to say, he'd made her laugh. "My point is that it's different with you. I never would've imagined it, but it's exciting to sometimes surrender control."

"It's exciting to me when you do." He drew her caressing thumb into his mouth and sucked deeply, revealing a never-before-realized direct connection from Sedona's left thumb to that wet, still-tingling place between her legs. "Maybe I should have Bram build a soundproofed room in the loft flat. For you to play shy young virgin to my kinky billionaire."

Oh, God. Could her life get more complicated? Conn had, apparently, moved their relationship to a level where he was picturing her being with him in that Guinness warehouse loft. Which just yesterday, she probably would have agreed to without a moment's hesitation. But that was before Annie's call that could turn her world upside down yet again.

They had to talk about it. Soon. But not now. Not when Conn had a concert to perform and a potentially uncomfortable dinner with his mother and birth father to get through.

"Ha," she said. "Wouldn't you be surprised if I took you up on that idea?" She slipped her right hand beneath his shirt to play with the dark arrowing of chest hair between his pecs. "Or perhaps we should turn the tables and I could be the billionaire's dominatrix." She playfully pinched his nipple, causing him to suck in a breath.

"Any time you want to show up in a black leather corset and thigh high stiletto boots, luv, you can count me in."

The shadows had lifted from his eyes, replaced by a sexy glint. The same way he could make her stop thinking, it seemed that she could lift him out of that dark place he'd disappear into from time to time.

They were good together, Sedona thought, putting that down on the plus side of her mental ledger sheet. The same way he'd trusted her enough to share the painful story of his birth secret, she, in turn, trusted Conn to take her places she'd never before imagined. As much as she'd admired her friends' relationships—Annie and Mac, Mary and J.T., Maddy and Lucas, and especially Kara and Sax, who still acted like sex bunny newlyweds—she'd never truly understood the depth of their relationships.

Conn had been right when he'd told her that there was more to their connection than just hook-up sex. But did they have what it took to last? Or was this just a hot, enjoyable summer fling, destined to last as long as a sandcastle and tan lines?

"Did you say something about a shower?" Conn asked, pulling her out of her tumbling thoughts.

She could have stayed just where she was forever. But unfortunately, it was time to return to reality. "That's right. You need to leave soon."

He lowered his lips to hers in a lingering kiss so sweetly tender it brought tears to her eyes. His brow furrowed. "I'm sorry. I could have the lads do the sound check."

"No," she said. "It's not that. I'm just feeling emotional right now."

"Good emotional?" Frowning now, he brushed away a runaway tear shining on her bottom lashes. "Or bad?"

"All good," she assured him. Okay, it was a lie. But only a white one. And, she told herself, for a good reason.

"Well, then. Let's get wet together, and this time I'll let you have your wicked way with me."

After taking hold of her hand to bring her to her feet as he stood up, he lifted her into his arms and carried her out of the suite's living room to the bathroom, where, as the hot water rained down, sluicing over their bodies, Sedona's brain stopped thinking as she proceeded to prove exactly how wicked, with the right inspiration, she could be.

46

ALTHOUGH IT WAS still more than two hours until show time, crowds had already gathered on the other side of the barricades outside the arena overlooking the River Liffey. Being a rock star, Conn had discovered, was living a paradox. On one hand it was gratifying, after the early years of struggling and buying cut-priced leftovers at restaurant back doors at the end of the night, to have people the world over love him solely for the entertainment and pleasure his music brought them.

On the other hand, the side of him that required some zone of privacy had an aversion to that aspect of fame. Whenever he wanted to just stuff the whole thing and walk away, he reminded himself how hard he and his band had worked on not just every single album but their entire career. Because another dirty secret no one told you when you started out was that the music business was a big frenzy of sharks, and if you didn't keep swimming forward, you'd be ripped apart by the other larger, more predatory sharks.

So, he'd reach out, sign autographs for the fans that queued up outside a venue, show up on the chat shows, travel the world, always working on building a bigger and bigger audience even as an equally strong part of him wanted to pull away.

Which was why he'd bought the warehouse. Why he was getting more into producing. And why, although he knew it probably wouldn't go over all that well with his band mates, he wanted to take more time to build a single career. It wasn't that he didn't want to share the fame and money. What he didn't want to risk bringing down on the others was the stench of failure. He was wealthy enough that he could afford to put out something not mainstream enough to appeal to the masses. Too edgy, perhaps, or too different to receive rave reviews from the critics.

But the lads, for the most part, were content with their music and their lives, so, not wanting to end in a breakup with bitter feelings, like the Beatles or Simon & Garfunkel, bifurcation only made sense.

Conn wasn't naive. He knew there'd still be conflicts, but every instinct he possessed assured him that this was a compromise that would allow him the privacy he needed while keeping him in the game.

In no mood to interact with screaming fans tonight, given what he was about to do, he decided that he'd have to initially disappoint those already queued up outside the arena and pull off a pop star ninja move by using the back entrance. Even then, before he got to the dressing room, three different gardai held out programs, requesting autographs.

Since the others hadn't arrived yet, he worked with the arena crew to make certain those in the top of the horseshoe-shaped tiered seats would be able to hear him as well as the fans who'd paid the big bucks to sit on the floor in front of the stage. Fortunately, the acoustics, like everything else about this arena, which was one of his favorite places to perform, were as close to perfect as possible, giving Conn one less thing to worry about.

Which also gave him time to place a call to Castlelough.

"Why are you calling me for a favor?" Roarke asked.

"Because Patrick's busy with the pub and working out the new farming plan with Declan. And you're the best of all of us when it comes to planning a secret mission."

"You've piqued my interest."

"I thought I might." In truth, Conn *knew* how to appeal to his older brother's ego. Which was easy when his statement was true.

"First tell me if you've seen our mother yet," Roarke said.

"I have. I also met my father."

"I *knew* the mystery friend was a man. And that she was holding something back."

"She was. I suspect because she wanted privacy to see if their feelings and connection had changed over time. It was obvious the minute I entered the room that the bond was still there. I'll tell you and the others all the details when I get back home. But I need you to do this one thing for me."

"Leave it to you to go for full-out extravagance," Roarke muttered after Conn had shared his plan.

"You obviously have spent too much time in war zones. Extravagance would have been fireworks over the Eiffel Tower." Which, at one time in his life, he might have considered. "Can you pull it off? By tomorrow evening?"

"Is the Pope Catholic? Don't worry, it'll get done. Now go rock their socks off and do the family proud."

Next to Declan, Roarke had always been the least talkative. Which, Conn considered, was probably a necessary attribute to have in the spy business. He was just wondering if he should have called Mary and asked her to double-check with his brother on the details of the plan, when the dressing room door opened and the other three members of Celtic Storm burst in and the moment passed.

CONN HAD ARRANGED for a car to take Sedona to the arena. The driver, she discovered as they made their way through the city to the dock area, was also part of the band's security team who'd be staying with her during the concert.

"That's really not necessary," she said. "I'm perfectly capable of taking care of myself for a couple hours."

"I'm sorry, miss," he said, meeting her gaze in the rearview mirror. "But I have my orders. But don't concern yourself. You won't even know I'm there." Since the man was the size of a Coke machine, Sedona sincerely doubted that, but she also knew it was futile to argue.

"Well, if we're going to be together for the evening, my name is Sedona. And yours is?"

"Brian, miss."

"Sedona," she reminded him. Although she hadn't given it any thought, of course Conn would have a security team. Which, along with the private planes, the hired man who'd shown up on that remote beach with horses and riding apparel, and the way he'd been treated like royalty by the hotel staff, brought home again how different their lives were. And had her wondering yet again if Conn could ever be happy living an ordinary life with an ordinary woman. A woman like her.

No thinking, she reminded herself. Especially not tonight. It had been a very long time since she'd gone to any concert that didn't involve Shelter Bay school children, and having never seen Conn perform, except for those videos on Celtic Storm's website and YouTube, she was looking forward to seeing how much of the man she'd fallen in love with resembled the rock star who'd be performing to more than fourteen thousand fans. Many who probably had posters of him on their wall, the same as she'd had that Heath Ledger poster on hers growing up.

The pass Conn had given her gained access to his dressing room, where she met Luke, the drummer, John, the bass guitarist, Michael, who played keyboard, and Matthew Dolan, the band's principal photographer. Another black-suited giant and three arena PR people played traffic cops, deftly directing the stream of top industry people, local media celebs, and wealthy fans who'd donated richly to the cause, all who were wearing passes around their necks.

Wanting to stay out of the photos as Matthew busily snapped away, Sedona had only enough time to wish Conn luck before escaping the room that had begun to make her feel like a sardine packed into a can.

She took her seat in the center front row, the hulk filling the one next to her, his don't-even-try-to-effing-mess-with-me scowl seemingly carved into his granite face as his eyes continually scanned the crowd. As the earlier acts played, Sedona couldn't help thinking what a contrast that dressing room experience had been with the man who'd grilled steaks in a cottage garden and raced horses with her on a deserted beach in the Connemara.

She wanted to ask the real Conn Brennan to stand up. But couldn't he be both? And if that were the case, if they were to try to build a future together, could she live with the high-profile rock star who traveled with his own security guards and, it seemed, didn't have a single private moment once he left the bucolic Irish West?

During their second night in that castle resort, he'd told her of an evening, earlier in his career, when he'd performed at Métropolis, a club in Montreal. Since he'd still been traveling commercial back then, he'd flown in a day early. Wanting to get out of the hotel the night before the gig, he'd gone to a movie by himself and had been standing in line, waiting to buy a Coke and a bag of popcorn, when a young man came up to him and invited him to sit with him and his family.

Which he'd done and afterwards they'd taken him to their townhome and fed him a very good French burgundy, a home-cooked *Tourtière*—a traditional Quebecois meat pie that had reminded Conn of shepherd's pie back home, if the Irish had caribou available as a protein source—and a maple sugar cream pie so sweet he'd practically felt his teeth sprouting cavities. Afterwards, the father had driven Conn back to the hotel.

He'd explained to Sedona that one of the perks of being a public person was that you occasionally had an opportunity to step into some total strangers' lives for a minute, or even a few hours. However, as lovely as that evening sounded, she wondered if it would be possible for him to do anything like that these days.

The concert planners had, unsurprisingly, opted to have Conn close the show. As time passed, the expectation grew so palpable, when he finally strutted onto the stage, people leaped to their feet, and shouts of "Connnnnn!" rocked the roof.

Onstage, he radiated the same personality he had when he'd played at Mary's wedding reception: powerful, confident, charismatic. But here, in front of an arena filled with fans, he'd amped it up a thousandfold.

After returning from the wedding, Sedona had listened to everything Conn had recorded, and noticed that his earlier cocky, almost buoyant defiance had gradually transitioned to more somber tales of small, hard-luck lives being lived on the rocky edges of society as he, himself, had matured.

Despite being larger than life, he somehow also seemed to connect to each and every person on an individual level, often making eye contact, and when a teenager raced up the center aisle, trying to reach the stage, only to be stopped by a uniformed guard, he'd invited her up to dance a few turns with him. An act of generosity Sedona imagined the girl would remember for the rest of her life.

Although she'd come to realize that he was not a man given to easily expressing emotion, on stage, he poured his heart out. Especially when he sang "The Devil You Know," a song she realized he must have written after Joseph Brennan had died.

His voice was rough and raw. And for him, as the band dropped off playing and he stood there in the center of the stage, with only his voice and that old acoustic guitar he'd switched to, row by row the crowd of fourteen thousand plus grew silent as he sang a hushed, agonized ballad of a hard-drinking, abusive man whose dreams had been crushed due to his own flaws. His own failures. A man who, on his deathbed, was an empty husk, eaten up by self-pity and hate.

By the time the last word of the ballad had drifted away, the room was as hushed as a church on Monday morning.

Showing instinctive timing, Conn, who, she'd discovered, had a habit of talking between songs, telling a bit about the songs and life, let the silence spin out long enough to increase the impact of the lyrics and what was obviously an autobiographical story he'd just shared.

Then, holding onto the hand mike, he looked straight out into the crowd and said, "For any of you out there who might have others in your life trying to crush your dreams, never, *ever* stop believing. Never let any fucking hater force you to surrender."

On cue, the lights lowered a bit, just for a moment, and in the lingering silence, Sedona heard a few sniffles. One woman a few rows behind her began weeping softly.

Then, handing off the guitar to one of the stage crew who'd brought out his red Stratocaster, he started belting out an upbeat rockabilly song about taking a road trip with the prettiest girl in the world. The one he was falling in love with.

The crowd, obviously relieved for the return of more fun songs, joined in on the chorus, and like the pro Conn was, he left the audience happy and calling out for more.

When it appeared they'd never stop chanting, stomping, and clapping, he came out from the wings to another deafening roar of applause to sing "Just One More Pint." The first hit coming out of Celtic Storm's pub band days, it was universally known, and even Sedona found herself singing along with everyone else in the arena.

Afterwards, as she made her way back to the waiting town car, it did not escape her attention that of all the songs that had been played during the nearly three hour long concert, the one tune people were humming was the bad-boy-meets-good-girl love story, "Road Trip."

47

THE LATE AFTER-CONCERT dinner with Conn's parents turned out surprisingly stress-free and enjoyable. Dennis Byrne reminded Sedona a great deal of Conn. The physical resemblance was so strong it was obvious at first glance that they were father and son. Their shared love of music also spoke to the power of genetics, as did the way they looked right into your eyes while you spoke, and occasionally nodded, not necessarily in agreement but in an unconscious gesture to reveal that they were paying attention to every word.

Eileen, who'd been a lovely woman when Sedona had met her at the funeral, had been transformed to stunning and looked at least ten years younger. Her face glowed with happiness and while she'd been friendly and gracious the last time she'd spoken with Sedona, tonight she seemed to be welcoming her into the Brennan family. Even more telling was Conn didn't disabuse his mother of the notion.

Another fun part of the late dinner was when Dennis informed Sedona that he'd met her once before, when her father had played a concert in Cork.

"Of course, you wouldn't be remembering it," he said. "Since you were a mere babe in your mother's arms at the time. Just beginning to walk, you were. I told Freebird and Skylark that you were the most delightfully sunny lass I'd ever seen." His smile was warm as it skimmed over her face. "You're obviously no longer a child, but you've remained a ray of sunshine."

"That she has," Conn said, taking her hand beneath the table. "I thought, when I first met her, that if they weren't writing their songs before she was born, I'd have sworn the Beach Boys had her in mind when they came up with 'California Girl.'"

"You never told me that," Sedona said.

"It never came up," Conn responded. "But it's true."

"It fits," Dennis decided. "That song came from Brian Wilson's first acid trip. He's said that he was sitting in his apartment and decided to write about girls, because, since he loved girls, he figured everyone else did."

"You won't get any argument from me," Conn said. "It hasn't escaped my attention that if you want a record to sell, you put a girl in it."

"Like you did with 'Road Trip' tonight," Eileen said. "Is that new? I haven't heard it before."

"It is new," Conn said. He looked at Sedona. "I was recently inspired to write it."

As much as that revelation pleased her, Sedona felt as if the obvious fact that she'd been the inspiration for the song had put her in a bull's-eye as his parents seemed to be studying her more closely. Measuring her, as if to decide if she'd be a good match for their son.

"Well, if the audience reaction was any indication, it's going to shoot up the charts," Dennis said. "I predict a number one slot the first week."

"First we have to record it," Conn said. "I only wrote it yesterday."

When they'd returned from their own road trip. Warmth, happiness, need, and too many emotions too complex to quantify rushed through Sedona.

"It was the first time we've performed it," Conn told his father. "I only had time to play it to the others five minutes before we went on stage."

"You never would have guessed from the way you all pulled it off. I predict it'll be a much faster session than 'California Girl.' When writing my book on Brian Wilson, I discovered that he'd insisted on forty-four takes on the instrumental recording alone. Then they dubbed in the vocals two months later. Everyone agreed he was brilliant but a perfectionist to a fault, which made him exceptional but not always easy to live with."

That comment had Sedona wondering if she should put her own perfectionism down on the negative side of her pro-con list. She'd been trying, during this time in Ireland, to loosen the reins on her need for control, but what if, after a few months, or years, Conn found *her* too difficult to live with?

"Yet the extra effort paid off," Conn said, reminding Sedona of his own insistence on precisely the right chord. Key. Word.

"It did, indeed," Dennis agreed. "It was one of their best-selling international singles and since it continues to get radio play, it's earned the most royalties of any of the

Beach Boys' songs. I suspect 'Road Trip' has the capability of topping it."

"Any success that comes from it, I owe to my muse." Conn looked at Sedona, then surprised her by leaning over and kissing her on the lips. It wasn't a long, embarrassing PDA but nevertheless had the power to curl her toes.

"So, Sedona," Dennis said, breaking the momentary silence that had settled over the table after Conn's uncharacteristic show of emotion. "I read your father's going to have his work performed on Broadway."

"He is. It's a rock opera based on a local legend surrounding a shipwreck in the Oregon town where I live." She gave him a quick synopsis of Captain MacGrath's tale.

"You should have him bring it here," Dennis said. "We Irish love our legends. And our tragic love stories."

"Conn suggested it play at the Abbey. When I mentioned it to Dad, he thought it was a grand idea." Another idea occurred to her. "If you'd like, I'd love to get you and Eileen tickets to the New York opening."

"Oh, wouldn't that be wonderful!" Eileen reached out and took hold of Dennis's hand.

When he brought that slender hand to his lips, Sedona was reminded of how Conn would do the exact same thing. "We could make it part of a honeymoon trip to New York City," he suggested.

"What an exciting time that would be! When I was a young girl, I dreamed of someday performing with the New York Ballet. Visiting there for our honeymoon will be even more grand." Conn's mother's eyes were moist through her smile, reminding Sedona how long these two had waited for their happy ever after. "That would be so generous of you," she said to Sedona. "And of course we'd have to take you, Conn, and your parents out for a night on the town to celebrate your father's grand success."

It appeared she'd already moved on to considering not just Sedona but now Freebird and Skylark as extended family. Not wanting to put a damper on what had been a perfect evening, Sedona merely smiled in response.

ONCE SEDONA AND Conn had finally returned to their suite after midnight, in contrast to his hot, almost angry sex before the concert, their lovemaking was slow, sensual, and so beautiful she'd almost been brought to tears again. Keeping to her vow of not thinking, she allowed herself to enjoy every exquisite moment. All night long.

During a late breakfast in bed, discreetly delivered by the suite's butler, Conn told her all the details about meeting his father. And how, after an initial discomfort, it had gotten easier. Enough that by last night's dinner, he'd felt as if they'd known each other for years.

"Which you have, in a way," she said. "Given that you met so many years ago, and not only has he been following your career, you've always read his columns and books."

"I have. And wondered why, given that he wrote so highly about me, he never interviewed me again."

"And now you have your answer. Along with your mother's reasoning."

"Which I'm less comfortable with," he admitted.

selfishly didn't want to ruin their last hours together in Dublin dealing with a decision that could complicate their relationship.

She padded across the carpeting in bare feet and began massaging the boulders that had bunched up in his broad shoulders. "I'm not versed on Irish tax law, but if there's anything I could do to help—"

"You've already been a help just by being here when I needed you." He turned around and met her concerned gaze. "What unfortunate luck you have to keep being the person who has to deal with me after I get news of my bastard status from Joseph Brennan or yesterday's, from Brendan."

"I don't consider myself unfortunate at all. While I ached for the boy you once were when you told me about the man who you'd believed to be your father, I was glad I was there for you when you needed someone. As for yesterday...as sorry as I truly am about your financial problems, I'm not about to complain about being so exhilaratingly ravished by a hot Irish rock star who most women only get to fantasize about."

His laugh was rich and warm. "And aren't you grand for my bruised ego, Sedona Sullivan? And I mean that in the most superlative definition."

It was her turn to laugh. "So, why don't you come to bed and let me grandly ravish you for a change?"

"There's nothing I'd like more. But unfortunately, Brendan brought one last piece of news. A reporter from the *Irish Independent* has dug up a piece of the embezzlement story and was only willing to hold off publishing it until after the concert if I agreed to an interview. Not that there's anything I'll be able to tell him, since he could well know more than I do, but I'm due to meet him downstairs in ten minutes."

"Well, then, of course you need to go," she said.

"You're an exceptionally understanding woman, luv." He bent his head and gave her another of those toe-curling kisses. "I shouldn't be long. And afterwards, perhaps we can get some shopping in before our tea."

"You're the exceptional one," she said. "I don't know many men who'd not only be willing to have a formal tea but who'd also go shopping."

"It's not watching you shop that I'll be enjoying all that much," he admitted. "But the idea of buying you some memento of our trip is more than appealing."

As he left the suite, Sedona thought that she didn't need any gift. Because whatever happened between them, the memory of this trip would stay with her for the rest of her years.

48

GRAFTON STREET WAS just as Sedona remembered. A bustling, wide road mostly closed to traffic, home to a plethora of shops, restaurants, and street entertainers. She'd always enjoyed shopping there while attending Trinity College, but this time was special as Conn pointed out all the corners that he and his band had performed as buskers while struggling to achieve their big break.

She bought a ceramic wind chime with Celtic symbols for Skylark to hang outside her art studio window, an Irish fisherman's sweater for Freebird, *Darina Allen's Ballymaloe House Cooking School Cookbook* for Maddy, a box of exquisite, handmade paper for Annie, and, of course, she had the painting Finnola had given her for Mary.

For Kara and Sax, who'd taken her in, she'd found a cloud-soft woven mohair blanket in the colors of the sea their home overlooked to replace the one their new puppy had chewed to scraps. And for everyone else, she'd bought enough boxes of exquisitely decorated artisan chocolates to give a serious sugar buzz to half the population of Castlelough.

"Well, you can't say you didn't give our Irish economy a boost," Conn said later that afternoon as they shared a brocade-covered sofa in the Lord Mayor's Lounge while enjoying the impeccable ritual of a formal afternoon tea. Though in this case, rather than the vast assortment of loose-leaf tea, although Sedona suspected he'd prefer a pint of Brian Boru Ale, Conn ordered the Moët et Chandon brut champagne to commemorate their weekend.

The food was an elegantly created mix of sweet and savory and even knowing that such behavior would be disapproved of, Sedona sneaked out her phone and snapped a quick photo of the raspberry and chocolate mousse with fondant pearls to show Maddy. Since there was no way she could remember the menu, she asked for a duplicate to take home to Shelter Bay's favorite chef.

And then, too soon they were back on the plane, and as the wheels left the runway, Sedona knew that her time had run out.

"I received some news myself yesterday," she said with a casualness she was a long way from feeling. "From my friend Annie."

"Who lost her scrapbook store in the storm." Not only had he been listening to her talk about her friends, he'd actually remembered these people he'd never met. Which partly explained his close feelings toward his fans, even going so far as to have dinner with strangers, simply because they'd invited him.

"That's her. Remember I told you that the developer had been going to turn the block into condos?"

"Bondurant." He nodded. "You referred to him as a cross between Scrooge before his redemption and Mr. Potter in *It's a Wonderful Life*."

"I did?" Sedona had certainly thought of the man that way enough times, didn't remember sharing the description with Conn.

"Aye. You did, indeed."

"Well, he overreached this time," she said. "The zoning council rejected his plan to build those tall harbor-front condos."

It was only because she'd been watching him so carefully that Sedona noticed the slight hesitation as he lowered his coffee cup to the seat table. "I see." His eyes were shuttered, like windows painted over. "What does he plan to do instead?"

"Nothing. He sold the property to another real estate investor. A friend of mine, Gabriel Lombardi, whose family owns a winery."

"Would he be intending to use it for a restaurant and tasting room?"

"No. He's rebuilding it much the way it was originally, but although it will still have that old-time coastal appearance, all the interiors will be updated and modernized."

She hesitated as she reached the difficult part of the conversation. Fiddled with the embossed gold Claddagh bangle bracelet he'd bought her at a Grafton Street jeweler. The two hands holding the crowned heart was a symbol created in Galway centuries ago. It stood for love, friendship, and loyalty. Which of those, Sedona wondered now, had Conn been considering when he'd chosen it?

"He's offering all the displaced tenants the opportunity to claim their spaces before he puts them on the market."

When Conn didn't immediately respond, just took another, longer drink of coffee, Sedona forced herself to press on. "And because he knew that I'd been eyeing the empty space next door to expand, he assured the realtor handling the property that I was more than welcome to take it over."

"That's what you wanted." His tone was deliberately neutral, giving nothing away.

"Yes. It was." She waited for him to tell her not to take it. To insist that she belonged in Castlelough with him.

"I suppose the logical thing would be to fly back to Shelter Bay and check out the space," he said instead. "Don't you have a friend who restores old buildings, the way Bram does?"

"Lucas Chaffee," she agreed. "I'd hired him to rebuild Take the Cake after the storm. Until Bondurant cancelled my lease."

"Well, then." Again, she couldn't hear a single clue in Conn's level voice. Nor read any emotion in his eyes. "It sounds as if everything has fallen in place for you. Exactly as you'd originally planned."

Sedona had been nervous about telling Conn her news because she didn't want to disrupt what she'd thought they'd created together. But he was giving her nothing here. No suggestion that they might at least try to come up with a compromise plan that would allow their relationship to continue.

While he'd been downstairs in the hotel, meeting with that reporter, she'd even been trying trying to come up with her own plan that would allow her and Conn to be together.

"Yes," she said, her tone as mildly remote as his. "Apparently it has."

They didn't speak during the short hop to Shannon Airport from Dublin. Still unsure what she was going to do, Sedona turned on her Kindle, and in no mood for the romance novel she'd been reading, she switched to Nate Breslin's horror tale about a Bermuda Triangle-type area off the Oregon coast that had supposedly caused many of the shipwrecks. Including the one that had sunk Captain MacGrath's ship.

Since his Dublin performance had been shown live on TV, getting through the terminal once they arrived back in the West turned out to be yet another obstacle course. Conn had put on his rock star shades, which, since the sun was hidden behind the clouds, Sedona felt made him stand out even more.

Did he wear them to be noticed? Or because he'd gone back into that dark, private place she'd witnessed him retreating into? Whichever, she was confused, and conflicted. She needed to talk with Annie, which was going to be impossible until she returned to the cottage and Conn to the house. At least she assumed he wouldn't be staying with her. Unless, for him, the past weeks had been all about sex?

No. He'd been the one who'd first broached the subject, insisting that whatever they had was more than just chemistry.

Not that there was anything wrong with chemistry, as Annie herself had pointed out.

She knew her friend would tell her to make a stand. To not do as Annie herself had done, because waiting for Mac to come out and tell her that he loved her and always would had been far more stressful than it would have been if she'd just been upfront with her own feelings from the beginning. Which had been exactly what Sedona had suggested to her all along.

But how was she supposed to tell Conn how she felt with the flight attendant standing nearby, waiting to jump into action and fulfill any request from the silent man who appeared lost in his own world, scribbling what she assumed to be lyrics into a spiral notebook? And wasn't it easier to give advice to others than to take it yourself?

49

Conn couldn't come up with the right words. He'd woken up with them in his head this morning. He'd silently rehearsed them during shopping and that tea, where he'd sipped French champagne like a proper gentleman rather than gulping down a pint or two and just coming out with the words that were stuck in his head and behind the damn lump in his throat.

He'd already come up with a plan. A plan he'd been determined to stick to. A plan that, thanks to some probably oversexed Italian winemaker turned property investor, appeared to have been blown out of the water.

Conn was accustomed to improvising on the fly. There was no way you could sing on stage night after night, especially when you were exhausted from traveling and the headaches that came with trying to keep all the damn balls that a tour entailed in the air at the same time without occasionally forgetting lyrics. Usually, he just threw in some words off the top of his head that fit the music, and since the crowd was often screaming so loudly, the substitution usually went unnoticed. Except for that time in Reykjavík, when, right in the middle of the second verse of "A Rainy Night in Dublin Town," his mind had gone as blank as glass.

He'd stood there for what seemed like an eternity, but suddenly, from somewhere in the crowd, a lone voice started singing the words. Then another. And before they got to the chorus, it seemed as if every one of the eighteen hundred people in Harpa's Eldborg Hall had joined in and saved him from professional humiliation. No matter how busy Conn might be, to show his appreciation, he returned to that city every year, not only performing at the Eldborg, named for Iceland's most recognized volcano, but taking part in the nightlife locals referred to as *jammith,* playing in smaller clubs throughout the city.

If only those loyal Icelanders were here to save his arse today, Conn thought after they'd managed to forge their way through the crowd and were heading toward the coast, where, if everything went according to plan, it might be possible to salvage what was left of the day.

As they approached the sea, the clouds lifted, which, thinking of Kate's belief in destiny, he decided to take as a positive sign.

"Are we going to the pub?" Sedona asked as he passed the turnoff to the cottage.

"No."

She seemed surprised by his lack of explanation. "Are you going to tell me where we're headed?"

"I am." He turned toward her and gave her an encouraging smile that felt false on his face as he struggled not to reveal his insecurity.

"When?"

Because it had been too long since he'd touched her, he reached over, took hold of her hand, and placed their linked hands on his jean-clad thigh. "When the time's right."

She shook her head, but he sensed her relaxing ever so slightly. "You're not an easy man."

"I doubt you'd find anyone who disagrees," he said easily. They were talking again, which he took as another good sign. "But the fact is that I have a surprise for you."

"Seriously?"

She seemed honestly surprised, which showed how badly he'd fucked up. But he hadn't gotten where he was by not being stubborn and single-minded. And tonight, the only thing on his mind was to convince Sedona Sullivan that she was not only his destiny, she was his soul mate. And his future.

He pulled into a turnoff overlooking the beach. "Would you be up for a walk?" he asked as the sun lowered over the water.

She shot him a curious look but nodded. "That sounds lovely. As much as I enjoyed Dublin, I'd forgotten how noisy and hectic it can be."

"It's easy to get accustomed to the peace found at the far edge of the continent," he agreed. "As I imagine you've discovered since moving to Castlelough's sister city."

He was pleased when she laughed at that, the silver bell sound ringing its way into his heart. "*City* might be more than a bit of an exaggeration," she allowed. "Given that I suspect that Shelter Bay may have fewer people than Castlelough."

"Yet close enough," he said as they walked down the winding steps carved into the limestone cliff to the beach, "that were it not for our castle and mythical Lady and your resident whales, it would be hard for a visitor from outer space to tell the difference."

"I suspect you're right." She drew in a sharp breath as she viewed the scene that met her. "Oh. Wow." She shot him a look. "How many people did you hire to pull this off?"

"None. I called Roarke yesterday. He set it up, with help from the others."

And hadn't he done a grand job, Conn thought, taking in the table for two draped in white linen and already set with champagne glasses, soft lights strung between poles set into the sand to brighten the gloaming, and a candle already lit in a lantern as a touch of romance.

"This is by far the most romantic thing anyone has ever done for me," she said.

Her voice quivered, making Conn wonder if she were fretting about how to tell him that their summer holiday was over and she was returning to her rigidly planned life. Or had he managed to touch her heart enough to have her wanting to be with him?

"You can thank my brothers for that." He pulled out one of the wicker chairs for her.

"And I will." She sat down and looked up at the lights, her expression one of a child who'd just seen her first Christmas tree. "But it was *your* plan."

"Not entirely." He sat down himself and reached beneath the tablecloth, pulling out a cooler of iced champagne and a selection of Declan's best cheese along with some water crackers. "Patrick said that he'd be the one choosing the dinner since my taste tended toward fish and chips, which, while a grand supper, isn't romantic enough for this occasion."

"I tell you, the man's as close to perfect as you'd ever find."

"Is that what women want?" Conn asked, truly curious. "Perfection?"

"Haven't we agreed perfection is an illusion?" Sedona said as he expertly opened the bottle and poured the champagne into the flutes.

"Then you'd be open to loving a man with flaws?"

"Of course. So long as he was willing to put up with mine."

"Which would be no hardship." He drew in a deep breath. "I've been giving a lot of thought to us."

"So have I."

He nodded. "Grand...So, as I didn't expect your building to become available, I hadn't factored that obstacle into my equation, but I understand that your logical side will require you to return to Shelter Bay and check the situation out. I also realize that you've worked hard to create a life there. Not just your bakery business but a circle of friends who mean a great deal to you."

"That's true. They do."

"And my work is here. The lads, the production studios I'm building that I can't abandon because I've already promised the opportunity to others. I may not need any more money, but other musicians haven't been so fortunate, and if I can help them achieve their dreams while keeping traditional music alive, it wouldn't feel right to abandon them."

"I wouldn't want you to."

"But what we have, what fate has meant us to share, shouldn't be torn apart by mere geography. I love you, Sedona Sullivan. More than I ever imagined it was possible to love a woman. And although I won't deny that I would want you to stay here, in Ireland with me, it's important that you understand that I'll do whatever it takes, including traveling back and forth between here and Castlelough's American sister city to make it work."

"You love me?"

"With all my heart. No. *More.* With every atom in my body. You're a woman men write songs about. And I intend to be writing a great many about you."

"I'm flattered. And honestly relieved, because I love you, too. More than *I* ever could have believed possible. And I also agree with some of what you said."

"And what part would that be?" Never before, not even the time he'd played for Queen Elizabeth and her sister Princess Margaret, had Conn's nerves felt like downed electric wires dancing and sparking on a wet sidewalk.

"That what we have shouldn't be torn apart by where we choose to live. Not that I believe it could. But it needn't be. Because I want to stay here. Not here on the beach," she said. "But in Castlelough. With you."

"But what about the building? Your building? Don't you want to go back and see how it would be? Larger and restored?"

"I've imagined that space more times than I can count over the past years while planning for expansion. It will be a lovely location for someone. But not me. Because I have other plans."

"Are you opening a bakery? Castlelough could use one."

"I've already done that. And while it was successful, I'm ready to move on. Though I believe I'd enjoy teaching classes to those women Patrick mentioned who'd be interested, my main job is going to be you."

She stood up and came around the table and sat on his lap. "Meet your new manager."

"You're going to take Diarmuid's place?"

"Not exactly, because I'm going to be a best friend you can trust. Not just with your heart but your money. I'm going to handle your finances, your various businesses, tour dates, and whatever else a manager does. I'll get with your Brendan Hennessy and between the three of us, we'll work out what you need. Including, if you'd like, my occasionally working on a score with you."

He ran his hand down her hair, which was fluttering in the breeze blowing off the sea. "I can't imagine being able to write without my brilliant, beautiful muse. We'll be the new Irish Paul and Linda McCartney."

She laughed. "Just don't expect me to sing," she warned. "I'll not be in the band, but after waiting for you all my life, I'll be your one and only groupie, *mo chuisle, mo chroí*."

The pulse of her heart. It was the first time she'd used her Irish with Conn and from the softening of his expression as he touched his knuckles to the side of her face, she knew that pleased him.

"As I've been waiting for you," he said. "Never knowing that you were across an ocean and a continent, standing on your own golden sand, waiting for me.

"And now, thanks to destiny, it's happy we'll be, *a stór,*" he sang softly against her lips as they shared a kiss that had music playing in her head. "Together. Beyond the sea."

The End

To keep up with publication dates, other news, and for a chance to win books and other cool stuff, subscribe to the JoAnn Ross newsletter from her website at www.JoAnnRoss.com. Also connect with JoAnn on Facebook, Twitter, Goodreads, and Pinterest.

Keep reading for a sneak preview excerpt of *Sunset Point*, the next book in the Shelter Bay series, coming in October, 2015.

Sunset Point

A Shelter Bay novel

JoAnn Ross

1

NATE BRESLIN HAD dreamed about her again last night. As always she appeared in the midst of a violent thunderstorm, the black crepe of her mourning clothes swirling about her slender body in the cold, harsh wind. Without a word she emerged from the tempest, gliding ever so slowly toward him, her hand outstretched as if reaching for his touch.

A gust of wind from the storm-tossed sea ruffled her black veil and a sudden sulfurous flash of lightning illuminated her ghostly face. In response to the overwhelming sorrow in those lovely, soulful eyes, he held out his hand, offering whatever comfort he could.

She was closer now.

In another moment their fingertips would touch.

Then, as always, dammit, she was gone.

—

GIVING UP ON any more sleep for the night, Nate sat on the porch of his Shelter Bay home perched on the edge of a cliff, gazing out over the waters of the Pacific Ocean. As he dank his coffee, he reassured himself—not for the first time—that the entire dream was nothing more than a figment of his imagination. Maybe even some weird PTSD thing he'd brought back from Iraq and Afghanistan.

He had, after all, seen a shitload of death. And rather than come home and try to forget it, Nate worked out his "issues" as the Marine shrink during his separation Transition Assistance Seminar had referred to them, by delving into the dark world of the supernormal.

He'd written his first novel after surviving Fallujah, the bloodiest battle of the Iraq War. His blog, which he'd mainly started to amuse himself during downtime, was part ground truth of war, part absurdities of military life, and part creative writing. It was his short story of gigantic camel spiders being sent out to eat enemy combatants while the bad guys were sleeping that had gotten him noticed by the *New York Times*, which had signed him to write for their "At War" blog.

The camel story, based on an exaggerated myth of an actual carnivorous arachnid, which did not eat people or camels, fortuitously happened to be read by an editor at a New York publishing house, who'd offered him his first book contract while he was still deployed. A book that went on to earn him a Bram Stoker award for best first novel, stellar reviews, and the rest, as they say, was history.

Ghosts, vampires, werewolves, ghouls—these were merely his fictional stock-in-trade, nothing more. It was certainly not unusual for a story idea to come to him in the middle of the night.

On the other hand—and wasn't there always another hand?—Captain Angus MacGrath, his resident ghost, had turned out to be absolute fact. Two weeks after Nate had moved in, the captain had shown up. Shortly after that, the mystery woman had started appearing in his dreams. The logical explanation was that she was nothing more than a potential character lurking in the dark depths of his subconscious. Even as Nate assured himself that she was nothing more than an enticing product of his creative, often twisted mind, he didn't believe it.

Not when he could still see the anguish in those lovely dark eyes even when he was awake. Not when the evocative violet scent of her perfume lingered in the rose-tinged early-morning air. Not when he could vividly recall the tingling of his fingertips when their hands had come so heartbreakingly close to touching.

Not when his midnight visitor seemed so…real.

So alive.

The only thing to do, he decided as he gazed down at the hulking metal skeleton of the capsized ship that MacGrath had been captaining when he'd drowned at sea, was to find her.

And learn the story she was so desperately trying to tell him.

2

THE MULTNOMAH COUNTY district attorney's was in its usual state of chaos. The incessant clamor of phones was escalated by the hum of competing conversations. Cardboard cups, doughnut crumbs, and wrappers from fast food take-out meals littered desktops. The atmosphere was laced with aggravation, frustration, stale coffee, and sweat.

Tess Lombardi loved it.

Tess had never minded the breathless pace that her work as a deputy district attorney entailed. On the contrary, she thrived in the midst of what could only charitably be called bedlam.

The daughter of a Portland Police Bureau detective, she'd cut her teeth on the rarefied discipline of the law. When her parents had divorced a week before her fifth birthday, Mike Brown and Claudia Lombardi had agreed that it would be best if Tess remained with her father. No one concerned had ever regretted that decision.

Claudia was free to travel the world like the beautiful, jet-set social butterfly she was, unencumbered by a growing child. While Mike, unlike so many of his divorced friends on the force, was able to keep his daughter under both his wing and the roof of his small, but cozy historic Craftsman bungalow.

When Tess was twelve—despite the Lombardi custom that all the women maintained their family surname—she'd announced to her father that she want to go to court and change her last name to his. Which was when Mike Brown had assured her that he'd always love her, whatever her name. But he also wanted her to never forget that her mother's wine-growing family could trace its direct lineage to seventeenth-century Tuscany.

Having arrived from Italy in the 1800s, the Willamette Valley Lombardis had become one of the first families to commercially grow grapes. The son of a drug dealer who'd been killed in prison and an alcoholic mother who'd often forget she'd left her infant alone at home, Mike had landed in foster care before his first birthday, moved to a group home for wayward and homeless boys at age three, then self-emancipated at sixteen. Appreciating the importance of roots, he'd encouraged Tess to recognize and embrace her own.

As usual, her father's instincts had been right. While she might not carry his last name, the big, outwardly tough man with the warm and soft heart was everything a father could be. His unreserved love had provided all the nurturing and encouragement any young girl could ever need.

Tess's fondest memories were of the times she was allowed to watch him testify in court. Detective Michael Xavier Brown was more than her father. He was her super hero—Superman, Batman, and all the X-Men (especially Wolverine, who was her favorite because—duh—what woman alive didn't crush on hottie Hugh Jackman?) all rolled into one husky, gregarious human being. Although she'd attended law school rather than follow him into the department, Tess never entered a courtroom without thinking how she was continuing her father's life work to gain justice for those unable to achieve it for themselves.

As she returned to her office to pick up some papers after court this afternoon, however, Tess was more than a little irritated. Punctual to a fault, she was running behind schedule, something she abhorred.

As she tossed her briefcase down, the woman at the neighboring desk glanced up in surprise. "I didn't expect you back. Aren't you due in Shelter Bay by five?"

"Five-thirty," Tess said. "Of all days for Larry Parker to play Perry Mason, he had to pick this one. You should have seen him on defense this morning. I could not believe one man, especially one with such a limited vocabulary, could be so long-winded.

"By the time Judge Keane declared a lunch recess, we were already running forty-five minutes late. Fortunately, the judge must've had a hot date, because he cut off testimony and sent everyone home early."

It hadn't escaped anyone's notice that ever since *Portland Monthly* magazine had named Judge Gerald Keane the city's most eligible bachelor, early adjournments were happening more and more often.

"The boost to his social life appears to have shortened the court day," Alexis Montgomery agreed. "But there's also the fact that ever since he decided to run for that vacant seat on the Court of Appeals, the judge hasn't passed up an opportunity to make a speech. I read that he was talking to the Business Alliance at a cocktail mixer at the downtown Marriott this evening."

"Finally," Tess said. "A reason to be grateful for politics. If I'd had to listen to Larry another five minutes, I'd have started slamming my head onto the desk."

"If you're driving down to Shelter Bay, it can only mean that Dana White is getting cold feet about testifying."

"She's apprehensive," Tess admitted. "But I can certainly understand her feelings. What woman would want to admit to the world that she was foolish enough to marry a man who already had twenty wives scattered throughout fifteen states?"

"Well, I wouldn't worry too much about the Shelter Bay Mrs. Dexter, if I were you. Fortunately, there are enough women out there who want to see the guy drawn and quartered that we shouldn't have any trouble getting a conviction. Especially with the case Donovan handed us all tied up with that pretty red ribbon."

Donovan Quinn was a detective in the Portland Police Bureau who'd tirelessly worked the bigamist case from the beginning, tracking down all the loose ends to make that pretty bow. Like all the cases he brought to the D.A.'s office, the investigation had been impeccable, making him a prosecutor's dream detective. Having dated him few times before they'd decided to remain friends, Tess also knew him to be one of the good guys.

"I know we don't need her," Tess agreed. "But I have the feeling Dana needs us. Her self confidence has taken a big hit, and she sounded shaky the last time I talked with her on the phone."

Alexis leaned back in her chair. "Sometimes I think you're too softhearted to be in this business, Lombardi."

"Why don't you try telling that to the much-married Melvin Schiff?" Tess countered. "One of the reporters down at the courthouse couldn't wait to show me today's *Oregonian*."

"That bad, huh?"

"Schiff was quoted as saying that I was such an icy bitch that if any man even was willing to have sex with me, his penis would freeze off."

"Shut up. They did not write that."

"No, they put in an asterisk for the 'i' in bitch and went with a 'certain part of the anatomy,' for penis, which, I suspect, is still a more polite term than he actually used."

"The guy's a real charmer."

"Isn't he? I can't figure out what all those women saw in him."

"He's a con man," Alexis said. "I suppose, looking at the big picture, we—and all those women who fell for his slimy grifter ways—ought to be grateful he isn't one of those sociopaths who kills his wives for their insurance money. His M.O. is to do a juggling act between families for as long as he can get away with it, clean out the bank accounts, then move on."

"Leaving them alive. But still devastated," Tess said. "And speaking of moving on, I'd better get going. As it is, I'm probably going to have to break every speeding law on the books to get there in time."

"At least if you get stopped, you can argue your own case. Want some company?"

Tess considered the offer for a moment, then shook her head. "I don't think so. You've been working around the clock on that arson case the past three weeks. Besides, don't you have a hot date?"

"I could cancel. It's not as if Matt isn't used to it."

Which was life as normal in the D.A.'s office. Tess couldn't remember the last time she'd had a date. Nor a day off, including weekends. There were even times when she thought that if her townhouse ever became a crime scene, one look at the contents of her refrigerator and cupboards would have investigators questioning whether anyone actually lived there.

"You just happen to be engaged to the man voted Portland's second sexiest bachelor," she reminded her best friend. "And we both know he only lost first place to the judge because you guys got engaged, which took him off the market. Besides, after the hours you've been putting in, you both deserve to get lucky."

Alexis grinned. "Now that you mention it, that's exactly what I'd planned when I went shopping at lunch." She'd reached beneath her desk and pulled out a shopping bag from Portland's premiere French lingerie store.

"Ooh la la." Tess lifted an ebony brow. "You're pulling out the heavy weaponry."

"You bet I am. In this designer bag I happen to have a bustier, garter belt and hand-dyed vintage stockings designed to knock Matt's socks, along with the rest of his clothes, off."

"If you weren't my best friend, I'd have to hate you," Tess, whose only sex life for too long had involved batteries, complained. She was still laughing as she left the office, headed to Shelter Bay.

The Shelter Bay series

The Homecoming

One Summer

On Lavender Lane

Moonshell Beach

Sea Glass Winter

Castaway Cove

Christmas in Shelter Bay (Cole and Kelli's prequel novella in *A Christmas on Main Street*)

You Again

Beyond the Sea (pre-publication title, *A Sea Change*)

Sunset Point, October 2015

The Castlelough series

A Woman's Heart

Fair Haven

Legends Lake

Briarwood Cottage

Beyond the Sea

The Shelter Bay spin-off Murphy Brothers trilogy

River's Bend (Cooper's story)

Hot Shot (Sawyer's story), early 2016

Orchid Island series

Sun Kissed, November, *2015*

About the Author

When *New York Times* bestselling author JoAnn Ross was seven-years-old, she had no doubt whatsoever that she'd grow up to play center field for the New York Yankees. Writing would be her backup occupation, something she planned to do after retiring from baseball. Those were, in her mind, her only options. While waiting for the Yankees management to call, she wrote her first novella—a tragic romance about two star-crossed mallard ducks—for a second grade writing assignment.

The paper earned a gold star. And JoAnn kept writing.

She's now written around one hundred novels (she quit keeping track long ago) and has been published in twenty-six countries. Two of her titles have been excerpted in *Cosmopolitan* magazine and her books have also been published by the *Doubleday*, *Rhapsody*, *Literary Guild*, and *Mystery Guild* book clubs. A member of the Romance Writers of America's Honor Roll of best-selling authors, she's won several awards, including *RT Reviews'* Career Achievement Awards in both category romance and contemporary single title.

Although the Yankees have yet to call her to New York to platoon center field, JoAnn figures making one out of two life goals isn't bad.

Currently writing her Shelter Bay series (set on the Oregon Coast, where her high school sweetheart husband bought her a bag of saltwater taffy, then proposed), along with a River's Bend Murphy Brothers trilogy spin-off (set in Southern Oregon ranching country, where she grew up), her multi-award winning Irish Castlelough series, JoAnn lives with her husband and two fuzzy rescued dogs, who pretty much rule the house, in the Pacific Northwest.

Dear Reader,

My grandfather McLaughlin (who kidnapped—with her consent—my grandmother, when her wealthier Cavanaugh family wouldn't permit them to marry) was a *seanachie*—an Irish teller of tales. My earliest memories are listening to the music of his lyrical brogue spinning grand stories of kings and castles, battles and banishments, magic and miracles.

Inheriting his love of storytelling, I wrote my first novella when I was seven-years-old and immediately decided to become a writer when I grew up. Taught by Grandda to think big, my youthful fantasies invariably involved me dashing off the great American novel in some Greenwich Village garret, hand carrying it to a New York publisher who would proclaim it brilliant and launch my career to both critical acclaim and commercial success, after which I'd move to Cape Cod and live among all the other rich and famous novelists.

Well, it didn't quite work out that way. I've written advertising copy extolling the wonders of everything from household appliances to diamonds to tires. For a few years, I wrote for a large metropolitan newspaper, only to feel more and more constrained by the rigid parameters of fact. It was then I reminded myself what I really wanted to do - what I'd always wanted to do: make up stories I could share with others.

Hardly a day goes by that I don't realize that by exploring my favorite themes of love, loyalty, family, and, of course, my favorite, redemption, I'm still following in my grandfather's footsteps. In all his tales, heroes and heroines ventured forth on perilous quests against seemingly impossible odds, slaying myriad dragons along the way. Tyrants were toppled, lovers united, the wicked were punished, justice prevailed in the end and the good always lived happily ever after. And isn't that what the best romance novels are all about?

Happy Reading!

JoAnn

Sign up to receive the latest news from JoAnn
http://joannross.com/newsletter

Visit JoAnn's Website
http://www.joannross.com

Like JoAnn on Facebook
https://www.facebook.com/JoAnnRossBooks

Follow JoAnn on Twitter
https://twitter.com/JoAnnRoss

Follow JoAnn on Pinterest
http://pinterest.com/JoAnnRossBooks

Made in the USA
Lexington, KY
10 December 2015